Colour Blind

Charlotte Milne

Published 2022 by Charlotte Milne Books

ISBN: 978-1-9162785-2-3 (Print)
978-1-9162785-3-0 (E-book)

Cover design and typesetting by Jane Dixon Smith of JD Smith Design Ltd

Printed and bound in Great Britain

Publisher
Charlotte Milne
26 Northcliffe House, Grove Place
Nursling, Hampshire, SO16 0AP

www.charlottemilne-author
charlotte@charlottemilne.com

This book is set in 2018 because I have found the Covid pandemic an irritating stumbling block to storytelling. Who wants to be reminded of face, space and lockdown?

Chapter One

It's the hottest day of the year so far, and I'm stark naked in a tepid shower in a Winchester sports centre. My shaky hands have tipped out far too much of my lemon-smelling, teal-coloured shampoo and the bubbles would fill a kids' ball pit. In my head there is a mill wheel revolving the endless who and why of my disaster and whether this coming appointment will solve anything. No matter how I consciously relax my muscles, they are exhaustingly taut again within seconds and my stomach is hard with tension. The water on my face isn't just from the shower, and that makes me furious with myself as well as furious with whoever has stolen from me. And, at this moment, I am soap blind.

Hands on hips, I put my head back and wait for the water to rinse out the shampoo. Eventually, I sweep my hair off my face, open my eyes and emit a strangled screech.

The cubicle door is standing wide and facing me are three men. I can't see them clearly but think that their mouths are open and their eyes are not on mine. There is what seems like quite a long silence. Men! In the ladies' changing room! How dare they! Grabbing the spray head in one hand, I turn the tap to full-on cold. In only a second, they are very wet and chilly. There is a satisfactory joint shriek, and they all disappear. I turn off the water and get my voice back.

After they, and every other occupant of the entire sports

centre, have heard my opinion of them, I realise my towel is outside.

'And if someone could retrieve their bloody manners, put my towel over the door and then get the hell out!'

It does indeed sail over the now latched door. Someone sneezes multiple times. Perhaps the result of being doused in cold water.

I can hear male sniggers which means they are still where they shouldn't be, and then a posh voice says, 'Excuse me, ma'am.' *Ma'am?* Have we strayed into an American sitcom? 'Perhaps you don't realise, but this is the men's changing room.'

I stop rubbing my hair and wrap the towel round me instead. It is not possible that this is the men's changing room. I came out of the pool and took a left. This is where I changed into my swimsuit, now dripping from its hook, and where I left my clothes, glasses and contact lens clobber in a locker, in the company of several other assuredly female sporty types. I mutter 'Balls!' under my breath while I try to analyse my route from changing room to locker, to pool, to changing room. An unmistakable sinking sensation overpowers me. I am not in my usual sports centre in Southampton but in the Winchester affiliate. And the layout may not be quite the same.

Dignity is hard to maintain when dressed only in a skimpy towel, hair in rats' tails, marching through a smirking crowd of men. I grimly keep eye contact where I can and at the door remember I have left my swimsuit in the shower. Beautiful, expensive, made of recycled plastic bottles and not disposable, as it is a demo model. But there is no way on earth I am going back for it, and no way on earth I will ever enter this sports centre again.

* * *

The heat is beyond any previous experience of the month of May as I make my way to my appointment with Mr Dominic Paget, investment banker. The air smells blood red and the pavements would sear a steak in a minute flat and indeed are threatening to sear the soles of my feet through my fabulous sandals. There is sweat on my carefully made-up face, not helped by my nervousness about approaching this person for money. The visit to the sports club at lunchtime was designed to cool me down, but obviously has not and although I try to squash the memory of my very public shower every time it surfaces, it seems to pop up like a bursting bubble, splattering me with humiliation. I squint at my brilliant, in every sense, toe and fingernails in an effort to gain the upper hand, the confidence, the cool poise I so badly need. Catching a blurred reflection of myself in a glass door, I wonder whether this wig is quite the right image for visiting staid bankers who might or might not lend me any money. It was certainly an unwise choice on a day as hot as this. Too late now.

In the mirrors that line the lift, the effect is startling but pleasing. Let's hope it's startling and pleasing to Mr Paget, too. It is my *raison d'être*; colour, design, eye-catching, unique. Recycled plastic bottles can be truly wonderful. The thin, apple-green trousers swish like cool silk around my ankles, catching the light as they swing, revealing a warp thread of gold.

I have a sudden longing to feed whoever has stolen from me through the vicious metal teeth of the plastic recycling plant. Think how pink the wastewater would be.

The lift sighs open and the receptionist's eyes widen over the top of her computer. I resist the inclination to tell her that yellow is not her colour and that tight does not equate to good fit. Some things I see perfectly well.

Like the face of the man who comes from behind his desk to shake hands with me. He smells amber.

Dear God, please, please may the green wig overpower any memory of a foul-mouthed, naked harridan in the men's changing room at his sports club.

He shakes my hand, looks at my green fingernails and then at the matching toenails in their beautiful four-inch heeled sandals, made entirely out of plastic bottles. There is a moment's silence, during which I apprehend that my prayer has not been answered, although his expression is unaltered.

'How do you do, Miss Hunter. How nice to meet you. I'm sorry we don't have air conditioning.' He indicates a chair parallel to the open window. Behind it is a wall-hung cabinet full of strange glass objects. 'This is the best we can do for a breeze. Would you like to sit down?'

I wouldn't like to sit down. I would like to go home.

I am tall. I can manage those hellish chairs with long deep seats which are designed to make people sit like wooden puppets with their legs sticking straight out in front of them. But I remain standing.

'No, thank you.' I can't pretend it never happened. 'After this morning, I don't think there is much point in this meeting. I doubt you would consider a capital investment to someone who confuses changing rooms.' I am not going to explain any part of why that happened.

He looks at me with considering eyes, fingertips on his desk, standing because I am standing. On the desk there is an In and Out tray, a photograph of a dark-haired girl playing with a little boy, a pen and notepad and my letter to Vermont and Paget. He is about fifty, with an old-fashioned haircut to match, looks weary, wears a thick gold wedding ring and is good-looking in a kind of city-suit-ish way. His was the posh voice that called me ma'am.

'Based on the information in your letter, I'm prepared to listen and to discuss the possibility of financial investment with my partner. Quite apart from the loss of your capital, your business is part of an increasingly important commercial sector given current concerns about damage to the environment, climate change and modern slavery. It's a sector that we are interested in.'

I shake my head, although I need his money. Despite my anger about the theft, I cannot bring myself to crawl to this man after what happened today.

'Thank you, but no. I'm sorry to have taken up your time, but I feel the business relationship couldn't possibly work.' I hope he hears the dry non-embarrassment in my voice. I have never felt so mortified in my life.

He nods regretfully, the weary eyes smiling, but not in an unpleasant way. He understands. And I am grateful – very grateful – that he has the good manners not to embarrass me further or try to make me change my mind.

* * *

Short of cash, I stop at a hole in the wall, queuing behind two other slow customers and trying unsuccessfully not to think about that very short interview. I am not a shy flower or easily embarrassed, but my skin flares with chagrin.

After a ten-minute wait, which makes me miss the next fast train, I fossick in my bag only to discover that my new debit card is not in my wallet. Or in any of the myriad pockets, or among half my life's debris in the bottom. What on earth have I done with it? The thought of having to cancel it and get yet another card with all the associated hassle is exhausting. No, today is not a good day.

As I stand, sticky in the heat, on the platform, a small marmalade cat exits the waiting room oozing belly down between the wheels of a baby buggy. It eyes the small person waving a chubby hand at it, and then the tail, oddly kinked, stands up straight in recognition of a kindred spirit and it jumps onto the child's knees. There is a squawk from an appalled mother and her flailing hand sends the cat flying. It skitters away, ears flattened, and comes to a tense halt under a luggage trolley. Both cat and I glare at the mother.

'It was only being friendly,' I protest.

'Filthy creature,' she spits, but she means, 'Mind your own bloody business.'

A recollection floats to the surface of my mind: Dad dropping my 'please be pleased with me' offering of toast, butter and marmalade into the bin, castigating me for my dirty fingernails and unhygienic hands. Sitting on the trolley I put a hand down in apology, but the marmalade cat backs off with a hiss.

'I don't blame you,' I mutter. 'And I know just how you feel.'

As the train clatters slowly towards Southampton, I reflect again on my failures and debate how much of my disastrous day I am going to tell Mike.

Smarting at his prediction that Vermont and Paget wouldn't be interested in my business, I had waspishly asserted I would get either a loan or investment from them. Now I am uncomfortably aware that I am going to be on the receiving end of 'I told you so', even though he might not verbalise it. When we were first together, there was none of the critical attitudes that seem to have crept in recently. The very opposite in fact. He had been so encouraging and positive about the business.

The heat makes my eyes feel gritty, and peripheral vision seems to close slightly.

* * *

Letting myself into the flat, I am surprised but relieved to find Mike home already. I walk into his comforting, familiar arms and lean against his chest, inhaling the blue-green smell of him. The colour of his smell has changed a little in the last few months, which I find vaguely odd as I tend to recognise people by their colour. But it is so subconscious that I am not altogether sure if a person's smell changes colour or not. I put it down to a new aftershave.

'Hello, my darling. You look exhausted. How was your meeting with Mr Paget?'

Pushing away the memory of today's fiasco I hide my flushed face in his shirt buttons. 'Not a hope. You were right. They weren't interested. Embarrassing really.' I'm aware that I'm gabbling.

'What a shame,' he says sympathetically. 'You were so certain you could persuade them.'

Guilt – that I walked out on Mr Paget, that I didn't even try, that now I'm telling Mike half-truths, lies – sweeps over me. Closing my eyes on my failure, I change the subject.

'On top of everything else, I can't find my new bank card. I suppose I'll have to tell the bank to cancel it and get another one.' My shoulders drop in irritable weariness. 'The process is so slow and cumbersome. A whole raft of accounts will now have all the wrong details.'

'Oh, Cass! You must remember to put it straight back in your wallet after you've used it.' His rueful despair rubs in today's failures. 'It's probably on your desk. Unless you left it in a shop. Where have you looked?'

'Nowhere yet. I haven't had a chance, have I? I haven't been shopping and I *do* put it back in my wallet.'

He shakes his head. 'You nearly always put your card back, but this time you didn't, and then there's a disaster. You're a bit careless about these things.' He grins at me, teasing, trying to lighten the moment. 'Like not noticing your account is empty.' But the teasing feels like sarcasm. Something I would normally shrug off, but after a day like today it feels like a wasp sting; unexpected, sharp and painful.

I snap peevishly, 'You're the one who said you'd look after the finances.'

He reacts badly to my resentment. 'But they're still your finances.' The rebuke is irrefutable and he continues more gently. 'You'd better ring the bank now and cancel the card before the rest of your money is cleared out.'

I am remorseful about my temper loss and exhausted at the thought of replacing yet another card. 'I'd better look for it first before raising the alarm.' I empty my bag onto the coffee table with a noise like a one-armed bandit giving up a week's worth of coinage and stir the assorted essentials without success.

'Good Lord!' Mike says as if he's never seen the extent of female necessities before. 'It's a wonder you don't have a permanently dislocated shoulder, carrying all that around.'

He helps me look, but we can't find it anywhere. I ring the bank and cancel it. A new one will arrive next week, sometime.

'That is so irritating.' I am nearly shouting. 'As if I haven't got enough to deal with without problems with my personal account as well.'

Mike's mouth compresses gravely. 'Carelessness has its consequences.'

'Thank you so much for your helpful comments. Don't be so bloody pompous.' There goes my temper again, but having my misfortunes laid entirely at my door, deserved or not, brings out the worst in me. My troubles are making me more sensitive these days, or he is getting fed up with my reactions. Or both.

'I didn't mean to upset you.' His hands lift defensively. 'It's just that so many things have gone wrong for you, I get worried.' He stretches out to touch my face and it is all that I can do not to twitch away from it.

After we've eaten, Mike suggests a spin in his new prized possession, a white Aston Martin with his personalised number plate. He is, I suppose, trying to mend some fences, but I am still feeling sullen. The open roof makes talking difficult and I am left with my thoughts, the ever-turning wheel spewing out the moment when I went to transfer the money for the new premises.

* * *

The colours of the figures were all wrong. Puzzlement lasted about three seconds before I clocked the balance. The savings account had only a few hundred pounds in it instead of many thousands. I'd enlarged the font to make sure I wasn't having one of my non-seeing moments, and then a blast of panic and horror hit me in the chest, expelling all the air from my lungs.

I closed down, pulled out plugs, and sat frozen, unable to think what on earth to do. Mike was in late meetings at his office, his phone turned off. I WhatsApped him with urgent *Ring Me*'s but knew he wouldn't and couldn't until he was finished. Do not jump to conclusions. Do not assume the worst. It could be a computer error. A bank error.

I punched in Wendy's number, but then hung up. Wendy designs clothes. More to the point she designs many of her clothes from the sustainable fabrics I source, but neither she nor I make a huge profit from the sector. Her impending retirement has coincided with my ambitions to expand. She wants to sell her premises and I want to buy them, and it had seemed the perfect answer for both of us. But there was not much point in giving such bad news to my biggest creditor before I had to. I spent long minutes trying to contact the bank fraud team and even longer explaining my disaster.

Eventually, Mike returned.

'What's happened?' he said, putting his laptop case on the hall chair.

I tried to get a grip on my disintegrating self-control. 'Ecolore's capital has gone. Disappeared. There's nothing left in my reserve account.' There was as near to a sob in my voice as there ever has been. He turned, frowning, as if he had misheard and misunderstood.

'What?'

'I went to transfer the money for Wendy's shop and the colours were all wrong. All the money has gone.'

Mike has never understood that numbers are colours for me, but he certainly understood what I was saying. He reared back like a horse faced with a striking cobra. 'You must have overspent.'

'I haven't overspent,' I said furiously. 'Don't be ridiculous! I don't use my reserves except for big projects. Someone has stolen the money.'

He went very still. 'That's highly unlikely. You must have made a mistake. Your eyes are so bad, you must have made a mistake.'

'I haven't. I've double-checked. The bank has confirmed the balance.'

He let fly a stream of questions I couldn't answer. 'How much money? When did it happen? Did the bank flag it up? Can they get it back?'

'Mike, I don't *know*! I discovered it this afternoon and I've been dealing with the bank ever since. Everyone, including me, is going round like headless chickens.'

He calmed down a bit. 'It must be a mistake. Someone at the bank has pressed the wrong buttons. Did you check the current account? Perhaps they've debited one but credited the other. It must be a bank error.' He put his arms around me. 'Darling girl, it'll be all right. It has to be a bank error.'

For a second a frail little seed of hope had germinated. Had I checked the other account? Yes, I had. All too quickly, the little seed died a death. 'It's not a bank error,' I said hopelessly. 'It was transferred out and they don't know where to.'

His arms tightened and a vein in his forehead pulsed. 'Cass, you must have done something and forgotten. Transferred it to another account. Put it in your ISA?' I was tense with indefinable guilt. What the hell *had* I done? What the hell *could* I have done? Something unbelievably stupid?

Later, we concluded that Richard, our bookkeeper, must be the culprit. Mike was mortified and furious because it was he that recommended and recruited Richard. I was filled with guilt because I should have kept a closer eye on the numbers. No, not a closer eye. Just an eye.

Now we are both getting over the shock and beginning to be a bit more sensible. The bank accounts have been safeguarded – not that there is a huge amount to be kept safe – and the bank was helpful enough to put me in touch with Vermont and Paget, private investment bankers. But today I had failed once again by walking out on Mr Dominic Paget because I was embarrassed. That door had now closed, and I must try a different one. How does one find an investor and why would they want to invest in a company with no reserves at all?

The open top of the Aston has blown slightly more refreshing air into my addled brain, and on return, I try to tackle some of the urgent business. Mike comes in and massages my stiff shoulders.

'Stop that and come and watch the news.' His hands go still. 'What's that, near the back of your filing cabinet?'

Scrabbling on the floor I retrieve my errant bank card. How on earth did it get there?

'Must have slipped between the desk and filing cabinet,' he says. 'Lucky I saw it.'

‘Sorry, madam,’ says the emergency number after another million security questions. ‘Your card has already been cancelled and a new one ordered. Don’t worry, the new one should arrive by Wednesday.’

Why can’t life be simpler?

Chapter Two

On Saturday I colour my hair blue in an effort to lift my spirits and, at Mike's suggestion, work at the sports club while he plays squash. My office in the flat now feels insecure and lonely, whereas coming to the club with Mike feels inclusive and supportive. Between games, he sometimes comes into the café and gives me a cuddle and a kiss. But I find it difficult to design sports bags while my brain is churning financial disaster like a demented washing machine.

'May I join you?' Again, it is that posh voice that called me ma'am when I was stark naked. Looking up I find it belongs to exactly that person: Mr Dominic Paget the investment banker who never was. He still smells, amber. I don't do blushing, and in public I wear make-up, but I have to make a genuine effort to be unsurprised. Cool. Severe.

Snapping the graphics tablet off, I fold my hands on top of it, trying not to fiddle with the pen. He is wearing a pink polo shirt and taupe chinos, both of them expensive.

Not taking silence for a negative answer, he sits down opposite me, opens his briefcase and gives me a flat package and a smile. My breath snags. The smile is lopsidedly attractive, and lots of little lines pucker around his mouth. I am shocked by the fleeting thought of how kissable that mouth is.

'I thought you might like your swimsuit back.' Oh, Mr Paget, you've no idea how much I needed it back. I had been dreading confessing its loss to Wendy. How the hell did he find me?

He answers the thought. 'Your mobile is off. I rang your office number, and you weren't there. So as it's Saturday I came inquiring at your local sports centre.' This is amazing sleuth work, not to mention a lot of effort. Nervously I hope he won't stay because if Mike appears it will be difficult to explain how or why Dominic Paget is here when I hadn't been entirely truthful about our meeting.

'Thank you.' My ankles are tying themselves in a knot under the table, but luckily he can't see.

He leans forward, elbows on the table, one hand folded on the other. 'I do see I am probably not the person you would want to deal with, and I am not touting for business. But your letter was – interesting. And if you hadn't taken off from my office quite so fast, I wanted to say that if you really think someone is stealing from you, I hope you have contacted the police and a good lawyer, as well as seeking investment.' Half my brain thinks this is a rather meagre excuse for searching me out when he could have phoned on Monday. 'We don't often come across an entrepreneur who is as passionate about their objectives as they are practical about their finances. One or the other, but not always both.' There comes that delightful crinkly smile again and the other half of my brain is flattered that he thinks I'm worth the effort.

I find that my mouth is open and shut it. Mike would agree about the passion, but not about the finances. Why is this man saying all these complimentary things and do I believe him? Does he have some ulterior motive and if so, what?

Trying to hide the fact that I am warmed by his interest and want to smile back, I say stiffly, 'My partner thinks I should gather much more information before going to the police.'

'Why?' The word is imbued with curiosity, not accusation. I don't know what possesses me to answer him.

'He's not convinced that it's been stolen. He says it may have been transferred somewhere else by mistake.' I wouldn't normally tell virtual strangers that Mike thinks I'm scatty, but to my confusion, this virtual stranger seems to be loosening my tongue.

Mr Paget's eyebrows go up. 'And do you think he might be right?'

'No.' I shake my head, hesitating. I am still affronted by Mike's insinuation that I may have forgotten what I've done with my money, but a little bit of me wonders if it could possibly be true. 'I'm just finding it difficult to say precisely what has been stolen, and when. Over what time period, and what happened to the withdrawals.'

'I would have thought that's what the police should be doing.' His voice is perfectly mild. Why do I think there is scepticism? I wriggle, hopefully only metaphorically. 'And do you have a lawyer?'

I'm beginning to get scratchy about this questioning and more nervous about Mike appearing. 'A lawyer is not much good to me if I don't have any evidence. And funnily enough, there is now not enough money to hire one. A chicken and egg situation, I fear.'

'You must have a lawyer, surely. You can't have a business like yours without one.' He looks concerned, but also I suspect he thinks I am ditzy. It is perceived that people who wear colour are generally ditzy.

'Well, I do have one, but I'm not about to confide in him.' Mike had suggested early on that we both use his lawyer as it was easier and cheaper. I hadn't liked the man's patronising manner much, but it had seemed sensible.

He looks at me a bit sharply, cocking his head to one side.

'Because?' When I don't answer him, a frown line

appears between his eyebrows. 'You don't trust him? You think he may be involved?'

'A lawyer? No, he can't be, surely! But I do find it difficult to trust anybody now, and my office doesn't feel very safe. That's why I'm here.' I wave a hand around the café. 'That's why I have been busy securing my bank accounts, both personal and business. Now, alas, with not much in them.'

There is a considerable pause while I watch some of his cogs turning. His nose is very straight. Mine, Mike says affectionately, has a dip in it like a soup spoon.

'You understand about hackers and scams?'

I shake my head slowly. 'As much as anyone else, I guess. I've got all the usual antivirus and malware programs. But I am a designer, not a technician. And I don't know whether I know whoever did this, or if it's a business connection, or a total stranger.'

I heave in a breath, tugging a hank of pale cornflower-blue hair behind an ear. I don't add that I am dead scared. I get to my feet, inviting a goodbye, a final handshake.

'Thanks for bringing back the swimsuit.'

He ignores my pointed invitation to leave and remains where he is, fingers linked under a clean-shaven chin. A solid, hard-muscled, mature man, considering me.

'Tell me more about your business. You must have started it when you were a teenager. How did you get your start-up funds?'

There is a subdued clatter from the café area behind him, and a cluster of sweaty squash players swarm for drinks at the counter, smelling dark plum. Mike is not among them, to my relief. I sit down again slowly. Now it seems there might be a second chance if I can only bury the sports centre humiliation.

'I started at nineteen, when I had to drop out of art school – lack of funds. I started making clothes from fabric offcuts which were being thrown away and selling them in the market locally. They were like patchworks; lots of quilting to hold them together. That's when I first realised what a huge amount of wastage was going on. Manufacturers were throwing away fabrics, thread, buttons, everything imaginable. Nobody recycled or sent it to those who could use it. It went into landfill. It made me furious.'

He is listening. He has grey eyes and a penetrating gaze. 'So, you started from nothing. How long until you made some money?'

'I made enough to feed myself and Mum from the end of that term, then Mum died and Dad sold the house. After that, it was a bit trickier cos I had to rent accommodation, and working space as well, but I was OK. I just made more stuff and by then I was learning what people liked. What they bought.'

His steady scrutiny becomes a little sceptical. 'And you made enough to live on, selling in the local market?'

'Oh no. I was finding other outlets. It was taking off. I had labels and flyers made. And I met a boy – a homeless refugee – who was a real wiz on the sewing machine. Then I bought another sewing machine. Then I rented more space and almost went under.' I grin, remembering a hungry time. 'That taught me a lesson about finance! I had to let my tailor go.'

My tummy is rumbling. 'Anyway, no start-up funds. Just sheer bloody hard work. Would you like a coffee? I need a slug of chocolate cake too.' I get to my feet, but he waves me down again.

'I'll get it. Don't go away.' He walks lightly for such a solid man. He's not gym-muscled, and he's neither fat nor thin but has the firmness of maturity. Attractive. And – I find myself approving – authoritative; the girl behind the counter serves him before the remaining sweaty squash players.

Returning with much-needed sustenance, he settles in his chair again. 'You said your father sold the house after your mother died. Did you not get any money then?'

I shake my head, remembering the utter thankfulness I felt at not having to be in the same house as him, and that my mother was free of his malice at last.

'No. I wouldn't have taken it if he'd offered. And he didn't.'

He looks a bit shocked. 'What does your father do?'

'He's an independent financial adviser. Not that he advised me, or only to tell me to get a proper job.'

Dominic Paget allows a moment's silence, his mouth compressing a little. Is that disapproval of my father? Surprise flickers. Why would he care?

'But you didn't go under. You now run a design business – how is it pronounced by the way? Ee colour?'

'Not quite. It's Ecolore. Echo loray. Eco and colour in Italian.'

He laughs. 'Of course. It sounds delightful – and clever. So, a design business based on sustainability and recycled materials, and you had enough in the bank to tempt someone to steal just at the point of expanding your business. And you are only thirty-seven if I calculate right. That is quite some achievement. Tell me more about how you got there.'

No one had ever put it like that or said that it was an achievement. A warm, grateful feeling begins to permeate the anger and the self-blame. I think I like Dominic Paget, although I have only just met him. I am wary of men after my experience of a father.

I tell him more about my passion for saving the world from drowning in plastic; how I searched out the scientists and engineers who could do miraculous things with plastic rubbish and how I persuaded them to let me loose with colours and designs on the results of their labours. How

I found manufacturers of clothes and shoes and wigs and accessories and household gadgets and persuaded them to use the beautiful fabrics and materials that gave new life to litter.

The grey gaze doesn't leave me as he takes a sip of his coffee. 'The green wig? That didn't look like plastic, it looked like real hair.'

'The wigs are made from recycled plastic too. It doesn't attract static, unlike other materials – nylon or acrylic for example. The clothes fabrics are the same. They're fabulous.' I lick the last of the chocolate cake off my fingers and catch a little grin as he watches me. 'Sadly, we don't make more than a tiny dent in the waste and landfill tragedy, but I suppose it's a beginning.'

'So you don't actually manufacture clothes or shoes or anything else?'

He is assessing the information. This man is asking business questions. Investment questions. I don't think it's just curiosity or polite conversation. A bubble starts deep in my gut, grows bigger, rises steadily into my diaphragm, and expands under my ribs. Forget the men's changing room, Cass, sell your dreams and your passion to this very attractive man. Save Ecolore. Save the planet. I blink and concentrate.

'Nope. I source the fabrics, design prints and colourways, suggest uses for the materials, source the manufacturers, get them made up and showcase them by putting them into retail outlets – usually small outlets. The big boys aren't interested because I'm not big enough. I'd like to be big enough because if you can scale up, costs come down. But it's difficult to tout the products around retail outlets. It takes a lot of time and I am a one-woman outfit and my skills are in textile design, not sales. Mike, my partner, helps me with the website and marketing ideas and finance, but I've been running the business from home and just can't go on like that.' I wonder if I'm sounding peevish and inject some hopeful aspiration.

'I want to expand. I need an office and a storage area and a showroom. I need an assistant and partners if I am to increase turnover and profits. This theft came at exactly the moment I was making that expansion. I need my financial reserves.' Quite an understatement. 'And I have considerable extra costs right now with a project involving carpets made from recycled plastics.'

He looks astounded. 'Plastic *carpets*?' His laugh isn't a laughing 'at' of scepticism, it's a laugh of fascination. 'It sounds scratchy! Tell me more.' His eyes hold something else. Respect? Admiration? The bubble inside me grows bigger.

He makes me feel like laughing too, which hasn't happened since my disaster. 'No, it isn't scratchy. It's silky – softer than wool, but much more easily cleaned and very strong. Plastic bottles are ground into small chips which are cleaned and melted. Then it's coloured and stranded into plastic thread and spun into carpet yarn.' If he's thinking about investing, he'd better know what he's investing in. 'It's brilliant, but the colours are so boring! Think of all the hotels and conference venues that would use it if there was a range of colours and designs!'

But nobody agrees with me, even Mike, who had been dubious about my ideas. Wendy thought the carpet project timing was madness, just as I was expanding into new premises.

'I've got colour samples being made up, and designs on the drawing board, but it was quite an investment and now I haven't got enough funds to go forward.' There I am, whining again. 'Sorry. I've been burbling on. So tedious of me.'

He shakes his head and smiles that very delightful smile again. 'Not tedious. Not at all. I think your business has got a great deal of potential.'

That sounds positive, I'm glad someone is impressed by the potential. My bubble expands a little bit more. 'So that's why the bank advised me to knock on your door. *They* weren't going to help, that's for sure.'

'No,' he says thoughtfully. 'The high street banks are not into risk.' He pushes his coffee cup away and gets out his mobile. I watch him keying in some notes and hope rises again. He has big strong hands and good nails. I always notice nails. Another batch of sweaty people swarms to the counter. Again, I am nervous that Mike is among them, and relieved that he is not.

'What's the present situation with your bank's fraud department?'

'They confirm that the online banking transfers were made to another account in my name. But it wasn't my account and I never had knowledge or access to it. But somebody used it – a lot. In any case, that account is now empty and closed. Initially, they thought the whole thing was a scam by me.' That had been an extraordinary shock, and even now my guts twist at the recollection. 'Honestly, you'd think they could trace the movement of funds!' I feel the frustration and anger taking over again. 'And because "I sanctioned it", it's "not their fault" and some withdrawals happened months – years – ago, so the bank isn't going to repay me.'

'And it took you and your partner all that time to notice the withdrawals?'

'The theft is from my reserves,' I say defensively. 'I knew what was in it and I didn't need to look at it unless I needed capital. It was when I came to use it that I found there were virtually no reserves at all.' I am reluctant to try to explain my weakness with numbers when I don't even understand it myself.

He leans back in his chair, his hands relaxed in his lap, but his eyes are intent. 'So it was you who found the discrepancies, not your partner who advises on your finances?' He waits for my nod of agreement. 'Did he know about your expansion plans?'

Can I hear an underlying criticism of Mike? 'Yes, of course,' I say shortly.

'And your carpet ideas?'

Even shorter. 'Yes.'

'And did he think these ideas were good ones?'

I hesitate, remembering Mike's cautious reaction. 'Not immediately. He thought it was a bit risky doing both projects at the same time.'

'And now there is no question of expansion because there are no funds.' His matter-of-fact statement is not quite a question and makes me want to fight back. Although I say nothing, he is watching my face, and there is a flash of something. Satisfaction? A confirmation of expectation?

I suppose my losses are probably peanuts to a banker. As he enters more stuff on his phone, I reflect on why he is so attractive. Perhaps it's because older men are much more at home in themselves; they aren't trying so hard to impress. Although his face is tired looking, the widely spaced eyes seem to see inside me. I doubt anyone would take him for a ride. Those grey eyes now pin me with intent.

'I'm going to give you the name of a friend of mine. He's a senior partner in a law firm in Southampton and you may need a good lawyer depending on how the police do. I think you'd like each other.' He looks up a number and writes it on a business card. 'You can quote my name. Do you have a business plan?'

My shoulders drop. 'Well, I did. A three-year plan and a five-year plan too. They've just gone gurgling down the drain,' I say bitterly.

He smiles briefly. 'I make absolutely no promises, but if you want to rethink your application, send those plans and any other previously considered capital expenditure, to my office and we will look at them. What you sent with your initial letter was not enough.' He leans back and taps on the table with his fingers flat. 'And should we consider your application, I would like to meet your partner, as he is your financial adviser, to hear what he thinks and why.'

Typical bloody man who thinks a woman can't run a business! 'He's not a financial adviser in that sense,' I say tartly. 'He's my partner and we discuss things. This is my business and I run it.' Too late I remember that I want this man's help. 'Sorry. Didn't mean to be rude, but I really am quite capable of making sensible decisions, even if I look odd.' Oh Lord, Cass! Don't make it worse.

Dominic Paget swings forward and laces his fingers together in front of him. The grey eyes are amused but at the same time sharply assessing.

'Oh, I can see that. That wasn't what I meant at all.'

He rises and adds an afterthought, 'I have a son doing software and systems security at Oxford but who is just at this moment at an irritating – irritating for me, you understand – loose end. I think you need someone to check on your security and to do it fast and discreetly. Money laundering is an art these days.' He waits out the silence.

'I can't pay him.' My tone is almost aggressive as I hold his gaze.

'No, I understand that. But I would pay to get the loose end tied up for an hour or two. Otherwise, students just come home and spend their days in bed.' The tired eyes are smiling.

Staring at him, I feel like Alice in Wonderland. 'Why are you doing this?'

He shrugs and the grey eyes are still on mine. It is only for a moment, but oddly it feels like an eternity. Then he smiles that warm attractive smile again and my tummy does a little pirouette. He shakes my hand, holding it for perhaps a second longer than necessary and the amber smell drifts in my throat.

‘I don’t like thieves,’ he says. ‘And I love the blue hair.’

Chapter Three

'A guy is coming to check on my computer and accounts security,' I tell Mike. 'Recommended by that investment banker, Dominic Paget.'

He leans back on the sofa and there is surprise in his voice. 'I thought you said they weren't interested?'

'I didn't think they were, but I may be wrong. He was trying to help anyway.'

There's a silence and then he says, 'How long do you think these withdrawals have been happening?'

'I don't know. The statements are all online and I haven't been able to go through them all yet and it's so ...' Why do I find it so hard to explain the lack of focus, the way the numbers slip and blur?

'I know, I know. You find it difficult to see the numbers. Don't fret, love. I'll sort it out. We're a team. Partners. You do the design, and I do the finance – or I should do – I'm afraid I haven't kept a good enough eye on it while it's been so hectic at work.'

My conscience squirms. 'You've got so much on your plate already. I should have been watching my own business, not relying on you as my voluntary CFO.'

He grins at my poor joke and kisses my cheek, and again I'm aware that his turquoisey blue has veered towards greeny blue. 'As I said, we are partners. In every sense.'

'It's like a stranger has come into the flat uninvited. Helped themselves to food and drink. Opened my cupboards, handled my clothes.' Not for the first time since this theft, I am feeling very shaky and Mike knows it. He pulls me gently across to the sofa and folds me in his arms.

'A violation. I understand. It's not surprising your emotions have got all screwed up. It's got me pretty twitchy as well.'

I don't want to hear that. I want a strong, competent man who is going to sort it out.

When life gets a bit much, Mike retreats to the kitchen. For him, cooking is unwinding. It's his creative spot, whereas mine is the graphics tablet. Tonight, even my tablet cannot soothe my fears and my eyes ache. Dominic Paget's look of respect and admiration has become obscured by Mike's anxieties. I close the tablet down and wander into the kitchen.

I see he has scooted all my rough drawings, which had littered the kitchen, into a pile on the edge of the counter, and I remove them as he does like to cook uncluttered. He is adding little pinches of this and that to a sauce on the hob. I dip my finger.

'Yum. Is that for the chicky?' He always buys free-range from the butcher. None of your supermarket tasteless.

'Yup. What colour does it smell?' He loves that I smell colour.

'Cobalt.' And why does he smell blue-green?

'What do you suppose that is?' he says, indicating a tiny black item marooned on a square of kitchen towel. I peer at it. Cumin? A chip of black nail varnish? A broken piece of my eyeliner pencil? I prod it cautiously with a blue fingernail and squint, but I can't see it properly and feel the need for a bit of levity.

'Mouse dropping? It's too big. More likely a rat.'

'Oh, God! That's what I thought.' He takes an appalled step further away from it. He has never quite got a handle on my sense of humour. 'Honestly, Cass, your kitchen cleanliness needs to improve *radically*. In fact, not just in the kitchen, if I'm honest.' He wraps the offending item in the paper and puts it in the bin, then sprays the granite top with Dettol cleaner and wipes it clean. 'Please ring a rat catcher tomorrow morning.' He sounds ratty, and like me, our circumstances rattle him.

'I think they're called pest control officers these days. But yes.'

I'm not perfect, I know, but I'm not dirty. I feel a bit hurt.

* * *

Monday morning I take Mike's Aston Martin to the car wash early to be valeted by the lovely Polish lads whose comments always make me feel joyful. Mike thinks the short weekly drive gives me a kick, which it does, up to a point. My troubles are shelved for a few minutes as I practise my Polish 'Good Morning', surrounded by the green watery tarmac smell, and the shouts of 'Beautiful hair matches your shoes, Missy Cass!'. Why do some women get uptight about being admired, whether for their looks or their achievements?

Dominic Paget flits through my mind as I walk back to the flat. I wonder why he really came to find me. Is Ecolore such a potential winner? The swimsuit could have been posted. He could have contacted me through my website. I recall that long moment when his grey eyes met mine and find myself smiling. His complete disregard, a seeming forgetfulness, of my previous behaviour and bad language, have disarmed me.

When I get home, I dig out my down-the-drain business plans. There really isn't much point in sending them but he did ask for them, so I email them over, even if they appear hopelessly unprofessional. When Mike had looked at them, he had been encouraging, but I think he felt they were amateurish and that my 'passionate obsession' for sustainability had run away with me.

I ring the pest control officer who sounds like a rat catcher should, all growly and Hampshire, and to my astonishment, he says he'll come round this morning at ten forty-five. The kitchen gets a quick clean-up as I think the rat catcher might give me a lecture otherwise.

The rat catcher is early and smells orange. Some type of oil? Young, thin beard, clean black hair down to his shoulders, round, black-framed glasses, clutching a laptop case and a motorbike helmet, which he puts on the hall table. Catching rats is more technical these days, it seems. His T-shirt says, 'Never under-estimate Binary Man', whatever that means.

'Hi,' he says. 'I'm Patrick. I hear you've got a problem.' He doesn't sound at all like he did on the phone.

'I have. Well, my partner thinks we have. Personally, I've never seen any evidence of mice, let alone a rat.' As I pour us both a coffee, he is looking slightly bemused. 'I always think of rats near dustbins, why would it come upstairs?'

'I don't know,' he says rather cautiously. 'I have to say that I don't know much about rats.'

'You don't?' We stare at each other. Surely a pest control officer must know about rats?

'I came about computer security,' he says, even more cautiously. 'Have I come to the wrong address?'

'Ah!' I say, hilarity trouncing my various tribulations. 'No, you haven't. You could say I've got two problems. You are Mr Paget's computer genius son, who I wasn't expecting, and not the rat catcher, who I was expecting.'

Patrick laughs too, and I notice that his smile is attractively uneven like his father's. 'I thought I'd see if you were home. It's not long on the bike.'

'I'm amazed that a student can surface so early.' I say in admiration as I put toast, butter and strawberry jam on the table. Why is he here and not in Oxford? Do they do any work at all?

Before all the toast has been eaten, the doorbell goes again, and the rat catcher introduces himself as Eddie and looks and sounds exactly as he should. He smells pinky purple and is tattooed everywhere I can see including his face. It makes me wince with transferred pain. What on earth will he look like when he's eighty? We have more coffee and discuss whether blue hair looks best matched to gold or silver nails. Eddie tells us that his wife is a tattooist – which accounts for his decorations – and experimenting with new watercolour inks. Maybe I will pay her a visit, although I have a low pain threshold. And I am nervous about that kind of permanence.

I explain that my beloved has thrown the evidence of the rat away. I do not confess to the possibility that the dropping was my eyeliner pencil.

'A rat within six feet of every person is rubbish,' he informs us. 'It's more like a hundred and fifty feet, and you're unlikely to find them in a house.' This is a relief to me. He finds no evidence, thank God, of rats, but for safety's sake he puts rat poison in ventilating pipes that I never knew existed but now know how to access with a Phillips screwdriver. Rat poison goes behind the kitchen kick plates, and he'll come back next week to check on results.

Patrick Paget has his father's eyes. He looks at things. The ceiling light fittings, the curtain poles, and the shelves of files in the office. He is itching to find evidence of skulduggery on my hard disk. His state-of-the-art building at Oxford has legionnaires' disease.

'It's in the ventilation shafts and they've sent us home till it's sorted.'

I suppose this accounts for him being an irritating loose

end to his father. I learn that a smartphone is far more of a liability, and six times more powerful, than my laptop. Also that everybody, but everybody, knows everything I do and say. But surely not what I think?

'I can't not have Alexa!' I bleat. He shrugs and grins.

'What other devices?'

'We've both got tablets.'

'All synced?'

'Well, my own accounts are.'

'Anybody else have access to your stuff?'

'I suppose in theory, my bookkeeper. My partner Mike keeps an eye on the finances.'

Patrick gets me to open my online banking but makes me stay and watch. He does some clever filtering and downloading.

'Someone's been into your savings account, for sure. The earlier transfers are for odd amounts, and in hundreds of pounds, but the withdrawals get bigger.' He reads out the increasing amounts. 'You don't think that's you?'

'No!' The heatwave is in full swing, but suddenly I am icy cold. 'That's insane! Much more than I'd realised.' Disbelief is making me light-headed. He looks troubled, logs out of the bank and returns to punishing the keyboard.

'Might take a while. I'll do a deep clean for malware.' He sounds concerned.

'Someone has hacked me, haven't they?' There is a fist in my innards, twisting.

'Yep. Afraid so.'

A new SIM card goes into my phone. 'Do you write down your PINS and passwords?'

'Some,' I confess.

He shakes his head. 'And where do you keep them?' He turns my laptop upside down to reveal the sticky labels with my essentials to life written on them.

For a twenty-two-year-old, he has a good eye-roll, and

I take the lecture on the chin. Later he hands my laptop, phone and tablet back, cleaned and scoured. Security everywhere, bleeps and alarms, stuff on the cloud, funny pop-ups, odd apps.

'New PINS the moment I've gone,' he says severely. 'And a new master password.' He gives me so many instructions on what I shouldn't use that I am left wondering if there's anything I can use. Then he hesitates. I can see he is uncomfortable but wanting to say something else. I put my head to one side and question him with a lifted eyebrow.

'What?'

'Can I suggest ...?' He blushes. 'After something like this ... you don't know ... it's a case of safety first ... it would be best ... if ...'

'If what?' I can feel something unwelcome is coming.

'Um – not to tell anyone about your new security details.'

'Well, I'm not about to shout them from the rooftops.' My voice has taken on that tone which heralds bad temper. And then I get it.

'Nothing to anyone? You're saying I shouldn't even tell my partner? Mike? I can assure you he is the one and only person in the world that I *do* trust.'

Patrick nods. 'Yeah. Right. Even so.' He collects his bits of kit. As he goes out the door he says, 'Silver nails with the hair.'

* * *

Mike watches me do a new nail design involving flicking blue onto a coat of silver. After all these years I am extremely accurate with both hands even with my short sight. I can feel his relief that there are no spatters except on the protective sheet.

'So, what did this man do with your security?'

I concentrate on my hands rather than look at him directly. 'He's installed various defensive programs. I have new PINS for everything. And I've changed all the important passwords on the password manager.'

He frowns. 'Well, whatever you do, don't forget your master password. Have you written it down somewhere? You're hopeless about remembering numbers and letters.'

'Well,' I say, 'I've written down the colours and I won't forget them.'

Mike's shoulders drop and he looks mortified. 'I should have checked. And you probably had them written down somewhere obvious. Open house for a hacker. I'm sorry I didn't help you more about all that.' So much for Patrick's reservations about my partner, who now feels guilty about what is my fault. 'I just can't believe you never noticed. That you never looked.'

'I didn't *need* to look. I knew – or thought I knew – how much was in that account. And Richard doesn't check it either. You told him to deal with the current account. There's nothing funny going on in the current account and if there was, Richard would have noticed and told me.' I've always thought of cautious Richard as a bit of an autumn shower and tend to dump the folder of orders and receipts on the desk, go out to clients and leave him to it. Perhaps that was a mistake, although it is hard to think of him as a thief.

'He wouldn't have drawn your attention to his dishonesty, would he?' There is a caustic undertone. 'Have you verified the entries on the current account?'

My brain feels like it's full of dried sludge. I close my eyes momentarily and pull myself together. I am Cass Hunter. I have created a healthy business from scratch; I am not a fool. I am a perfectly sensible businesswoman with skills and talents.

'Can we get this straight? The current account is irrelevant. Nothing wrong with it. It's my capital funds that have been stolen. Transferred, and not to my current account.'

For the umpteenth time, he says, 'Are you sure?'

This time I'm shouting. 'Yes! I am sure. What the hell are you saying, Mike? That you think all this money has been transferred out of my savings and into my current account and then removed? And you think one of us wouldn't have *noticed*? Why on earth would anyone do that anyway?' The stupidity of this conversation is getting to me, and my mental processes are being tied up in knots.

Mike's hands clench and he frowns. He isn't used to me arguing the toss.

'Have you spoken to the bank fraud department?'

'Yes, of course, but they need me to confirm which transfers weren't mine. And I don't have those details yet.'

'Why not, for God's sake?'

The way he says it stings. He knows I hate having to admit that my short sight slows me down.

'It takes a long time because I cannot see properly,' I hiss. 'The printed statements are so hard to see. On the computer you know I have to enlarge the font, and then it doesn't fit on the page, so it's really difficult to find the headings and make sense of it all. It takes so long to sort it out.'

As often happens, his aggression suddenly disappears. His shoulders drop and he puts a hand on my shoulder. 'I know. Of course, I know how difficult it is. I'm sorry to be so cranky when I know your eyes are not your fault.' He goes to get us both a drink and yelps over a sticky puddle on the glass tabletop.

'Aargh! This place is filthy. Look at the dust. Though I suppose you can't see it. And I wish you'd clear up this mess.' He indicates my sewing machine and what I think are perfectly tidy piles of fabrics. 'Look, I'll go through the statements and then you'll have the details for the fraud department. OK?'

I am heartily relieved that he is going to help, although it feels like the days are slipping past without them having the information.

'Darling, do you think you could rustle up some dinner while I try to catch up with work? Delving into your disaster has taken up rather a lot of time.'

'Of course I will.' My annoyance dissipates with his apology. I feel bad about keeping him away from his work, as well as being a lousy housekeeper and, as it turns out, a poor businesswoman as well.

Over supper, he keeps suggesting unlikely causes for my losses.

'Wendy didn't approve, did she?'

'Approval didn't come into it. She wanted me to be careful about big expenses at the same time as expanding the business. But she's a friend. And a customer.' Without Wendy designing clothes for my fabrics and selling them in her shop, I would have had much less of a successful business. And she is my go-to mother figure.

He narrows his eyes thoughtfully. 'Perhaps she didn't want the idea to go any further.'

I take a deep breath and count to three. 'All she had to do was say so. It was Wendy who announced she wanted to sell up and retire.'

He rubs a hand across his eyes, trying for some other explanation. 'Perhaps your financially astute father is still trying to do you down.'

My breath hitches for a flustered moment and then I screw up my face in disbelief. 'You know he hasn't a clue where I am or what I do and nor would he be remotely interested. No, it can't be him.'

Mike sniffs. 'Every time we say "It can't be him," it reinforces the fact it must be *someone*. And your father was horrible to you, so you just don't know if he's still being horrible. Perhaps he does know where you are and what you're doing.'

Anxiety trickles down my spine. My father had tended to scare both my mother and me by seemingly knowing what we had been doing – or not doing. As I grew up, I concluded they were simply good guesses, but I hated his unpredictable meanness. The way he would push a stool in front of her and then laugh when she tripped. Or drop the house keys someplace she couldn't find them or put the little radio out of her reach.

'Don't say that. Of course he doesn't know. Or care.'

Mike shrugs again and his expression clearly says, 'OK, you think what you want to'. Getting up, he prowls restlessly around the sitting room.

'I'll check the accounts. I've got to be in London again tomorrow night – a client conference all afternoon, then dinner with them and our team, then an early staff meeting on Wednesday.' He groans at the thought. 'And we tread carefully with Richard until we know for sure what's happening. Tell him we're concerned about cash flow and must watch the outgoings more carefully and then I'll sack him.'

'We can't just sack him!'

Mike looks grim. 'Yes, we can.'

I turn my head into Mike's neck and breathe him in. Over the past few days, he has reverted to his lovely turquoise smell, but I sense a growing impatience in him which began long before I discovered the theft and wonder whether it's with me, or his job. Mid-life crisis?

'I wish you could be here and talk to him,' I say to Mike, clutching him round the chest. My throat is dry, and I swallow. 'This dinner is very short notice, isn't it? Where are you staying?'

His face scrunches up. 'Can't remember. The office does it. It doesn't matter anyway, as I'll have my phone on me. Text me rather than ringing if you have any problems.'

‘OK. Mr Paget says I must report the theft to the police, and he gave me the name of a lawyer too.’

Mike’s enfolding arm tenses. ‘Good heavens! That seems a bit of a knee-jerk reaction. No need for the police until we know more, and we’ve got a perfectly good lawyer of our own. I’ll give him a ring because he won’t charge just to advise. Don’t panic, babe, I’ll make sure everything is OK.’

Chapter Four

To my surprise, and a strange uplift of heart, Dominic Paget rings me. He sounds faintly apologetic.

'I never know whether Patrick takes in anything I say, and though I wrote down your address and phone number and he mumbled OK, I don't know if he spent the entire morning in bed and then went to the pub. Did he come?'

'Yes, he came. Surprisingly early for a student. He was amazing and I feel very safe now and have all sorts of new security stuff installed. I mistook him for the rat catcher at first.'

Dominic laughs a delightful full-throated laugh. 'Have you got rats?' I laugh too. The Pagets seem to have the ability to make me laugh.

'The rat catcher, when he came, thought it unlikely.'

He inquires how I am feeling (still murderous towards the thief), whether my bank has come up with a refund (no, and not likely to), and whether I have contacted the police yet (no).

'Any good reason why not?'

'Mike thinks the bank will sort it all out.'

'Maybe they will, but you should still report it. It's not a small thing, you know.' It certainly is not, and it's reassuring to know that he's taking my troubles seriously.

'If you want us to consider your business plans,' Dominic goes on, 'we'll need to see that you've taken every opportunity towards getting your money back. I'm sure you understand the implications of not reporting it.'

My fists clench involuntarily. 'You mean it would be a condition of whether you would invest in Ecolore or not?' Somehow, I'm not sure how, my walk-out from Vermont and Paget has metamorphosed into walking in again.

'We would certainly wonder why you were reluctant to inform the police.' His voice is quite even, but there is a firm undertone.

I've been slow on the uptake and my clamped hands suddenly feel as if too hot water is running over them.

'Oh! In case it was me stealing my own business?!' The bank had considered that possibility too, and I am dismayed that Dominic might have thought it. Mike had implied the police would consider it too trivial. 'I'll do it today,' I say meekly.

We discuss the old business plans I sent over and to my surprise, he seems to think they had been well developed and thought through.

'I would like to see a new business plan for the next three years, based on limited investment, say £50,000,' Dominic says. 'How soon could you do that?'

A three-year business plan! Here was I fearing the business was going tits up in a few weeks. I think over my diary and what needs to be done to contain my disaster. 'By the end of next week? Does this mean you might reconsider my application?'

There is a smile in his voice. 'We never rejected it. It was you who walked out on us.'

I don't think I've ever come across such a forgiving character. 'Thank you so much,' I say gratefully and hope it sounds as heartfelt as I feel.

* * *

Unable to face putting this whole mess down in writing, I visit the police station in person. Getting to the right department, and the right police officers, takes forever, and then it still has to be written down.

Mike phones after his staff meeting and nervously I tell him that I've reported the theft to the police.

His disapproving tone tells me immediately that he thinks that was a bad idea. 'You have no idea what's happened, or when, or where. I told you it wasn't necessary and now you've ignored my advice and the whole thing is going to get clogged up in bureaucracy.'

I feel extra hot and move to the open window. 'It was necessary! This is a major theft!'

'If it was a theft at all. You'll have a lot of egg on your face if it turns out this is all your fault, which seems perfectly possible. Why didn't you check with me first before making ill-considered decisions?'

The heat burns up my face. This is traitor talk. 'Mike, Ecolore is *my* business, and I am entitled to make decisions about it, whether you think they are ill-considered or not.' I am trembling and can feel the sweat gathering on my face, trickling down beside my nose to lie salty on my tongue. I want to think it is rage, but it is apprehension as well. I have seldom heard him so angry and dictatorial, but then I have seldom argued the toss to this extent. 'An investment or loan is dependent on my reporting the theft to the police.'

'You don't know what's missing, if anything. Your accounts are hardly accurate, half the receipts aren't there, let alone the bills.' This is surely not true as well as irrelevant, and I am taken aback by his vehemence. 'They'll only say they'll "look into it" and then not ask the right questions or interview Richard. They'll label you a time waster.'

'You can't sack Richard on suspicion,' I say angrily. 'But the only people who can check whether his bank account is full of money which he hasn't earned are the police.' I am getting louder. 'I do not understand why you are so against it when it's my business that has been ransacked.'

He sounds exhausted. 'Cass, I'm feeling rough after the office dinner. I simply haven't got the time to sort it right now. If only you had kept better records it would be easier. You are pretty disorganised about your filing and paperwork, to put it mildly.'

I don't have the energy to argue with him any longer. 'Mike, I have to go, Richard is due any minute.' I cut the call.

Am I disorganised? I'm not sure how to be *more* organised. I stare at my coloured filing system, which I always thought worked perfectly well. What does he mean, my accounts are hardly accurate? The support he has always given me seems to be melting away like ice cream in the sun. My anxiety and confusion are gradually becoming anger and hurt, and my mind skitters about like an aspen tree: silver one moment, murky green confusion the next.

* * *

Dominic rings to clarify some details of the business plan. I don't mention Mike's reaction to my telling the police, but instead tell him about my meeting with Richard.

'It was awful. I didn't know whether to be angry or apologetic. He was horrified – stared at the accounts like a skydiver who had changed his mind a second too late. Swore he never had and never would touch my money. Said he only used the bookkeeping program. He was very, very upset. But I don't know if that was because he was being wrongly accused, or because he was guilty.'

My eyes have that gritty feel again and I want to take my lenses out. I am out of my depth and all my certainties are uncertain. My brain deals with colour, shapes, shades and sustainability. It doesn't deal with betrayal, money, greed, deviousness and plain old dishonesty.

'Did you believe him?' Dominic asks.

I don't answer immediately because my answer has consequences. If someone looks dishonest, you wouldn't trust him with your money, would you? I have difficulty thinking that honest-looking Richard, grey and characterless, is cheating me. Dominic doesn't press me. He just waits.

'Yes,' I say wearily. 'Yes, I believe him. But what do I know? My judgement is not exactly reliable, is it?'

'Better to trust than distrust until proved wrong,' Dominic says, which is kind of him. Mike would advise the opposite. 'It must have been an unpleasant and unsettling meeting.' I am touched by his empathy. I had expected a banker to consider only financial implications, but here was a positively human one. Lucky wife. Lucky children. Does he have other children besides computer genius Patrick?

* * *

Guilty about our quarrel over Richard and conscious that Mike is struggling with my problems as well as his own work, I resolve to do a bit of tidying and cleaning, which I know will please him. I'm also conscience stricken that I feel so attracted to Dominic Paget.

In his turquoise-smelling dressing room, I fold, hang up, and put away clothes and drop old receipts and grubby Polo mints into the waste bin. After a dust and vacuum, it all looks immaculate. Colours prick at my subconscious. Yellow, blue, grey, ochre. His expensive leather shoes smell sky blue, the same colour as the number four. Pale yellow furniture polish.

When he returns, late, tired and hot, I am pleased that the cleaning is noticed.

'My dressing room looks gorgeous, darling. It hasn't had such a spring clean in ages!' He leans across and kisses my cheek, the scent of him again oddly greeny blue. 'Thank you. Much appreciated. And the kitchen too. Not a sign of a rat!'

I try to cuff him, but he grabs my hand and kisses my throat, moving upwards until he reaches the side of my neck where he blows a gigantic tickly raspberry. I screech and dissolve in giggles.

'Eddie the Rat Catcher is coming back on Monday to check.'

'Let's hope Eddie finds no sign of a rat either.'

Over supper, Mike tells me he is meeting with Vermont and Paget. Without me. Without consulting me. Tomorrow. Into my gobsmacked silence, he also mentions his fortieth birthday and how we must celebrate – something that had quite slipped my attention due to Ecolore's troubles. Any possible birthday enthusiasm is eradicated by the news of this very unwelcome meeting between Vermont and Paget and my partner.

'Why you?' This is another reference to women in business being unreliable and incompetent. I can feel my indignation mounting.

He shrugs. 'I don't know. Dominic Paget asked me to meet them.'

'Don't you dare tell them that you disapprove of my plans.'

'Of course not! But I will give my honest opinion on any questions he has.' That's what worries me.

I'm so cross, I phone Dominic in the morning after Mike has left for the office. 'It's my business,' I protest. 'I should be there.'

'It's OK.' Dominic is firm and patient. 'If you're present,

he won't say what he really thinks, and you will interrupt, and we won't get the information we want. It's not because I don't trust your judgement, we just want to have Mike's take on it too, and if he has been involved in advising on your finance, we have to take all facts and information into account.'

I still feel deeply insulted that he wants to discuss my business finances with Mike rather than me. I have an underlying suspicion that he thinks Mike's opinion of me and my business may be entirely different from mine.

* * *

When he arrives back at the flat, Mike is in a good mood. Evidently the meeting has gone well. I am seething with a volatile mixture of anger, insult and anxiety.

'I rather liked him,' Mike remarks. 'Sensible sort of guy, and a good listener. He and his partner were extremely interested.'

'In what?' I ask stuffily. 'My business, the finances, or your opinion?'

Mike chooses not to notice my stuffiness. 'In everything. I was able to give them the facts and figures, and they seemed very satisfied.'

'They've already had the facts and figures. What do you mean, "satisfied"?' My fingers lace themselves into a bad-tempered knot. 'Have you got anything more concrete? Are they going to offer any finance?'

'Oh, well. We didn't really discuss that. No doubt they'll have to calculate whether they'd get their money back, and how they'd advise you to do future business.'

A fizzing sensation runs up my back and down to my fingers. My voice rises to a squawk. 'They'd advise me how to run the business?'

'I would assume so, if they are thinking of investing in it.' His eyes flicker to mine and away again as if to calculate my reaction. 'They asked a lot of questions about it, and what my advice would be.'

'And what were those questions, and what was your advice?' If I don't sound dangerous, I certainly feel it. My jaw hurts and I consciously unclench my teeth and loosen my hands.

He shrugs. 'They asked mainly about your marketing and financial planning. We didn't discuss your future expansion plans in any detail, though I said I was cautious about your intentions and couldn't honestly advise going ahead.'

'And why would you be giving them advice on how to manage Ecolore, which I have run successfully for seventeen years on my own until I encountered a thief?' Sarcasm and fury vie with alarm. 'A business about which you know virtually nothing, and have no interest in?'

Some cold, detached bit of me thinks that he looks hurt to make me feel out of line.

'Don't be so scratchy! I've been involved in it for six years and know a great deal about it. Of course I'm interested! Have you forgotten how much marketing I've done and all the financial advice? I only want to help you and you don't seem to be at all grateful.'

Not much help when someone can help themselves. He must be unaware of my tense anger because he ruffles my hair fondly as he takes a sip of his gin and tonic. 'Don't worry. I'm sure they'll invest, or at the very least offer a loan.' He says it in a way which means he isn't at all sure and I very nearly slap him.

* * *

On Monday the heatwave and Eddie Rat Catcher return, and there are no warfarin casualties in the ventilation shafts or behind the kick plates. Mike will be relieved.

After Eddie departs, I talk to the bank again who have nothing helpful to add to their last unhelpfulness. The carpet manufacturers reluctantly agree to a deferred payment for my samples; I have never had to do that before and feel ashamed of requesting it.

After an uneasy weekend following our bad-tempered exchange, I again find myself wanting to do something Mike will approve of. Cleaning up some of the office mess is one of those things. The office is what an estate agent would consider to be the dining room. Because it joins the kitchen via a generous archway, conversation can flow easily between the two, if one of us is cooking and the other doing paperwork. It's usually me doing paperwork because I've been out to manufacturers or retailers all day, but Mike is often unaware that conversation, concentration and poor sight are too much to cope with simultaneously.

Both our desks look out of the north-facing window, to dreary grey buildings across the street. There are two two-drawer filing cabinets between the desks. Mine is bright red and his bright blue. The red one always has several stacks of files and samples all over it. The blue one is, like his desk, tidy, but his filing tray tends to overflow, perhaps in the unfulfilled hope that I will do his filing, like a secretary. He is a hoarder. I have never understood why he prints everything off the computer – onto new white paper which enrages the planet-saving-me – and then files it. The wall opposite the window is shelved floor to ceiling and stacked with box files and lever arch ring binders. Mike's have perfectly ordinary names like Insurance, Utilities and Investments and go back in time to the age of T-Rex. Mine are thin, unnamed but colour-coordinated. They make perfect sense to me. Everything else is on my computer.

A good deal of stationery detritus has ended up in the space behind our desks, along with a spaghetti junction of cables liberally coated with dead flies, dust and spiders. I have a strong aversion to spiders. I look at the mess in distaste and pull on my rubber gloves.

At the back of my mind, despite all my busyness, I want to know exactly what went on at that meeting last Friday. Do I ring Dominic Paget, or do I ignore the insult to my competence? Maybe Mike is right, and I'm not competent. Perhaps my judgement is not as good as I thought. I may well be a victim of self-delusion as well as a victim of fraud. I don't ring Dominic.

I give the cables and floor the scouring of a lifetime and sort out paperclips, drawing pins, pens and pencils into their allotted little pots and boxes. I love little boxes. I am left with Post-it notes covered in passwords for who knows what, old receipts, business cards, and dead spiders and tip the whole lot into the bin. Yellow, blue, grey and ochre chip at my subconscious again, but I haven't got time to reflect on what's bothering me and if the bits were on the floor, they can't be important.

Among the residual paper is some documentation for Mike's Aston Martin which I dump onto his pile of filing.

It all looks a lot cleaner and tidier, and I am hot and exhausted. I will tackle our bedroom tomorrow. Sipping a mug of tea at my desk, a thought strikes me. Taking my debit card out of my wallet I try pushing it between the desk and the filing cabinet. No way does it go through. The edges of the desk and cabinet are tight against each other. So how on earth did it get where Mike had found it?

It is not till the afternoon that Mike emails from his office with the promised statement details. I enlarge the attachment, more than a little annoyed to find he has concentrated on the current account, despite my denials of its relevance, querying certain transactions which I know to be correct. There is also a comment about how much I spend on my hair, nails and clothes, and perhaps I should reduce this expenditure. His inspection of my reserve account is less detailed, but to my relief, although I am also surprised, the list of queries is not long, and most of the amounts are not large. He hasn't listed the three major withdrawals this year, but I have already raised the alarm about these, so I suppose he thinks he doesn't need to list them again. I don't feel his analysis is very thorough and therefore it is probably inexact, and crossly think his effort may have been a waste of time.

At the computer, I'm finding that full stops look like commas, and certain letters are on the slant, so the rest of the afternoon is spent preparing samples for my meetings in London tomorrow. Second only to the actual designing, I love these meetings with distributors and buyers, where I can enthuse about sustainability, responsible work conditions, recycling and design, to my heart's content. The icing on my cake is when I see the sparkle in a buyer's eye. I shall take my zigzag laptop case and the colour designs to the head office of Together With in Covent Garden. They are always up for one-off quirky ideas which no one else has yet snaffled. My quirky ideas have come good in the past, and they'll come good in the future. I will fend off any interference in how I run my business and that attractive banker will recognise my talents and offer to invest vast gold. I may have had a business catastrophe, but in my bones, I feel an upturn around the corner.

Chapter Five

After my meetings in London with some useful offers to stock accessories under my belt and an enthusiastic visit to Together With, I feel much more cheerful about my computer cases although it's only a tiny order. How can computer case manufacturers want to stick to boring black instead of my zippy, coloured, individual, unable to get muddled with anyone else's, recycled plastic bottles computer case? I nearly have an expensive Italian lunch and a glass of wine to celebrate. Pulling myself back from the brink and remembering the expense of the train ticket, I stick with a sandwich and coffee at a table in the sun and contemplate how to make good use of half a day. I decide on visiting Mike's office, wandering around the Wimbledon shops in search of more business and coming home with him.

I have spoken on the phone several times to his secretary Laura, but I have never met her before, and she is drop-dead gorgeous. I contrast her size 10 to my slightly squeezed size 14 and prefer my curves to her bones. Even in the heat, she looks perfect in a sharp beige business suit, gleaming black chignon, flawless marketing make-up, brown legs out of a bottle and expensive black, three-inch stilettos. I can smell Armani's Acqua di Gioia, an irritatingly beautiful greeny blue. I shall never be size 10 or look perfect or wear a business suit, but my crazy clothes and crazy make-up and crazier hair give me more 'Water of Delight' than anything Armani can come up with.

'I'll tell Mike you're here,' she says, taking in the peculiar girlfriend and her even more peculiar clothes and accessories with obvious disdain. 'And bring you a coffee.'

'Thanks,' I say when Laura clicks the coffee down on the marble table with an air of 'I hope you're grateful because I've got more important things to do'. Why is she so hostile?

I can do my own brand of putting down. 'What a pretty bracelet that is.' And it is pretty, with unusual gold links and discreetly gleaming diamonds. Which are probably paste. I make it clear I wouldn't be seen dead wearing it and smile at her amiably.

I am delighted that she is scandalised by my non-conformity; her face is stiff with annoyance as she withdraws the braceleted wrist rather sharply before clacking away across the marble floor. The company have spent a fortune on marble.

Mike's office smells of spray polish and coloured marker pens and there are a lot of people perched on corners of desks talking earnestly into telephones. I get the impression that my visit is not an entirely welcome surprise and I have interrupted Mike's busy working day.

'Hi, Cass. If you'd rung, I would have changed my schedule. I won't be able to stay I'm afraid. Did you have a fun day in London?'

It sounds as if he thinks I was partying. 'Yeah. Quite a few orders, and lots of good networking. Thought I'd mooch around Wimbledon and visit a few outlets and then come home with you.'

'Yes, OK. Fine. Look, I can't stay. I'll text you when I'm ready and you can wait for me in the lobby downstairs.'

No question of him waiting for me in the lobby. Not for the first time, it occurs to me that Mike puts his convenience first, not mine. His gender attitudes could do with a bit of realigning.

I do some good networking in Wimbledon shops and when we get home, he suggests going for a spin in the Aston and having a meal at a favourite gourmet restaurant in Ringwood.

'Wear something glamorous for the Aston.'

I am irritated. When he says glamorous, I know he means smart, rather than Crazy Colour Cass. He has never enthused about my clothes, but I have never kowtowed to his obvious hints to dress less oddly. He puts up with it reluctantly because he loves me, which is rather flattering in a way. It took me some time in our early relationship to discover that outward appearances, possessions and a show of affluence are more important to him than to me. His attitude has never bothered me much, but I am an embarrassment to him on occasion, and I think that's why he's never taken me to meet his parents. Their disapproval has not given me any reason to want to meet them either. He had told me his parents had had to sell their house after some disaster, and I knew he resented their resulting 'poverty'. The Aston Martin is important to him as a mark of wealth, not as an object of engineering beauty.

My way of thinking, after nearly twenty years with a domineering, controlling, and self-opinionated father, is laissez-faire. Each to his own. Be tolerant of one another. As he drives, much too fast, down the dual carriageway, I reflect that he has become less tolerant recently of my peculiar passion for eco-sustainability, colour and weird clothes, and a little frisson of disquiet trickles down my spine.

When we reach the pub, coincidentally there are friends of his there who think the Aston is *gorgeous darling*. I feel vaguely as if meeting them wasn't a coincidence.

* * *

Nine fifteen am. I have been at my desk since seven thirty and have just given myself coffee number four when the phone rings and Dominic Paget comes up on the screen.

My voice is immediately crisp and business-like. 'Eco-lore. Can I help you?'

Still roiling like vegetable soup in the blender, a bit of me quickens with pleasure at the sound of his voice. Another bit is a stubborn lump of annoyance about that meeting with Mike, another embarrassed at what Mike may have said to him, yet another hoping like hell to have some encouraging financial news.

'Good morning, Cass. Haven't heard from you for over a week, and I wondered how you got on with the police?'

'Didn't Mike tell you?' Try not to sound so shirty, Cass.

His voice is amused. 'Yes, a bit. That's not the same as you telling me.'

There is a little pause while I digest that. 'Well, after the most ridiculous waste of time being kicked from department to department and being told "the officer you need is not here", I eventually got some sidekick who took notes and said he'd pass the information on. Haven't heard anything since.'

I am squinting through today's heap of mail and see a relevant envelope. 'Oh, hang on. There's a letter just come.' I give it a quick peer. 'They've acknowledged receipt of my complaint and will be following it up.'

He grunts and then asks if I have contacted a lawyer.

'Mike said he'd ask his – ours – for his advice. I haven't heard anything.'

'Perhaps follow that up too. You could let me know what he says.' I wonder if his discussion with Mike will be mentioned, but he moves on.

‘We’d like to have a chat with you and discuss the three-year business plan you sent. Could you manage this week? Tomorrow or Friday?’

Really? A frisson of excitement ripples under my ribs, closely followed by cautious wariness. Mike had said they might want to tell me how to run my own business, so I foresee an unwelcome makeover attempt. On the other hand, I need their money, if they’re offering it.

Chewing my lip, I contemplate my diary. ‘Late Friday morning I could do. I’ve got an appointment at ten – Winchester Cathedral shop as it happens – so could be with you about eleven thirty. Otherwise, it would have to be next week.’ I’m not going to make it look as if I’m begging on my knees.

‘Eleven thirty would be perfect.’ He sounds pleased. ‘We could have an early lunch as well if that suited you. Before your next round of appointments.’

I can’t help laughing, my suspicion and ill temper in temporary abeyance. ‘Before your next round of appointments too. Well, I’m always hungry, so OK. Thank you.’

Would he bother inviting me to lunch if he wasn’t going to at least consider a loan or an investment? Might they demand a greedy percentage of Ecolore and then try to change my business ideology? I wasn’t sure whether I truly minded if they did or not; I can always turn it down. Lunch with Dominic Paget would be very pleasant anyway. I wish I didn’t like him. It would be easier to be tough if I disliked him. Focusing my mind, I think seriously about how much money I need to keep Ecolore on the road, and what percentage of my business I would be willing to give up to achieve it.

* * *

Dominic introduces me to his partner Peter Vermont, a browny, bronzy, shambolic looking man, whose brain is not at all shambolic, and we sit down in Dominic's office for a chat. I am curious about the strange glass objects in the wall cabinet and am told they are 'toddy lifters'. He hands me one and I bring it close to my eyes to examine it. It looks like a mini decanter with a long neck and a bulbous onion-like base, but there is a hole in the bottom as well as the top.

'Obviously not for holding liquids then,' I say, puzzled. 'Something used in a chemistry lab?'

He laughs. 'Yes, liquid, but not chemistry.' And demonstrates by lowering the bulb into a water glass where it fills up to the water level. Holding his thumb over the top hole he lifts it into the air. 'No drips!' He releases the liquid by removing his thumb. 'Around the middle of the eighteenth century a lot of silver was melted down and there was a shortage of punch ladles. These were used for transferring drink from punch bowls to wine glasses. I collect them. I have always been intrigued by the solutions people find for their problems.' He glances at me with a faint smile and puts the object carefully back in its place.

'Neat,' I say.

They ask me questions about sustainable manufacturing, the processes, the products, the valuation of Ecolore, the costs, my gross and net figures. They ask me why, and how and who and where and what, and I have a lovely time, getting passionate about the planet, without feeling that they are anything but interested.

At twelve thirty Peter disappears to a lunch appointment and Dominic gathers me up to ours. It's a table in a garden, with an umbrella. He sits in the shade; I revel in the sun until even I feel broiled and move into the shadow opposite him. It's the sort of place Mike wouldn't choose because the tables are far apart, and no one is looking at us. Dominic offers me alcohol, but we both have mineral water. I go with his recommendation of mackerel fillet with rhubarb because it appeals to my colour sense. The plate smells maroon and deep pink.

We chat as easily as ever, but it's time to get real. I take a deep breath.

'Dominic, you've asked me lots of questions about my business, but you haven't said whether you are interested in investing in it and if you are, with what parameters. Nor have you said whether you would consider a loan, and if so with what conditions.'

He smiles that slow reassuring smile again. 'There are some things that Peter and I need to consider before we make a decision, apart from analysing what you have told us this morning.'

'Like?'

'Like who stole from Ecolore in the first place, and why, and whether they might do it again, this time from our money.' He sees my frown. 'I know you have secured your business accounts now, but the fraud happened, and so far, no one knows who or how or why.' The grey eyes are direct. 'I think you have to consider that it may not be just greed, a random plundering. It may be something else. Something more personal.'

I stare at him silently. I have never considered that I am dislikeable, that someone might have a bone of contention so large that they would want to destroy me. I can't think of a single person who might feel that strongly. Except possibly my father, and as I've already told Mike, the idea is ridiculous. Utterly ridiculous. I shake my head at Dominic.

'But why?'

He beckons for the bill and picks up his jacket. 'Why indeed.'

Chapter Six

For my appointment with Dominic's lawyer friend, I have scrumptious streaks of scarlet and gold in my hair rather than a wig, and gold lipstick. Although it is raining it is still hot, and I am trying out one of my new designs, a demo model mac, semi-see-through with gold streaks, over a scarlet and berry jumpsuit. Some people say you shouldn't put clear red with blue-red, but you can: it looks great. Gold waterproof thigh boots which the shoe designer raved about. Naturally, everything is manufactured from recycled and sustainable materials, and I am pleased with the whole effect. Lots of furtive photos from the public as I tote my curvy umbrella – also see-through with gold streaks – sashaying to the law office, fire in my belly.

Rising to his feet to shake hands is the most gorgeous man I have ever seen outside a magazine. Tall and lean, incredibly smart even in the heat, with ingenuous brown eyes. I return his smile with a false 'I am not impressed by your gorgeousness' expression. His name is Zev Mahindra, and he is ultra-sexy and smells lemony yellow.

'Cass?' he says. 'Is that Cassandra?'

'Cassia.'

'Ah. Cinnamon. And a lovely flower.' Not many people know that. He must be a gardener, which surprises me. He doesn't look the type. Mum was a gardener too before she went blind.

He tells me the hourly fees and I have a near heart attack.

I explain everything, and he asks lots of questions.

'It would be helpful to have your bank statements with the entries you are concerned about marked up. Do you bank online?'

'I've got the bank statements here.' I hand them over. 'Yes. Mike said banking online is the most secure option, and it's more convenient for him.'

Zev looks faintly puzzled. 'What do you mean, "more convenient for him"? Is he your accountant?'

'No, but he checks the statements. He deals with the finances, mostly.'

'So he can access your accounts as well as your book-keeper Richard?'

'Well, yes.'

Zev straightens slightly in his chair. 'Can I get this clear? I had understood Ecolore was your business alone, but are you telling me it is jointly owned by you and Mr Benton?'

'No, Ecolore is mine alone. He helps with the finances and marketing.'

His eyes are considering. 'I see. And how long has Mr Benton had access to your business accounts?'

I stare at him, my chest tight. Mike is my partner. I trust him completely. If this man is implying that Mike might be implicated, he really has got it wrong.

'Five or six years.' I'm cross and brusque. 'He's always helped me and it's always been very good advice. He keeps an eye on my company's finances, but he's been very busy, so he didn't query these withdrawals – he thought it was me.'

Zev apparently doesn't take offence at my tone. 'And have you, as a couple, had any major outgoings in the past? Property? Yachts? Cars?'

I can't quite work out whether Zev is insinuating something shady about Mike, but he has never met him and can't know that he is a wealthy man in his own right, so I put him straight. 'Mike has an extremely well-paid job. He really does have plenty of money – he has substantial investments and collects paintings and sculptures.' I must sound defensive and try for a more neutral tone.

'He bought our flat, although we have a joint mortgage, and this year he sold his Mercedes and bought an Aston Martin. A car is not a major thing for him.'

Zev nods and moves on, flipping through the bank statements. 'I see you've highlighted a large online transfer in March. So that wasn't Ecolore business?'

I shake my head. 'Definitely not.'

Zev confirms that we need evidence in order to accuse someone of stealing. As if I didn't know that. There are explanations about letters of engagement. Do I want to engage them, if so, please sign here. I am terrified of the financial implications, but despite my hesitations, I sign. He will do some preliminary work.

His brown eyes are laughing every time he looks at me. I don't mind. I enjoy bringing happiness to people. Think of the evening conversations as they all go home, 'You wouldn't believe who I met today …'

* * *

Mike thinks I'm mad to be hiring another lawyer. 'Ours is perfectly competent and would be much less expensive than this fancy one Paget has recommended. You've no evidence to give them. They charge for every second. You can't afford them at hundreds of pounds per hour, and I suggest you don't engage them. At least not yet.' He sounds like a censorious headmaster, and I feel like a schoolgirl on the mat.

'All lawyers charge about the same. Anyway, I think he's

already started.' Am I sounding wimpish and uncertain? I think of that 'preliminary work' the gorgeous Zev Mahindra said he would do.

'Why didn't you ask me first?' he says, emptying the dishwasher with far more vigour than seems necessary. 'That's how they reel you in – they try to make it impossible for you to back out because they've already done several hours of work. Which they will now charge for. You should let them know right away you don't want them to go ahead.'

I am beginning to fear for the plates. 'I can't do that. I'd look an absolute fool. I only saw him today.' My stomach tightens in a panicky out-of-control feeling.

His face is tight with annoyance. 'You're an idiot to have engaged them without thinking of the outcomes. I'll cancel them for you.'

Pulling myself together, I force my annoyance to get the upper hand. 'No thank you. I don't want you to cancel them. Ecolore is mine, and I want to know who is stealing from me. I'll decide whether or not we go ahead.'

In another life, I would just back off. This time I dig my heels in although I am feeling distinctly shaky in the face of his displeasure.

There is no comforting arm when he eventually comes to bed, a good hour after me, and I lie, eyes closed, breathing deep, feigning sleep.

* * *

After an edgy sexless weekend, Mike announces he has to stay the next Tuesday night in London because another early morning meeting has been scheduled. I nearly ask him why on earth he can't get up early like anyone else to go to an early meeting, but I know he is fed up with my short temper and preoccupation. But for the first time I wonder, why can't he? There are early trains, Southampton is not exactly a village in the sticks, and he has a season ticket so he's not saving money. Is the company happy to keep paying for so many hotels?

I am still pondering this when Zev Mahindra asks me for personal instructions after Mr Benton's email.

'What email? What are you talking about?' Alarm bells are ringing, but I have no idea why. Something is wrong. 'What email?'

'Instructing me to go no further with Ecolore inquiries. I'll forward it,' he says calmly. And he does. The font is Mike's unreadable size 11 and I enlarge it. Even then the letters are frisky and out of focus.

'Cassia Hunter does not wish you to engage in any further inquiries about Ecolore due to lack of funds. We will be in touch should the situation change.'

Mike didn't tell me he'd done that, and I choke as if I'd inhaled vinegar. How dare he! This is interference as never before and I don't understand it. Through the vinegar fumes, I give instructions that Zev should continue.

I have too many balls in the air, and one of them is a nagging feeling I should make an appointment with the optician for a stronger prescription. Too much to think about just now. I'll do it later.

* * *

In the early hours I wake, sweating from the heat. Neither of us had initiated sex last night and maybe that was why I was wakeful. The bad dream dies away instantly, but my visual memory has number colours imprinted on it. I don't need to go to my diary to know what those colours and numbers are: yellow Tuesday, blue one and grey five, ochre May. I may not be too good at remembering numbers, but for me, every number has a colour. Every day and every month has a colour. And I remember colours.

Why am I dreaming about Tuesday 15th May? I try to go back to sleep, but the colours hover, refusing to fade. We sleep with only a sheet, kicked down now into a crumpled tangle, and the windows are wide for the non-existent breeze.

Turning my head towards Mike, his face is a pale blank until I slide my glasses on. His muscular body would normally make my tummy cramp with desire. Not now. One arm is thrown up, bent around his head like a halo. But the colours of that faded dream are still with me. I need to see the diary entry.

I slip, naked and silent, out of bed and into the office. Turning on the desk light, I squint at my diary. It confirms exactly what I was hoping it wouldn't, *'Mike overnight London'*. The night of the office party. The air is warm but I suddenly feel cold.

Yellow, blue, grey, ochre. I have seen those colours somewhere else. I have seen those dates somewhere else. But where? Standing in the middle of the office for several minutes, I let my memory untangle itself until it comes to me.

Forgetting to empty the office waste bin has paid off. Along with the fluff, dead spiders and pencil shavings, there are all the bits of paper I threw out last Monday. Among them are three mini bank statements. The tiny print and its associated colours dance before my eyes. Date, time, place, balance. Yellow, blue, grey, ochre. He had a very busy day when he was supposed to be locked in important client meetings.

In Mike's dressing room the waste bin has not been emptied either. I collect all the bits of paper together and slip them into an old envelope which I put in the bottom of one of the drawers of the Victorian cabinet which had belonged to my mother. Mike hated it and named it Ugly. I don't want him waking up and padding through to see what I'm doing.

Tuesday 15th May. Yellow, blue, grey, ochre.

I lie sleepless, clammy with sweat, nerves tingling and itching on the surface of my skin, heart thumping as if I'd sprinted for a bus. Rubber balls are bouncing around my brain, scattering grey cells in every direction. I am confused, bewildered, puzzled, disbelieving. Suspicious.

* * *

When he's left in the morning, I take the envelope out of Ugly and sort the bits of paper out. Tuesday 15th May. Dinner for two at a Wimbledon restaurant called Callaloo. On the night he said there was a big office evening.

My pulse begins to race again, shortening my breath, and making my hands tremble. This cannot be happening. There must be an explanation.

Checking further I find a receipt for the same date from a jeweller in Wimbledon for 'One gold link bracelet set with crystals' for £103. OK, not a king's ransom but I remember a pretty bracelet on Laura's wrist. Mike seldom gives me jewellery because my idea of decorative is big and bold and his preference runs to little and cute. Once, early in our relationship, he produced a silver(ish) neck chain with a tiny teddy bear charm. Even he noticed me throwing up. I think he found it in a charity shop. No, it is less than likely that this bracelet was bought for me. I remember Laura's abrupt withdrawal when I admired her bracelet. I remember her hostility, and I remember the blue-green scent of Acqua di Gioia.

My eyes ache from straining over the faint and tiny print of the card receipts. The darkness at the edges of my vision seems to have crept further towards the centre. But worse than my aching eyes is the ache in my heart, the beginnings of the possibility of betrayal.

None of this is more than vague suspicion, and yet the ache is becoming a twisting knife.

Is he cheating on me? Is his recent impatience and irritation an indication of his changing feelings towards me?

The question circles my mind as I pace around the flat. Onto the balcony, where we have our companionable evening drink in the cooler air. Into our bedroom, place of passion and his wild lovemaking, round the sofa and the oak table under which my sewing machine is tidily stashed because he dislikes it left out. Through the kitchen where we often prepare together the food we love. The office, scene of discussions, advice, mutual help. As I pass the bathroom, I pick out one of Mike's discarded shirts from the laundry bin and bury my nose in it. It is turquoise. Mostly turquoise. But beneath it is a hint of blue-green. Zev wouldn't call my instinct proof. He wouldn't say my deductions were evidence.

The bony, brown-out-of-a-bottle, oh-so-immaculate Laura? The clichéd office romance? My legs are pacing and my heart is racing.

I crumple to the floor, still holding the shirt whose blue-green scent becomes less ignorable by the second. A numbness stupefies me. Am I letting my imagination run away with me?

I think he is cheating on me with his secretary.

Or is he? I must be mistaken, there are explanations for those cards and receipts and bills. He couldn't and wouldn't do what they appear to be telling me. It could be a client he took to dinner at a restaurant called Callaloo. The bracelet on Laura's wrist could be a present from her parents. There is a bracelet awaiting me for my birthday. Mike works with her, so it is not surprising that he has absorbed her greeny blue smell. He really does have that many business appointments, that many hotel stays.

But smells, colours, numbers, dates and receipts all line up. Is this paranoia? Is Mike lying? Is Mike cheating? I swing from disbelief to misery to fury. If he's cheating, I need to find out for sure.

Chapter Seven

I ought to do urgent Ecolore work, answer emails, delay payments out, ask for payments in, and update the website. In fact, I go to see Wendy, in the premises which I thought would be mine by the end of May, but which probably won't be mine ever as I can't pay for them. The disappointment makes me feel sick.

Wendy has got a series of clients and is juggling machinists because her best one is off with a poisoned finger, so I have to wait. Every time we have eye contact her expression is not so much disappointment as annoyance. I am not flavour of the month. I occupy myself playing unfunny games with my eyes. Covering my left eye, there is a faint dirty beige cloud right in the middle of the right eye. Wendy specialises in the mature figure and looking at her sizing list I take comfort again in my own generous proportions. I am amazed to see that she has a heretofore unknown size 19 dress. Squinting closer I see that I have misread size 16.

'I've had to put it with an agent,' she says, briskly replacing her fabulous clothes in their correct places. 'This is a bugger for you, but it's also a bugger for me. All sorts of spokes in both our wheels, sadly. Have you heard from the bank?'

'Nothing further. They say there was nothing wrong with the transfers, and that I did them. Which I didn't. They were transferred to a current account at another bank.

Why the hell would anyone have two current accounts? And I never got the debit card, someone else did.'

'What an unholy mess,' she mutters, throwing her hands up. A customer comes in, and she rearranges her face. 'I'll have to go. Can you wait? We really do have to talk.'

'Sure,' I say. 'Can I go in back and do some work?'

'Fine. I may be half an hour or so.'

When her client has gone, we sit at the showroom table. She is sympathetic about the theft, but she's also a tough businesswoman as well as my friend. I tell her some of what Dominic and Zev have said. When I tell her that Mike's colour has changed recently, she knows what I mean. Wendy understands my sense of smell. She knows that she smells apple green. She knows that Mike smells turquoise blue. Eventually, I get round to the point of my visit.

'Am I right in thinking that you got your father a sort of tracer gadget, ages ago, for when he went AWOL with Alzheimer's?'

'A GPS tracker, yes. It worked, so long as I remembered to charge it.'

'Have you still got it, and if so, could I borrow it for a while?'

There is a pause, and she eyes me thoughtfully. 'I think I must still have it at home. You'll have to re-register to your computer.' There is a further pause, and she glances at me sideways. 'It's much simpler to use Google location finder on your phone.'

And Google would undoubtedly tell Mike I was tracking him. 'There's a good reason why I can't.'

Wendy is of an age which gives her authority to be motherly, in the sense of keeping me on the straight and narrow, but at this moment she looks helpful. She is not stupid either. She and Mike have never hit it off. She has never said anything negative about him to my face, but neither has she ever enthused about him. She was clearly wiser than me.

'I'll tell you sometime. I'll collect it if you find it.'

* * *

Wendy texts to say she has found her GPS tracker, which I collect the next day and charge while poring over the Dutch instructions trying to discover how the damn thing works. A movement at the edge of my vision makes me jump. Turning my head sharply I see a large Hampshire spider sprinting across the office floor and then disappearing between the floorboards. While the air is still reverberating with my spontaneous shriek, Dominic rings. I keep one eye on the point of the spider's disappearance and hope I sound calm and collected.

'There's an exhibition at the Winchester Gallery called "Impressionist Colour". Would you like to come tomorrow?' He sounds slightly hesitant. Shy even. 'They have air conditioning.'

Vaguely surprised, because it sounds like a sort of date, I spray the floorboards with spider repellent and say, 'Ooh! How could I resist air conditioning? I'd love to.' The air conditioning will be pleasant. Seeing Dominic will be even more so. I should be resisting this temptation to go out with a potential investor, but I'm not going to. What I think Mike is doing to me, means that I don't have any qualms about accepting the invitation. I am going to have difficulty playing the innocent lover attending to his every whim, so being absent will let me off the hook for one night at least.

As I nestle the tracker in the deepest recesses of Mike's computer case while he is showering after work, I inform him that I will be going to an exhibition in Winchester tomorrow evening. He doesn't appear to mind and doesn't ask to come with me. In days gone by I would have been rather hurt, but as it is I am just relieved.

I think of that spider ignoring the repellent and coming out again and I leave nothing on the floor. I have noticed before that spiders like to crawl underneath clothes.

* * *

All day long the tracker has made uninformative bouncy location icons on my laptop screen, and I wonder how long the battery will last. The thought of having to replace it when the 'Battery Low' message flashes up makes me fearful that Mike will catch me in the act of inserting or removing it. He may also explore the lump under the case lining which would be extremely unfortunate.

When I join Dominic at the gallery the heat has hardly dissipated. I have dressed up and my theme is cool blues: wide floaty trousers with a sequined tunic and matching scarf. My nails are all different blues too, and so is my hair. It's too hot for a wig, though there is a fetching Prussian-blue bob with a fringe on the warehouse shelf.

'I hope Mike didn't mind,' he says. 'I didn't get the feeling that Impressionism was quite his style.'

'Mike's style is abstract modernism,' I say. 'We don't really enjoy each other's taste in art.' This makes me gloomy because he doesn't enjoy me anymore either.

We wander the gallery until it closes, sometimes together exchanging comments, and sometimes apart, staring as long as we want at pictures which take our individual interest. I go up close and drown in those colours – the greens and yellows and blues, the dabs of scarlet. Pure throat-stopping pleasure. It is peaceful and undemanding and something Mike and I seldom did together because although he purports to have an interest in art, in fact his knowledge is superficial, and he is more swayed by price than pleasure.

In the sticky heat outside the gallery, Dominic says diffidently, 'Have you got to go back, or would you like a quick snack and a glass of wine here?' He indicates the tapas bar a few doors down. I hesitate. Is he just being polite? Isn't there a Mrs Paget waiting at home? Mike will be back from work, but I really don't want to talk to him.

'It seems a pity to waste that gorgeous outfit. And the hair.' His voice is now persuasive and the smile widens into a grin. It does seem a pity. I'm getting the impression that he fancies me, and a little spark flickers in my midriff. When was the last time Mike told me an outfit was gorgeous? Or that he liked blue hair? Is it just because I'm suspicious of Mike that I'm allowing these thoughts to creep in?

I find myself smiling back. 'That sounds lovely. It's thirsty work, taking all those pictures into one's soul.'

The quick snack is not so quick, and not so much of a snack either. And the glass of wine becomes two. We talk about the exhibition, and I tell him about the three modern eyesores Mike bought.

'Painted by a pretentious artist called Milo Szorski-Czyz. Mike had masterminded his marketing campaign and Milo graciously helped with the hanging of his huge, miserable black works in the sitting room. He really put my back up by saying that colour was so yesterday.'

Dominic is greatly amused, and I am suddenly aware that someone has genuinely laughed at one of my stories. Mike does not laugh at my stories. Well, he might laugh at, but not with. I have managed to be discreet about my suspicions of Mike, but I do tell him that Mike cancelled Zev Mahindra without informing me and that I have reinstated him.

Dominic raises his eyebrows. 'And how did Mike react to that?'

'I haven't told him yet. I'm waiting for him to tell me.'

He considers that for a moment, the grey eyes speculative, turning his wine glass slowly between finger and thumb. 'And if he doesn't, will you?'

'Yes,' I say decisively. 'I'm awaiting my opportunity to cut him off at the ankles.'

'Oh dear!' Dominic's face registers misgiving as well as amusement. 'Rather him than me.'

My problems are shelved and we are quickly into our very different politics, our very different book choices, his music (and a crush on Enya) and mine (with a crush on Boyzone), my art and his art.

'Let me guess,' he says, giving me a long judicious scrutiny. 'Gustav Klimt.'

'Mmm. How perceptive. *The Kiss*. Those clothes.'

'More like *Judith and the Head of Holofernes*,' he says dryly.

I'm disconcerted. Does he think I'm vindictive?

'My turn,' I say hurriedly. It's difficult because I suspect the outward convention hides wide interests. 'Lely. Vermeer. Turner.'

He grins. 'What if I said Francis Bacon?'

Like a flower opening, I expand in the warmth of his attention. Did I ever have this interest from Mike? My midriff now has lots of sparks fizzing about. I like this man's company. I like this man. And I probably shouldn't, because there must be a nice wife in the background.

'You said you had to drop out of art school because of lack of funding. Which one was it?' he asks.

I grin. 'Round the corner. Winchester School of Art. I did textile design and wish I could have finished it.'

'You ended up in the school of life instead. Probably more useful and enjoyable, especially as design is what you seem to do naturally.'

'Hmm. Not sure that I *enjoyed* all the school of life.' But his comment gives me a little glow inside to add to the sparks.

'I doubt you'd learn anything more than you've already learned in the big wide world, even if you did go back and finish it. Probably you should be a lecturer and tell them how to use their art degree and run a successful business at the same time.'

The little glow gets brighter, and I feel myself giving a great wide smile to this person who makes me feel good about myself. My father's take on my educational failure had lodged itself in all the cracks, and I'd spent half a lifetime painting over them by trying to make a success of myself.

'What about you? University of course, but where? Did you read maths?'

'I went to Oxford, and no, I didn't read maths. I did history. I've always loved history, and at one point I wanted to teach it.' He makes room for another plate of tapas. 'I don't quite know what happened there! I got a holiday job with an uncle in his bank and found I enjoyed it, and just stayed with it.'

Reaching over to refill my glass, his fingers fleetingly brush mine. The electric kick is so sharp I am certain he must notice, and I drop my eyes in case he looks at me. With the result that I don't know whether he looks at me or not. I am good at hiding my feelings and my conversation doesn't falter. Is this attraction a result of Mike's betrayal, or would I be feeling it anyway? I ought to be ashamed of myself.

Sport and music. Books. How I do my hair and nails. His work and mine. Science and mathematics, new technology and old archaeology, countries and cultures, our friends and pet hates. I have discovered that he sneezes in sixes, and that red wine can set him off. His eyes are humorous and twinkly and I more than like him. He can give me electric shocks.

I have an epiphany about my relationship with Mike. Yes, we talked, but there was not much beyond the superficial. Nothing deep or heart-searching, no debate, no exchange of opinions. He didn't like me arguing a point, and he always knew better; he was often dismissive about my interests or knowledge. I wonder now whether he was afraid of me knowing more than him.

Dominic wants to know about the technology of plastics or the statistics behind global warming. If I ask Dominic a question, he doesn't treat me like I'm an idiot. It's refreshing and affirming. I'm beginning to see what I've missed.

'Thank you for lending me Patrick. He's lovely. I expected to be overwhelmed by techy talk, but he didn't.'

He glances at me, amused. 'Aren't you the lucky one! He overwhelms me with techy talk, but you probably understand it more than me.' He sighs ruefully. 'I don't think I made a very good job of the teenage era. He always did know best.'

So where was his wife if *he* didn't make a good job of his teenager? I can't imagine anyone divorcing Dominic. 'Your wife – his mum – isn't around?'

He glances down at his hands. 'She was killed. A skiing accident.' Nudging the tapas nearer to me, it covers the little hesitation. 'A long time ago. Patrick was five.'

I am jolted. My own parental disasters seem minuscule by comparison. 'I'm so sorry. What a tragedy.' What is it about commiseration that makes it so difficult to sound genuine?

'Thank you,' he says. 'Time does heal though it leaves a scar, but I always think life is easier with two of you.'

'I don't know.' I feel sad. 'I thought so too, but in my case, I think I got it wrong.' I'd rather not dwell on my poor choices. 'You never married again? Sorry – Mike's always saying I'm so bloody brash.'

He seems quite relaxed about the question and laughs.

'Think about it frequently! But no, never met quite the right person to take on a boring banker and teenage tantrums. But now the teenager is all grown up and doesn't spend much time at home.' He stops, and I think – he's lonely.

We talk about her. She was called Penny and she had been an archaeologist. He had duly become fascinated by digging up the past.

'I go to an archaeological dig in York for a week most seasons and will probably go back in the spring. I just hope it doesn't rain next time.'

'Have you ever found anything?'

'Oh yes. Lots of things. I found a brooch last year. From the time of the Jewish pogrom in 1190.'

I contemplate the likelihood of a piece of my jewellery lasting underground for eight hundred years. 'It rained? It sounds as if you must have got dirty.'

His eyes crinkle up when he laughs, and my stomach tightens in a ridiculous desire to touch the crinkles. 'And some! We were so thick with mud you wouldn't have recognised your best friend. I dropped a bin bag of work clothes in a skip on my way home.'

Gazing at Dominic Paget, remembering his well-cut business suit, and seeing now his immaculate, though slightly unclear, chinos and crisp shirt, I find the whole idea impossible to visualise. I think he sees my disbelief.

'Better not to make assumptions about what people are,' he says, twinkling. 'The old clichés of not judging a book by its cover or a horse by its teeth apply to clothes as well.'

That's a direct reference to me, isn't it? Those grey eyes are as penetrating as ever, but they are smiling too. And kind. From the point of telling myself I would never rely on a man again after my father, he gives the impression of reliability. Only an impression, I tell myself sternly. I'm not about to rely on anyone other than myself.

Eventually, I sigh and tell him I must go home.

'I need to locate a spider which I know is still lurking in my office.'

He looks bemused. 'Why?'

'Because if I haven't disposed of it, it means it's still in the flat and will attack me when I'm not expecting it. I had a very bad night last night knowing it was going to crawl into the bed, and onto my face.'

'Really?' he says, his eyes widening in amazement. 'A real arachnophobe? What brought that on?'

'My father,' I say flatly.

There is quite a silence and then Dominic says cautiously, 'Your father is afraid of spiders?'

I laugh, without too much amusement. 'When I was twelve, Dad put a whole family of spiders – big ones – in my bed. Between the sheets, under my pillow, under the cover, everywhere. He knew I hated them. He thought my attack of hysteria was the funniest thing ever.' Even just telling the bones of that episode makes me shudder with the horror of it, and my throat closes just as it did then, when I truly thought I was going to die.

Dominic looks shocked. 'I think that would have given anyone nightmares for life,' he says slowly. 'Would you like me to come and assist in the hunt, or will Mike help?'

He doesn't comment on my ghastly father, which means I can't continue to criticise him either which I would like to. This frustration is coupled with the safety, the security, of grasping that Dominic does not indulge in gossip or backbiting.

For the first time in many moons, I wish the flat was totally empty and that he would not just visit but stay. I ensure my voice is very firm.

‘Thank you for even thinking of it, but I wouldn’t dream of allowing you to. I have an armoury of sprays and gels and spider catchers. And Mike will be home.’ I intend to give the impression that Mike being home will be helpful in a spider hunt, but truth be told, I don’t want them meeting again.

With a little nod, Dominic’s eyes meet mine. ‘Of course,’ he says, and I know that he understands perfectly.

Chapter Eight

It is six pm and Mike seems to be in Wimbledon. Enlarging the map, I find the tracker is bouncing in the middle of a residential street called Sedgewick Road with a greengrocer and corner shop at one end and a nail bar and bookie at the other. It's a couple of miles from his office.

There may be a perfectly good reason for him to be in Sedgewick Road, but I would like to find out what it is. I text him.

'Where are you? Are you on your way back?'

'Still in office meeting. Leaving in about 1 hr.' My heart hammers more than it has been already. He's not at the office. He's lying. There's a pause and then he texts, *'Are you OK? Problem?'*

No, I am not OK. I'm swirling with confusion, and a peculiar misery envelops me. To be lied to so directly is somehow worse than having the truth that he's tired of me said straight out. It smacks of 'can't be bothered', of having two cakes and eating both. A tiny bit of my mind shouts, 'We're not married. Both of us are free to go.'

I can't confront him with lying right now, as I'd have to admit to the tracker, and I need to keep a grip on what I want to say. But it's time to squash the misery and at least let him know how angry I am about Zev.

'Yes. Can we actually speak?'

'I'm in a meeting,' he types crossly. Funny place to have an office meeting. I ring anyway.

'You may recall,' I say when he eventually answers, 'that my problem is that Ecolore's reserves have been stolen and I'm trying to discover who, and how and why. And I now find that you have taken it upon yourself to cancel the lawyer who was employed to do the who, how and why, without telling me. So yes, there's a problem. Like how dare you do that when I specifically told you not to interfere?'

There's an echo on the line. A door closing. Like a door closing on our relationship.

He sounds fatigued. 'It was for your own good. You don't need or want a lawyer.'

'That's not for you to say. It's my business and it was my decision.' It comes out croaky and I clear my throat.

'And as usual, you're making bad decisions.' As *usual*! You creep! 'My lawyer said it was entirely unnecessary and I know that he's got our best interests at heart. This fancy lawyer you've found is just wanting to get his bloated fees paid. You'd have gone bust years ago if it hadn't been for me keeping you afloat.'

'*Afloat!* Since when have you ever put one penny into Ecolore! As if I'd accept it anyway!' He's deflecting into another subject, and stupidly I have allowed it to happen.

'Guess why I never offered! I'm not in the habit of putting money into a failing business.'

I only just manage to keep a lid on my rage at his sudden and unexpected spitefulness. 'It is not a failing business. Vermont and Paget wouldn't be considering investing in it if it was a failing business. It's a bloody good one, and I'm not going to let some lousy thief take it down. And if I want to hire a lawyer, that is my decision and you have absolutely no right to try to reverse it. And to do it without telling me was even more underhand.'

He's a mixture of scorn and disparagement. 'I was trying to save you from wasting your money, but as ever, you're so pig-headed you'd never admit it, so I did it anyway, knowing that you wouldn't have the grace to thank me. And,' he adds nastily, 'you're kidding yourself if you think Paget will invest. He won't.'

The point of my pencil snaps with a crack. 'What the hell do you know about it?'

'I had a meeting with them if you remember. I'm afraid it's a given.'

I have a sudden frightening awareness of a malevolence I have never experienced from him before. 'What did you say to them?' It comes out as a shout.

'They asked me questions and I answered them. I asked them what they were going to decide. They were quite clear.'

My wrist is hurting and looking down I see I am pressing the broken pencil point into my flesh. I put it down precisely on the desk. This does not add up. Surely Dominic had not said they wouldn't invest in Ecolore, just that they wanted answers first. But I am confused now and remember that there had been no mention of finance on the evening of the art exhibition. Had they already decided not to invest? My chest contracts as disappointment and rage take my breath away. Why do I fall for the wrong men, trust the wrong men, and get influenced by the wrong men?

'You intentionally influenced their decision against me! How could you do that? *Why* did you do that?'

'Don't be pathetic! Of course I didn't. I told them the truth and they made their decision based on the facts.' His voice changes to pompous business mode. 'I can't go on discussing this now, Cass. My colleagues are waiting, I have work to do, and this conversation is a waste of time.'

He cuts the call. We have never had a row like this before and I feel physically disjointed, as if a bus has run over me. I would dearly love a strong drink but have a strong coffee instead.

The bastard. He's lying about being in the office and he deliberately wrecked my prospects with Vermont and Paget. The mean, malicious, devious bastard. All that play-acting, despising me as I continued to behave like a little loving, submissive wife, cooking and cleaning and running his errands. And all the while he stayed in London with his new lover, lying about office pressures and team meetings. Lying cheat.

I think of him and pretty Laura laughing about my simplicity, my naive belief that I am the one and only. I'm literally burning with fury and humiliation, my skin flushed, and my stomach bruised.

At least I managed not to throw the accusation of his cheating at him. It will be kept for another day when I can control myself so that he can't take pleasure from my hurt. Kept until I am strong enough to use it as a weapon, not a cry of pain.

* * *

If this feedback about the meeting is true, why the hell was Dominic Paget discussing the business at all? What was he doing asking me to an art exhibition and then for an evening out if he had no intention of following up on that offer? Not because he thought Ecolore was worth a punt but because he wants me in his bed? An offer of investment in return for sex? There had been the occasional glance, moments seemingly unchoreographed when his hand touched mine. Attraction on my part, but what had it been on his part? I feel exhausted by my own naivety, and my poor judgement of men: Dominic is no different, and I am staggered by my disappointment.

I can manage without his money, even if he offers it. I'll prove them all wrong. I will rebuild Ecolore and make it not only profitable but a success. I've done it once and I can bloody well do it again. In fact, I'll make it a national name. A global influencer. They'll all regret they underestimated Cass Hunter.

I run down to the docks and back. Pushing myself fast, trainers slapping onto the hot concrete, sweat flying, T-shirt sodden. Brain in stalled mode; don't think, don't analyse, keep running, don't fall. At the dock gates I crash against the netting for a few seconds, then turn and run back. Pumping impossible adrenaline in impossible heat. At the street door my legs fail, and I collapse on the steps, blinded by sweat which pours off me in rivulets and puddles on the stone. Somewhere in my befuddled miserable fury, I comprehend that Mike's maliciousness must stem from having a new lover, from falling out of love with me. This isn't a lovers' tiff. This is a life-changing malfunction in our relationship. My perspectives have shifted, and I don't recognise this man at all.

I am calmer now; showered and in my right mind. I ring Dominic Paget.

'Mike tells me you've already decided not to invest in Ecolore! Why did you ask to discuss my business if you had already decided Ecolore wasn't worth your while? Why get me to employ an expensive lawyer if you think Ecolore doesn't even have a future? You're just another chauvinistic man who can't believe – doesn't want to believe – that a woman has the brains to run a business. This whole episode has been a waste of my time, and I assume your time too.'

He has to wait until I've finished what I have to say and then he says ruefully, 'Can I speak?'

'I don't want to hear it.'

'Oh, yes. I think you do.'

'I will probably be very rude.'

'My dear Cass, you've already been very rude. If you listen, you might well be nicer to me.' He doesn't sound offended. I am silent and exhausted and bruised. If I was the sort who cried, I would feel like crying.

'We told Mike that if your management of Ecolore was as he described, and if your financial handling of the business was as he described, then there would be no possibility of our investing in the company.' I take a breath. 'Please don't interrupt, Cass. We listened very carefully to everything he said. Then we looked again at your business and your aims and your forward planning. Then we spent some time talking to you. Then I spent some more time talking to you.' I remain silent because I am confused. What's he saying? That they think Mike is right? Or wrong? Do *I* think Mike is right or wrong?

He goes on. 'In fact, we don't think Mike's analysis *is* accurate, but some questions do still remain, and until those are sorted out, we won't be coming up with any hard offers of financial help.'

That's blunt, to say the least. 'What questions remain?' Even to myself, I sound defensive and brusque.

'Any chance of this conversation continuing face to face, either here or with you? The airwaves are unsatisfactory.' He sounds patient and calm. I would have taken offence at me some time ago.

'I've just had a monumental row with Mike, and I don't think it would be helpful if you were here. I don't want to be here myself. I'm going to ask a friend for a bed for the night.'

'Would this friend do? I've got a spare room. I could collect you in twenty minutes.'

Huh? Am I hearing this right? It takes me some seconds to crank down to some semblance of civility.

'I have just been, on your own admission, extremely rude to you. Are you now saying that you consider yourself a friend, that you would drive from Winchester to pick me up, take me back to your house and put me in your spare room for the night?' My hands make spontaneous fists at the infelicitous phrase 'pick me up'.

'Yes.' It sounds as if he's smiling. Muscles which were stiff with tension now slump in defeat. Is this man being kind or is he just trying to manipulate me?

'What's the deal?'

'No deal.'

I say nothing. There must be a deal of course, but it's hardly likely to be rape, mayhem and murder. But do I really want to know what these remaining questions are?

'No deal, no catch. I'm not saying I wouldn't like there to be a catch, but I promise there isn't. Pack a bag and I'll be with you in twenty minutes.'

* * *

The 'remaining questions' seemingly revolve around Mike's position advising on my finance.

'I've told you. He doesn't hold any position in the company,' I say defensively. 'Ecolore is just me. But of course, I did ask his advice and take soundings. He says I'm liable to be too spontaneous, that I act before thinking, and he thought my ideas for expanding the company were unwise and premature. But then I got this opportunity to take up Wendy's offer and I said I was going to go ahead. I felt it was the right time, and I had the capital reserves to do it.'

'And how did he react?'

I stare at the vague outlines of Dominic's apple trees against the sunset. 'Um, not very well. He told me that my judgement was unreliable. I was too young, too inexperienced. It would end in disaster.'

'Which it did,' Dominic says thoughtfully.

I turn my head sharply. 'Not because of my judgement, or my age or inexperience.'

'Certainly not inexperience after sixteen years. No. Your disaster was man-made. Quite coincidental, don't you think?' I don't answer. Coincidental with what? 'It is always interesting,' he goes on, 'to hear the same story from two different perspectives.' He sips his whisky. 'So Mike advised or at any rate had strong opinions about how you ran the business financially? And he had access to your accounts?' I nod uncomfortably. 'Does he still have access?'

'No! Your son was very fierce about only me having access.'

'I don't want to say this, but there is a possibility – an extremely unpalatable one, I know – that I think you need to consider.'

The penetrating grey eyes make me feel like a butterfly pinned to a board although he is looking at me with a good deal of sympathy. 'Over the years, Peter and I have developed a good working instinct for investment opportunities, and along with that goes a good working instinct for people. We always write individual reports before discussing the proposal, and interestingly neither of us liked nor trusted Mike. I would say he likes to be the centre of attention and praised and admired. I think he may have a devious, greedy and controlling personality.'

I gasp at this blunt assessment of my partner. How rude to say he didn't like or trust him! If anyone else had said it, I would think it was jealousy – sour grapes. But what has Dominic Paget got to be jealous of? My stomach cramps.

'Are you suggesting that he might have something to do with my losses?'

Dominic looks at me steadily. 'At this time I'm not suggesting anything concrete because there is no evidence. I'm telling you what Peter's and my assessment of him is. It is entirely up to you how you deal with that. You can take it on board, or you can ignore it.'

What he doesn't say is whether Vermont and Paget

would continue business discussions if I ignored their assessment. It's virtually blackmail and I don't like it.

I shake my head in repudiation of the suggestion that Mike is financially untrustworthy.

'He's a wealthy man in his own right. He's given me good advice and he's always been supportive of my business ethos. About four years ago he rebuilt my website and it's really good. Would he have done all that and then stolen from me! I simply don't believe he's got anything to do with it.' If I say it firmly enough, it has to make it true. 'Devious, controlling and greedy? That's a huge indictment. I never saw any sign of that.'

But is that true? Mike got his way with the flat – how it was decorated and furnished. With the car parking space which was always his. With where we went on holiday. My lovely competent man. Was that control? His suggestion that I 'paid my way', that our expenses should be equal: food, meals out, event tickets, holidays, mortgage. Because as a woman in business I was equally as capable as any man. That was certainly my own instinctive attitude, but was it devious greed on Mike's part so that I didn't cost him anything? I am silent, staring inwardly at Mike's behaviours and my reactions. Uncertain of him. Uncertain of me.

Dominic doesn't say anything, and I go on slowly. 'But I do think he's playing away.' I hadn't even said that to Wendy. Not in so many words. It's the first time I've admitted it out loud. He still doesn't say anything, but he's listening.

I take a breath, steadying myself. 'Someone in London. I think it's his secretary. He's often away overnight, on business. Her colour is on Mike.'

'Her colour?' His face creases uncertainly.

'Mike's colour – his smell – has changed over the past few months, and when I met his secretary, her colour is different, and it's on him.'

‘Colour? That’s not exactly evidential.’ Dominic is cautious, not understanding.

‘It is to me. Everybody has a smell and the smell is a colour. Mike is turquoise blue, and his secretary is greeny blue, and they are quite different. People don’t change their smell unless they are up close. When Mike comes back from an ‘office event’ his colour is greeny blue. He smells of Laura.’

Dominic stares at me. ‘Everybody has a smell! It sounds horrible. Even if they’re showered, clean undies and everything?’

I find myself smiling. ‘Clean is the true colour. Sweaty squash courts and the people playing all smell the same. Sweaty. And the colour is a dark purple – like a plum. Mind you, people can smell the colour of their soap, or their scent or aftershave.’

I thought Dominic would laugh at why I think Mike is cheating on me with Laura. People don’t understand my dominant sense. Smell is insignificant to most people, so I am surprised that he is not more sceptical. But he is perfectly serious and curious about it, appearing to accept that there is another dimension.

‘Can you smell more than other people? I mean, I don’t normally smell people, and certainly not in colour. Do I smell a colour?’

Laughing at his note of alarm, I say, ‘You smell the colour of dark honey. Amber. And yes, my sense of smell is more acute than most. I smell things other people don’t notice. I could tell you what spices or herbs are in a sauce. I smell things long before anyone else. So you see, when Mike’s colour changed and it coincided with one of his office events, it made me wonder. And it isn’t just smells that are colours for me, but numbers, days, months.’

‘How extraordinary! But it still couldn’t be considered evidence of cheating on you. After all, she is his secretary, and they could work physically quite closely.' His face compresses slightly. It is not disbelief but more a thoughtful assessment of possibility.

'It's not the only evidence.' I know I sound childishly stubborn. 'I found a receipt for dinner for two on the date of a big office dinner, and a bill for a bracelet bought on the same day. And just before I spoke to you today, he lied to me about where he was. He said he was in the office when he wasn't.'

Dominic looks amazed. 'How do you know?'

I have passed the point of feeling guilty about this. 'Because I'm tracking him. He was in a private house about two miles from his office.'

Is he shocked? He looks impressed if disconcerted. 'That's interesting. But there could have been a reason. It's still not evidence, not in a court of law.'

'I'm not in a court of law,' I say tartly. 'I'm in a flat which is supposed to be my home, living with a man who I had hoped to have children with, running a business which was perfectly stable but is now teetering on the edge of bankruptcy. A bankruptcy not caused by me, but if it happens, I think that's legally the end of my business career.' I pick up a pink blossom fallen from a begonia, turning pale brown at the edges.

'I suppose that's a bit like Mike and me,' I say, cupping it in my hands. 'A relationship going rotten.'

There's a little silence and then Dominic says, 'What will you do?'

I drop the limp flower back to the grass. 'Leave him,' I say sadly. 'I don't believe he has stolen from Ecolore – why would he? But he's allowed to fall out of love with me. We're not married.' Heat-desiccated apple leaves twist themselves off the twigs and float to the grass. One lands on my fingers and I crush it into powder. Bitchily, I think having an affair with your secretary is about as downmarket and clichéd as you could get, however drop-dead gorgeous she is.

The temperature has dropped with the sun, and we retreat indoors. Dominic tops up my white wine and produces spaghetti and bolognese sauce out of a jar while I make a salad. This Edwardian terraced house is unremarkable from the outside but has spacious rooms and high ceilings. I itch to update the kitchen. In my search for a salad receptacle, I clock an enormous dog bowl with 'Eat Me – But Slowly' written round the rim.

I love dogs, but I can't smell one here. 'Why the dog bowl? You haven't got a dog, have you?'

'I did have. A golden retriever. He was called Buzz.'

'What happened to him?'

'He died of old age, and because Patrick had grown up I hadn't the heart to replace him. Buzz used to come to the office with me, but it seemed a bit crazy to get another dog. I miss the company though.'

The conversation comes around to his wife Penny and how he managed to bring up a little boy single-handedly after her death. He doesn't appear to resent what could be taken as my curiosity.

'My mother came to live with us for a while and took over running the house and looking after Patrick. Then she and Penny's mother alternated.' He grinned. 'A difficult mix, mother and mother-in-law. Brilliant apart. Less good together.' He looks out of the kitchen window to the garden. 'Mother-in-law took a long time to get over losing a grandchild as well as her daughter.'

What am I hearing? Losing a grandchild? 'You had another child? Killed in the same accident?' I am so horrified I can hardly get the words out.

'No. Penny was five months pregnant.' My hands clench on my own stomach in protest.

His eyes focus back on me. 'A little girl, they said.' I see only sadness, no railing against a bitter fate.

'I am truly sorry.' Embarrassingly, my eyes go even more blurry at the thought of a lost baby, and I try to dissipate my tension. 'I suppose it was one thing I never had to cope with – a mother-in-law I mean.'

He smiles. 'She's very good news and an excellent grandmother to Patrick. Keeps him accountable. Did you get on with Mike's parents?'

'I never even met them.' He looks surprised. 'He's not at all family oriented and hardly mentioned his family and so far as I knew, he never visited them. I was vaguely surprised that he never suggested dropping in on his parents, even over Christmas. I got the impression they didn't want to meet me, and he wanted to protect me from their disapproval. I suppose that's not particularly surprising, and it was no loss, I guess.'

'Why would they disapprove of you? I mean, what is there to disapprove of?'

'Well, I'm not very – conventional.'

His mouth goes up at one corner. 'Oh dear. A non-conformist. Unorthodox. Speak first, think second.'

I sniff because I don't blush. 'Sorry I was rude. I was pretty angry.'

He smiles again. 'You were.'

He is a man who listens. A serene man comfortable in his skin with none of the angst or self-centredness of many of my contemporaries. Or Mike. He asks about my family, and I tell him briefly that Dad was not the most brilliant father and had no time for art or anything associated with it.

'My mother went blind over about ten years. As her sight got worse, he bullied her more and more.' I shrug slightly. 'He was frustrated by her I think, always trying to make her do things she couldn't or was too frightened to do and it just made her more scared and helpless. If I argued or stood up for her, he took it out on both of us – it wasn't physical, only verbal, but – ' I can feel my face twisting. 'I think that he was ashamed of her, and she embarrassed him. He resented her, how she held his career back, how he was unable to give smart dinner parties, or have clients come to the house.'

It's a long time since I even thought about my father, let alone spoke about him. I daresay Dominic can hear the underlying antipathy. He listens but makes no judgements and his grey gaze is thoughtful.

'Was your father always – difficult?'

'Difficult?' I consider that. 'He was very quick, always on time or early, very precise, clean and tidy. Easily irritated when things weren't just so. Nothing you could say could make him change once he'd made his mind up. Mum moved quite slowly and was always late for everything. She never worried about doing the washing up immediately or tidying. He was most uncomfortable to be with – always in a hurry. And she was very comfortable, always had time to chat, read stories, ask about school, play games.'

'And which of them do you think you're most like?'

I laugh. 'Oh! Mum! No doubt about it!'

He stretches and gathers our dirty plates. 'You're also punctual, clean and tidy. Easily irritated. And stubborn.' That easy grin takes the sting out of his remark. 'We're all products of both our parents.'

Sometimes you don't want too many home truths thrown at you. I nearly ask if I am uncomfortable to be with, but I don't want to hear another home truth.

We wash and dry the few supper things. 'Dad was always impatient. He wanted both Mum and me to do what he wanted, not what we wanted. Mum gave in, for a quiet life, peace at any price sort of thing, but I didn't, and it drove him nuts.'

'Is that what happened with you and Mike? Did you give in for a quiet life? Peace at any price?'

I turn and stare at him. Water drips from the pan I've just washed, leaking down my wrists. Jeez! He's said that in the same tone of voice he might ask whether the cake I baked is chocolate or coffee. Did I? Was what I called tolerance, a form of giving in?

'The more she gave in,' I say slowly, 'the nastier he got. By the time she was completely blind, he had made her utterly dependent, and he despised her to the core.' Is that what happened to Mike and me? The more 'tolerant' I became, the more he despised me? Until eventually I was so dependent on him, so uncertain of my own abilities, that he took me for the ride of my life.

I take a deep breath and hand him the saucepan. After a moment he hands it back.

'Reject. Sorry, it's got bolognese all over the outside.'

I peer at it and run my fingers over a crust of cooked mince. 'Oops, sorry.' I scrub it off and hand it back.

After a while I say, 'Maybe I'm too much like my mother. Peace at any price.' The lesson to learn is: if you become dependent, you become despised.

'Cass?' He hesitates. 'Is something wrong with your eyes too?'

I stiffen. Every bit of me tensing into flight mode. 'No. Why?'

'You were having a problem reading the art exhibition information. Bringing the catalogue very close. And you didn't see the spag bol on the saucepan, you felt it.'

He waits out my silence.

'I don't think anything's particularly wrong. I'm very short-sighted, that's all.' I pause and then say, 'I do need new glasses.'

A little bit more fear creeps into me because I too have been wondering if there is something wrong with my eyes.

* * *

Dominic's spare bedroom smells the pale yellow of aerosol furniture polish beloved by cleaning ladies. It is clean and tidy and the bed is already made up. Restless in the heat, I churn over a tumultuous day. Is Mike curious as to where I am? Did he even come home? I have left no message and nor has he.

The churning becomes sadness. A loss of what I thought was commitment, permanence and faithfulness. A future, mutual support, mutual everything. And now there was nothing but broken dreams and an uncertain future on my own. Even trying to rescue Ecolore seems a bit pointless now, like climbing a mountain with endless false summits. Dominic had asked what I was going to do, and I had put into words something I had never wanted or intended.

I am assaulted by loneliness, a longing for the soul warmth of another human. Somewhere along the line, I failed to fulfil my father's expectations, and I suppose I have failed to be the woman Mike wanted. I want to creep into Dominic's bed, to spoon against him, his arm heavy across my body, his breath warm on my neck. I want some comfort as my life assumptions disintegrate, and I think he is a man who would give comfort without blame. I push back the sheet and the smooth floorboards are cool under my bare feet. At the door I hesitate, hand on the doorknob. This is not the right moment, whatever you feel, whatever you want. Stiffen up, Cass. Back to your own bed.

Back under the sheet, I think of that comfort only a few steps away, but it might as well be on the moon. When he said there was no catch, I think he really meant it.

Chapter Nine

I wouldn't have found anything wrong unless I'd tried to register some new design copyrights. And even then I thought I'd just forgotten how to do it or was entering an incorrect username or password because all I can think of is that I so nearly got into Dominic's bed last night.

I go quite sweaty with mortification at my narrow escape. What was I thinking? What would he have thought of me? I had queried *his* motives, and he said there was no catch. No deal. And there wasn't. And I so nearly blew it.

With an effort, I try to concentrate on this particular problem of copyright. Because my eyesight seems to have got worse, so much so that even Dominic has noticed, I tend to put my computer hiccups down to not seeing clearly. But after failing several times to get into my account, and wasting an inordinate amount of time, I eventually ring Patrick, the son of the man I nearly seduced last night, who is back at uni now that the air conditioning has the all-clear, and ask him to look at it remotely. I have to trust someone. Surprisingly he answers his mobile and seems to be pleased to have something to do other than revising.

While my cursor darts about clicking things all on its own, I make an optician appointment because I have allowed this situation to go on too long and I must stop being an ostrich. I must stop hoping the problem will just go away.

Peering at my jumping screen I see unknown names

dotted about and Patrick gives me some extremely unwelcome news.

'Looks like your design copyrights from Ecolore have been regularly transferred to a company called Brainbow. Postal address PO Box 7793, London, email address brainbow@gyproc.com.'

Not my email. Not my address. Nothing received by Cassia Hunter. *Transferred?* A great lump of fury lodges itself between my ears, expanding until my head feels about to burst. How can that be done without my knowledge? This is copyright for God's sake. It's supposed to give you rights over your work. Why wasn't it protected? Don't they check? Send an email? Write to me?

I stare at my laptop as if it might bite me, shaky enough to spill coffee on the desk, and thanking Patrick, allow him to return to his revision.

I report this theft to the police as well. Somebody languid will leave a note for the DI. I find the police unsatisfactory and would dearly love to let off steam by yelling at them.

This is no ordinary theft. This is my life, my existence, my achievements, my answer to my mother's failure and my father's scorn. This is someone targeting all that I am, intending to destroy me. I consider what Mike said about my father being horrible to me, and how it could be him stealing and destroying. I had left and made a life thinking he wouldn't care; he would be glad to be rid of me. But what if he still wanted a punchball? Was he frustrated by no longer having a hold on me? Was he targeting me to bring me under his thumb again? It could be my father stealing my IP and the company name; he is, after all, a financial expert. Anger is being steadily eroded by a remembered childhood fear of his omniscience. But why after all this time? Why would the success of my business trigger such malice?

Mike and I have superficially made up our differences, agreeing to disagree about whether Zev should be employed or not, but I have stuck to my guns despite his continued disapproval, my resolve hardened by the suspicion that he is cheating on me. Continuing to live with him, shop, cook and eat with him, and sleep in the same bed, doesn't seem to affect him much, but I am finding it incredibly difficult to respond naturally to his remarks without a frosty silence, to do everyday things without seeming to avoid him. My disinclination for sex must surely be raising questions in his mind. How can you have a normal life with someone who is living a lie? I am terrified that I will say or do something which will reveal my suspicions before I am ready to. But I know I must bide my time before facing him with his unfaithfulness. I need undeniable evidence that he cannot slide out of. And an unacknowledged segment of my mind refuses to accept it.

Nor am I giving house room to Dominic's suggestion that it is Mike defrauding me. I simply don't believe it. He doesn't need to, he's got a brilliant well-paid job, and he's been constructively involved in the business all these years. The more I think about it, the greater the likelihood is of it being my father. After all, it wouldn't have been impossible to find me if he'd wanted to. I do business under my own name, my registered address is here, and the business is run from here too. All these years I have assumed he wouldn't want any connection, that he wouldn't be interested in whether I lived or died. But now I think I may have been wrong.

When Mike gets back in the evening, he smells his normal turquoise blue, and I can't help but enlarge on my latest catastrophe.

'The money isn't the only disaster for Ecolore. Someone has been into Companies House and registered the company and my copyrights in a different name. I found it this morning when I tried to register some copyrights.'

His expression freezes in disbelief. 'What! They can't have!'

'They have. And they've changed my address and the email address too.'

'How extraordinary!' An incredulous frown creases his forehead. 'It must be another company with the same name, and they've confused the entries. I'm sure you can easily straighten that out.'

'Well, I don't think it can be straightened out that easily. And I don't think it's confusion. Correspondence has been sent in my name, but to a PO Box address in London, which someone else has picked up.'

Mike now sounds angry. 'God forbid! Cass, this is surely the result of poor security. What a mess!' He scrubs his hands through his hair. 'I'll try to check tomorrow.'

I'm thinking if it ought to be checked, it should be checked right now – the internet never sleeps, does it? And how would Mike check, and what would he check? In any case, it's not checking I need. I need my business back in my name.

'It's not poor security on my part. It's dishonesty or spite on somebody else's part. I've let the DI know, and this is what I have a fancy lawyer for. He can bloody well earn his fees.' Anxiety ruptures my balloon of determined calm. 'It can't really be my father, can it?'

Mike slaps our supper ingredients onto the kitchen counter in a temper. 'Yes, of course it can! He's the only one with sufficient know-how who loathes you enough to do that sort of thing. Getting the police involved is pointless, and the lawyer won't do a thing, just charge you money.'

I stiffen at his use of the word 'loathes'. Surely my father never *loathed* me? No doubt I irritated and angered him, and he was certainly malicious on occasions. But loathe?

'Why would he loathe me?' I can hear the confusion in my voice even as my father's most hurtful insults flash in my memory.

‘I’ve often wondered. I expect your mother had a lover. Maybe he had to bring you up knowing you’re not his child.’ Dumbfounded by this off-the-cuff remark, I take a step back and get a punch in the kidney from the microwave handle. Mike pauses in his wiping down the counter, seemingly surprised by my shock, ‘Had it never occurred to you that you might be illegitimate?’

‘No,’ I croak. ‘It hadn’t.’

* * *

Zev listens without interruption to my suspicions that it might be my father trying to ruin Ecolore. He will try to discover who made the Companies House alterations and the copyright transfers and will get everything back in my name. How many hours will that take, I wonder, mentally wincing at the cost.

I can’t settle to work and pace restlessly around the flat. I need a distraction and finding out more information about Mike and Laura, if she is indeed his new lover, would certainly be that. Before he gets back, I go through all his cupboards and every pocket. Nothing. Flipping through his old diaries there are plenty of female names, including a Laura Beauchamp of 54 Sedgewick Road, Wimbledon. What a coincidence. On the other hand, she is his secretary and it’s not a crime to have your secretary’s phone number. But if he was in Sedgewick Road on company business, why say he was in a meeting in the office?

I search the bright blue filing cabinet and the lever arch files and boxes on the shelves and find a batch of recent mobile phone bills for a phone I don’t recognise and don’t know about. One set of number colours recurs more than any other and it’s the same one as in the address book. Laura Beauchamp of Sedgewick Road. I hear an odd little noise and it takes a few seconds to realise it's coming from me. Putting a hand on my painful stomach I find it's as hard as a rock. Massaging out the tension, I try to reason why Mike might need a separate phone to call her but fail. My chest is pounding and my fists are rubbing angry tears into my burning cheeks.

How long have I been the useful housekeeper, collecting and delivering his life? And when he isn't in Laura's bed, he can be in mine. One body being as good as any other.

Now the humiliation of his betrayal has metamorphosed into something different. My hands convulse as if they were throttling the life out of him. At this moment I want to kill him. I want to kill him slowly and painfully, but it would be far too good for him and inevitably I would be caught.

The heat of my anger is so physical that I go out onto the balcony to get some cooler air, my fingers gripping the cast iron railing so hard they turn white. I will leave him, leave the flat, leave my life. The actual process begins in my mind. Boxes, suitcases, packing, storage. And then reality steps in.

Leaving Mike is not quite as simple as it sounds. Over six years our life has intertwined in ways which can't be untangled in an instant of walk-out. My office is here, my business address, utilities, mortgage, bank details. I will certainly leave him to his new lover, but I must think this through carefully. My walking out would only be a relief to him. All his problems would be solved with my departure. But I want to punish him. I intend to punish him and I intend to make my revenge hurt. Gazing unseeingly across the park, I think about what Mike values most and what would hurt him most to lose. It obviously isn't me.

By the time I am finished, he will truly regret messing with Cass Hunter.

Chapter Ten

I ring my personal techno wizard and Patrick is tickled by my desire for revenge on a cheating boyfriend and even more tickled by my ideas for making it hurt.

'I've got no lectures on Tuesdays, so I'll come down on the bike tomorrow. Did you find out who nicked your IP?'

'Not yet, although I've got a good idea. Someone from my past. I've told the police and the lawyers are looking into it.'

There's a little pause. I remember his injunction to change all my passwords and to keep my master password secure. From everyone.

However, he just says, 'Whatever you do, don't tell my father what we're planning. He'd freak out.' I feel uncomfortable about that, but I would also feel uncomfortable telling him because I know he wouldn't approve. I don't want Dominic's disapproval, but my desire to punish Mike is stronger.

I park the Aston as close as possible to the back entrance and Patrick hacks into the electronics. It takes him about three hours and I feed him tea and chocolate biscuits, and then sausage and bacon butties as he sits on the back doorstep with alternating cold gel bags under his laptop and an extension lead to the hall socket. We gaze at the Aston as it performs some peculiar tricks. I hope the neighbours aren't watching.

Later, I go to the car wash and have a conversation with

Stefan the manager who is quite a mate of mine and is teaching me Polish phrases which I practise on the assorted workforce.

He throws his head back in a guffaw. 'You naughty, Cass! But how could he cheat on the most beautiful girl in all England? He is not a good man to do that to my favourite lady. Of course, I would like to help you, but how?'

'I want him to have to drive through the car wash. The full works, the big wash for really dirty cars. Not me, just him in the car.'

His eyes become slits and he rocks on his Nike trainers. 'But how this punish bad boy? Is just a wash, yes?'

I grin. 'Only a wash, Stefan. I'll organise the mud.'

He goes Polish guttural. 'What you planning, Cass?'

'If I don't tell you, you won't know. And if you don't know, you can't be held responsible.'

For a long moment he looks at me searchingly and I think he's going to refuse. He's wondering how on earth a car wash could punish Mike.

'An Aston Martin! You must be so, so careful nothing is my fault. The insurance! If anything goes wrong here, Mr Benton would sue me, you understand? So I must hear this plan.'

So I explain my harmless plan which consists solely of timing on Stefan's part. He gives me that searching stare again, but after a minute's thought, he nods reluctantly.

'Perhaps only me will know, not my brothers. Yes?'

'I understand, Stefan. Only you and me.' We shake on it and I say, 'Now, I've got the hang of "Good morning" and "Thank you". How do I say, "That's a lovely Polish polish"?'

Stefan gives me an old-fashioned look. 'All this teaching, Cass! I'll have to charge!' He takes a notebook out of his pocket and writes the phrase down and then writes it phonetically underneath before tearing the page out for me. I practise till I've got it to his satisfaction and when I come back to collect the gleaming car, perform my latest language trick on the valet, Stefan's young nephew. The effect is way beyond my expectations. The young man goes beetroot red and backs off as if I'm a vampire, and the surrounding workforce doubles up with mirth.

By the time I discover that I have actually said, 'Last night you made very good love, thank you,' the nephew has disappeared, and I am unable to apologise. Stefan gets a thick ear.

* * *

A week later Mike is due to drive to A Really Important Meeting with new clients at some swanky hotel in the New Forest. Unfortunately, when he gets to the Aston, in his new suit and expensive shirt and silk tie, he discovers that overnight someone has smeared it with a lot of dirt, and swear words are daubed all over it in black grease. I am not even dressed, and definitely not going to be seen dead driving crude words around. He'll have to take it to the car wash himself. He is furious and flings his computer case on the passenger seat. He is Going To Be Late. And, I think revengefully, Humiliated.

I haven't even time to put on make-up before Patrick arrives to pick me up on his motorbike, handing me a battered helmet.

We get to the car wash shortly after the Aston. Kicking the stand down at a safe distance, he takes the two twenty-pound notes for his artistic work on the Aston with gratitude, gives his helmet to me and gets his phone out.

'You're sure no one saw you?' I am anxious and slightly sweaty.

'Nope, there wasn't a soul around. And I had my lid on just in case.' He seems unnervingly sanguine about it. 'Took ten minutes.'

I keep my helmet on, feeling nauseous with a mixture of triumphant expectation and self-hatred and nearly lose my nerve and cancel the operation.

There is one car in the car wash and five waiting for hand wash, as carefully pre-ordained with Stefan.

We can hear bits of the horrified conversation between Stefan and Mike.

'Handwash in only twenty minutes, sir. Well, maybe twenty-five, thirty.'

'Can't wait. Late already,' wafts over to us, desperation clear.

'Car wash, sir, but you'll need the heavy wash, sir, that's oil. We do extra polishing job at end if any oil left.'

The brushes stop spinning and the car in front moves out. Stefan waves him through and Mike shoves his token into the machine before driving into position. Patrick's finger hovers.

'Wait!' I hiss. 'Not yet! Wait for the soap.' Oh, God! That beautiful car! Tears are running down my face under the helmet but I rev up my hatred for Mike. How dare you cheat on me, how dare you ditch me for some other woman, how dare you love this car more than you love me.

The machine rumbles into action, water spraying, the spinning brushes coming up and over the beautiful white bonnet, the side brushes stroking over the wheels, and down the sides. Back they spin, and the spray bars deliver their cargo of detergent as the brushes spin again. I have regained the fury and buried the regret.

'Now!'

His finger taps lightly. Just once.

All four windows and the sunroof open fully, simultaneously.

Oh! The joy! The sweet, sweet taste of perfect revenge. I have starbursts of vermilion, cirrus clouds of rose and ruby, gusts of magenta and cooked lobster.

He doesn't jump off the tallest building in town, but I am pleased he looks like he wants to. As the doors are opened, a waterfall of soapy water pours out. The leather seats are a definite goodbye, the walnut dashboard oozes foam, and dials, gearbox, bells and whistles are all wonderfully waterlogged. The Aston is photographed inside and outside. The Poles Twitter and Facebook, and the public are open-mouthed and wielding smartphones on a man in a saturated suit, hair dripping onto the sodden shirt and limp tie, shiny shoes squelching and bursting little soapy fountains. He coughs detergent out of his lungs and staggers to the front of his car where the rude messages are faded, but still perfectly legible. Leaning forward he throws up. Before we depart, Patrick reverses his electronic wizardry, but is uncertain whether it will succeed, due to excess water in the works.

By the time he drops me back home, my elation has dwindled with the receding adrenaline, tinging the clouds of rose and ruby with grey. It had been a lovely car.

Why don't I feel more triumphant?

Perhaps my sense of depression is because he doesn't know it is a punishment.

* * *

After he'd changed into dry clothes and done all his essential phone calls, Mike catches me crying. Well, not crying, because I don't, but sniffling. He thinks I feel sorry for him, but in fact, I feel sorry for myself.

'You are so sweet to mind so much.' He puts his arms around me and I feel utterly traitorous. 'I expect I'll lose the clients, which is a hell of a blow, and my boss wasn't at all understanding, but I'm alive though I did think I was going to drown.' He shudders. 'It was truly horrible – all those bloody brushes feeling like alien worms and stuffing detergent in my mouth. My suit is completely ruined, as is that new silk tie.'

'And those very expensive shoes,' I add, blowing my nose. 'I'll take the suit and tie to the cleaners. They may be OK. Your laptop and phone are buried in rice in the kitchen. You should leave them there for forty-eight hours apparently, but don't hold your breath either of them will work.'

The pockets of the sodden suit reveal nothing beyond change, pens and a soggy Kleenex. His leather wallet is only damp, so I remove the contents, shoving some receipts down my bra until I can have a proper look at them, then dunk the wallet in more water and spread the bank cards and cash out to dry on tea towels. He comes into the kitchen and looks at it all with an uncertain frown.

'What on earth are you doing?'

'Drying out your wallet. It was sodden.' Shoving little bits of kitchen towel into each compartment I prop it up on the tea towel like an open book. 'It shouldn't take long. Have you rung Aston Martin?'

He nods, the frown deepening into financial worry. 'They'll collect it tomorrow. They maintain water couldn't have been the reason, that it wasn't possible, but as there can't be any other answer, I hope to God there won't be any argument about insurance.'

'Well, I hope so too. Look, I must do some work. I abandoned everything when you called. You'll have to buy another phone as I can't do without mine.' I wonder if he will, as he has another mobile somewhere already. Thinking of documentation, I remember the contents of his wallet are in my bra. I make photocopies of various receipts and bank slips before returning them, damp, to the drying wallet contents in the kitchen. There are also two seats for *Les Misérables* at a West End theatre for next

Wednesday. Hmm. I wonder when he'll ask me. It's a bit short notice now.

* * *

Since planning my pointless Aston revenge on Mike, I have felt guilty about asking Patrick to enable it, but much worse is his request that I don't tell his father. The guilt of not being able to tell Dominic has turned into an unhappiness I cannot fathom. I'm a girl with not much of a conscience. Until now. I have never felt so bad and I just can't understand it.

The result is, I haven't communicated with Dominic since and there is an empty sort of ache inside me which has nothing to do with Ecolore's adversities. Therefore, his unexpected invitation to go with him to see the roses at Mottisfont Abbey is both welcome and yet unwelcome at the same time. For a start, it obviously isn't business, so is it a date? I'd be letting Patrick down and getting him into trouble if I confessed about destroying the Aston. And if I did tell Dominic, would he be angry as well as disappointed? Perhaps he wouldn't want to have anything more to do with me. That prospect makes me feel utterly wretched. But it would be very odd not to tell him the Aston has been ruined, as he's likely to find out. I suppose I don't have to mention Patrick. I accept the invitation with an uneasy conscience. When I tell Mike I'm going to see the gardens with a friend, he just shrugs and says OK. He doesn't even ask who with. Maybe he hopes I'm having an affair because then he could kick me out with impunity.

* * *

'This is unbelievable!' I have smelled the perfume long before we reach the garden and as we come closer the fragrance is overwhelming. 'I want to drown in it.'

The colours are like the satellite pictures of storms, curling and swirling, swinging and sweeping. Ever moving, ever turning. Inside the pink brick walls, I close my eyes and am almost blown away by this ecstasy of beauty and scent. 'It makes me want to cry, it's so incredible.'

I am oblivious to the many rose lovers around me. They may see, they may even smell a great deal, but they don't receive what I receive. They do not sense the depth of this aroma, the clearest, deepest blue of sea over sand.

'Are you going to look at them as well?' He sounds gently amused. For the first time, I realise that not only are my eyes shut, but I have turned into his chest and his arms are around me. People ease past us on the narrow path, ignoring what must be the slightly strange sight of a woman blindly clutching a man at the entrance to heaven.

'Oh! I'm sorry! So sorry!' Opening my eyes, I see in his face a warmth and tenderness that I can't remember ever seeing before, in anyone. 'How crazy of me. But the smell of them!'

Releasing him from my embarrassing grip I step into shadow and inhale the colours again. We wander the paths and little open spaces, sit in gazebos, and perch by fountains. The vast spectrum of red, pink, yellow, cream and white; the clusters and single blooms, the spires of white foxgloves. I am in a different universe. Why have I never discovered this before?

Gradually I understand that every rose has a different scent, and every scent a different colour. I breathe in splendour and glory, a fragrant paint palette of happiness.

When we eventually leave, it is a bereavement, even though he compensates with tea and sticky cake in the café.

‘I have a sudden urge to have a garden,’ I say. ‘I’d fill it with old roses and sweet-smelling herbs.’

‘Lilies and lilac.’

‘Sweet peas and freesias,’ I sigh. ‘But I don’t have a garden.’

‘You could share mine,’ he says, putting the plate of cakes next to me. ‘If you do the weeding, I’ll fill it with old roses.’

I think he’s just joking, but I look away, aware of a little leap of my heart. But now I’m even more aware that I am withholding something important from him. The longer the car isn’t mentioned, the odder it will sound.

‘Any progress towards leaving Mike? Or is it too soon to say?’

‘No progress really. It seemed so simple, but the realities of life are more complex than I’d thought.’

His expression doesn’t change, but I’m aware of a sadness in him.

‘You’ve changed your mind about leaving him?’

My fingers have laced themselves into a Turk’s head knot. ‘I haven’t changed my mind if it’s true, but I won’t drop six years of commitment in the waste bin of history without final and irrefutable evidence.’ I take a deep breath. ‘I didn’t tell you. Something went wrong at the car wash and Mike’s Aston got wet inside.’

He stares at me. ‘Really? Did he forget to shut the windows?’

I shrug. ‘I guess so.’

After a moment’s silence, he says, ‘How wet?’

‘Very wet.’ I lift my eyes and think his penetrating ones are puzzled. ‘It’s a write-off I think.’

‘Is he very upset?’

‘Yes. Can’t say that I am, though.’ I grin at him cheerily and feel relieved that I have told him the very bare bones. I just hope I never have to put flesh on them.

* * *

There is a message from the insurance company, asking for the Aston Martin paperwork. Zev's queries about Mike's liquidity and spending have been subconsciously sculling around my brain and this is virtually permission to pry. As I unlock his blue filing cabinet it occurs to me for the first time that it is a bit strange to lock your filing cabinet in the family home. The key to my red cabinet is identical to his, but that has never crossed his mind.

There is a sinking feeling in my gut as I look at each page of the Aston folder in his Car file. The sub-totals and totals are hair-raising, with additional accessories worth thousands of pounds. Four forged black alloy wheels at a cool £4,400! That is outrageous!

There are no repayment dates; he has paid outright for this baby. A clear stamped receipt: 'Paid'. How could he possibly have had that money? All the dropped hints over the years about what a burden the mortgage was, and how necessary my contribution was. How we must share all our costs because I was so expensive to run! Without success, I try to recall why I had the impression that he would be paying monthly instalments on the car. Was that an assumption on my part or had he told me?

Nausea creeps up from my stomach because the colours of what Mike paid for the car are dancing in front of me. I see that my defensive assertion that Mike was independently wealthy was more for my own reassurance. Zev had seen that the huge withdrawal of funds could have been connected with Mike buying the Aston. I had convinced myself that it was pure coincidence, but the coincidence is becoming less certain by the moment.

My heart is racing as I stare blindly at the documents, my fingers abstractedly crushing the papers.

Zev was not wrong. Patrick's and Dominic's instincts were not wrong. It was my instinct that was wrong. My judgement that was faulty. Mike had spent much of my stolen funds on the Aston, an asset which I had just destroyed instead of recovering. I'm glad no one is here to see my chagrin, my hot cheeks, my tears of humiliation. And now my anger.

You had access to my money, you greedy rat, and before I could spend it on my business you thought you'd spend it on your pleasure. No more free cash would have been a real downer so there was no point in hanging back. Let's go for the big one, shall we? An Aston Martin would be nice. How about a yacht? A villa in Greece? Sorry there wasn't enough for a private jet.

Banging the file drawer shut, I storm through to the balcony. The flat, my home, my office, is suddenly tiny and claustrophobic and I run downstairs. Blood-red heat beats at me, and there are no shadows in the empty street. I head for the park where the trees are indistinct beckoning sentinels of shade.

He was the one person I trusted, the person I had been hoping to find innocent – or at least had been hoping not to find any evidence of guilt for. Did he think that my difficulty in working with numbers would prevent me from seeing what he was doing? Or did he just think that it would never cross my silly little mind? He was right on both counts I think bitterly, running the pads of my fingers over the rough bark of an oak tree. The smells are of warm resin, unfinished picnics, the cobalt of newly mown grass. Early summer.

The cheating, thieving scumbag. The lousy, despicable jerk. The worm, the lying two-faced creep. What did I ever do to deserve him? Having an affair with another woman hurt enough but to find he has deliberately ruined my business as well! That takes his betrayal to a whole new level. And I have been an *idiot*. A stupid, blind, pathetic idiot not to have seen in his eyes, to have heard in his voice, how he despised me. But why? Why keep me with him all this time if he hated me so much? Just because I was the cash cow who couldn't – wouldn't – see it coming? Well, I can be a cow all right. You'll find this cow has teeth, and I will bite you. I inhale the smell of the tree again. Dry on the outside, but inside running with the water of life.

I may be dry on the outside, but inside I too am running with the water of life, and I return to my office with much less self-delusion and much more resolve.

I ring Mike. 'The insurance company have just rung. They want the Aston documents scanned over immediately. Do you want me to do it? If so, where's the key to your cabinet and where are the documents?'

I don't think I'm imagining the slight pitch of panic in his voice. 'Why the hell didn't they ring me directly? I've got all the papers here. I'll do it.'

Without a doubt, he doesn't want me in his filing cabinet.

'Oh. Good. Because I've got a lot to do, and I really don't think I can sort your calamities as well as mine.' I'm going to put the cat among the pigeons a bit more and spoil his theatre evening with his new lover. 'By the way, I saw in the paper that *Les Misérables* is on in London and I'm dying to go. Why don't we try for next week? I'm due to be up there for a meeting on Wednesday so I could meet you at the theatre. It'll cheer us up after all our disasters.'

There's a palpable hesitation. 'I can't on Wednesday. I've got a meeting that might well run late. Sorry.'

I add a bit of bite. 'What a shame. I think I'll go anyway. They've always got single tickets at a discount.' This spoke in his wheel is a minor victory. He'll have to cancel if he thinks I'm going, and I hope Laura will be very disappointed.

A little compensation for my bruised ego and wounded

feelings, but as I hang up, I am vaguely surprised that my broken heart doesn't seem to need too much mending.

Chapter Eleven

Of course, I continue to scrabble about in Mike's files and dip into Legal.

Legal contains fairly recent correspondence with his lawyer about, oddly, Callaloo, the restaurant I found a receipt for, on the night of an office dinner. He seems to be buying or refitting it, and I am puzzled as to why. And with what money? Mine? Mike has never been into property development to my knowledge, but of course, my knowledge about Mike is not what I thought.

Then I find another folder in Legal for a company called Brainbow.

Brainbow! I sit bolt upright in shock. Patrick had discovered that my copyrights had been transferred to Brainbow. My company had been transferred to Brainbow.

My chest feels as if it is going to burst as I read that file. It wasn't some anonymous hacker and it wasn't my father – here is evidence that it was Mike, to add to all his other foul activities. And he has left the proof *here*, in my *office*! My hands are trembling as I squint fiercely at the papers.

I get out my bank card remembering the day I had first gone to see Dominic Paget when I thought I had lost it. The day Mike had come home early, found the card under my desk, and then castigated me for carelessness. Had he copied the new number and CVV intending to go on stealing? Or had he just done it to annoy, to emphasise my inefficiency, to sow more seeds of doubt about my competency, to accentuate the irritation of replacing it? I send for yet another new card and change my PIN.

The printer is drowning my naive dreams as it spits out the waterfall of evidence. He had tried to make me believe that my father loathed and hated me so much that he would ruin me. He had insinuated that my mother had had an affair and that I was illegitimate. Why? Why would anyone say that? And it wasn't new, it wasn't just a result of falling out of love with me and falling in love with Laura. This had been going on for much longer. This had been a targeted hate campaign over a long period of time, and I had never realised it. Never recognised that this man who I loved and who I thought loved me, not only disliked me but must actively hate me. My brain stalls in incredulity. How could I have been so stupid, so blind?

Sliding the photocopies into an envelope, I scribble a shaky note to Zev and take it to the post office. Outside, empty-handed, I take off my glasses and heel the moisture from my cheeks. The external world becomes a swirl of fuzzy curves, figures that are shapes without features, patterns that slide in and out of focus. My internal world is equally disoriented, and I am cracking inside. This road which I had thought was heading to lifetime safety has ended at a cliff edge, and the shock has left me bewildered and lost. My Aston revenge now seems a pathetic little slap for Mike cheating on me with another woman, discarding me down the drain like sour milk. My shock turns to dismay when I remember that if the insurance company doesn't pay up, I have probably written off an asset which had in fact belonged to me.

Dominic and Zev, and indeed Wendy and Patrick, had tried to tell me that it was far more serious than being unfaithful, but I had stubbornly ignored their warnings.

Now I must concentrate on unscrambling our joint life of six years; I must face Mike with what he has done and demand recompense. But I feel utterly powerless and alone. I don't even know what I should be telling him, demanding of him. At this moment I would give anything for a strong man to take control and fight my battles for me. I would dearly like Dominic to be in charge.

I need thinking time before going back to the flat so I walk down to the Red Jet quay, hardly taking in the vast cruise liners or the busy crowds boarding the Isle of Wight ferry. Pull yourself together, woman. You are not helpless. You've been stupid and overtrusting, but you've got a brain and it's better than his. What needs doing first? Stop paying the mortgage and the utilities. Tell the police. Tell Zev. Tell Dominic. Humiliating but necessary. But should I face Mike with the fact that I know what he's been doing, or will that enable him to cover his tracks?

Cancelling the mortgage standing order to Mike will be simple enough, but the cliff edge of leaving Mike means that I must leave my home too. Anxiety fills me as I realise I have no idea what the complications are of getting six years of mortgage contributions back. I need to have account information before ringing the mortgage provider.

When I get back, I make myself a strong cup of coffee, cancel all payments to Mike and force myself to embark on his Mortgage file. But it makes no sense because I cannot see my name anywhere. Maybe there is another file with my details in it, but I can't find it, and my concern grows along with the frustration of not being able to see clearly. I ring the mortgage company who confirm the policy number but state categorically that there is absolutely nothing in my name, that I do not own half the flat and that Mr Michael Benton is the sole mortgage holder.

Dropping my phone onto the desk, I stare at my rigid hands. There simply cannot be another major disaster. I shall scream, or cry, jump out of the window. What the hell do I do now? Someone, somewhere, do the thinking for me, take over, know what to do. If I ring Dominic with yet another Cass calamity that will surely be the end of any financial assistance I might have hoped for. I groan at my imprudence and Mike's duplicity and an icy curl of fear creeps up my spine as I ring Zev.

'I pay half the mortgage, but my name is not on the deeds, or anywhere in the paperwork.' My voice is cracking. 'The company have never heard of me. And I paid it to Mike direct. Not to the mortgage company. For six years.' It is more than embarrassing to confess that I have been unbelievably unwise.

There is a small silence.

'Oh dear.'

'I know, I know! I never thought it through, I never *thought*. I believed him when he talked about "our" flat, and what a good investment it was for me. I trusted him all the way.' I can hear the bitterness in my voice.

'Not in cash I hope?'

With relief, I say, 'No. By standing order to his account.' And my memory goes back to the occasional request for cash payment because he is short of cash, and my refusal because I know I should have some form of record for something as important as a mortgage payment.

'Was there a reason for that? I mean, why not direct to the mortgage company?'

'Because he said it was easier. More sensible to have one payment going to the company instead of double payments which would be more expensive.' I take a deep and wobbly breath. 'I never asked to see the deeds, I never signed them. I thought I was a savvy businesswoman, but I'm a total idiot.'

There is another silence. I'm hoping he is just thinking and not reduced to speechlessness by my idiocy. Please tell me I need not worry.

He doesn't. He goes into the detail of what I pay, and

when and how, and says he'll follow it up. He tells me to send him everything I have found and to tell the police.

'Should I tell Mike that I know everything he's done? What if he won't move out?'

'I think you should wait until we've all the ducks lined up. There could be explanations for all this.'

Could there be? It seems highly unlikely. It dawns on me that not only is my business going under, but I could be on the verge of losing the roof over my head, and I am attacked by a headache that borders on migraine. The tsunami of Mike's treacheries washes over me in a surge of life debris, smashing through everything I have built. My independence, my financial security, my relationships, and my future. This surely cannot have been happening for six years at the same time as we lived a happy and fulfilled life together. Could there be an explanation for any of this? And am I now imagining the subtle changes in his attitude as those years progressed? That the love and laughter submerged into a prosaic routine? That teasing became mockery, that suggestions became instructions?

* * *

Through my mind mush is the vague and slow comprehension that Dominic's calls are no longer business calls; they are regular and personal. He is cautiously asking me on dates; he wants to talk to me. Feebly, I ditch my concerns about Vermont and Paget's possible investment in Ecolore and clutch at this friendship hoping like hell that my judgement is not faulty this time. I don't ring him, but when he rings me, I blurt out my latest disaster.

'You can stay with me,' Dominic says, his voice full of concern.

'I can't! You know I can't. It would solve nothing. If I

leave Mike, I leave my home and my office and I'll never get it back. Zev is uncertain that I'll get back any of my money. I mustn't leave Mike; he must leave me. And I need him not just to leave me in the flat but to leave me full possession of the flat.' But for all my creativity, I cannot for the life of me think how I can force him to do that.

'But you can't stay there, living with him, when you know he's done all this!' Dominic sounds appalled.

I can't even imagine how I could pretend to live a normal life with someone who has betrayed me to this degree. How would we have a conversation, have sex or make plans, with these lies and deceptions unacknowledged between us?

All my certainties are melting away, and I want a lifeboat. The thought of moving in with this calm, wise and attractive man is so alluring that I give it serious consideration, but reality rapidly takes over.

'I must,' I say grimly. I don't know how I'm going to do it, but I must. For the moment anyway. I run my business from there, it's my office as well as my home.' I find my sense of humour recovering. 'And you have no idea how much stuff I've got.'

And how can I move in with you when you haven't so much as made a pass at me? Ever.

My computer sends me a reminder about my optician appointment tomorrow. I very nearly cancel it as I am drowning in disasters which need to be dealt with, but stronger glasses would be helpful.

* * *

The optician doesn't say much as he slots the eyepieces in and out, turns screws, and puffs air at me. I know I'm not doing well on his tests, and he spends an inordinately long time peering inside my eyes and taking photographs. His long and silent assessment is concerning because I had just assumed I needed stronger lenses. I feel very alone and wish that I had told Dominic about this appointment. He was the one who had noticed. I'm here because of him, not Mike.

'What's the verdict?' Although there are certain verdicts you'd rather not hear.

He is putting away his kit and moving equipment. 'There is deterioration since your last examination – which was over three years ago – and you also have a cataract in your right eye which really needs dealing with. When that has settled, we'll order new lenses, but before then I would like a specialist ophthalmologist to examine you at Moorfields Eye Hospital in London where they have equipment which I don't have.'

'Moorfields? That's not a destination to confirm a cataract, surely?'

He doesn't turn his head from tidying up his instruments. 'You say your mother went blind but you don't know the cause. There are many diseases of the eye, some genetic, and the specialist will make a much more detailed examination.' He is sombre, and even if he doesn't know exactly what is wrong, it is clear that something is not right.

There is a lot of information about referrals and appointments and dates and letters, but I am not really listening. Did Mum have glaucoma, or macular degeneration, about which I know nothing except that there is dry and wet, and I think it's genetic. I thought it was something that happened to old people. Feeling a bit shaky and light-headed, I go to stand at the shop doorway and watch the busy street while the optician taps away at his computer. The sky is as dull as my brain and there is a strong steel-grey smell of curry from the Indian restaurant next door. I have a stupid desire to get to my computer and do research, and at the same time I don't want to know anything, and then the problem will go away. And what is an ophthalmologist, anyway?

When I get back to the flat, I Google eye diseases and ophthalmologist and am not comforted. I have a sudden, urgent and irrational desire to tell Dominic and to be comforted by him, but though I finger it, I don't pick up my phone. He is more than a business acquaintance, but he's not a lover, and his kindness and friendship are purely part of his character. I am not going to add to the weighty millstone of the misfortunes he already carries on my behalf. In terms of a developing relationship, girl meeting boy, I hardly know the man, even if he has asked me to stay. In any case, until I see this ophthalmologist, there is no crisis. There is no scary diagnosis. I would be making a fuss about nothing: a mountain out of a molehill. There is nothing to tell anyone.

Chapter Twelve

Shop windows reflect the fuchsia colours of my dress, thin and floaty as silk, another demo model borrowed from Wendy, and the shiny pinks and purples of the sandals. I am not outrageous because today I must have an old head on my not-so-young shoulders.

It is hot again, and stuffy; charcoal-smelling as if thunderstorms loom, both physically and emotionally. I might look good outside, but inside is a mess. From long ago, I hear Dad's voice. 'Pull yourself together, Cassia. All this pretentious, arty talk won't get you anywhere. You need to work, my girl. I'm not paying for this art school. Get a job, earn some money, stop expecting the world – me – to bow and scrape and support you. You're behaving like your mother – a loser.'

The lawyer's office is the same peaceful, quiet oasis of clever people using clever words to make clever decisions. Clever is not an adjective applicable to me, and now my many unwisdoms are coming home to roost.

The gorgeous Zev lopes into reception, a large plain girl in a dark skirt and white blouse (is it an office uniform?) trailing in his wake. He introduces her as Lucy, one of their researchers, and we troop into a conference room. A young man sidles in carrying a pad and sits in a corner. He is apparently a trainee and will take notes.

Within minutes I am drowning in official incontrovertible evidence. Up the creek, out of my depth with no lifebelt. Why am I feeling like a punchbag? None of this is new to me, but I realise that I hadn't totally accepted my own discoveries. I had thought – I had hoped – that there was a possibility I was wrong. I have the sensation of being locked into an unstoppable train.

No stranger has wormed their way into my business; no disaffected bank employee, no customer or client, and not Richard whom we had sacked. I am again dumbfounded by the betrayal, the sheer meanness, of the man I had loved and trusted. It has reduced the hard-boiled, self-sufficient me to a jelly, and a publicly humiliated one at that. Lucy's list of withdrawals goes back almost to the time Mike and I first met. The police have found, and the lawyers confirm, if not direct connections with money leaving Ecolore, then indirect ones with similar amounts of money subsequently going into Mike's account.

How mortifying to think of the pleasure he had had, taking me for the ride of my life. Now I had to admit to these people I was not the businesswoman I had thought myself. Mike's assumption that I am a ditzy, arty freak is absolutely correct. All my high-minded, save the planet, eco-sustainable gobbledegook isn't worth a bean in the face of large plain Lucy's laser mathematics and bloodhound doggedness, all laid out in spreadsheets on a shiny conference table. I now see that some of what Mike had done had been purely to make trouble for me; to annoy, to irritate. His transfer of the company name and my copyrights can't have brought him any financial gain but caused me fear and anguish and an undoubted financial cost. He used and then 'lost' my bank card and enjoyed the trouble it caused me. He laundered what he'd stolen through the restaurant called Callaloo, seemingly assisted by his – our – lawyer, making regular credits to an offshore account in Nevis. The non-existent mortgage, all the financial thefts trailing back through six years of evenings cooking together, wine on the balcony, holidays, parties and restaurants, advice, discussion and football. He hasn't just been cheating on me with another woman. Here is the confirmation that he's been stealing from me as well, and he always has done. He had planned it all from the beginning of time. And I have no idea why.

Suddenly, it is all too much. I push my chair back so hard it rocks drunkenly and hits the wall. Going to the window I stare down at the indistinct street below, at people going about their business unaware of the disintegration going on inside me. I can't even swear. I've seldom been rendered speechless before, but then betrayal has never been like this before either. I am aware of pain in my hands and looking down I find both palms adorned with little half-moon cuts, and there is blood under my perfect purple nails.

It hasn't taken long to officially destroy six years of happiness, security, a home, and a future.

Lucy and the note-taker depart but Zev Mahindra ignores my extended hand and asks me to sit down again.

'You need to fully understand the financial situation,' he said, 'and you need to make a decision based on that information.'

I sink into the chair, all my bones like cooked spaghetti. Considering how many rotten decisions I've made already, I'm surprised he's asking me for more.

'The funds in Nevis cannot be retrieved,' he goes on. 'Only Mr Benton has access to them. The Nevisian government find it convenient to keep those accounts secret. As far as your mortgage payments are concerned, without your name on the deeds, I'm afraid you do not own half the flat. You have been paying Mr Benton a direct unsecured monthly allowance.'

Zev looks at me as if to assess whether I am taking this information in before continuing. 'The issue of the ownership of your business and the theft of your intellectual property will be complex, but I think can be rectified quite quickly.' He steeples his fingers against each other. 'You have to decide whether you want us to try to retrieve any money remaining in Mr Benton's accounts in the UK. The costs of doing so may be higher than what you will get back.' He sighs regretfully. 'The police will try but may not succeed in gathering enough evidence to persuade the CPS to prosecute. If they don't, they won't charge him.'

I stare at him in despair. A dizzying, sweating wave of apprehension sweeps through me and I have a sudden desire for the comfort of Dominic's enfolding arms. This is ridiculous and I push the thought away.

Taking a pathetic pull at self-control, I feel tears flood against my eyelids and have no idea what to do.

'So your advice is what?' My voice cracks.

He taps his pen on his notepad. 'Think carefully before you commit yourself to anything. Sometimes retreat is the correct strategic – and financial – decision.'

'You mean cut my losses? Forget it? Let him get away with it?' My tone is bitter.

He is sympathetic but firm. 'My fees would be worth it if there was money to be reclaimed, but only Mr Benton has the power to access funds in Nevis. The law is toothless in this respect I'm sorry to say.' The pen suddenly stops tapping. 'Yes, my advice would be to cut your losses now. I doubt you will forget it.'

Justice before punishment is what the law recommends, but I can see justice could be a long time coming, and probably never will. I can't afford legal justice however much I want it and I have ongoing business costs. And I still have to live with the man who is cheating me financially as well as cheating on me. No, I'm not going to let him get away with it. I will make him pay somehow. I must make him pay, in every sense.

My tears have dried behind my eyelids and my voice is

firm. 'Please get Ecolore back in my name at Companies House, and my copyrights. Both as quickly as possible.' Shock and fear are already changing into something different. Something much tougher.

* * *

Naturally, I don't mention the meeting to Mike nor that I know he has betrayed me in every possible sense. We are inexorably drifting apart. We go on living in the same flat, and my behaviour has changed ostensibly because I am worried about my business. I cook what I have to and speak when I have to. Any advances for sex I turn down with various excuses – too tired, too worried, PMT. Mike initially didn't seem to notice, but now I see the odd puzzled, slightly apprehensive, glance, and he hasn't queried my cool attitude. The bonds between us have weakened and are now falling apart like wet paper.

There was a certain amount of satisfaction in telling him that my Wednesday meeting in London had been postponed and therefore I hadn't gone to *Les Mis*. His efforts to conceal his annoyance are some compensation.

He spends more nights in Sedgewick Road, according to the GPS tracker, to return smelling blue-green instead of turquoisey blue. I wonder why he doesn't ask me to leave. Why he doesn't just say he's fallen for someone else. I guess it's because I'd find out about the mortgage.

Dominic's now daily calls of concern and support keep me sane, and our friendship strengthens. He understands my reluctance to leave the flat, but the offer of moving in with him is always there and oh-so-tempting. I am not at all sure that either of us could remain 'just friends' if we were living under the same roof, although neither of us has admitted to the obvious chemistry between us.

Underneath all my anger and anxiety the same old questions go around like pastry in a mixer, getting thicker and more obscure by the moment and no one can give me an answer. Why? Why has any of this happened? What did I do, or say, to make the man I loved and who I thought loved me, into a monster? A mean, greedy, malicious monster. Jealousy could not account for that. Could it? What could he be jealous of? He often made jokes about Ecolore with our friends, and I had never really minded, thinking it was just his sense of humour. Now I feel it had been an intended denigration, and my skin cringes in retrospect. How could any human being do this to another? What was wrong with his own job and salary? Why did he pretend to love me? What pleasure could he possibly get from my ruin? His malice is sneaky, hidden, secretive. Unfathomable. Unforgivable. He is a rat of the first order. I too must become sneaky and secretive. To survive I must force him to return what he's stolen and if he won't or can't, then I must prevent him from taking the flat and six years' worth of my mortgage contributions. The cooked spaghetti of my backbone is drying out and stiffening.

If Zev Mahindra can't deliver, then I will. I have the beginnings of a plan.

* * *

'I still can't understand why he would want to do this to me,' I fulminate to Dominic as I print out some new information leaflets about eco-friendly products. 'Zev says that legally there probably isn't anything that can be done to get my money back, but I'm still being advised not to tell Mike I know what he's done.'

Dominic picks up one of the leaflets and glances at it while drinking his pale-blue-smelling coffee. He's been doing business in Southampton this afternoon and has dropped in to see me. I had been startled by the thrill of surprise and pleasure I got on opening my door to him and by how easily and quickly we have developed a friendship far beyond our business relationship. Not that the business relationship has progressed and I fear it won't.

He's thinking about what I've said, not really taking in my leaflet. 'That's tough and must make living in the same house extremely difficult.'

'It does,' I say with feeling. 'I am living a lie, and I hate it. I am also living with the possibility of letting the cat out of the bag by mistake. My nerves are all jaggedy. Which is why I escape to Winchester more than I should. I'm surprised Mike hasn't queried it. I'm surprised you haven't queried it.'

Dominic smiles. 'You can escape to Winchester any time you want. A welcome awaits.'

It's certainly a welcome, but so far, it's a purely friendly one.

'You'd think he'd notice there wasn't a welcome here. The police and lawyers are making slow to no progress, which must give him great satisfaction. But I think I have an idea to force his hand, although it will force my hand too.'

'And what's the idea?' Dominic sounds cautious.

'To make him leave because I will make the flat uninhabitable and unsellable. The only downside is that it will be uninhabitable for me too until such time as he returns all my money including my mortgage payments. Then he can have it back.'

He sounds even more cautious. 'How are you planning to make it uninhabitable? Flood? Fire? And if it's uninhabitable, where will you live and what will you do with all your possessions? What about your office?' He puts his empty mug on the leaflet pile and his elbows on his knees and looks at me searchingly.

'I'll tell you if it comes to anything,' I say evasively. 'If it does, I'll move as much of my stuff as possible into the storage container I use for my samples and stock.'

'And the remainder?' he says wryly. 'And you can't live and run your office in a container, can you?' I shrug because I don't really know the answer. 'You could bring a certain amount to my house. You could bring yourself too.' He swallows the remainder of his coffee and the mug hides his expression. 'If whatever ghastly plan you're cooking up works, I guess it will only be temporary.'

Does he really mean it? The idea of moving in with him is extremely appealing although I don't think the invitation includes his bedroom. I wish it did.

'Thank you so much for offering. That's an inadequate response to your generosity I'm afraid, but I'm really grateful. I hope to goodness I don't have to carry out my dastardly idea, but whatever happens, I won't be staying with Mike and will have to make alternative home and business plans at some point.'

'It isn't anything illegal or dangerous, is it?' I shake my head, not very emphatically. 'Promise?' He now looks faintly anxious, as if what he's come to know about me might give him cause for alarm.

'I'm not one hundred per cent sure and I never make promises unless I'm certain of keeping them.'

'I'll visit you in prison,' he says with resignation.

Chapter Thirteen

'We've had a horrible few weeks, and I know I haven't been much fun to live with,' I say with a sigh. 'We need something to look forward to after all our bad news.' I breathe a prayer that Mike will like my suggestion. 'We never decided on how to celebrate your fortieth, so what do you think about a party, in the flat? It needn't be grand or expensive, neither of us has the funds for that, but it would be fun to show off the flat to a few of our mates.'

Mike is a social animal. 'It needn't be that small. This room will take thirty people easily. Yeah, good idea.'

I open my phone and peer at the calendar. 'Your actual birthday is a Saturday, which is pretty convenient, but it's less than six weeks away – we need to move fast and get invitations out, and I need to get organising.' I straighten up and look positive. 'Let's do a guest list and I'll design an invitation.' We talk names and then I take a deep mental breath. 'I'd have given you the party as my present, but sadly, as I haven't now got any funds, I can't. I'll have to get food and wine and stuff. Are you sure you can afford it, what with losing the car and everything?'

As I thought, he resents my suggestion he hasn't got the means for a decent party, and hands over his debit card. 'Don't go mad.'

'Certainly not,' I say puritanically. I intend to go very mad.

* * *

Eddie is a bit bemused to be asked for a drink in the flat. We exchange enthusiasms. His for Southampton Football Club and mine for eco-sustainability. When I get around to mentioning it, he is even more mystified by my request.

'Dead rats? You want some actual dead rats?' He puts his beer down and sits back slightly on the balcony chair. It seems he needs an explanation.

'I want to freeze them, so I can draw them. I'm thinking of a design for a hoodie, and I like to draw from life. Well, not quite life, a live rat would be a bit alarming.'

Eddie stares. He suspects dirty work at the crossroads but can't quite fathom it out. 'You could get a white one at the pet shop, they make nice pets. And there are some excellent photos on the internet.'

I give him my best wide-eyed pleading look. 'Just a couple of dead ones, Eddie, as a favour?'

Eddie is firm. 'I can't give you any rats – dead or alive – but there are plenty of guys who keep snakes as pets, and they need a vast supply of rats and mice. The rats are farmed then gassed and frozen.' He debates with himself for a moment. 'I could probably buy a couple for you.'

'You're an angel, Eddie.'

Eddie looks thoroughly baffled and takes himself off shaking his head, and in due course complies with my rat request. Please collect them from his wife at an address in Bournemouth. Bring a cold box.

I ring to confirm a time and despite the usual problems of being unable to decipher building numbers, find her tattoo and body piercing establishment, where we recognise each other as kindred spirits. Jade is tall and slim and smells a silvery olive green – disinfectant, I think – and wears a thin yellow mini dress under the white coat which she takes off as I enter. She is a walking advertisement for her trade, covered in delicate designs from her hairline to the ends of her toes as if she has had a shadowy lace veil thrown over her shining black skin. What goes on in the middle only Eddie knows, but Jade makes it clear she wishes she had twice as much space to draw on.

I'm fascinated. 'Who does the bits you can't reach?'

She laughs. 'I haven't done any of mine. There's a community of tattooists and we tend to specialise in particular procedures and types of decorations.'

I am impressed by her premises – modern and hi-tech, spotlessly clean. More like a hospital theatre, though the outer office-cum-waiting room is a friendly space with books of designs and explanatory leaflets festooned on little side tables and delicious pale blue nutty coffee smells emanating from a little kitchen.

'Have to be a hundred and fifty per cent over and above standard requirements,' she says, putting down a cappuccino for me before cleaning up her workspace after her last customer. 'I sometimes wonder why I married a man in Eddie's profession when he puts unmentionable packs like yours in my freezer.' She has the biggest, whitest grin I've ever seen. 'My curiosity is killing me!'

I confide that the unmentionable packs are to be delivered to my very own rat. Jade's huge black eyes open wider as I start to explain, and before I know it, I am telling her everything from start to finish.

'I'm sorry. I never meant to say all that. I can't think what came over me.' I force a laugh, disconcerted to find I have poured out a great deal of stuff to a perfect stranger. 'I obviously needed to let the rat out of the bag. But I think rats for a rat might just do the trick.'

The swathe of honeysuckle encircling Jade's forearm seems to move as if in a breeze.

'Shouldn't you prosecute rather than use dead rats?'

‘My lawyer isn’t convinced the police will be able to make a case, and it’s unlikely they can get the money back. And God knows what a court case would cost.’

I get to my feet. ‘I’d better remove the offending items from your freezer and put them in mine. I’ve brought a cold bag and ice blocks.’ She picks up my cold bag and removes a package from the kitchen freezer drawer. Her eyes are gleaming with firm reinforcement. ‘In that case, go get him, girl!’

* * *

It’s only when I get back to the flat and look again at those thick sealed polythene bags (single-use plastic, which I heartily disapprove of) which clearly hold two frozen rats, that I think our freezer is perhaps not the best place to keep them. Mike is the one who uses the freezer most, in and out for ice, frozen herbs, lemons, and if I have been inefficient about the shopping, for meat and veg. Chewing my lip, I ponder the problem. Could I double-wrap and label them as something he wouldn’t touch? Possibly, but not for certain. Mike was quite liable to do the opposite of what was expected, and he would almost certainly have a look at any food. What else might I keep in the freezer? My mind is a blank.

I go upstairs to Susan Mayhew’s flat. She is a conservative widow of about sixty who disapproves of me, my clothes, and especially of the fact that Mike and I are blatantly ‘living in sin’.

‘Hi, Susan,’ I say cheerily, clutching my packet which is now bound with wide parcel tape. ‘I’ve been given a whole salmon. Might you have space in your freezer for it? Just until we can eat enough to make room for it?’

She eyes it warily. ‘Sorry, Cass, I’m afraid I can’t. My

freezer is full to bursting and I couldn't get something that size in.'

I retreat down to the ground-floor flat, but they are out. Back in our flat, I label the package 'Ecolore freezer samples. Do not open or expose to air' and put it at the bottom of the deepest freezer drawer until I can think of a better solution.

* * *

After a noisy session with the liquidiser, Mike appears from the kitchen holding a package containing two frozen rats. I nearly choke on my heart which has leaped into my throat.

'What's this? I want to freeze my courgette soup and need the space. We don't have enough room in the freezer to house Ecolore samples. Samples of what, anyway?'

Since I put it there, I have had time to think of an answer. I stuff my heart back where it belongs. 'A new fabric for wrapping food. To replace cling film and plastic bags, but it's being tested to make sure it doesn't become brittle when frozen over time.'

He looks interested. 'Why don't we try wrapping food in it then?' He starts to attack the parcel tape and I shriek in protest.

'Not yet! The tests are over various time periods. Leave it alone. We'll experiment with it later.' I get up and organise enough freezer space for his soup, thoroughly unnerved and terrified his curiosity will find me out.

* * *

Within a few minutes of his departure for work in the morning, the rats are extracted from the freezer. I have a moment of frustration as the two plastic bags are frozen together. A hard bash on the edge of the sink frees them and I start to do the most difficult one first, which entails the step ladder and a screwdriver to get into the ventilation duct. Halfway up the ladder my phone rings. At this point in my life, I can't afford to ignore phone calls, and in any case, it might be Dominic, who I would love to talk to, day or night. Sadly it's not Dominic, but a distributor who has a great many queries which culminate in a long and complicated order. After discussion with several manufacturers, I get the order organised and the invoices printed. This is all money coming in, but it is also rat installation time slipping away. My heart rate increases.

My sight, blurry at best, hates ladders and screws and I am terrified I might drop one because if I do, I'll never find it on the rug. I aim my eyes fractionally to one side of the screw because anything in my central vision just disappears. Eventually, three screws are out and safely in my pocket and the grill swings drunkenly from the top left.

I carefully climb down the ladder, retrieve the frozen rat and climb back up. Breathe deep, find the oxygen. Don't fumble. Get that bag open.

An aeon later the zip slides back, and the stiff body slithers out and into the duct. The smell is yellow-red dust and dirt. Distaste becomes revulsion as I push it as far back into the dust and cobwebs as I can. Taking more deep breaths in an effort to calm my pounding heart and trembling hands, I carefully replace the cover. There are tiny scratches on the paintwork and coving where the screwdriver has slipped, but there is nothing I can do about it. I climb circumspectly down the ladder, put it back in the hall cupboard and put the screwdriver back in the toolbox. I feel as if I've run a marathon.

The street door clunks, and someone is coming up the stairs. Could this be Mike coming back? Did I sleep-talk my evil plot? Hurling the remaining rat into the hall cupboard, I grab my mobile and press it to my ear, pretending to be in a non-existent conversation. My thundering guilty heart sounds like galloping horses, but the footsteps pass, and I let out a gasp of relief. Susan Mayhew going to her flat. God, I'd be hopeless as a spy.

Taking another deep breath, I retrieve the second rat and tackle Mike's latest expensive acquisition, (did I pay for it?) a huge square coffee table. Sliding the heavy glass top, engraved with writhing Indian gods, to one side, I begin to feed the rat into one of the brass filigree legs when it occurs to me that a rotting rat will leak liquid – I shudder at the thought of what that effluvium would comprise – onto the carpet and Mike will see it. But if I open the bag and slide it and the rat in together, it will still defrost, decompose and smell revolting, but hopefully, the plastic bag will contain any liquid. I shove the glass top back into place and walk round the table critically, trying to see if the bag and rat are visible through the filigree and decide they are not. At least, not to my eyes. But Mike has sharper eyes than mine; I wonder how long the rats will take to start to smell.

* * *

After a mashed banana and brown sugar sandwich and dealing with myriad phone calls, I put part two of my plan into action by stitching ziplock bags, each containing two prawns, under the curtain linings. The zip is closed for the moment but can be opened through the material without touching the actual bag. My guilty, trembly hands, and shoulders and arms which cramp from working above head height, are not helped by my lousy eyesight. Some biblical prophet had to hold his arms out for the duration of a battle and needed guys to take the weight and I could do with some of that. I am not cut out for this cloak-and-dagger stuff. Revenge should be a joy and a triumph, and it isn't.

My phone rings yet again and the needle drops from my shaky fingers. It slides off the thread and disappears into Mike's Persian rug.

The carpet samples, madam, where would I like them delivered? I had totally forgotten they were coming.

'Where are you?' Oh Lord! About ten minutes away. And I have to find that needle before anyone steps on it. The rug pattern of the tree of life in the Garden of Eden is far worse than a haystack. There still remains a piece of haddock I was going to put behind the bookcase and clearing up to do. And what will Mike say about piles of samples cluttering up the hall? I find another needle and manage to get the second bag attached and about an inch of seam sewn up before the bell rings.

'Please put them there.' I indicate a spot in the hall, and the delivery driver goes to get the second enormous pile of 100 by 50 cm samples. On his return, he is followed up the stairs by Mike, only about three hours earlier than he should be. All my veins empty.

'What the hell is all this?'

'Ah! Mike! Sorry, I'll explain.' My brain behaves like a car being started in gear. Jolt, crash, stall.

'Sign here, love.' The driver thrusts a delivery sheet and pen at me. My signature is unreadable.

Mike is standing at the kitchen door, staring at the evidence.

'What on earth is going on?'

'Fish,' I say feebly.

'I can see that.' His lip curls. 'And smell it. What sort of fish? It looks revolting.'

'It's fresh haddock. It smells maroon. It was going cheap

and I thought I'd make a fish pie for later.' Quite good for an off-the-cuff explanation, I think. He looks at the haddock in distaste and goes to take his jacket off in his dressing room. I do a quick scooping of ingredients back into the fridge. I had better make the fish pie even though the haddock had been cheap because it wasn't very fresh.

Mike is now standing by the ladder, staring up at the curtain rail with narrowed eyes.

'Why are you sewing the curtains up the ladder?' He can obviously see the needle and thread in the fabric, which is more than I can.

The evildoer will reap the whirlwind or some such long-ago message from my father.

'A hook had come off one of the rings over here,' I pull back one of the other curtains and Mike's gaze swivels round. 'And when I checked the other curtains, I saw the thread had broken on the seam, so I was mending it. As I had the ladder out.' How was that for quick thinking? 'Then I dropped the needle when the bell rang, and I can't find it. Why are you back so early? Is everything all right? Have you got the insurance straightened out?' Do I sound as tense as I feel? Why didn't he phone to say he was coming back early?

Mike is disagreeably uncommunicative but solves the needle problem with a magnet. I feel very exposed as I finish sewing up the seam as if he can see everything I've done; the scratches on the ventilation duct, the rat in the coffee table leg, the bulge of the ziplock bags in the curtains. I don't dare look at him as I put the ladder away. In the hall, the samples wink at me and despite my nervous tension I am dying to look at them. Taking a few into the sitting room, I perch on the sofa and pull them out, opening my laptop to my carpet designs.

'Oh! Look, Mike! Aren't they gorgeous! And they feel like top-quality wool. It's incredible.'

I rub the pile sideways, and it behaves like wool too. Tight, close, smooth like velvet. New carpet smells cream, whatever colour it is. Mike stares for a moment and then shrugs.

'Quite nice I suppose. But they're just carpet. Nothing to get excited about.' He glances at the designs on the screen. 'The plains are OK, but the designs …' He screws up his nose. 'Well, let's just say they're not to my taste.' When it comes to taste, we have never agreed, so I am not surprised. But as always, his comments are deflating even though I now know why he makes them.

'But the colours! Even these four shades are glorious!' I don't deserve his condescension. I had been waiting for them for so long and had had so many arguments with the manufacturer about the quality, the textures, the colours, the backing. 'Well, you might be a bit pleased for me, especially when I really need some encouragement after what's happened.' I get the rest of the samples and lay them out in their gradations from pinkish white through light pink, through amaranth to rose and cerise. Fourteen good-enough-to-eat feasts for the eye.

He toes the samples with a derisive foot. 'You can't afford to do it,' he says flatly. 'Nobody would want these, and if you go ahead, you'll go bankrupt.'

I sit back on my heels and look him straight in the eye, a crazy risk-taking sensation rising up in me. 'You sound as if you want me to go bankrupt.'

'Don't be ridiculous! I spend my life trying to stop you making stupid decisions!'

It's a remark which doesn't deserve a response. But of course, I can't resist.

'That's a particularly nasty thing to say, and it's untrue. What the hell has got into you that you've suddenly become so spiteful? And I feel that you do want me bankrupt, for some reason I have yet to fathom. You want me to hit the skids, go belly up, fail. Why?'

He gives me a look of utter contempt. 'I don't have to want it, Cass. You're taking yourself there without any help from me.'

If he just wanted to walk off with my money and the flat, I could understand it; greed is a human weakness. But it's more than that, and miserably I wish I knew what the more was.

Chapter Fourteen

As I take the morning mail to my desk, I'm aware of a distinct lavender smell of eggs and bacon floating from some nearby flat. My stomach rumbles. Still exhausted and wretched after yesterday's tensions, I see one of the letters is from Vermont and Paget's business address. Unfolding the dense sheet of typescript, I have to read it twice using the magnifying sheet. The words still squiggle about the page, either because my hands are now trembling, or because my focus is more off than usual.

In view of my three-year business plan and business record, Vermont and Paget are willing to provide a capital investment of £75,000 for twenty-five per cent of the company's value, or a loan at seven and a half per cent interest over five years. I let out a spontaneous yell and throw a fist in the air. They surely would not be offering me money if I was a bad risk. Suddenly my belief in myself is restored. Suddenly there is light at the end of the tunnel. Suddenly I know that with careful planning and some drawing in of the horns I will succeed, and Ecolore will not go under. Plastics will be re-used; the planet will survive.

It took them long enough to decide that I am a reasonable financial gamble. Was it my declaration that I would disassociate myself from Mike that finally unlocked the coffers? I doubt it has anything to do with my burgeoning friendship with Dominic. Looking at their options in more detail, I sober up. I feel disinclined to give away so much of my company and wonder if I could possibly meet the loan repayment requirements given the battering the company has had. If the worst happens and Zev really can't get any of my money back, and my rat tactics to retain the flat for some reason don't work, I will have the expense and outgoings on new office premises as well as having to find somewhere to live. The familiar thump of anxiety fills my chest as I contemplate how I might slide into homelessness and poverty unless I accept Vermont and Paget's offer. Or even if I do accept. I have to force Mike's hand.

I realise that I have read only half their letter. The second half is more deflating. Their offer will only be valid if and when the ongoing legal inquiries about the theft from Ecolore are satisfactorily concluded. What do they mean, 'satisfactorily concluded'? They know that I'm not at all sure that legal inquiries will conclude at all, so this offer is unlikely to come good.

I need to make sure that my rat tactics work.

* * *

Whether I should or shouldn't accept Vermont and Paget's offer gives me a headache and a restless night. Mike's suggestion that they might want to change my business model preys on my mind. Wendy tends to be dubious in response to my various enthusiasms and encouraging when I am uncertain, which means I need professional advice. Although Dominic and Zev are lifetime friends, I am certain that they are both professional to the hilt and there has not been and will not be any cross-business communication. I make an appointment with Zev, brush blue and silver into my hair, and dress with my usual exuberance in a shiny blue mini skirt with a matching bamboo fabric top. No point in having good legs if you never show them off.

As I get into my broiling car, burning my backside on the seat, I do wonder if this heatwave will ever end. I love the sun; I love the crackling black smell of hot tarmac and the slushy blue smell of disapproved-of lawn sprinklers, but this has been going on for so long that even I am longing for rain.

As I enter a roundabout I feel a jolt, sense a crunch, and hear a yell. I see nothing untoward, but something has definitely hit me. Or I have hit something. Heart crashing, I pull into the side and stop. I still see nothing until I get out, narrowly avoiding having the driver's door taken off by a passing lorry who stands on his horn. Behind me on the verge is a bicycle with a bearded rider still trying to disentangle himself from wheels and pedals. I rush to pull the bike off him as a gaggle of people converge on us.

'I am *so* sorry,' I gasp. 'I didn't see you. Are you hurt? Are you OK?' I don't even know if I am to blame, but assume I am.

The disentangled man staggers to his feet and seems to be shaking as much as I am. 'I don't think I'm damaged. Much more concerned about my bike. That's several hundred pounds worth.' We both scrutinise it anxiously, me looking for bent wheels, he inspecting the gearing, and the gaggle of onlookers give us the benefit of their opinions about women drivers, bloody bicyclists, should be taken off the road, be shot, get the police, should have flashing lights, what can you expect from women dressed like that, et cetera, et cetera. The bearded bicyclist and I both feel censured for having wheels and in mutual self-defence profess ourselves unhurt and apologetic, exchange telephone numbers and insurance details and go on our wobbly ways. I look very carefully at each intersection, anxiety clutching at my throat, my hands gripping the steering wheel to stop them from shaking.

The optician had told me that I should think seriously

about not driving, and this accident has underscored my foolhardiness in ignoring his advice. The thought of having to give up the car fills me with desperation but my heart pounds as I think how close I came to killing someone. Independence has never been so precious and so easily lost. How do I run my business, if I even have one, without a car? How do I visit friends, meet customers, or carry samples? It would be the beginning of a whole new way of life which I can't even contemplate. Why did I not see that cyclist? Why was the optician so uncommunicative, and why am I being sent to a specialist eye hospital in London, albeit not at any great speed?

I'm late, but Zev's face creases in a warm amused smile. He leans, lemony yellow, and kisses both my cheeks.

'You look terrific. You enhance my reputation as a trendy lawyer.'

It's good to be complimented but my run-in with the cyclist takes the gilt off that particular gingerbread. Zev is sympathetic about the accident, and I don't mention my sight problem.

Studying Vermont and Paget's offer, he listens and dismisses my somewhat incoherent concerns about legal inquiries being satisfactorily concluded.

'They will just want to know that we have done all that is possible to get your funds back.'

'And Mike suggested that Vermont and Paget will try to change my business model if they put money in. Could he be right?'

'That's unlikely. I would think what they are investing in *is* your business model. But all you have to do is ask them. I suspect they'd leave you alone to get on with it.'

'But twenty-five per cent!'

'Try fifteen. You might end up at twenty. I'd be inclined to take the investment rather than the loan if you really think you couldn't meet the repayment terms. I don't think they'd interfere, and you could get some good business advice there, if you wanted it.'

'Well, the repayment terms are too short. My outgoings in the next five years may be huge. I did a rough budget on the worst-case scenario and came out leaking blood. Then there's the lawyer to pay'– I close my eyes in comic dismay – 'my own flat to sort out. What I really, really want is Ecolore's money back.'

His mouth twists slightly. 'The police haven't got enough solid evidence for the CPS. Even if Mike was faced with prison, it wouldn't reduce his sentence much if he returns your funds, so he'll probably keep it safe in Nevis for a rainy day. You are just going to have to slog back up the road of building your business all over again.'

That sinking feeling. All the dreams and plans down the drain. The sinking feeling threatens to become something far worse and I have to stamp on it once more. Even if Vermont and Paget's offer still stands after the legal failure, their money might cover my immediate needs, but it won't do anything else. Depression settles on me like a fog and even the thought of Dominic fails to cheer me.

When I get home – except it is not my home, it's Mike's – I contemplate the ventilator cover and the coffee table. Very soon the rats will start to smell. Filling a few bags with my least-used possessions I take them to my warehouse container. Dominic is absolutely right. There is no way I could either live or work in a container.

Chapter Fifteen

I know the rats must have thawed because the heatwave is still with us, but as yet there is only a vague whiff of something I doubt anyone else would notice.

Still touchy after our harsh words over the carpet samples, we both confined our conversation to essentials. I'd gone to bed early and he came to bed late. No sex was proposed so no requirement to rebuff.

But the next day he puts down his coffee cup, lifts his head like a bloodhound and sniffs, frowning.

'Is there a funny smell in here?'

He knows I have an exceptional sense of smell, so I don't deny it. 'Fish? Chartreuse green, but quite faint.' That smell is going to be worse tomorrow, and my plan is coming alarmingly to fruition.

I pack some more clothes into a suitcase. Fabrics are the first thing to take on smell, and the last to let it go. I do not wish to smell of dead rat. I don't really want to take up Dominic's offer in case it smacks of using him as a convenience, but on the other hand, I can't have all my clothes in the container as I need to wear them. I am going to have to tell him about my rats and hope that he doesn't retract his offer in disgust.

'It's the heat,' I tell Dominic despairingly. 'I never expected them to thaw quite so quickly. So if you could bear to have a few bags stashed under a bed in your house, that would be – very kind. Wendy says I can use her garage, but there are mice so I don't want to put any clothes in there.'

'Yes, of course you can bring a few bags. Are you as allergic to mice as you are to spiders?'

'Oh no! I rather like mice. Not so keen on rats though.' Dominic snorts with laughter.

* * *

The next day the pale chartreuse green has become stronger chartreuse green and at breakfast I add to his nose anxiety by letting on that I have asked about sixty people to his party. I have tried to become slightly more friendly, but it is an effort.

He nearly drops his toast. 'You what?! You're going way over the top! Sixty? What's all this costing, for God's sake?'

He's probably thinking he hasn't got sixty friends. And worrying that he's going to have to pay for it because my depleted bank accounts are not available to him.

'It's an important birthday, and you're an important man.' I shrug. 'So I've asked lots of guests.'

Apprehension is beginning to creep into his eyes.

'Who?'

I hope my expression is irritating him. 'Good grief! If I told you who I've asked, it wouldn't be a surprise, would it? But it will be a surprise. You have lots of friends.'

Apprehension gives way to suspicion. 'Not that many. What are you up to, Cass? Who else have you asked?'

But I'm not saying. I wrinkle my nose. 'This smell is not good, is it?'

After he's gone, I nervously email Vermont and Paget asking them to consider a twelve per cent stake in Ecolore rather than twenty-five. Will they then withdraw their proposal completely? I am trying my best to separate Vermont and Paget from Dominic Paget, but it is Dominic who phones at lunchtime and after discussion makes an offer of the same amount of investment but for a seventeen per cent stake in Ecolore. I say I will think about it and tell him about the state of the rats.

He sounds concerned. 'You can't stay in the flat. It's not healthy and you'll smell of rat too. Why don't you bring your stuff and come and stay here?'

I would dearly like to, but I hesitate. Should I do that in the middle of financial negotiations? His partner might well consider it unethical and in any case, Mike and I are still officially together. Just. I have hesitated too long.

'No catch, no deal,' he says evenly. Oh, Dominic, that's not my problem. My heart does a little jig of excitement at the idea of staying with him, even if it is just in his spare room.

'The smell's not that bad. Yet. I'll ask Wendy if I can stay with her.'

But I am disconcerted, if rather pleased, to find that Wendy's bereaved mother is staying with her for a few weeks, so the option of her spare room when I am smelled out of the flat has gone. There are other friends, but they will require some sort of explanation for my homelessness. I don't want to go to any other friends, I want to go to Dominic.

Is this a sign from heaven that I can accept Dominic's offer? He can't possibly be making it without some sort of motive, and he has definitely become a friend rather than a business acquaintance. I would like that friendliness to develop into much more. Would he like that too? No deal, no catch is not at all what I would like. Just the thought of him brings that amber scent into my skull, swirling behind my fuzzy eyes, resting on my tongue, filling my sinuses. I can feel his fingers on my bare shoulder and all my nerve ends spring into awareness.

* * *

On this hot morning the mustard yellow smell has become unpleasant and Mike is definitely alarmed. Both of us have slept very badly, our backs turned to each other.

'Something must have died,' he says wildly, looking anxiously round the sitting room as if whatever had died might be lying on his Persian rug.

'Perhaps there was a rat after all, and it's died from the poison,' I suggest helpfully.

'You'll have to get someone in to deal with it if you can't find what it is.'

I shake my head. 'No can do, sorry. I told you I had meetings all day. My problems with the company mean I'm twice as busy as normal and I'm simply not here. I'm afraid you'll have to deal with it.'

For once, obliging Cass is going to disoblige. It's your problem, dear Mike, and I am going to enjoy watching you trying to solve it.

Tempers fray. No amount of verbal bludgeoning shifts me, and the new Cass is impervious to blame, accusation and demands. I watch and listen as my erstwhile lover becomes as unpleasant as the smell and we leave the flat in silence, me carrying my laptop and tablet and all necessary paperwork. Dominic says he has left me his spare key under a flowerpot, and I can work at his kitchen table.

Today has been scorching again and this afternoon I have had a steamy hot visit to an upmarket catering company in Maidenhead to persuade them to exchange their nasty plastic for my beautifully designed bamboo takeaway bags, napkins, cutlery and plates. It is nearly seven when I get off at Winchester. My possessions are now spread between the flat, the container, Wendy's garage and Dominic's house and I am not at all sure which property has what in it and spend time searching for a particular item in the wrong place. I wonder when or if Mike will notice.

* * *

Dominic is already home, wearing tatty shorts and nothing else and he is painting his garden fence with wood preservative. He has no idea, I don't think, how incredibly sexy that is. The solidity of his nakedness, the natural bulk of muscle in his arms and chest, dry my throat. My inclination is to tear the shorts off him and wrestle him to the grass, but instead I inhale with my eyes closed.

'What colour are you smelling?'

'Sky blue. Summer sky, deep blue.' Amber overtakes the blue. There is a gentle kiss on my cheek, and I find him arms wide, paint pot in one hand, brush in the other. He smiles and I melt.

'Is it just smells you see in colour or taste as well?'

'Both, I think. Smell and taste are part of the same sense, aren't they? But I'm not going to taste your paint to find out.'

'Touch? Sound?'

I lie down on the grass and am mesmerised by the steady strokes of his brush, the movement of his shoulders and the undulations of the arm muscles.

He turns inquiringly and I say hastily, 'Sorry. I was trying to work it out. No, touch and sound aren't colours. But numbers and some letters are.' I think for a moment. 'Some words too. And days of the week. And months. And probably more things, but it's normal for me so I've always taken it for granted and used to assume everybody was the same. I didn't know for ages there was anything strange about it.'

'Same colour for the same things?'

'Oh yes. Monday is always pink. Thursday is pink too, but more yellowy pink. Lots of graduations. Some things are a mixture or even stripy.'

'And always the same colour for the same numbers?' I nod. 'Has it got a name, this ability?'

'Yes, but I've quite forgotten what it is. I discovered it when I was at art school.' I sit up and try to eradicate my sexual fantasies.

Dominic puts down the paint pot and balances the brush across the top. He takes his phone from his pocket. 'Smelling in colour. Yes. Synaesthesia.' He reads for a few moments. 'It's fascinating. There are all sorts. Numbers, letters, words. People can see or smell sounds, especially music, or colours can smell.'

I pull my knees into my chest and concentrate. 'Colours can smell? Not for me, I don't think, but smells are colours. And numbers.' I hesitate, trying to think what is colour. 'Not sounds though. Certain colours *relate* to certain smells, I suppose. And every number is a colour – one to nine I mean.'

He looks up, suddenly intent. 'So, when you looked at your accounts you saw a colour picture, is that right?'

'Yes. I do see the numbers, but I don't tend to remember them. I remember the colours. A sort of colour wash.'

'So when you found the discrepancies in your accounts, was it because the colour of the accounts was wrong, rather than the numbers?' Was he going somewhere with these funny questions?

'Not so much wrong but changed. The colour patterns were different. I've never been too good at remembering actual amounts, but I remember the colour patterns.' I try to put a brain function into words. 'It sounds as if I don't see the figures, but I do. Lots of noughts make a green block, so when the green fades …'

'So do the thousands.' His eyes narrow in concentration.

'Your accounts were different colours in different places from what you had remembered?'

'Yes. Then I started looking back, and not just the colours. I concentrated on the actual figures.'

'Did Mike understand all that? That for you, numbers are colours?'

I stare at him. This is the first time anyone has even vaguely got it. Eventually, I shrug. 'I don't know that he understood. He thought I was hopeless with the balance sheets. He sort of knew that for me Monday the third of May was pink, red and ochre. It made him laugh.' Remembering Mike's laughter catches my throat. Had that laughter been genuine amusement, or something else?

'Why all these questions about – what's it called? Sin something?'

'Synaesthesia. It occurs to me that Mike knew and used the fact that your brain works better with colours rather than numbers, but he didn't understand that there are other ways of skinning a cat.' He glances at my face. 'Other ways of analysing information. I wonder if he thought you'd never notice; that he'd get away with it for far longer. Some frauds go for decades without being discovered.' The way he says it makes me feel I hadn't been as stupid as I thought I'd been.

'I suppose he might have done – got away with it – if I hadn't been intending to use that money. He certainly tried to discourage me from using it.'

Dominic grunts and finishes his painting. I make mugs of tea and as we lie in the shade of the apple tree, I dream of tearing his shorts off again.

I tell him that the smell is already upsetting Mike. And about my plans for his party and am inordinately pleased to have made Dominic Paget laugh out loud.

'Whatever Zev says, I'm going to have to confront him with what he's done. If he agrees to return everything he's stolen, including the mortgage payments, I'll stop the smell and he can have his party or I'll cancel it if he wants to. And we'll go our separate ways. But if not, I'll tell all his friends and his company what he's done. At that point, I'll have to prevent him from selling the flat from under me.'

Dominic rolls over onto his stomach and his face is suddenly very close to mine. The grey eyes are intent. Please kiss me, Dominic. Touch my face, put a finger on my lips. I want to touch your face and kiss your lips. But he doesn't, and nor do I.

'Why don't you just leave him? And move in here?'

That sounds quite different to, and much more attractive than, 'no catch, no deal', but I sigh. 'I can't. Not yet anyway. The smell won't last forever, and if I've left him, I won't have any access or right to the flat, and all those mortgage contributions will disappear, with everything else, into his pocket. I've got to get him to return my money or move out and leave me the flat.'

My phone vibrates and a quick glance tells me that Mike's train is at Basingstoke. Soon that tracker will need to be recharged again.

'Quarter to eight! He's working late,' Dominic remarks.

'If he's been working.' My dry tone probably gives the impression of judgmentalism. 'And on that note, I must go back because he'll be home soon and I need to collect some paperwork for an appointment in London tomorrow.'

'Another client? What are you persuading them to buy this time?' I had told him about the Maidenhead caterers. He notices my hesitation and turns his head to me. 'Sorry. I didn't mean to pry into your business.'

'It's not a business appointment.' I keep my voice light. 'I've got a cataract and it needs specialist photography or something at Moorfields.' He gives me a keen glance and then nods.

When the taxi arrives, he declines my thanks and says

he's coming too, holding the car door for me and getting in the other side. 'I just have to experience the rats.'

* * *

A faint mustard yellow swirls in the air as we go up the stairs, but as the door opens it hits both of us with a physical blast to the chest. There is an extraordinary buzzing sound.

'Good Lord!' Dominic exclaims. 'Who'd have thought a smell could be so nasty?'

I am so stunned by the speed and power of the smell that I find myself speechless. There is no way on earth that I or anyone else could sleep here.

Slamming the door, he takes my wrist and tugs me coughing downstairs and into the street. 'I bet the neighbours will have something to say about it.' On the beat, Susan Mayhew erupts from the house. She must have heard my door slam.

'Cass! Cass Hunter!' She has caught up with us. 'What is that dreadful smell from your flat?'

'I don't know, Susan.' I gasp. 'But I'm not investigating. It's Mike's responsibility and he'll be home any minute.'

Dominic ushers me into the taxi, and it drives off leaving Susan wailing on the pavement. Having gone round the block, she has disappeared, and we park outside again.

'Looks like you've smelled both of you out very successfully. You can't possibly sleep there. I think you'd better move in with me for the foreseeable future!' He looks at my face which I suppose expresses a mixture of gratitude and discomfiture. 'Can you hold your breath and go get what you need?'

'Dominic – I can't just move in with you. I didn't mean that to happen and I had no idea it would be so awful so quickly.' Again I'm thinking: his reputation, his quiet life, what will his friends say?

'Why can't you? It would save me traipsing up and down the M3.'

I take a deep breath. 'Look, Wendy isn't the only friend I've got – there are lots of people who'll take me in.'

He smiles. 'Well, yes. Of course there are. But I am here and no phone calls need to be made and no explanations required. It's a bit late to be cadging a bed for the night, isn't it?' He looks at my face again and laughs.

'You are the nicest man,' I say gratefully.

His mouth compresses with amusement. 'Go get your essentials, and the suitcases, and bags, not forgetting what you need for your appointment. We'll wait' – he indicates the driver – 'until you've finished wiping the floor with your partner.'

I try rather feebly to decline all this kindness, but he shovels me out and I meekly do what I'm told.

The buzzing sound is caused by flies and I try not to inhale either them or the mustard gas by opening the window every half minute or so for a gulp of fresh air. I want to keep the atmosphere inside as nasty as possible for Mike as I gather the last remnants of my belongings: make-up, toothbrush, phone charger, clothes, files. My life.

Distinctly nauseous, I stagger downstairs with my possessions and the driver puts them in the boot, just as Mike turns the corner into our street.

He sees me on the steps outside the street door.

'Have you lost your key?'

'Nope. I was waiting for you.' He smells blue-green. He has been for a drink with Laura, although I suppose he may have just been working with her.

He frowns, not quite sure about my tone of voice, and neither of us moves to kiss each other.

'Have you solved the smell?'

'Nope. You haven't either. I don't think you're going to like it.'

The frown deepens into worry as he lets us into the lobby. The mustard yellow smell seeps gently down the stairs, trailing softly over the treads like a Dali watch. He opens the flat door and lurches away as if he's been punched. I am standing well back on the landing holding my breath.

'Jesus! What the bloody hell is that?' He's coughing tears. 'It's a health hazard. You must ring the council to check the drains!'

'The council! At this hour? You were supposed to have done that this morning.' We are retreating down the stairs. 'But *you* can ring the council tomorrow to check the drains.'

'I tried this morning. I couldn't get through.' He sounds sulky.

'Welcome to the time-consuming world,' I say dryly. 'You'll have to try again. I've got a lot to do and I'm going somewhere else to do it.'

He looks utterly astounded as we disgorge onto the pavement. Cass is never that bolshy.

'My clients are rather more important than your little …'

If I had a gun, I think I'd knee-cap him and he suddenly looks as if he realises it. 'It's your flat, Mike. Your smell. Your problem. Your party coming up.'

'It's your flat too.' But his voice is less certain. He doesn't quite know what's going on, but he knows something is. 'We can't have the place stinking like a – a cesspit. Check the other flats and see if they have the same problem.'

I shake my head. 'Only yours. Though the others are complaining about it.' Heaving in a deep breath, I take the plunge.

'I'm sure I could deal with the smell if only the status quo – my money – was restored,' I say thoughtfully. I wait for his reply, but it's as if he's had a chop to the throat. Head goes back, mouth opens, and no sound comes out, so I continue. 'I've arranged to stay with a friend. You can stay in the flat, of course, if you want to.'

He stares at me. A lying lover, a perfidious partner, a betrayer. A thief. I walk away.

Getting to the taxi, I am externally calm and internally disordered, and I don't think Dominic is fooled by the calm, judging by his assessing glance.

'I virtually told Mike I suspect him of taking my money. Probably not very sensible. Zev had said he might put the money out of reach if he knew I suspected him, but I think it's out of reach anyway.' I feel my hands trembling in my lap and link my fingers to stop them.

I think Dominic has noticed. He says quietly, 'It's done now and probably just as well. Your rats are certainly strong leverage. Quite apart from him not wanting his friends to experience it, he won't be able to live there, let alone think about selling it while it smells like that.'

On arriving back at his house, I take up his suggestion of a relaxing bath. As the tension seeps out, I think again how pleasant a bath is after years of standing upright in showers. I think about how I stood up to Mike and how shocked his reaction was. There haven't been many occasions when he has been rendered speechless and I am gratified to have knocked him off his superiority platform.

My stomach growls. I will ask Dominic for an apple and a biscuit, but when I go downstairs, he is watching the news and there are two generous plates of smoked salmon and buttered bread on the coffee table, along with a small glass of white wine. This man is a dream, a downright delightful, delicious dream. Mike would have expected me to produce it for him, and he certainly wouldn't have clocked that I might be hungry.

'You could have hot chocolate instead of wine if you

prefer,' he offers, switching off the TV. He has a most soothing ambience. There is an entirely unassuming confidence about him, the way he speaks, the way he moves, which is extraordinarily attractive. Mike's self-confidence is arrogant; Dominic's is self-effacing.

'The wine looks wonderful, as does the smoked salmon. That is so kind and utterly delicious. I can't think of anything more perfect. I've had no food since a Maidenhead sandwich and I was beginning to notice.'

I squeeze lemon and grind pepper and he gives me the morning lowdown; breakfast, his departure to his office, mine to London, keys, food. I hope I am taking all this in.

He doesn't say much about my repellent flat, or my repellent ex-partner, and in due course sends me upstairs to his spare room and the comfortable bed which still feels distinctly lonely. No catch, no deal. I wish there was. I would dearly love to be in Dominic's bed. The more I see of Dominic, the more I like him. He seems to know exactly what I need and when, and his kindness and thoughtfulness are a revelation after being frequently treated, I now see, with offhand disdain by Mike. Not for the first time, I wonder how on earth I did not see what Mike was doing to me. Trying to look back at our years together, there was surely a time when we truly loved each other, when there was no disdain or criticism. What happened? And when?

My attraction to Dominic, his kindness and support, the dreadful smell and the uninhabitable flat seethe endlessly behind my closed eyes. Together with the underlying and hardly acknowledged anxiety about the appointment at Moorfields tomorrow, my racing pulse prohibits sleep. The rats are doing exactly what I intended, if much faster than I intended, but the fact is that it's not just Mike who can't go to the flat, it's me too. Where am I going to run my business from? How long will it take to get Mike to hand the flat over?

I check the time on my phone. Two am. My relationship with Mike has fallen off a cliff and I am in shock at the speed of its fall. Why am I not devastated by grief, instead of infuriated by my stupidity? I'm also shocked by the speed of the transfer of my affections. How can I have fallen so suddenly for another man? Am I a shallow superficial woman, to throw a long-term partnership so easily into the emotional wastebin and pick up another? If I am, do I care? Anyway, although I might want to pick up another, Dominic has only offered his spare bed, not his own bed, so dream on, Cass.

Chapter Sixteen

Eventually, I fall into an exhausted sleep, and it takes several repeats of my phone alarm to pull me out of it in the morning.

I manage to get the London train but I'm not really thinking about the appointment. I'm thinking of Mike's malice and my retaliation. I've never thought of myself as vengeful, but here I am, full of it. Doing things I never thought I was capable of. But then, where would I be if I hadn't taken some decisive action? On the street, no doubt.

My reverie is interrupted by a text from Mike. *'Are you mad? What on earth did U mean last night?'* And because I don't answer, another text arrives later. *'Don't be childish. You need to explain yourself.'* My silence infuriates him and a stream of increasingly abusive texts pours in over the day. I consider deleting them but think I should keep them for Zev or the police.

* * *

'I'm sorry, Miss Hunter, but you have no appointment today.' The receptionist has hunted through her digitised books and is quite firm. 'I will do a search under your name and see what has happened.'

It doesn't take her long to tell me that I have come a month too early, and the consultant is on annual leave.

Only when it doesn't happen do I realise how apprehensive I had been, and how enraged at the thought of having to do this all over again on the right date, furious that the only person I can lash out at is myself.

As I travel on into central London, nursing the embarrassment of a fairly major mistake, I mull over yesterday. Where did Mike stay last night? Did he go back to the blue-green Laura? Surprisingly I find myself not caring as much as I did about his betrayal with Laura, and I can't be bothered to look up the tracker locations. Keeping Ecolore afloat has become more important than him moving on to a new lover. Does he think I know what he's done, or that I'm only guessing? Will he return any of my money? The pain of what I've lost is morphing into outrage at his behaviour and mortification at my self-delusion. Now I can't seem to think of anything much except Dominic Paget and how he is the absolute opposite of Mike. I wouldn't have met Dominic without all this happening, and that is the sugar sprinkled on this whole bitter story.

I am goaded into responding to Mike's texts.

'I'm in London and can't do anything about either the smell or the flies until Ecolore's finances are sorted and the money back in my account. Don't worry about the party organisation – all under control, everything ordered. Acceptances arriving regularly.' That should surely induce some sort of panic reaction, I think grimly.

My afternoon appointments pass in a haze although the success of getting my matching designs on socks and T-shirts into a new sustainable clothing store exhilarates me, and I am encouraged by the shoe designer saying she intends to eliminate all nylon and plastic by the end of next year. That may be wishful thinking, but these paradigm shifts take time.

On the return journey, the thought of being with Dominic makes my tummy flutter with anticipation. Mike would have been sarcastic about my stupidity this morning, had he known, but I am certain that Dominic won't be.

When I get back, out it all pours. From my disastrous morning at Moorfields, through to Mike's horrible texts, and Dominic's understanding is balm to my self-inflicted ignominy.

'It's hardly the end of the world. At least you know exactly where you're going next time. Concentrate on your business success and put the appointment mistake down to having other things on your mind.'

It's Dominic who is on my mind. 'And I feel awful just moving in on you,' I say, mortified that my actions have ricocheted into his life.

He hands me a mug of tea and stirs forbidden sugar into his. 'I can see it's not ideal from a working point of view and your flat will have to be resolved at some stage, but it will give you time to work out what you should do.'

'Thank you,' I say, with heartfelt gratitude. 'I will try to be an orderly guest.'

There are still so many unresolved issues to be fixed before I can move forward – before I can even think about putting my old life behind me and embarking on a new one. 'I'm going to meet Mike and have this whole thing out in the open, whatever Zev says. In any case, the law seems to be the one in handcuffs, not Mike.'

* * *

I text Mike, a reasonable non-ranting text, without accusation or blame, and we agree to meet in Winchester as the flat is unusable. Armed with a bottle of wine we sit opposite each other in a pub garden. I know that I must be strong and decisive but inside I am like soft butter and fear all my resoluteness will melt away. How odd that I have always known in some deep part of me that he manipulated me with words, but I never acknowledged that it was manipulation at all. Had my desire for security and acceptance obliterated my common sense?

He starts with the problem of the smell and doesn't even mention the elephant in the room, but I need to get everything off my chest before I either lose my nerve or sink a broken bottle into his face. I intend to hammer the final nails into his coffin. The memory of Dominic's gentle strength and kind words stiffen my resolve. Mike won't want a noisy embarrassing scene, witnessed by dozens of fascinated pub-goers. This is the moment of moving across the border, changing universe.

'Never mind the smell, Mike. You can pay the council to fumigate the flat, but it won't make the slightest difference.' He hears the assurance in my voice and looks at me with sudden sharp attention. 'Much more importantly, I know exactly what you've done. Everything. How you've been milking me and Ecolore for years. The ultimate parasite, sucking my business dry.' These are words that have been chasing around my brain for days and now that I have actually said them, his betrayal becomes reality.

His mouth opens in a stupefied gape. 'What on earth are you talking about? Sucking your business dry? Are you completely mad?'

'No, I'm not mad. I've paid for all those expensive holidays, the antique furniture, the so-called treats, the restaurants, the theatres and films, other people's jewellery, even the flowers you so romantically gave me.' There haven't been flowers, even paid for by me, for a long time. My fingers are laced together so tightly they hurt.

'So that's where your comment about restoring your funds is coming from!' His eyes bulge slightly above flaring nostrils. 'Where have you got these crazy lies from? Who's been filling you up with this rubbish? Is this something that lawyer has dreamt up? To make it look as if he's actually doing something?'

There is a pounding in my ears, making my gripped hands quiver. 'Even I, stupid blind me, eventually discovered that the Aston Martin was paid for in one fell swoop. A cool £70,000. At that point, I didn't know that it was you who had raided Ecolore's reserves, but I did wonder where that money tree suddenly appeared from.'

'How dare you poke your nose into my affairs? How I pay for my car is none of your business.' His tone deepens, but I can see that he is trying to keep his voice down as there are people at adjoining tables in the beer garden.

I'm almost amused by his choice of words. 'It's my business if it's my money you're using. But an affair *was* what I was poking my nose into. You smelled different, Mike. You smelled of Laura every time you stayed in London on so-called company business.' He sits back abruptly, as if distancing himself from my sense of smell, and with pleasure I give him more bad news. 'That's when I decided to punish you by trashing the Aston at the car wash.'

He is stunned. 'Trashing the Aston! You couldn't have. You wouldn't have had a clue.'

I smile and stare straight into his eyes. 'Of course I couldn't have.' I don't want to get Stefan into trouble, but it's enough to make Mike question how it happened.

'You are talking complete drivel.' His incredulity is edged with doubt.

I straighten my spine. 'And then I found you paid for the car outright with money taken from Ecolore.'

'I did not! You can't possibly prove that!' He looks as if he's just had an uppercut to the chin.

'I can. I have. You said you had the papers but, in fact, I'd found them in your files. And then I found it was you, not my father, who had used Brainbow to take the company name and my copyrights, though why you did so is still a complete mystery as you couldn't profit from it. I have to say, it was a bit astounding to find you'd never loved me at all. Ever.'

Unexpectedly he looks unhappy rather than guilty. 'That's not true. I did love you. I fell in love with you.'

'And you expect me to believe that?' I say caustically. 'You loved me until stealing was more fun? Until you fell in love with someone else? Or was it that my business success got up your nose? You couldn't bear some feeble little woman to be more successful than you?'

'No,' he said, and his voice is almost pleading. 'No, that wasn't the reason. You don't understand.'

'If that wasn't the reason, what was? And what don't I understand?'

I wait, but his mouth tightens and as it's obvious he isn't going to say any more I continue.

'I found loads of other things too. You were very careless. After that, I really did poke my nose into your affairs. I have shedfuls of evidence, collected over quite a long time. Receipts and documents, the phantom mortgage payments, bank statements, financial movements, money laundering through Callaloo, Nevis.'

My apparent assurance is doing what I'd hoped. His colour and temper gradually go from jalapeño pepper to blanched celery.

'I know where you go,' I continue, 'Sedgewick Road, dinners with Laura, bracelets, you name it, I've got it. It's all been evaluated and checked by the lawyers. The flat will smell until you return everything you've stolen. If you don't, the smell remains and everyone at your party is going to hear what you've done, birthday boy, even if it has to take place in the street.'

He looks briefly terrified. 'I'll cancel it. No one will be there. *I* won't be there.'

I plaster on my assured smile. 'If you could cancel it, it

would save me a lot of trouble, but I fear you won't be able to.'

Then there is silence. A shift in his attitude. His face muscles are twitching and straining under the skin.

Eventually, he says, 'I can't. I haven't got your money. It went on the car. It's a write-off. No insurance.'

I knew the car fiasco would come back and bite me. 'Oh yes? I haven't seen any confirmation of that. In any case, you've stolen much more than the value of the car. But if you won't return my money, then it's time to hand over the flat to me. I know that you never put my name on the deeds even though I was paying my share of the mortgage.'

His Adam's apple bobs. 'Give you the flat! You must be joking! It's worth far more than ...' He realises what he's saying and stops.

'Far more than you've stolen? Well, you have the choice. All the money, including all my mortgage payments and all my costs. Or the flat.' I stare into his eyes for a few seconds and see that he is utterly despicable. 'And while Her Majesty is housing you, you won't need the flat anyway.' I tell him what the lawyers and police have calculated he's taken and what he must return.

He is wide-eyed at the figure. 'I won't give you anything. You can't stop me from selling the flat and you won't get a penny of it.' His tone is vicious.

Why have I never understood he has no principles, no moral compass? The rising bile, a constricting, burning, volcanic lava begins to bubble up again through my chest grabbing at my throat.

'Oh, but I can. And I will. No one is going to be buying that sweet-smelling property, are they?'

He makes a noise in his throat. It could be a sob. Or a snarl.

He forgets where he is. 'I don't have the money.' His shout carries not just to the next-door table, but much further. The turned heads may well think he is being blackmailed by this odd-looking woman. I don't care if they do, but Mike does and he is enraged by my apparent amusement. He bangs his empty glass on the table and gets up.

I won't let him have the last word. 'You do have the money. We know exactly where it is, but if you don't return it, then you give me the flat. I'd prefer the money, but one or the other. Then I'll deal with the smell, but not before. Either way, you'd better be quick otherwise your party will be a very pongy as well as a very public affair.' I hope that sounds serious. 'And the police will be visiting your office as well, of course.' I am not so sure about this last assertion.

He has never known me like this because I have always wanted to please – or appease – him. I can see he is not just taken aback, but genuinely alarmed by the threat of the police, as well as by my ultimatum. A wash of satisfaction acts like an antacid on my volcanic stomach. I have been riding for this fall ever since I fell in love with him over my scattered groceries six years ago. I may have been a bloody fool, but I am bloody well not going to lose to him.

'Don't forget to try cancelling your party,' I call after him as he stalks off, and I realise that after six years I have just finally and irrevocably tipped my lover overboard. What will he do, or not do? Can my rat tactics really do what the law cannot?

I am still confounded by the fact that I was convinced of his love, or at any rate, his affection for me. How can I have been so sure of that and yet not realised what he was doing? I am adrift on an ocean of anchorless life. And yet there is Dominic, my lighthouse, waiting for me.

Walking back to his house I am surprised to find my senses at full alert; the rustling of heat-shrivelled leaves under my feet, the dry yellow smell of thirsty gardens, the narrowing darkness of my perimeters yet a widening awareness of my surroundings. There is a lightness in me. A vast relief that I have done this thing, cut the umbilical cord.

* * *

At Dominic's door, my hand hovers at the bell that his cleaner has polished to the brilliance of a solar flare. Somehow I cannot use the key he gave me to let myself in. It feels too possessive, too assuming. The world has shifted on its axis and I'm not sure where I am.

Opening the door, he looks at my face and drawing me inside holds me against him. Protective arms demanding nothing but giving all I need. Relief makes me sag against him and suddenly I am trembling like a loose filament in a broken lightbulb.

'It's done.' My voice sounds thick and grainy. I am free. Free of Mike, free of his manipulation, free of his denigration.

Dominic's hands, full of my brilliant hair, massage my skull until the tensions begin to seep away. This is the first time he has touched me in such an intimate way, and I find myself revelling in the sensation, astonished that the chemistry between us is mutual when I had worried that it was only me feeling the attraction. His fingertips are sensitive but firm, like the perfect hair wash in the salon and I can feel myself smiling, almost purring. The loose filament reconnects.

I can't stop myself. Lifting my face, I lay my cheek to his, every nerve end sensitive to his skin, the faint end-of-day prickle, the warmth of his breath at my ear, fingers stroking down my cheekbone and under my jaw. And then those fingers lift my chin. He is a slow kisser, first my lips, then teeth and tongue. He tastes herby, he smells amber.

He is exploring, enjoying, discovering; I am lost in him. I am happy as I have never been happy before. I do not care about the past. He is the future.

He has a dreamy, almost spaced-out look. 'Beautiful Cass. What have you done to me?' He drops his head to my shoulder for a moment. 'What the hell are you doing to me?'

He is just holding me now, and I try to regain a semblance of normality, to take in this man who in such a short time has had such an extraordinary effect on me. The future is right here. At this moment, as Dominic caresses me with hands and eyes, I feel there is an eternity to come, an ocean to swim in, a vast sky to fly in, realms of colour and potential, new vistas, new ideas. I am free to imagine what I have been pushing under my consciousness, not allowing myself to dream of.

We manage to talk and drink; we cook and eat, and I tell him about my meeting with Mike. He wraps himself around me again and kisses me. First on one cheek, then the other. Then the tip of my nose. Then my mouth. But not a deep kiss, just a gentle kiss on my lips. A cloud of amber mists my senses. Am I speaking normal words? How can this be happening to the self-controlled me? His hands stroke my face, moving on my skin like a sculptor smoothing clay. My whole being is liquid and beautiful. Desire roils in the pit of my stomach. A deep desire to be naked under his hands and body, touched and held by him forever. And he kisses me again, and this time he opens my mouth and there is no need and no opportunity to verbalise anything. In the bedroom, he slides the silky clothes off me as I unbutton his shirt and he laughs as I push him to sit on the bed and fumble his shoes and socks off. He is kissing me again now, and I find he has unclipped my bra and we are suddenly where I have longed to be, my belly cramping, my skin firing with a million nerve ends, skin to skin, breast to breast, loins to loins, my lips swollen, my own fingers seeking, touching, holding, gentling. I am greedy, he is hungry. He brings into being all that I can give, and he gives all that I can take. The amber scent of him fills my head and my heart. There is no space for anything else.

The summer night has long since dropped into luminous darkness as I lie spooned against him, his arm lax around my waist and the amber scent flowing over me. We sleep until that darkness dissolves into pearly amber-smelling dawn, a delicious fresh coolness drops from the open window and nerve endings ripple in my hip, up my ribs and along my upper arm. My shoulder, neck and the corner of my jaw by my ear are drawn into a springing awareness by a gentle finger. I turn slowly to face him, the grey eyes holding mine, smiling. The muscles of my belly spasm under feathered fingers and my breasts harden, silently shouting for more of his touch.

'Good morning,' he says softly and inclines his head to kiss me. His lips are light but not diffident. His hands are gentle but supremely knowing. He wakens all of me, slowly, until I am half mad, arching into him, begging for release. His skin is smooth under my lips; his teeth draw my nipple to his tongue. I can hear myself. 'Please, please, please. *Now. Please.*'

He is lying on his back, and I am on one elbow with my other arm draped across his chest and my toes rubbing up and down his shin. His eyes are on mine, but half closed against a shaft of morning sun and his mouth is curved into a peaceful and contented smile.

He brings a hand to my face and with one finger traces slowly from temple to jaw, around the edge of my lips where I never knew there were so many nerve endings, up the side of my nose and around each eye in turn. The lightest of touches on the socket bones, smoothing the eyelids, tracing the contours of my eyebrows.

I replay the memory of his lovemaking, so very different to Mike's. Generous, slow, building my pleasure as much as his own. Mike had always been passionate, fast, grasping, unable to wait for fulfilment, and certainly unable to wait for mine. Often, he would hurt me, with teeth and hands, apologetic when I protested, but citing passion as an excuse for rough handling.

I have come home, out of the cold, away from the tension I had never acknowledged was there, from demand to giving, from seeking to receiving, from wanting to needing.

Chapter Seventeen

Zev sent all the documents by email and hard copy to every conceivable address and to the police, but there has been a deafening silence.

I email Mike and copy it in on WhatsApp. *'The flat will remain unsellable until either my money is returned or you sign the flat over to me. I am about to add more people to your guest list.'* I don't tell Zev as I think it could be construed as blackmail. Dominic affects to know nothing about it.

Sunday morning Mike phones and says he is at the flat – or perhaps he's outside it, as the smell is worse than ever. It is less than a week before his party. I stab the loud-speaker button with a shaking finger so that Dominic can hear. Mike is brazen. 'I've told everyone it's cancelled. No one will come. And I won't be there either.'

I laugh a stage laugh. 'Well, good. I hope you found *everyone*. Of course, you may be uninviting a whole lot of people who weren't invited in the first place. They may be very offended. Did you find all the caterers too? The billing address is your office by the way.'

I try to make my voice steely hard. 'It won't matter whether you turn up or not, because if you haven't refunded what you've stolen or handed over the flat, the police will arrest you. Think of your reputation!' I hope this threat will never have to be activated as I am fairly convinced the police are uninterested as well as unable to gather enough legal evidence. They won't even give him a slap on the wrist.

This bluff will not stand any scrutiny. But Mike doesn't know that and he sounds defiant and furious.

'Your accusations will never hold water.'

'They already do. Which bit of the paperwork do you not understand? We have a veritable reservoir.' There is silence. 'If you have gone and bought yourself some luxury villa and a yacht, that was a mistake. I'll take you down, Mike. You'll go to prison for embezzlement, fraud, and money laundering.'

There is heavy breathing, but still no comment. 'So, do you agree to sign those papers? If the lawyers confirm they are one hundred per cent watertight, I won't tell your friends and colleagues what a nasty piece of scum you are. But if you don't sign, or there's any doubt about the legality, well, you've taught me a bit about marketing and publicising, so I'll put it to good use.'

'You know quite well I haven't done anything you're accusing me of. No one will believe you. You're trying to blackmail me. I'm not signing anything.'

'It's up to you, Mike. Is that your final answer?'

My nerves are at screaming point. There isn't anything else I can do. If he really has told his friends the party is off, and he doesn't come, the whole event will be a fiasco, my rats will eventually stop smelling and he will eventually sell the flat from under me. He will walk off with everything, leaving me bankrupt. A great writhing lump of despair is materialising in the pit of my stomach, thrashing through my chest, twisting through my head. A shriek has formed in my throat and I take in a huge breath to let it out.

'OK!' he shouts furiously. I hold the huge breath. 'You can have the fucking flat on condition you keep your bloody little mouth shut about these false accusations. I want your word on that.'

I let my breath out very, very slowly so that he can't hear. I am not convinced. I am suspicious of his surrender, distrustful of his admission of defeat. Incredulous that I can have forced his hand.

'I'd prefer all my money back rather than the flat, but I already told you I will expose your dishonesty to your so-called friends if the lawyers are not convinced. So convince them, Mike.'

'You little *cow.*' There is a vicious emphasis which reduces me to broken filament mode again. I pray that he cannot hear the tremorous squeak of my voice.

'And you haven't got long to do it.'

'So come and get the bloody papers and get rid of this fucking smell.' He may be defeated but he's still trying to order me about.

'In exchange for your signature on the documents, I'll come over this afternoon with a friend, or friends, just to be on the safe side, you understand, and show you how to clean up the flat.'

As I hang up, I feel as if I've been mauled by a predator. Mashed, bruised, exhausted and empty.

Dominic folds me into his arms and promises to come with me. My nervousness diminishes and I feel I can take Mike on so long as I know Dominic is within reach.

'I'll phone you if I think anything is going wrong. Just knowing you are there makes me feel safer. He doesn't know about us, and I'd prefer to keep it that way.'

He doesn't argue and hugs me again. 'Remember, when he has signed, tap my number and I'll come and collect the papers. You don't need to say anything. I'll be there immediately.'

I want to tell him how much this means to me. To say I think I love him, but I only touch his face and tell him how grateful I am for his support. I'm in the unusual place of needing someone other than myself, and I don't know whether that's love or dependence. Maybe both.

* * *

The smell is still the colour of Dijon mustard made with balsamic vinegar. Utterly disgusting and stomach-turning.

'My, you have been busy!' I say with satisfaction, standing in the middle of the sitting room in my grottiest trousers, T-shirt and trainers, a scarf tied round my head like a thirties housewife.

'Where are these fictitious friends?' He doesn't believe I've brought any.

I grin. 'They don't fancy the smell and are downstairs. I said I'd text them every now and then to say I haven't passed out or anything.' He is giving off murderous vibes and I shall keep my distance from him.

Bluebottles dive-bomb and loop the loop and sail in and out of every window and their dead antecedents carpet the floor. 'Find anything yet?'

The flat looks as if a hungry hippo has thoroughly explored it. Table lamps on their sides, the bases either screw-driver-ed off or the baize ripped back. In the kitchen, the kickboards are out and stores are spilled over the counter-tops; jugs, bowls and gadgets are upended, and the freezer contents are on the way to thawing. In the bathroom, the bath panel is off, and the shower drain unscrewed.

He lifts a sickened face from peering underneath the beautiful rosewood chest of drawers which he has pulled away from the wall and crouches to peer behind it. His skin is blotched with livid red patches.

'What is it? Where? You are a bitch. A total bitch.'

He struggles up from floor level coughing and stands rocking in front of me. I guess he'd inhaled a bit too much. My borrowed sanding mask is not effective against the smell and I feel a bit faint myself.

'For God's sake, Cass, you promised, you *promised*, to

get rid of this—' He waves his hands in a despairing circle. Smells are hard to encompass with a facial expression and a gesture, but he manages it.

'As soon as you sign those documents.' I manage to keep my tone tough and unemotional. 'And I'm not going to clean up the flat. You are. Under my instructions. Let me remind you that I can prevent *anyone* from wanting to buy this place simply by reinstating this unpleasant experience.'

I am not nearly as cool as I hope I appear. Sweat is dripping down my back and between my breasts. I am scared of what he might physically do to me. I'm already feeling as drained as a can of kidney beans.

He has a good effort at killing me with just a look, but eventually pulls Zev's documents out of an envelope. 'I hope you rot in hell.' I hear that even though he mutters it under his breath.

The bluebottles circle like vultures through the miasma of decomposing rats. The ziplock bags in the curtains may have exploded too, given the heat and their contents.

'Sign both copies. We'll send you one in due course. Care of Laura at 54 Sedgewick Road, I assume?'

I politely hand him a pen and there is a long hesitation before he flaps away dead flies on the table and signs, then the second copy. His hands are heavy on the documents, and he makes no move to hand them over. I'm thinking that he is trying for a last-minute let out, and apprehension tightens my chest.

Then he turns his head to me, and though I can't see his expression clearly, I know that he really would like to do me some damage. He tosses the pen on the floor and sends the documents fluttering after it.

'You can pick them up, bitch.'

Calling me a bitch makes me feel like being one. 'No, Mike. *You* pick them up. Nicely. After all, there is work to do here and you need all the time you can get.'

In all his life, I don't think he has suffered humiliation like this. All those years I was so 'tolerant' – anything for peace, for a quiet life – how could I have thought it was mutual love? What on earth was I doing? I let him control me to keep the peace, in the same way that my father controlled my mother.

The documents and pen are thrown back on the table, but I make no move towards them. I don't want a crack on the back of my head.

'Now, would you like me to show you how to get this place decontaminated? It's only a few days to your party. I don't know for sure whether it will smell of roses, but it needn't be as bad as it is now.'

'You could cancel the party now you've got what you want, you devious little cow.'

I shake my head. 'Too late. If you'd done this sooner, I could have. But until the mortgage is confirmed and the lawyers have everything signed and sealed and they're one hundred per cent sure, I'm not letting you off the hook.'

And you've still to explain why you did it in the first place. But now is not the time or place. Both of us are in danger of keeling over from the toxic smell and there is work to do.

Arming Mike with rubber gloves and my cleaning arsenal, I indicate the ventilation panel. 'There's a dead rat up there. You'll need the step ladder and a Phillips screwdriver.'

While he is up the ladder, I retrieve the documents and check he has signed them properly. The signature looks shaky, but I hope it will hold up in court if it has to. They should give me some form of concrete assurance, a safety net as this part of my life falls apart. I tap Dominic's number, and the knowledge that he is there is the most extraordinary relief. As I thankfully hand the papers to him at the door, he grips my hand, his concern clear. I mouth, 'Thank you.'

A curious mix of triumph and dissatisfaction fills me. None of this is what I had wanted. My life with Mike has dribbled away, like a basin with a leaking plug, and I am left with a broken relationship, a flat and mortgage I don't want and can't yet sell, and an insolvent business balanced between life and death. And I am still wary of what he might do to invalidate the flat assignment. Only Dominic stands solid between my empty past and uncertain future.

Mike teeters dangerously at ceiling level, batting at the flying missiles, his eyes streaming as he coughs up his stomach contents into the bag intended for the rat, and eventually gets the putrid remains scooped up. Heat and flies equal maggots and there are a few squillion maggots in the rat. I pass up kitchen towels, bleach, more bags and a bathroom smell remover which came with a guarantee I doubt it can fulfil.

I send him deeper into the sofa springs, under the bottom drawer of the rosewood chest and underneath the desk and watch him periodically losing his stomach contents as he removes the maggoty remains. I help a bit by vacuuming dead flies. By the time everything – actually by no means everything – has been bagged and binned, and the flat doused in bleach and Dettol with blasts of smell remover for good measure, he looks very sick indeed. At last, he departs, taking with him another few bags of his clothes and papers, and acute worry that the smell is still very nasty and the flies still like the fourth Egyptian plague. From the balcony I watch him stagger down the street towards the station, and the impression, even from my faint distance, is of a beaten man. I hope this isn't wishful thinking. A cautious sense of accomplishment creeps into me and relaxing my tense muscles I find myself floppy with relief.

Dominic appears from downstairs. 'The smell is still pretty awful,' he says, pinching his nostrils together.

‘That’s because I didn’t tell him where the other rat was. It’s too good a hiding place to give up, and I may just need it in the future.’ Armed once more with my rubber gloves I remove the plastic bag and its disgusting contents from the coffee table leg. Sniffing at the curtains I can’t tell if the bags of prawns are still intact. We leave all the windows wide open.

‘Leave a light on,’ Dominic says. ‘It’ll deter burglars.’

Only a few of my moveable possessions are still left in the flat, most having been transferred to Dominic’s house, Wendy’s house or the Ecolore container. Only my office papers and Mum’s cabinet are still here, and when the smell has really gone, I will move back to work here until I can sell. The flat is no longer my home, my past, or my future. It can just be my working area.

Gradually, the weird and wonderful sensation of a new beginning is filling up my soul until I am ecstatic, terrifically, wonderfully, thrillingly filled with the thought of Dominic. Dominic is my future, and now there is nothing to prevent us from being together. And despite the smell, I am laughing as he smiles the smile that makes my stomach turn over.

‘You look beautiful, Cass Hunter. Especially in the cleaning lady outfit.’

Chapter Eighteen

All week I have cleaned and disinfected and vacuumed up dead flies. Dominic and Wendy have helped in the evenings and the windows have been standing open. The smell is almost gone, though it clings palely to curtains and rugs.

The thought of the party tonight, and what I may have to do, tightens my lungs and shortens my breath. I could have cancelled it with just a few emails, but I didn't dare. Zev has not been able to confirm all the legalities, or that the mortgage can be transferred. Mike has left it so late that I am terrified of losing this leverage on him, so my threat to expose him remains. He knows that if he doesn't turn up, some of his friends, or so-called friends, will, and I will tell them what he has done. Zev has agreed to come and is bringing his partner Sam. Part social, part business. Part protection? And I'm hoping like crazy that he will confirm the flat handover.

The caterers arrive with the chill cabinets, sniffing the air suspiciously. The champagne arrives and the blue and silver plastic (recycled, of course) paint-tube-shaped ice cubes. The champagne flutes, also recycled high-quality plastic, are blue for the boys and silver for the girls. They can keep them as a memento of a memorable evening. And as a nudge about Ecolore. The decorations are silver-dusted, blue-veined white lilies, and silver-dusted birch branches and cornflowers. As I swing my indistinct gaze around, I have to say it does all look fabulous. And expensive. The flowers smell blue as well, but it clashes with the faint sickly yellowy green smell still emanating from curtains and carpets. Along with the sharp edge of bleach and disinfectant, it is like a loose tarpaulin over decomposing corpses.

Jade and Eddie are some of the first guests to appear. As Eddie inhales, his eyes make little letter box shapes, and his nostrils narrow. I smile at him a bit nervously and am relieved when he takes a Kray-brother-looking back seat and enjoys the sensation his wife causes.

Mike's eyes dart to the door every time the bell rings and seeing his boss Kendrick, two work colleagues and Laura arrive together puts him into a state of nervous paralysis. He certainly didn't expect his boss to be either asked or to come. But he has come, mainly because I sent him a flattering note along with the invitation, mendaciously intimating Mike's admiration for him, but asking that his invitation remain a secret.

Jade and I have spent tipsy hours with Wendy, who as dress designer has clothed all three of us in outfits made of recycled plastic bottles, and as I introduce Kendrick to Jade, I see his sharp intake of champagne. His eyes slip helplessly from her hair, plaited into the thinnest strands and interwoven with silver thread, down the delicate tattoos to her fabulous cleavage and over the skintight silver dress to her long, elegant legs ending in silver four-inch stilettos. He forgets the faint sick room smell as she lifts her champagne flute to her full-lipped mouth. She knows exactly what sexual effect this has on him. As I leave them, I hear him ask her throatily which house she models for. Eddie drops me a wink as I pass him. There must be a great deal more to Eddie than meets the eye, otherwise he couldn't have snaffled Jade.

I'm not surprised but I am relieved that Mike has come to his own party. He needs to make sure I keep my promise not to tell the world what an immoral, dishonest, mendacious criminal he is. I drop a stray fly corpse into his champagne as I hand it to him. He obviously didn't have the nerve to try to cancel his guests, because they keep appearing, and he is acutely worried to see so many other acquaintances here. The girls wear calf-length slinky, silky dresses, long hair drifting over strappy shoulders. The men are Mike clones, conventionally attired in chinos and linen shirts which already look saggy and damp.

Laura gives me a hostile glare and that now familiar greeny blue smell. Eyes rove in fascination to me and my friends who are infinitely more interesting than Mike's. All are aware of the faint morgue smell. My apparent serene confidence and charm towards his friends are unnerving him. He doesn't know for sure whether signing over the flat will prevent me from landing him in shit with a public exposé. As the guests trickle in, he sees the noticeable twitching of noses and a drift towards the open windows and balcony.

I welcome Wendy who also sniffs the air. 'Lordy, Cass! There's still a funny smell in here.'

'And some,' I say grimly, handing her a champagne flute. 'Anyway, you look great. Almost as good as Jade.'

She peals with laughter, her enormous bosom heaving, and all twenty stone of her wobbling with hilarity within her tent of filmy baby pink.

'Love you, darling. Now, who shall I charm first?'

'Mike, please.'

'Oh! What joy! Lead on! I will be Bottom to Titania's enchantment of your beloved.'

Dominic and Patrick arrive together. Patrick has come down from Oxford and is in jeans, T-shirt, and a ponytail. He gravitates naturally towards Eddie as an old acquaintance. I catch Mike glancing at these strangers in nervous puzzlement. As he has so often told me, I am a loose cannon and a potential embarrassment in his social environment and many of these strangers look as if they might be loose cannon too. Dominic's smile makes my heart turn over. His cheek on mine in the diplomatic kiss, and his hands on my arms, make my skin vibrate.

'You look so beautiful,' he says softly into my ear.

Zev arrives fashionably late, looking perfectly exquisite. His partner Sam is a revelation. Short, stocky, untidy in some unfathomable way and with a bald patch. He has the most mischievous expression I have ever seen, and I warm to him immediately. Greeting Zev, I ask nervously, 'Do you have good news for me?'

He grins. 'I do. You are the proud possessor of this flat. All legal. And the mortgage, which may, of course, still bankrupt you.'

My knees go all rubbery with relief. 'Don't spoil my fun. I will cross my bridges when I come to them, and I will be eternally grateful that you have saved my skin.' With this news, I am not going to have to expose Mike. 'Now, come and meet the famous Laura.'

Zev turns his head sideways – so sexy – as I introduce him to her, prising her away from a little office cabal. She almost licks her Botoxed lips at the sight of him. They are offered sushi on a slate platter, and Laura asks Zev what his job is. She is wrong-footed when he tells her he's my lawyer. I think she thought he was a male model. It strikes me that all my friends are playing their parts perfectly, most of them without even having been asked to.

Introducing Sam to Eddie and Patrick, I discover that Sam is a horse-mad amateur jockey and leave them discussing steeplechasing and how to keep rats out of stables. The tiny mouthfuls of canapés are delicious, the guests are plied with champagne, and the open windows induce a breeze which further dilutes the faint yellow-green smell. I network like mad through Mike's friends and colleagues and Ecolore is well marketed. The little piles of my business cards carried on each drink and food tray reduce steadily, and Jade and Wendy are both brilliant ambassadors for my fabrics and designs. The decibel level rises in line with the amount of alcohol consumed. Dominic and Mike's boss are deep in conversation, and I wonder what about.

As I move towards the blue and silver podium between the windows, Mike is suddenly at my elbow. I have this feeling that he hasn't enjoyed his party. He looks pinched and small as if he has an acute stomach ache. I should feel pleased to have the upper hand, but I don't.

'Cass, please. You promised. Please don't. You won't, will you?'

His desperation seems genuine, and my resentment transmutes into a shamed recognition that I had intended to place myself on the same level as him, had Zev found any loopholes. If I had succeeded in ruining him, what would I have done to myself? To my own reputation? To my business? What would anyone think of a vengeful woman who destroys her enemy in public? Dominic would be disappointed in me at the very least and I definitely, for sure, no question, do not want to be a source of his disappointment. I sense his sombre waiting gaze from across the room and turn to smile reassuringly at him. I am surprised to find that having Dominic in my life has changed my priorities. Before Dominic, I would have taken that revenge without a second thought.

But I am not about to tell Mike that he's off the hook quite yet. Let him sweat a few minutes longer. I whirl my long, recycled plastic skirts in a flurry of royal blue and silver so that I am standing with my bare back to the room. Wendy has excelled with this outfit and it empowers me.

'The flat is yours. Please don't.' He puts a hand on my arm, but I delicately pick it off with my blue and silver-tipped fingers.

'I never wanted the flat,' I say bitterly. 'You've lost it through your own greed and spite. I loved you, but you never loved me. This is payback time.'

'I did love you, Cass. I really did. I know I messed up, but it was too late to change it.' He looks bleached and desperate under the designer stubble.

'Too late to change what?' I'm confused by his words.

He ducks his head and doesn't answer. After a pause, I straighten up, stepping past him and onto the little dais. There is a gradual reduction in conversation until I get silence. Public speaking has never been a terror for me. I am an exhibitionist at heart and relish the power, but my speech is shorter than first envisaged. Everyone gets thanked for coming: friends, the boss, Laura and his colleagues. Mike has edged back towards the door, but he can't go far or fast.

'As you all know, forty years is a milestone in anyone's life. And this is Mike's. I've only been in it for six of those years, but boy, have they been memorable! This party will live on in his memory and hopefully yours too.'

I can see that he thinks I am going to do the dirty on him. He is desperate to get out of the flat but is hemmed in by the guests and by Patrick, Stefan, Sam and Eddie who have congregated by the door. A solid phalanx who won't shift easily. They are grinning like Chinese dragons. Mike's pallid face is shining with sweat, and he looks as if he might pass out at any moment.

'Mike, our suave man about town, has qualities which some of you would not recognise, but many of you may soon know what they are.' They can puzzle on that one until the police get involved. If they do. 'In the meantime, we have his birthday to celebrate, so please raise your glasses and wish Mike a happy fortieth birthday.'

Mike is pushed forward to the front again, but the congratulations and back-slapping pass him by, as does the magnificent birthday cake, flaming with forty reigniting candles. I had wondered how on earth the caterers were going to light them all, but they have. There is an embarrassed rendering of off-key 'Happy Birthday to You', which to my delight makes most of his guests cringe.

Mike understands that he has escaped the fiery furnace and recovers his mojo with insulting speed. He doesn't thank me for not exposing his treachery.

'Lost your nerve when you realised no one would believe you?'

'No. Unlike you, I keep my word. I didn't particularly want to degrade myself by coming down to your level. But I'm still curious as to why you stole my IP. And the company.'

He laughs, and it sounds triumphant. 'Why? Just because I could. And you made it so easy, Cass. It amused me because it got you very worked up.'

Just because he *could*? What sort of reasoning is that? 'Why didn't you just say you were tired of me?' He shrugs infuriatingly.

'But why make Ecolore bankrupt? Was there a reason? Why? Why did you do it?'

Mike curls his lip and gives off vibes which tell me I am being dense.

'Oh, there was a good reason. Your bloody father was the reason.' There is a viciousness in his voice which makes me shudder and my mind jolts to a halt. I don't understand what he is saying. How could my father be the reason for anything?

'It was easy to find you and pick you up. Easy to reel you in. But you were so easy to manage I really began to fancy you then. But gradually you got obsessed with your bloody business. You never saw the silliness of your little enterprise – how badly you ran it, your pitiful eco-donkey-cart compared to the global technology express.

You chattered on, boring everyone rigid with your stupid fixations about sustainability. You believed it when people said you were so creative, so clever. You were never going to change the world, but you clung onto your pathetic little ideas and dug in. Like a tick. And in the end, the itch got the better of me and I had to get you out. You can't even read a bank statement, let alone a balance sheet, but you were so deluded, you never took that on board.'

His hatred and derision are a new thing, open and brutal. Why did I not see this in his jokes to friends about his funny girlfriend with daft clothes and hair, and cuckoo ideas on saving the planet? I am so hot that I can feel the sweat running down my skull, clagging in my hair. *You really hate me, don't you? You despise me.*

Finding my voice, I demand, 'But how was my father the reason to make me bankrupt? You don't even know him – you've never met him! And I haven't seen him since I was eighteen!' My throat constricts as if he has his hands around it.

'I don't know him, thank God,' he says venomously. 'But he ruined my parents and, in the process, destroyed my inheritance.' Was that the reason why he never let me, the daughter of their nemesis, meet them? 'He stole every part of my birthright from me, and I was left with nothing. What he has taken from me, I decided needed to be given back, and you were the one to do it.'

I take an involuntary step back from him. *What he has taken from me?* The words feel like a physical hit. 'But what did he do! What was this "birthright" you're talking about?'

'You wouldn't understand.' Dismissing me as too stupid to comprehend an explanation infuriates rather than intimidates me.

'I don't understand because you aren't making sense! Why the hell should you punish me for something I never did in the first place and never even knew about?' Every bit of me is hissing and vibrating; a rubber band stretched to breaking point.

Unnervingly he looks at me almost with glee. 'Why not? But it wasn't just you I punished …' He catches himself as if he's said more than he intended and as he looks over my shoulder, his expression changes from vicious to blandly polite. I see little on the periphery of my vision, but I'm guessing Laura is advancing on us. Swinging round to face her, I find to my relief it is not Laura but Dominic. He puts a steadying hand on my trembling shoulder and his voice feels like warm oil on the sandpaper of my soul.

'Congratulations, Cass, on a triumph of organisation and a splendid speech. And what a great party, Mike. You've been very generous to us all.' His fingers tighten a little and I feel his solidity and tenderness. 'Amazing food, delicious champagne and excellent company. And I've had such an interesting discussion with Kendrick.' At the mention of his boss's name and an interesting discussion, Mike visibly stiffens. For all Dominic's outward courtesy there is a steely core, and Mike doesn't miss it. He suspects that Dominic knows everything that I know, although I don't think he has ever suspected how deep our friendship is and certainly not that we are now lovers. He knows that Zev knows all about him. He knows that he can't influence me anymore. I can feel the tense muscles in my back and shoulders ease under Dominic's hand.

As the flow of champagne lessens, and the canapés are served less frequently, I can smile and exchange civilities as our guests depart, and to my relief, Mike leaves too, with Laura.

'Let me know when you want to collect your furniture,' I tell him. 'Even though I paid for most of it, I don't want it.' Turning to Laura I know that my smile is warm in the face of their hostility and silence. 'I wish you joy of him.'

Chapter Nineteen

The caterers have gone, food and bottles are gathered in the kitchen, and basic tidying is done. I turn my clouded eyes on my newly acquired property and feel no particular triumph.

'I feel sort of empty, even though Zev assures me the flat is mine and that means Ecolore will be safe.' Dominic has his arm around me and I rest my head on his shoulder.

'It'll take a while to get used to the idea. But that is hopefully the last time you'll see Mike, and from now on it's going to be us. You did brilliantly this evening, and I guess you're as glad as I am that you didn't publicly destroy him.' I hope he can feel me nodding in agreement. My throat is all choked up.

He puts a finger under my chin and lifts my head. 'Cass, it's over. Finished. Your business is safe; Mike is gone.' Into the quiet, he says, 'But something's wrong, isn't it?' How does he know that? 'What's wrong? Are you still in love with him?'

I can hear a faint tremor in his voice and my fingers dig deep into his wrists. 'No! I see now I never was. I thought it was love, but it was only me looking for – acceptance and security. I never understood I didn't really love him until I met you.' Heaving in a breath I burrow into his embrace. 'It was what he said, just before you joined us. It wasn't a chance meeting, him and I. He picked me up – he picked me off, to punish me for something my father did to his parents. But he said, “What he has taken from *me*.” Not what was taken from his parents. Whatever that was. He wouldn’t explain. Said I wouldn’t understand. Something my *father* did! How is that even possible?’

‘I have no idea. And what do you mean, “picked you off?” Surely you just met and got together?’ He seems puzzled by the idea.

I begin to dry the wiped trays and think back to how Mike and I met. As far as I was concerned, it was a happy coincidence. He had been crossing the street, dodging traffic, and bumped into me on the pavement sending me and my groceries flying.

‘He was full of apologies; helped me up, picked my shopping up, concerned that I was OK. Could he please buy me a coffee, he felt so bad about his clumsiness.’ I pull the back of my hand over my face, remembering how grateful I was, how great to meet this nice, good-looking guy. ‘The coffee led to chat, and my phone number, and then a drink at the pub, then dates. Then he was buying a flat in Southampton and before I knew it, we were an item and sharing the mortgage costs and making plans for the future and I was over the moon. So happy.’ I can feel my shoulders have risen, and consciously relax them. ‘So, yes. It seems he knew I was Dad’s daughter, and he picked me up on purpose. He says he fell in love with me later, and we did have some really good times, but it does make me feel so naive, thinking he liked me for who I was, when in fact he was plotting to steal from me before we even met.’ Did I sound bitter? I certainly felt it.

Dominic takes my head in his hands and his lips are against my forehead. ‘That’s horrifying. I knew he must have said something to knock you sideways. You were so confident, so in control, and then suddenly you were in pieces.’

Had anyone else noticed I was in pieces? Dominic had

seen it from across the room and had come to help me.

'In any case, whatever happened was nothing to do with me, it was a generation ago and if Mike wants to drag it into his present, that's his problem and it doesn't have to be mine.' The bravado is evident. 'It's over. I'm going to try to put the whole thing in my brain dustbin. I think he was saying all those things because he knows any mention of my father winds me up and gets me upset.'

He pulls me gently into his chest. 'Mike is gone, and you can dismiss his malicious allegations. Tonight is for celebrating that you are the proud possessor of an extremely valuable bit of real estate. Tonight your business is safe. Tonight is for you and me and being together and nothing need keep us apart from now on.' His hands are firm on my shoulders, and amber floods my senses.

Peace begins to wash through the mental uproar and I lift my eyes to his steady grey ones. 'Yes, tonight is for us. And the future is all new and shiny.' Suddenly I am feeling shy, like a teenager on a first date. 'I'm not quite sure how it happened, but I seem to have fallen out of love with Mike and into love with you.' The shyness is verging on worry. Is this because Mike and I have disintegrated? Because my relationships are all messed up? Am I on the rebound? Are my feelings genuine or will they pass?

'I love you too.' He sounds ruefully amused. 'I don't know how it happened either, considering how dissimilar we are, but it has, and I'm just grateful and thrilled and happy to be with you. Tonight is victory and happy ever after.'

I take a huge breath. It really does feel like an entirely new beginning, a new birth, a new life. My lungs are full of air that is lifting me off the ground, like a hot air balloon, into a place of blue skies, above the mist, fog and clouds of the past weeks and months.

'I cannot begin to thank you for what you've done for

me, and I want you to know that I really do love you.' As I actually speak the words, I know this is the real thing. Genuine, true, lasting. 'I love you very, very much. And I always will.'

* * *

A week later, the flat still has an odd smell, but seemingly it is only me that is aware of it. I sniff gingerly at the curtains where it appears the bags of prawns still haven't burst.

'Mike will take his furniture at some point, so I'm leaving the prawns in the curtains for the moment in case he tries anything dastardly. It's a miracle they didn't explode in the heat.' I inhale deeply again. 'Can you really not smell anything?'

'Truly, I can't.' Dominic is laughing. 'All your sprays and carpet cleaners have delivered on their promises and leaving the windows open has done wonders. It's as fresh as a daisy.'

He has brought back a load of my business files in his car, as I am reinstalling myself in my office. There is much more space now that Mike has taken away all his paperwork. Dominic respected my stubborn refusal to part with more than sixteen per cent of Ecolore's value and I have accepted their investment offer. Already I feel more in control.

'When Mike takes his furniture, I'm going to lay my recycled carpet before moving the contents of the container in here,' I tell Dominic. 'Then I won't have any warehousing costs and it'll be much more convenient. I'm beginning to reduce stock and orders too. Giving up the car will save money as well.'

I tell myself that selling the car is more for financial reasons than poor sight, and I have also managed to put the forthcoming correct appointment at Moorfields in the bottom drawer of my mental filing cabinet. I refuse to be thrown off my pinnacle of happiness.

'Do you think I can take these horrible pictures off the wall?' I ask Dominic doubtfully. 'I'll have to stack them somewhere and the hall cupboard is already stuffed.'

'Yes,' he says firmly. 'I'll make room somehow. What will you put there instead?'

'Clothes. Fabrics. Hooks are some of my favourite objects. After boxes.'

'Boxes?' he asks, lifting down one of Milo Szorski-Czyz's black horrors. 'What sort of boxes, and what for?'

I laugh. 'Come and meet Ugly,' and temporarily abandon the stocking of my files. 'This was Mum's cabinet. Mike named it Ugly, which it is, but I love it dearly.' The top drawer is filled with little boxes of all sizes, shapes and colours. Enamel, papier mâché, stone, cardboard, wood, tin. Dominic looks amazed.

'What's in them?'

'Explore. What isn't in them!'

I return to sorting my office, and I can hear him chuckling next door, and the sounds of lids clicking on and off, and contents being stirred, picked up, replaced. Strange contentment, happiness and pleasure surge through me, that this friend and lover is privy to my silly secrets which have lain hidden all these years, with no one but me to touch them, to remember.

He comes into the office carrying a folding chair and the Red Box. It is in fact Indian pietra dura, but everything inside is red, and it smells a faded red too.

'Tell me,' he says, sitting on the chair and opening the box.

'This is a holly berry,' I say, taking out the first object to hand, wrinkled and now grey rather than red. 'A friend and I went sledging – the first snow I can really remember

– and I tried to pick some holly for decorating the house, but of course, it was too tough, and I got prickled. So we picked the berries instead, and I kept one forever berry. I knew not to eat them.'

'How old were you?'

'About six, I guess.'

'And this?' He has picked out a thick strand of bright red wool, with a thinner strand of yellow twisted round it.

'I made Dad a scarf for Christmas one year. I was about ten then.'

Dominic turns his head inquiringly. 'Did he like it?'

Thinking back, I surprise myself. 'Yes, I think he did. He certainly wore it.'

'So he wasn't always horrible to you?'

I ponder that. 'No. But when I was little, I was always trying to get him to be pleased with me, and he never was, so I became pretty contrary.' I haven't thought about this for years. 'He got angry very easily, and I certainly didn't help. I remember once I had the back window of the car open and he shouted at me to close it. Because he shouted, I wouldn't shut the window and he stopped the car, came round and pulled me out and drove off, leaving me on the verge! I hadn't a clue where I was.'

'Good Lord! Did he come back?'

'Nope. I hitched a lift in a lorry having walked to a service station. The driver drove me into Basingstoke town centre and I walked home from there.'

'What on earth did your mother do? Was she blind then? How old were you?' He is obviously horrified by this tale of paternal fury, and I laugh.

'Nothing my mother ever said had the slightest effect. She was already having sight problems, and I was thirteen.' I reflect for a moment. 'I learned a bit. How to cope on my own. The consequences of what you say and do. Funnily enough, I didn't hold it against him really. I knew I kind of deserved it.'

Dominic grins and ruffles my hair. 'So, it taught you not to be rude to someone you should respect and obey?'

I grin back at him. 'Not really. He had a terrible temper and I was stubborn. I suppose I was a real pain in his neck.' I pick out another object and lay it in the palm of his hand.

'A cigarette stub?'

'Another two disobediences! He forbade me to smoke, on pain of disinheritance, or to wear make-up. Admittedly I wasn't even a teenager then, but this was my first cigarette – nearly the only one, as I made the mistake of inhaling – and it's in the Red Box because I nicked Mum's red lipstick for the experiment. In front of the mirror. Mata Hari.'

He gives a snort of amusement. 'What a wicked woman! Did he catch you?'

'Naw. Even I didn't have the nerve for that. Not that it would have made any difference to the disinheritance.' Reflecting a moment, I say, 'I've never shown anyone my boxes, or told what was in them. Mike wasn't interested in my past – only his own. You're the first person. Like Carter finding Tutankhamun's tomb. No one's touched my past ever before.'

He looks at me gravely. 'I'm honoured.'

I put the butt back in the box and close it. 'Well, that's one of the boxes. It'll take you a lifetime to get through them all.'

'I look forward to it,' he says, smiling that slow smile again.

'Me too.' I lean forward and kiss him lightly. 'Me too. I love you, do you know that, Dominic Paget?'

Chapter Twenty

I had the sense to confirm the appointment this time and turn up at Moorfields in the right week, on the right day, and at the right time. Whatever is wrong will get fixed. Nothing can destroy the happiness that Dominic and I have. But my chest is constricted and my breath short, nevertheless.

The tests take forever, with long waiting periods while eye drops take effect; staff are either standing around talking about the latest film or frantically rushing about clutching clipboards and files to their chests. In the heat, which has permeated the depths of these hideous corridors, the silvery smell of disinfectant fights with a nasty yellow-grey of floor polish.

The senior consultant is absent and I am seen by a dusky-pink-smelling registrar who has not the first idea about bedside manners. He says it like it is. I tell myself I would rather have it straight than any saccharine sympathy. But it is not so. I want to howl. Instead, dry-eyed, teeth clenched in lockjawed tension, I gather the notes and information leaflets on retinitis pigmentosa and the instructions on monitoring it and put them all carefully in my cobalt blue tote. This is not reality. This is dreamland.

I watch myself from somewhere above me, rigidly uncomprehending, disbelieving, denying. My world is imploding. All the misery of Mike's betrayal had been mopped up by the happiness of being with Dominic and now that happiness is melting away like mist blown by the wind.

Old people go blind. Not young designers. People like me don't fumble their way down strange streets tapping with a white stick, seeking addresses and shops they cannot see. People like me are vibrant, dancing, in love with Dominic and in love with life. Building a business from ground zero, drawing, painting, observing. No, no, no. He's got it wrong, this stupid man with no manners. Trying to dramatise his boring job by exaggeration, inference and lies.

This man is not the senior specialist, and he has got it wrong. He is reading the wrong test results and looking at the wrong notes. He is confusing me with someone else. Someone who doesn't use their eyes to build a business, who doesn't find pleasure in the perfect design, who doesn't need to see the minutiae of line and shape and colour. Was this what my mother felt as her world darkened about her?

'So, no treatment? No cure?' My voice sounds cracked, grating as if used for the first time in years. There must be treatments, nothing in this modern technical medical age is untreatable. Of course there is a cure. There is a cure for everything.

He shakes his head. 'Only for the cataract.'

'Couldn't you give me completely new ones?' I joke because that's what I do *in extremis.*

He shakes his head again, failing to hear my poor effort at lightening up. 'No. Perhaps one day, but not in my lifetime.' And not in mine either.

Belatedly he remembers the bedside manner. 'I'm sorry. No. Gene therapy is only in its infancy.'

In the Uber to Clapham Junction, my phone vibrates. My heart does a mad expansion on seeing Dominic's text.

'Where are you? How was it?'

'Train in ten minutes. Not good.' I debate before sending and then delete *'Not good'*. I type, *'Not so bad. Eye man has*

no sense of humour. Need a cataract op.' I require thinking time.

Commuters are leaving their offices and I can only find a backwards-facing aisle seat. I like to see, however vaguely, where I'm going, and now I can't. My eyes feel gritty and more distorted than usual from the drops they used to help them peer inside the spheres which are letting me down, just as they let my mother down. In just a few weeks I have virtually lost my business, and now I'm on my way to losing my eyes.

Towns and country unravel, a dropped spool of ribbon, with unstoppable velocity, and as I compare this speed with my own life unravelling, self-pity bubbles up and I cringe inside like a lemon-juiced oyster. Why me? What have I done to deserve this? Why should I have been given the gift of colour only for it to be made useless? The consultant said among a welter of information I either didn't hear or didn't take in, that the vision in my master eye had already reduced to 20/200, but I had failed to ask how quickly I'd lose the rest. I'd failed to ask anything at all. How will I read instructions, draw designs, meet customers, carry samples or visit friends? I want to weep on Dominic's shoulder, spill everything, have his strong, warm arms around me, feel the touch of his hands, his sensible comforting advice to bring me back from anxiety to common sense. I want to be enveloped by his love forever.

And even more than that, I want to give him everything I am, everything I can. I have never felt or experienced that before. But now? What do I do? If I tell him I am well on the way to going blind, what will he think? What will he do? He'll be sorry for me, of course. He'll say he wants me to stay, that he doesn't mind, that it'll make no difference, that he loves me anyway. Maybe now, but what about the future? What could I bring to the party?

I will have to decline Vermont and Paget's investment

because they will lose their money if I am blind. Ecolore is at the same point as it was ten years ago but now its future is bleak, not hopeful. There won't be a business if I am blind. I will be a useless burden on the state. The terror comes in a huge wave. There is no family to fall back on, and my pension savings are minimal. How do I earn a living if I'm blind? I fell in love with Dominic, found such happiness and contentment, such a meeting of mind and spirit and now it will all disintegrate. How can such glorious fulfilment be crushed so quickly? A vortex of fear and misery spirals in my mind, blotting out all optimism. Why should I have discovered the one person who could make me happy only to have to lose him?

My bones are melting, my vision blurring, and I hear my father once more, having failed my maths GCSE for the third time. 'You are totally useless, Cassia. You're stupid. A waste of space.' I hear once more the door slamming with me on the outside. Stupid, a waste of space, like your mother, clumsy, pathetic, weak, whining. Useless.

* * *

An imperative tap on my arm makes me jump. A small, dark peachy girl thrusts a soft toy at me.

'Put it on him please.' Her frustration is palpable. Her pale pink mother is asleep across the aisle.

I peer down at a floppy-limbed monkey and see a tatty yellow felt waistcoat has been forced onto one shoulder, but the other armhole has only got as far as the opposite wrist. The garment seems about three sizes too small for the monkey and smells rich pink of dog.

'He's cold,' says the dark peach child.

I set to work. 'It's a very hot day.' The waistcoat has got mysterious holes all over it, and I fear I am expanding them.

'It's not hot compared to his jungle.' The small girl is firm.

'Who does the waistcoat really belong to?' It patently does not belong to the monkey.

'Mr Bird, but Daddy threw him to William, and he ate him.' I throw a glance at the grave little face. 'I cried and cried all day.' Typical father, I think, instantly disliking this one.

'Is William your dog?' She nods. 'Was the waistcoat all that was left of Mr Bird after William ate him?'

She looks wistful. 'There were some bits but they were all wet. William didn't mean to. He's only a baby. He's a black Labrador and he's got little sharp teeth. Mr Bird was my bestest, but Daddy did him a funeral and now Cronk is my bestest.'

Cronk. It's not even the noise a monkey makes. 'With Mr Bird's waistcoat.' I have at last managed to clothe the new best friend with the chewed relic and contemplate a child's ability to move on in the face of disaster. I need to take a lesson here.

'I like your hair,' she says, staring at it. It is blue and green this week, like tropical forest meeting Indian Ocean.

'I like yours too.' She has thick dark brown French braids, almost down to her waist.

She strokes my deep blue nails. 'You're beautiful.' Which is one of the nicest things anyone, other than Dominic, has said to me this week.

Mother and child and Cronk also get out at Winchester, and we exchange smiles, this six-year-old and I. I let them go ahead of me and walk slowly back to Dominic's house. Why did Mike throw my life to the dog, to be chewed up till it was a soggy mess, full of holes? Only fit to have the funeral rites spoken over it.

The peachy child's disaster is as great as mine. All things are relative, disasters included. And blindness comes in all sorts of packaging.

* * *

I am no further forward in my thinking on how or what to tell Dominic, so I say as little as possible, and only mention the cataracts. Cataracts are common and minor and reduce the whole mess to manageable proportions.

He's perplexed. 'Why were you sent to Moorfields if it's only cataracts?'

I shrug. 'I don't know, but they can be done in Southampton. They only do one at a time. Apparently, it's painless and quick.' I put my mug of tea carefully on the grass beside my garden chair.

He probes a bit more. 'Did they say why you've developed them? Aren't you rather young to have cataracts?'

'No. I should have asked. But I could do with having this funny cloudy effect removed.' That is true, although it is far from the whole truth. The whole truth may be incorrect, for all I know, so there's no point in having a drama unnecessarily, is there.

His eyes are searching. 'Was that all?'

I shrug. 'He was the registrar, not the consultant. I'll see the consultant next month.'

I have an uncomfortable feeling that he knows I am not divulging the entire story, but he does not press me further.

I can't just walk out on him, not after all our mutual loving, all his kindness. I think I am behaving normally and being my usual chatty self, perhaps a bit too chatty, and manage to keep the conversation away from Moorfields.

I know I should not allow him to make love to me, but how can I do that? And how desperately I want him. His arms around me, his hands moving on my skin, his kisses everywhere. In my guilt I know I am not responding quite as usual, and I grip his body tightly in my longing to keep him close.

Afterwards, I lie awake, staring at the blurred patterned cornices edging the ceiling and the gyrating shafts of lights from cars passing in the street. Faintly I hear a child crying, quickly silenced. The young family next door. We have stopped to make faces and laugh with the two-year-old and chat with his pregnant mother on several occasions. One day Dominic bought the toddler a fleecy white rabbit with floppy ears and pink button eyes. Dominic loves children and I'm sure he would like more. For her, the bump is heavy, hot and tiring but I am insanely jealous because it is unlikely I will ever have a baby, and it would be totally irresponsible to get pregnant. The specialist was clear: retinal dystrophy, or more accurately retinitis pigmentosa, is passed on genetically. My mother passed it on to me, and a parent gave it to her. And possibly generations before them. Before science, before bloody consultants. Before Mike, thank God, refused to have children. Any child of mine would inherit my blindness.

My exhausted brain turns cartwheels in the night, tossing impossible situations and nightmare conversations. My whole body aches with tension; guilt that I am keeping this diagnosis from Dominic, anger that it has happened just when life seemed to have only good and wonderful things in store, when this gentle lover promised true happiness and fulfilment. I am fearful about a future without him. I am sad about broken dreams, about Mike's betrayal, and confused as to why or how my father could possibly have come into the equation. Sad about Ecolore, about having to reject Vermont and Paget's investment. But it is utter misery rather than sadness when I consider how this idyll with Dominic may have to end. I should not allow the complication of a man – any man, let alone a good man – just at the point of going blind, of being as helpless and timid as my mother. His life frustrated and ruined, constrained by having to look after a dependent partner.

He shouldn't have the complication of me, although I cannot believe he could become like my father. But I am beginning to feel I must find a way to let him go.

* * *

Goodbye to new premises. Wendy has found someone else to buy her out. But with that out of the way, her normal motherly self takes over and I feel able to tell her about my diagnosis. I fill her in on retinitis pigmentosa, the out-of-reach expense of treatments which have no reliable outcomes and a cataract procedure in the not-too-distant future. She is wonderfully matter-of-fact, which prevents me from falling to pieces.

'Have they given you a date?'

'No, but I should think weeks, if not months, away. I'm not expecting it to work miracles anyway.' I shove my fists in my eye sockets. Wendy is far too astute for me to pretend that I have my act together. 'This bloody diagnosis has come at the worst possible time.' It will be the end of Dominic and me. The end before it has even really begun.

'At least Mike is finally out of the picture. I never did like him,' she says darkly. 'Far too smooth, arrogant. Always talking himself up, and other people – you – down.'

I frown. 'He wasn't like that at first. But, yes, he could be a bit scornful I suppose. Why the hell didn't I see that?'

She rolls her eyes. 'I don't know. He was always bored by what other people had to say. Always wanted to talk about himself, how clever he was, and how important his "work" was. For heaven's sake, it was just a job in marketing.'

'I wish you'd said.'

'Don't blame me. I came on the scene long after Mike. Any opinion of mine wouldn't have made the slightest difference. He love-bombed you and you were besotted.'

Contemplation of my besottedness is bad for morale. 'Anyway, you're rid of him now, so thank your lucky stars.' Wendy swivels to face me across the kitchen table and tops up our glasses. 'You've been living in Dominic Paget's house and, I assume, sleeping in his bed. I hope you haven't jumped out of the frying pan into the fire. Not very healthy sleeping with the banker I wouldn't have thought, not that I've met him.'

Flicking a glance at her, I think she may have a point. 'I don't think I should let him be involved with someone whose business will rapidly go down the drain – he didn't bargain on that. I'll have to turn down the investment, and I ought to end the relationship.' I really want Wendy to understand this. 'I adore him. He is the nicest person I have ever met. He's clever and kind and humorous and generous. He's great in bed. And I wouldn't have met him if it hadn't been for Mike, so for that, I'm grateful to Mike. But I shouldn't let him get more involved with someone who's going blind, I know what can happen. I couldn't bear to do that to him. If I become like my mother.'

Wendy knows a bit about my parents. Her eyes narrow and she says sharply, 'Well, the answer is not to become like your mother.'

'Maybe that's easier said than done,' I say sadly.

'History doesn't have to repeat itself, and Dominic doesn't sound like your father, though I suspect Mike was. And what does "more involved" mean? A long-term love affair? Partnership? Marriage?'

'No – I don't know. Just that it's dishonest to go on without telling him. We haven't discussed the future, but he's not the sort of person for one-night stands or multiple affairs. And he would want more children, and I shouldn't have children because they would go blind too.' I feel helpless in the face of her pragmatism. 'It's so new. So wonderful. I don't know what to do.'

Wendy almost sniffs. 'So you haven't told him about the retinal thing?'

I shake my head. 'No. He only knows about the cataracts. I wasn't thinking straight after the diagnosis. I was panic-stricken about the finances, how Vermont and Paget would have to cancel, and how embarrassing that would be for him. And me. And then I thought he might feel he had to keep the relationship going because he's kind. You know. Wouldn't want to let me down.' I trail off, not quite able to put it into words.

'So you think you love him more than he does you?'

I can feel my face screwing up. 'No. Well, I don't know, do I? But I do think he loves me, and I love him too much to want to be that sort of burden on him. I don't want him to have to make a huge sacrifice to keep me, or to have the guilt of letting me go.'

She pushes the fresh olives towards me and there is silence for a while. 'Life is full of choices, and you seem to have three here. Either you finish it, or he finishes it, or you stick together and make a go of it.'

'You make it sound so simple,' I say wryly. But just the fact that I have voiced this horrible secret to someone has given me a clearer head. Dominic doesn't have to make the decision if I make it for him.

Chapter Twenty-One

For an entire month, I have been trying to convince myself that the previous registrar got my diagnosis all wrong. I read or listen to every article I can find on RP but am no wiser as to whether this is my problem or not. Every now and then, I catch Dominic glancing at me with a concerned expression and he offers to come with me to the appointment. However, I insist on going alone, citing what a waste of his day it will be for him to sit through all the time-consuming tests. If there really is bad news, I want to be in charge of dealing with it.

I am finally seen by the consultant ophthalmologist who is much older than the registrar, has a silvery olive smell which reminds me of Jade, and a thatch of grey hair which reminds me of Donald Trump, or maybe the Foreign Secretary Boris Johnson. He has actually read my notes.

As he carefully and slowly confirms the diagnosis of retinitis pigmentosa and explains how the condition may develop, I feel that my ability to take in his words has ground to a halt like a frozen screen. I hear the words, but they are set in concrete, solidly immovable, meaningless. I am going to go blind. That's all I can see or hear or understand. No more and no less.

After a while, I hear silence and come back into focus. The consultant is patiently waiting for me, unsurprised by my shock and denial. He seems to have all the time in the world to draw diagrams and to ask and listen to questions.

He makes endless notes. He sets about boosting my morale and giving me tips and tricks to make life workable. In fact, he seems to find the whole idea rather exciting. I become more disoriented by the minute.

'You can inherit this condition from one gene from your mother who you have told us became blind – called autosomal dominant – or from both parents. We would need a DNA test from your father to establish that.'

'I'm not about to ask him,' I say, rather more firmly than I mean to. 'Would it make any difference to my diagnosis?'

He leans his head back and the lion's mane flips away. 'No. No difference to you. And you have no siblings, so no problem there. We would need to discuss the risk for any children you might have in the future because, as you know, the likelihood of passing on this genetic condition is high.'

My stomach cramps.

'The loss of your peripheral vision will increase gradually, and eventually, you will only see what is directly in front of you. When you look straight at it. Tunnel vision is how it's described.' I am already beginning to experience that. 'Colours will begin to change and fade but your brain will learn how to manage spatial variations and discrepancies. I expect you have noticed wobbly or curved lines instead of straight ones. Cataracts don't help and we need to deal with the most advanced one now. Then at least you'll have a clear lens. In time your central vision will contract as well, but it may take months, quite possibly years, to lose all your sight.' He pauses. 'There is no guarantee, but most people with RP always retain some perception of light and shadow. It is very unlikely that you will become totally, fully, dark blind.'

That happens with detached or destroyed retinas. By now I have read, or rather listened to, a few books on blindness. Professor Hull wrote about entering a tunnel from which there is no possibility of finding a light at the end of it. A tunnel with no end. Terrifying. The stuff of nightmares.

He is watching me, I think, from under his mad thatch, and giving me time to assimilate some of this.

Eventually he asks, 'What about night vision?'

'I feel very unsafe – as if I'm stepping into deep space.'

'Use your phone to see at night in an emergency. There are gadgets you can buy, but don't rush. They aren't wonderful.' He retrieves another leaflet from a rack and adds it to the pile. 'Every single person is different. The retinal damage may develop very fast – meaning maybe a few months – or very slowly, over several years. It can slow down or speed up.' He swipes back some of the hair so that it sticks up briefly like a badly designed mullet. 'But I'm afraid you will be blind eventually.' The leaflets are being tapped into tidiness and he gives me a very direct look. 'You have five senses, Cass, and each of the other four will become more sensitive, more enhanced, better used. You have already told me you have a highly developed sense of smell. You will find that smell, sound, touch and taste will become your eyes. Wind, sunlight, your partner's skin, raindrops – they will begin to speak to you. You must develop your own strategies for coping, but believe me, you *can*. Blindness can be a curse or a blessing. It's up to you whether you choose to be a victim or a victor. There are blind skiers, mountain bikers, yachtsmen, acrobats and jugglers. Blind authors, painters, sculptors and musicians.'

He chuckles. 'There are no blind drivers on the roads, officially. And so far as I know, no blind surgeons, but there are blind doctors, lawyers and MPs.' His chaotic haircut flips towards me. 'You can do whatever you want to do, with your eyes or without them. You will have to work harder, change your methods, change your mindset, that's all.' His face compresses into a thoughtful frown. 'Now. We could think about treatment if any.'

'But I thought there was no treatment!' Am I in the same hospital which just a month ago told me I was a hopeless case?

'Oh, there are treatments. Just no cure. Yet. And most treatments are not proven and very expensive.' The hairy highland cow effect mesmerises me and I wonder how this eye specialist can see through it. 'As you know, the cataract in your right eye is more advanced than the one in your left. The left one is at medium to late development and could wait a while, but I think it best to deal with the ripe one now, on the NHS, so that you have the best sight you can get for as long as you can get it. There is an excellent eye hospital at Southampton General so you wouldn't need to trek up here to get it done.'

'Oh!' Such an insult to have cataracts in my thirties. 'Expensive treatments are not an option. I'm fresh out of cash and my business is on the brink of going under.' I give him a smile which feels a bit wobbly, steeling myself to think positively. 'Coping strategies are my best bet.'

So we discuss, among other things, Braille, and how long to learn it; dogs, and how much looking after they need; canes, people, and my remaining senses. Google dictation and text reading, Amazon Echo, computerised information delivery, RNIB gadgets. Overwhelmed almost to the point of tears by this deluge of material, I realise he has given me a full hour of his time.

'You will have many questions in due course, but probably not yet. When they come, make a note of them and either ring or ask me at our next meeting.' And with a cheery 'See you about a month after the cataract is done,' he sends me on my way.

I return to Winchester, dealing with my enlarged print emails on the way, revolving the oncoming disaster through the mush of my thoughts. There is a text from Dominic asking how the appointment went. I tell him about the mad hair, having the cataract done at Southampton General, the recovery time. Everything except confirmation of the diagnosis. I cannot bring myself to put my fingers on the letters, to text the truth, to allow the impossible to become possible.

Why should I have discovered the one person who could make me happy only to have to lose him?

But I must resist him. I must resist the magnetic pull of him, resist his kindness, resist his lovely company, the enjoyment of just being with him, the fascination of learning about strange things from him. Resist his body and his lovemaking. Because I know, with terrifying certainty, that in the short time we have been lovers, he loves me too. Loves me as I love him. I love him enough to prevent him from being shackled to a blind woman becoming dependent, not independent. I will be a liability, not an asset. I will become my mother. There will be a repeat of my parents. I love him too much to allow him to go further down this road and I must erect a Stop barrier.

Even as I think it, I have no idea how to do it. When you love someone, it is unbearable to hurt them, and I have never been down this road before.

* * *

Dominic gets back from his office and while he is changing into cooler clothes, I bring mugs of tea and melty chocolate chip cookies into the garden. The grass scritches on my bare feet but under his apple tree it is softer and cooler. The smells are of hot dehydrated summer, spiky and brown. It is a recipe for happiness, and I am utterly miserable. I cannot put this off any longer because courage and willpower are oozing out of me like toothpaste from a squashed tube.

I take a deep breath. 'I've been thinking. I've changed my mind about your investment offer. I don't want to give away any of Ecolore's value, and I am certain that I couldn't repay the loan within the contractual period.' He has his mug in one hand and his chin in the other.

'I see,' he says. His calmness throws me into internal agitation. 'Are you saying that the figures you gave us are inaccurate?'

'No. I just think it's the wrong thing.'

He pauses for a moment, puzzled. 'OK. You must have a reason to think that. Is this something to do with our relationship? Mixing business with personal?'

That assessing gaze is directed straight at me. He has the ability to pull back the curtains on my soul and peer inside, but I can and must draw the curtains again.

'Yes, partly. I now think it's wrong for the business and wrong for us.' I have to heave in oxygen before I can verbalise what must be said. 'I've changed my mind about us. I'm sorry. Really sorry.'

'Changed your mind about *us*? What does that mean? And sorry about what?' There is bewilderment in his voice as he asks me to explain the unexplainable.

I can't explain. 'It's not ethical. Being together. I'm going to go back to the flat.'

He doesn't say anything for a few moments. 'But if there's no business arrangement there's nothing unethical about us being together, is there?' That penetrating gaze pins me down, and I am unable to articulate anything else.

When I don't answer he pushes. 'Cass, you can't just say you've changed your mind about us, with no explanation. What about us? You don't want to be here with me? You want to live independently? You suddenly don't love me as you said you did?'

Tears are pricking. None of those things. I want to be with you, to be part of you. I love you more than you could ever know, and all of this is unexplainable.

'I have to go. I'm not what you need. I'm exactly what you don't need.'

There is sharpness behind the confusion. 'Why are we talking about need? I love you. Is this coming from Mike? Are you going back to Mike?'

'Oh! No! Of course not.' What an appalling thought.

'Then it's what? You suddenly don't fancy me? You've found someone else? The boring banker really is too boring?' I can feel his hurt. 'You want to leave me?'

I must back off from Dominic. We fell in love, and now we must fall out of it. It must be done but it can't be done nicely. So I do it nastily. Like cutting off a gangrenous leg to save the rest of the body.

'All of that, yes.'

He is staring at me in disbelief. The garden is suddenly noisy with birds, the rustle of dry leaves and the sound of traffic beyond the house, but our own silence is profound.

When he speaks his voice is jagged. 'Is this something to do with Moorfields?' I shake my head and don't look at him.

'Cass,' he says, not sharp now but quiet. 'Is this to do with your appointment today? I know there's something wrong with your eyes. It's not a cataract, which is not serious. It's something else which is serious. You don't see much at the side – you have to turn your head and look directly at something. What is it?' I bury my face in my tea.

'Darling girl, ever since your first appointment you have not been – you. You've been bright and witty and superficial. Underneath you're unhappy and, I think, frightened. You don't have the joy you used to. Now you're desperate and I know you lie awake half the night. But I don't believe you've fallen in love with the consultant. I think you've had news that you haven't shared with me, for whatever reason.'

I can't manage to hold it together any longer, so I leap up, grab the biscuit plate and leg it to the kitchen, then lock myself in the downstairs loo. What the hell am I to do? I can't even walk out on a man successfully. If I tell him the truth, he will either try to keep me and end up hating the burden I will become, or he will do the sensible thing and let me go. It's one thing for me to leave, like I left home, like I left Mike, but something quite different if he lets me go like my father did. I will be lost forever as if I've stepped out of a spacecraft without any means of getting back in again. Floating helplessly in deep dark space while he shoots off to distant galaxies.

I realise that I've been sitting on the loo for ages and pull myself together. I can't live the rest of my life here.

I will tell him I'm leaving, and then I'll leave. The logistics of moving my life again flit across my brain. A great many of my possessions are in Dominic's spare room, having seeped in by degrees. Two suitcases are not going to be sufficient.

He is sitting in his favourite armchair. Head back. Not reading, not doing anything, except thinking that hysterical women are a total pain, dramatising life as if they were being slowly boiled to death.

I am not going to be a hysterical woman. I am going to be calm and sensible and firm. I sit opposite him, gripping my hands between my knees.

'I am deeply sorry to do this. You've been so kind, and I really, really appreciate it. But I've made up my mind, and I have to leave. Please don't argue. Please make it easy for me. Something we can always remember as good times, without it ending badly.'

He is turning his mobile end to end on the arm of his chair. Round and round, thumb and middle finger swinging it face to back, to face to back, the grey eyes direct and sad.

'You're not going to tell me what's wrong?'

'No.' I can't hold his eyes. 'Nothing's wrong.'

Again, that noisy silence, hot air dancing. I can smell the summer scents, mown grass, pollen, flowers, hot tarmac. A kaleidoscope of colour. Dominic is very still.

'Can we remain friends?' I sound desperate. I'm walking on dangerous ground. Mines underfoot. Red flags waving. A clean break is what is required, not a daily ripping off of the scab, but to lose him as a friend as well as a lover is more than my heart can take.

'I have no idea,' he says slowly. 'But the nature of friendship means there has to be trust and truth, and at this moment you are giving me neither.'

* * *

The horrible Mike episode. How to manage my business without Dominic's investment. How to cope with going blind. All of that is wiped off my brain at the prospect of leaving Dominic. No doubt it will all pop out into the here and now, unexpectedly and painfully, like a bulging hiatus hernia, but at this moment it is all totally irrelevant.

How on earth can I leave him. How will I live without him, without his voice, his touch, his slow smile, his grey eyes caressing me?

I pack, supplementing my two suitcases with a lot of black bin bags, and spend a sleepless night in his spare room. In the morning Dominic goes to his office early. He moves past me without even a peck on the cheek and mumbles, 'Bye, Cass. Take care.'

Are you trying not to cry too? Touch me, please. Why don't you try to persuade me to stay? Say you forgive me. Am I so easily let go? I am too wrung out to even speak. My hands are gripped together behind my back in case I try to hold onto him. Desolation greater than anything I have ever experienced fills me. I asked him not to stop me from leaving and he hasn't stopped me. This is my doing, my fault, my actions, my words.

His hurt at my unexplained withdrawal is an agony. How can I have done that? How can I possibly have let him go? Why did I have to hurt the one person who I would never in a million years want to hurt?

Chapter Twenty-Two

Even though I have been back in the flat for nearly a month, it is still a meaningless, unwelcoming space. The silence of just me is like a weight of water, thick and heavy, obscure and impenetrable. My work is here, my food, my bed, my possessions, but my soul is somewhere else. I may live here, but I am in Dominic's house, in his amber-smelling bedroom, straightening the amber-smelling duvet, plumping the amber-smelling pillows. I see his pen and notepad and the pile of books on the bedside table, and on his chest of drawers the little bowl which Patrick made for him in kindergarten where he drops his loose change every evening. I am in the old-fashioned avocado bathroom with its wicker laundry bin and cork-topped stool. I am cooking lemon and garlic chicken for supper, in a frying pan which is losing its non-stick, pouring a glass of wine, touching mine to his, receiving that slow smile, giving him my flashing one. He is the other half of me and without him, I only half exist.

Zev may have got my company back in my name, but I know that unless I pull myself together there won't be any income. Somehow, I have to get my thought processes into work mode. High summer is not the time to sell designs, nor to sell a property – everybody seems to have gone on holiday including Wendy, although it won't be a holiday coping with her still grieving mother. Wendy seems taut with worry, and I know it's caused by me.

'I am not going to do anything daft because of this,' I tell her robustly. 'Go and have a good time with your mum and forget about me being left miserably alone for a whole week, weeping into the gin and lying in a bus lane.' We both grin at each other. I know she feels better when I take the mickey. 'I truly do have a lot to do to get this business up and running again, and I'll do it a darn sight quicker without you distracting me.' She goes, still worried, and rings every morning to check that my speech is not slurred.

Today, after updating my website, I embark on carefully selected overdue payments. I don't have Vermont and Paget's money to fall back on, but much worse, I don't have Dominic, and I physically ache with longing and unhappiness. There doesn't seem to be a single moment when my mind is not on him, his scent floats in my nostrils in a kind of hallucinatory amber cloud, and my clouded eyes see him clearly at street corners, reflected in the delicatessen window, in passing taxis. This obsession threatens my ability to think and plan and I am almost frightened by it. It gets no better, only worse. Planning my outfits has lost its sparkle, I am apathetic about my hair and can't see well enough to do my make-up and nails.

There is no word from Dominic, even as a friend, and I do not have the courage to contact him after what I have done. I feel inexplicably abandoned; but after all, it was me who abandoned him. It was me who did not give him truth or trust.

* * *

By the end of the week, I am determined to be more positive. I am going to make a new mental start. Ecolore must survive without money, and I must survive without Dominic. I must survive being blind. I must survive. I will survive.

Turning off my phone, I settle down again at my desk and to my surprise achieve urgent lampshade designs by midday, although the design software is rather less defined than it used to be. Every time I log on to any device, I reposition my glasses, move my head so that I look directly at an object, turn my head to avoid the cataract cloud, check the perimeter, peer in close, and stand away. I wish I could have contact lenses again as the glasses are less than helpful. Checking my messages, Wendy is back and suggests meeting for lunch, and as my mid-morning carrot cake has given way to lunch hunger, I text agreement.

I trip up – thankfully not down – the restaurant steps. Was it just a trip, or did I not see the change in level? Usually, I am careful to watch where I'm placing my feet. I ignore the humiliation of splattering myself at ground level and will put leg make-up on to cover the grazes. I hope the cataract op will make a difference, that it will disperse the dirty mist that obscures the clarity of my increasingly limited sight. I am now impatient to have it done, to use every available pixel, to sharpen what is inside that misshapen circle.

Wendy casts a jaundiced eye over my lasagne as she eats her pathetic little salad. 'You really do deserve to be my size,' she says sourly. 'It is so unfair. The less I eat the larger I get.'

'The more I eat the hungrier I get. All this walking is making me even hungrier so I'm not taking any weight off.'

'Oh, you're losing weight all right.' I look at her solemn expression in surprise. 'All this hassle with Mike and the RP and your face has gone all pinched and bony.'

It's not the hassle of Mike or the RP. It's the loss of Dominic.

'Well, thanks for the compliment. Pinched and bony sounds so attractive. There are other ways of describing it, like "interesting cheekbones".'

'Pff.' She is dismissive. 'It's only my jealousy. Has there been any interest in your car then?'

'Nobody wants to buy a pink car covered in the Ecolore logo.' I wave my fork at her. 'Might it be possible for you to take me to Southampton General next Monday for this cataract op? It's hideously early I'm afraid. And collect me? I can easily get a taxi, but every time I do, I remember I'm spending money I shouldn't be.'

'That is just so inconvenient. I was planning to sleep in all morning on Monday.'

'You're a star. And you are hopeless at sarcasm. I don't know what time I'll be out though.'

She shrugs. 'Call me fifteen minutes before they let you leave.'

I close my eyes briefly. 'What did I ever do to deserve you? Would you like some of my lasagne as a reward?'

'Yes, but no thank you.' Her self-control is astonishing. 'Talking of this cataract op, why didn't you tell Dominic Paget your RP diagnosis?'

'Why do you think?'

'No idea. Well, there are some possibilities, I suppose.' I tilt my head in a 'such as?' expression.

'You still think that being involved with a blind woman would be bad news for him?'

'Yeah. Don't you? How would he extricate himself from that? He's not like Mike, who would just walk away. He would feel responsible. Obligated. Kind.'

'You think he might feel sorry for you.' She absorbs my crossness. 'You don't like people feeling sorry for you.'

'Quite.'

'Perhaps he wouldn't want to extricate himself.'

'Look. You're the man-hater. You said all men are like Mike. Of course he'd want to get out.'

She is quiet for a while. 'I don't know. I like him.'

'I like him too.'

In the afternoon, morale boosted by sending off the lampshade designs to the manufacturer, I do some serious and overdue financial calculations. After calculating three months' outgoings and worst case scenario three months' income, I know caution must be the order of the day. I tell some of my clients that I will not be restocking for them unless they can give me guaranteed sales, though this may mean I lose customers. My future projects, in particular the carpets, mean that I have bitten off far more than I can chew, and the lawyers' fees are huge. Too big a step for a small ripped-off business. My current account is at virtual zero. Though I am deeply reluctant to do so, I substantially reduce the carpet colour series. Even so, the figures are quite enough to bring me out in a cold sweat despite the heat. It is quite a gamble. And I have no idea how soon, if ever, I can recoup any of it. I should have been marketing it for weeks, and I have done virtually nothing. Gathering myself and my calculations together, I ring the carpet manufacturers and schedule a meeting with the managing director.

Chapter Twenty-Three

Surprisingly, Zev emails to say he's having a barbecue, do come. My state of mind wants to dig myself a hole and get buried, but I accept the invitation because you can't exist for long in a hole.

He lives in a little Queen Anne village house overlooking the Test south of Stockbridge, which seems quite out of character with his debonair urban persona. The Uber driver is impressed by its charm, but for me, it is uncomfortably rural. There are horses in the field at the bottom of the garden and a group of unknowns leaning on the fence looking at them. Zev and Sam are poking at the newly lit barbecue and carting bottles and glasses around.

'Cass! How lovely to see you.' Zev looks utterly edible, in a pair of dark jeans and a white T-shirt, with deck shoes on sockless tanned feet. His skin is walnut brown, smooth and well-muscled. 'Let me introduce you, while Sam gets you a drink.'

Sam puts a drink into my hand, and I see his bald patch is already sunburned.

'Sam, do I know you well enough to suggest a sun hat?'

He grins. 'I need to borrow one of your wigs. A green one, I think. Do I know you well enough to tell you that before Mike's party Zev described you as a walking plastic bottle?' His eyes are twinkling up at me. 'In fact,' he continues, 'I've never seen anyone look less like a plastic bottle. Don't go anywhere near my horses in that outfit though.'

I laugh. I am wearing scarlet cut-off dungarees with recycled glass decorations all over them, which make me twinkle like a disco ball. 'I'm so glad I don't look like a plastic bottle. It would be too awful to look like one's product! Are all those beautiful horses yours?'

I suddenly smell amber. I can't see him, but I know he's there. Electricity fizzes up my arms and hits me in the chest, expelling all the air. When I gather the courage to glance around, I find him deep in conversation with two women and he looks like his usual relaxed and charming self. Pure jealousy burns in me.

Sam thankfully has turned towards the horses, explaining that they belong to him and his sister who lives up the road and that's her in jeans and a green shirt leaning on the fence. He tells me that he and Zev have been together for eight years and that they bought this house together. I am going through the motions of listening and responding, but it is only Dominic I am aware of. Sam reintroduces me to a couple of girls, starting the conversation rolling before going off to pour more drinks. I wonder if I am making sense or whether I am an inarticulate mess. It had never crossed my mind that Dominic might be here, but of course, he and Zev are long-time friends.

I see Dominic heading towards me and my heart jams itself into my throat, cutting off all the oxygen as I try to stuff it back where it belongs. I force myself to meet his eyes, expecting either hurt or contempt but see instead the old familiar tender smile. My glass seems to be leaking over my fingers and I am leaking perspiration. The scent of amber washes over me again and my teeth nearly go through my bottom lip.

'Hello, Cass. You're never going to melt into the crowd!' While I struggle to articulate anything beyond a croak, he entertains the two girls with an informative explanation of Ecolore and my planet-saving objectives as I try to recover my equilibrium. Somehow, he manoeuvres us into a twosome and we ascertain that each of us is OK.

'I've missed you. Are you all right?'

Nothing to what I've missed, and no, I'm not all right. I am in splinters. I am unable to move or speak or think. I must appear hypnotised like the rabbit in headlights. Dominic is looking at me with that crooked half smile that ties my stomach up in tangles of desire and love.

I manage, 'I'm fine thanks. Busy.'

There is a Jane Austen-type silence between us. He puts out a hand and I know that when he touches me all the splinters will explode. But he doesn't touch me, he only carefully tips my glass upright in my petrified fingers.

'You're spilling champagne all down your beautiful outfit.'

After a stilted conversation, Dominic introduces me to some man and goes off to chat with lots of people he obviously knows. I have drunk my champagne as if it was orange juice and feel as if my brain has been sucked out with a straw.

It's a lovely party, and I feel totally wretched. At the end, someone gives me a lift back to the flat. But it isn't Dominic.

Chapter Twenty-Four

The weather has suddenly broken into cold wind and rain, paralleling my mood. The earlier heatwave is a dim and distant memory. The leaves which fell in the heat are cluttering the gutters and smell robin redbreast red and there are eddies of steel blue and copper green in the air as if autumn were already here. I miss Dominic with peculiar intensity.

On the National Health, you must take your operation date when they offer it, however inconvenient. Just because I am going through my worst life crisis, it's not a reason to quibble about a date. In some seldom-opened cupboard in my mind, I see an eye surgeon wielding a laser in an unsteady hungover hand, going just that little bit too deep, cutting not just the lens, but back into the retina. There is not a gradual descent into dusk, but sudden total darkness. I start to concentrate on deep breathing, on emptying my lungs before inhaling, on telling myself that they are only doing one eye, not both, and that I will see more clearly after it.

And on Monday, the surgeon seems delighted with his efforts, and I am almost persuaded that my sight will improve radically, that all my problems will be solved. The efficient conveyor belt spits me out, armed with bottles of eye drops and an elegant white plastic eye protector held in place by white masking tape crisscrossed from forehead to cheekbone. How extraordinary that they can chop a lens out with a laser without you feeling a thing.

Wendy brought me here, make-up-less, at some unearthly hour of the morning, and now she is here again, to take me back to her house. Friends are the most valuable asset a girl can have, and I tell her so.

The following morning the eye cover comes off and vision is just as blurry. If not more so.

'Stop whinging, girl. Of course it's blurry. I've never known anyone who expected so much so quickly.' She puts the bottle of drops into my hand. 'Three drops and I'm watching you. You must learn to be patient.'

Wendy ensures the cover goes back on at night and I stay indoors as the surgeon had wagged his finger at me and said, 'No make-up! And definitely no eye make-up for at least two weeks. Not until I say so.' The thought of being in public without make-up is not good.

Next lunchtime Wendy reluctantly takes me back to the flat, after I have promised faithfully to put the drops in and do what the doctor ordered.

'I absolutely must do the invoicing. They all make good use of the twenty-eight days' grace, and I need every penny as soon as I can legally get it. You know the bank won't deviate from their interest charges on the overdraft.'

'You're an idiot to have turned down Vermont and Paget,' she says with a sniff as I turn the key and open the flat door.

We both stand there, speechless. Frozen with astonishment.

* * *

Without my glasses, my one remaining eye is hopelessly distorted and unfocused, but even that one eye can see that there is not a stitch of furniture in the place. The empty hall gapes onto the empty sitting room, the curtainless windows, the bare boards of the floor. This is how it looked six years ago, exciting, beckoning, the opportunity for us to shape it and bend it to our will, our taste. Well, Mike's taste as it happened. I am so astonished that I begin to laugh.

Wendy isn't laughing. 'The rotten little bastard!'

I sober up as the seriousness of the situation hits me. 'Do you think he's left me my office?'

But I think that my business files are intact even though they are on the floor as the free-standing shelves have gone.

Wendy is furious. 'He knew the police really would have come down heavy on him if he'd taken your company.'

'He's taken everything moveable, even though I paid for much of it. Thank God for fitted cupboards!' I walk into the master bedroom to find the bedding on the floor but no bed, and no other furniture. It takes a moment to register.

'Oh, Wendy! He's taken Ugly!' An entirely strange sensation overtakes me – disbelief, panic, pain – for something which was virtually valueless and supremely hideous. 'It's the only thing of hers I've got.' This is not just shock, but an inexplicable sense of loss, a tie from the dead to the living undone, a root of belonging cut. 'It was Victorian and awful, but it was hers, and my grandfather's before her.' My one eye can't see anything now for tears of outrage. 'And what is more, it was full. The drawers were stuffed with all my things. He can't have taken it without emptying the drawers, surely!'

But he had. All my memory boxes. Batteries and belts, tools and costume jewellery, old letters and school certificates, and the few photo albums that Mum had made. An entire lifetime. All my sewing kit, the curtain hooks and tape, the buttons, a million coloured cotton reels. And paperwork, old bank statements, receipts and guarantees, personal stuff I didn't get mixed in with business stuff. And those receipts of Mike's.

Flopping down on the duvet on the floor I shamingly blurt out 'I want Dominic' in exactly the same way as a small child demands Mummy. This is so appallingly pathetic that I am galvanised into action. I stumble upstairs, and Susan Mayhew comes into her own by remembering the name on the furniture van. Oh, blessed curtain twitcher! She doesn't remember seeing Mike. The removals company confirm they have collected a load from our address but refuse to divulge anything else. I ring Mike's office but am told he no longer works for the company. This is not a surprise, but it is frustrating.

The doorbell rings and I am taken aback to find Dominic on the doorstep. In fact, I am paralysed, in both speech and movement.

'Hi, Cass. Wendy phoned me. Saying you have a problem,' he says laconically, moving forwards. Only the likelihood that he will touch me ends the paralysis and I leap back in soundless alarm. Can I throw myself into his arms? No. Do I look cool and cucumberish? No. Do I look elegant, nicely made up, with interesting nails and glossy hair? No.

'You look as if you've been in a punch-up.' This is not lover-like and I'm not even sure it is friendly. He is irritatingly brisk in the face of the end of my world, but I would bawl him out if he showed compassion, let alone pity, and he probably doesn't want to be bawled out. After ascertaining some basic requirements, he takes himself off again. When I go to the bathroom to put my drops in, the distorted vision of myself in the mirror makes me recoil in horror. I do indeed look as if I've been in a punch-up.

'You said you wanted him!' Wendy exclaims with ridiculous on-purpose misunderstanding when I hiss invective at her.

Dominic eventually returns with some IKEA flat packs, by which time I have got over my paralysis and found my voice again.

'If I'd known, I'd have opened those bags of prawns in the curtains. And put fish down the coffee table legs and chicken livers in the brass bar on his silent valet.'

Wendy rolls her eyes. I don't know what Dominic does, as I don't look at him. We start cutting open packs and putting a desk and chair together. I mention petulantly that he hasn't brought back a bed.

'Even if I'd found one, I wouldn't have got it in the car,' he says defensively. 'You'll just have to sleep on the floor.'

Wendy adds grimly, 'With the spiders.'

This time I steal a glance at Dominic who grins. 'Don't worry. You won't even see them in your present condition.'

* * *

Later, as he puts the shelving system together, with Wendy reading him instructions on what order to insert which screws, he suggests trying to find Laura, who might know where the furniture had gone to.

'She won't be there,' I say. 'She'll have absconded with Mike. But I suppose the office might tell me something.' I ring again, with no expectations.

'Could I speak to Laura Beauchamp please?'

To my total astonishment, the receptionist says, 'Hold on please, I'll put you through.' Good grief, she never even asked my name, or what my business was. Very sloppy. I hang up quick. My brain isn't functioning well enough to speak to her at this moment.

'The furniture might be in Laura's house,' Wendy says, handing Dominic the Allen key.

'By the time I'm finished with her, she'll wish she'd never set eyes on either Mike or the furniture,' I say grimly.

When I ring Laura later in the evening, she sounds embarrassed rather than angry.

'Oh. Was it you who rang and then rang off? I should have contacted you ages ago, but I lost my nerve. I felt such a fool.' I don't quite understand this, but her reaction has taken the wind out of my sails. I switch to loudspeaker so Dominic and Wendy can hear. They are both still trying to make the flat habitable.

'I'm so sorry. You have no idea how sorry I am,' she says, and I'm baffled by the apology. 'I took everything he said for the truth. How you took his money, how you bullied him into buying expensive clothes, and the Aston, and making expensive alterations to the flat.' She stammers to a halt, breathing heavily.

'Well, it's the furniture I'm ringing about. Do you know where it is?'

'The furniture? What furniture?' She sounds genuinely confused.

'The flat furniture. Quite apart from the fact that I paid for most of it, Mike has removed it all, my own personal possessions included. And the bed. Isn't it in your house?'

'No! Of course not! My house is tiny! I have no idea where it is.' She is astounded. 'He said you had taken all his mortgage contributions but only put your name on the deeds, so you'd stolen his flat and all its contents as well, and he had nowhere to go. I felt really sorry for him. He was so gentle and kind and unhappy and homeless. He said you had stolen all his money.'

Oh, good Lord! How can two intelligent women possibly have been conned by this inveterate liar? I glance blearily at my two good friends. Wendy's hands are clutched dramatically to her head, and Dominic is taking files off the office floor and putting them neatly on the new shelving. I can't evaluate his expression but he is shaking his head in an 'I can't believe what I'm hearing' way.

Laura hasn't finished. 'After the party, he was very twitchy. Telephones, the doorbell, letters even, made him jumpy. There was a lot of shouting about how you had ruined his life. That was the point when I began to – you know. Go off him.' Her voice cracked slightly. 'He shouted at me as if it was my fault. He was quite scary.'

By this time, I am squirming with guilt. Laura is never going to swim in my pond, but I recognise that she was caught in the same net as me.

'And then the police came to the office and started interviewing everyone.' She sounds utterly defeated. 'They wanted to interview Mike too, but by then he had disappeared.'

'Disappeared? Where to?'

She sighed. 'I don't know. He just didn't come back. No one at the office knows where he is, and his clients are rattling the bars. I assumed you and he had concocted the whole thing between you and had gone off somewhere together.'

Two women made fools of by the same man. We exchange email addresses for future information.

* * *

We are all exhausted from installing basic furniture and my eyes hurt. Dominic gives me a friendly goodbye peck on the cheek which doesn't have the plastic cover on it while my head is screaming for a full-blown lovers' kiss. Wendy carts me back to her house again and puts me to bed. I haven't even started on the invoices.

The next day I get an email from Laura. 'The police handed back his laptop. The furniture went to a storage facility attached to an auction house called Wedbury and Burton.'

A phone call to Wedbury and Burton has the usual effect of no information being forthcoming. I am going to have to be more subtle about my inquiries. Everything I do now takes twice as long, as my glasses only work with one eye, and the optician won't do another lens for two months to let it 'settle down'. Infuriated, I send for an expensive low vision reading magnifier.

Wendy has taken it upon herself to inform Dominic of progress and to my vexation and slight alarm she has accepted his offer to drive us to Wedbury and Burton's storage. How should I behave with him? He is so 'just friendly' that I can't bring myself to be either apologetic or offhand. Has he forgotten what it was like to lie in bed together, long lazy foreplay, making love, the murmuring gentleness of the aftermath? I want to weep with frustration but manage to be 'just friendly'.

Wedbury and Burton's premises are a complex of red brick barns surrounding a large, gravelled turning space, in which two enormous furniture vans are manoeuvring through torrential rain. Wendy and Dominic make a dash into the cavernous auction room to inspect the acres of junk while I do the preliminaries with the lady behind the reception desk who is harassed by swarms of dripping interrogators. There is no record of Michael Benton storing or selling furniture and behind me are two van drivers who need to unload, and where, please.

I escape back into rain so cold it is nearly sleet, leaving Wendy and Dominic still ogling appalling pictures and crates of costume jewellery and chipped crockery, but I am looking at one of the big barns whose double doors are open at an angle of about forty-five degrees. Behind them is a tall, shadowy mass of dark wood furniture. Crossing the puddled yellow hoggin in the pouring rain, I poke my head into a badly lit warehouse piled high with stuff which by rights should have been bonfire material years ago. The smell is as dull brown as the contents: dust, ancient sweat, rancid polish. There is no one in sight and I creep off down a narrow alley between wood-wormy chests of drawers and tables Olympic-ringed by ancient mugs. Every item has a hieroglyphed luggage label attached. With my limited one-eyed vision would I spot Mike's antiques in all this tat? I turn myself half upside down to peer at hidden coffee tables and rickety chairs along the myriad alleys, but of small black Victorian drawered cabinets there is not a sign.

'Cun I 'elp yer?' The voice is not helpful, but suspicious, and when I get vertical, it belongs to a small, weaselly man with greasy grey hair and a dry tufty grey face. He smells the colour of wet leather. 'This storge ain't fer t'public.'

'I called,' I say untruthfully. 'And nobody answered. I was told to come and look, but I haven't found my furniture and it's much better quality than anything in here.'

The tufty beard juts at me dubiously. 'Wrong place. Who told yer?'

I tilt my head towards the main building. 'Some chap over there.'

He sniffs, a filthy hand rasping across dripping nostrils. 'Stupid sods. Quality stuff ain't here. Got a docket then?'

'He didn't give me a docket,' I say irritably. 'Just said "It's over there".' Over his shoulder, I can see Wendy and Dominic approaching and hope they won't say anything truthful. 'Is there more storage for better furniture?'

'Yerse. Next door. Should have a docket.'

'Well, he didn't even mention it.' This time I drop my shoulders with an exhausted sigh. 'I just want to check if some particular items are here or not. I'll recognise the pieces immediately. Can we forgo the docket this once, considering the weather and everything?' I indicate my partners in crime. 'My friends here know what we're looking for, so we'll be even quicker.'

His whole face slips stubbornly sideways. 'Must have a docket. Match the name see.'

'That, unfortunately, is the problem. We think it came

in under the wrong name. It was all going to different people at different destinations and some things didn't arrive where they should have and maybe ended up here for auction when they shouldn't have. We know some of the names but not all, but we can recognise the furniture you see, and then I can contact …'

Thank God he gives in before I run out of fatuous lies. He shuffles off towards the doors, blowing his cheeks out in a stupid bloody woman expression, and locks them behind us. Wendy and Dominic detour around a large puddle but my combat boots follow doggedly in his gaitered footsteps across a sleety gap between buildings to an altogether more upmarket storage facility. Obviously, docketless women are highly suspicious so he keeps a sharp eye on us until our paths diverge to such an extent that he can no longer split his chaperonage.

There is a faint shriek from the interior. 'Found them!' Good for Wendy.

There are the sofas and the coffee table. There is the rosewood chest of drawers, the side tables, the chairs, the bookcases, the old banking desk, the rugs, and the curtains, complete, I assume, with their bags of prawns. And there is my Victorian cabinet. I yell with triumph and open the top drawer, thankfully and amazingly still full of my boxes.

Every label's hieroglyphics include W Davies. Who the hell is W Davies?

'Where are the pictures? Have they been sold already?' Those horrible black daubs cost me a fortune and I'd like to recoup some of it.

The old man indicates the deeper recesses of the unit. 'Kept in back.' He peers at the labels. This lot's fer next sales.' He sputters a smoker's cough and I step back from both smell and spray.

'Which are when?' asks Dominic sensibly.

'Toosday next, furniture. Froiday next, ceramics.

Tursday fortnoight, pictures. You done? Want to find them pictures?'

All the labels on the pictures are W Davies.

'Who'd *buy* these?' I ask. The unframed black abstracts look much worse here than they did in the flat.

'Not me,' Wendy says. 'Not anyone in their right mind.'

'They'll sell all right,' our minder says sourly. 'One man's poison. S'long as there's no reserve. They want canvases and frames. ''E'll get fifty quid maybe.'

'Blimey! He paid thousands!' Well, I did.

'Wassa problem wiv der name?' Back in suspicion mode again.

'Wrong one,' says I. 'Should be C Hunter, not W Davies. I'll be sorting it out with your boss. And that cabinet shouldn't be here at all. It's mine and full of my things and got taken by mistake.' Possibly taken by mistake. Or possibly not by mistake. I check the other drawers and they are as full of my beloved tat as they ever were.

'Yer can't take it without a docket,' Minder says morosely, and to all our relief shuffles off. We hear him coughing his way out.

'You bet I can,' I say forcefully.

'I think,' Dominic says to Wendy, 'that as sober citizens we should leave Cass to break the law.'

I do the sorting. I check the sale reserves, get a copy of the list, and note that sale receipts are going to W Davies at an address, which I note down for the police should they be interested, in Essaouira in Morocco. I don't really care anymore whether the police follow up on W Davies or not, but I do want Ugly back and after enough fuss to make Wedbury and Burton fear for their reputation, I am allowed to take it home.

Sorting the problem seems simple really, as I divert the Morocco address to my own in Southampton and monies to W Davies care of C Hunter.

W Davies even gets a new email address because someone has hacked his old one. Abroad is too complicated for W Davies, I tell the boss.

My triumph is obvious, combat boots dancing up and down in the puddles, and Dominic says, 'Do not tell us what you did, or how you did it. And if Ugly is going to be stuffed into my car, we'll have to put the back seats down and stuff you in beside it. Woe betide you if we get stopped by the police for you not wearing a seat belt.' Ugly is full and extremely heavy and we both get soaked during the loading operation.

He pulls up at an off-licence and buys a bottle of victory champagne which we consume in the comfort of Wendy's sitting room. I can't keep the grin off my face and don't even worry about my one-eyed and make-up-less condition. When he goes home, I can't help but give him a smacking kiss along with my heartfelt thanks and I hope his quirky smile means we really are friends again and I have been forgiven.

Chapter Twenty-Five

But that's the last I hear from him for what feels like a millennium, and I am in an agony of exasperation, frustration, and vexation. Please, Dominic, text me. Send an email or a WhatsApp. Communicate dammit. Any minute now and I will follow up my thank you email with another one. And that will be chasing him. Harassment. Stalking. I'm angry about the fact that he is doing exactly what I asked him to do.

I don't even get to be tetchy with Wendy because I have moved back into the flat along with Mum's cabinet and am sleeping uncomfortably on a friend's camp bed with a mattress about three centimetres thick. It makes me so stiff that I am up by six and get a lot of slow work done. The cataract operation has certainly clarified what I see, but what I see is distorted, bounded by an uneven dark brown ring and is only directly in front of me. I mutter my mantra of all the things I'm grateful for, dividing my time into slots of invoicing, bookkeeping, bill paying, techy talk with nerdy students and scientists, website updates, the phone calls to outlets and manufacturers, and then release myself back into ideas mode and design.

Of course, this does not really work, and the road to a bust business is tarmacked with longings for a man who wanted me to stay and who I walked out on. He tramples in my mind, clumps about my brain, speaks in my memory, touches my body, kisses my lips. Stupid Cass, pride coming before bankruptcy.

In the middle of updating the website, the phone rings and it is Dominic. I am alarmed to be so ecstatic at hearing his voice and hope our conversation doesn't reveal my desperation.

After he has inquired about the furniture and the auction, he says, 'One of my god-daughters is going to be seven next week and as usual I haven't a clue about the appropriate present and you might solve my problem. Could you think of something brilliant and bring it next Saturday?'

He must be kidding!

'A present? For a seven-year-old? I haven't a clue either! My seventh birthday was thirty years ago, and my memory is poor. And I can't come on Saturday – I'm busy.'

'Doing what?'

I huff. 'I need to go buy some more cheap furniture. And the business is hanging on by its fingernails. And I'm having supper with a friend.'

'Well, that's OK then. I'll come and buy cheap furniture with you. This is a birthday lunch at Pizza Italia with Arabella and her parents. You've met her father, Peter Vermont, my business partner. I'll get you back in plenty of time for supper with a friend.'

I fell into that one, didn't I. 'But I haven't any idea what a seven-year-old might like.' Chippiness alternates with defeatism and self-hatred. This is exactly what I have been waiting for and now I'm being nasty again.

Needless to say, I end up agreeing. But if I'm honest, I agree because I want to agree. His absence has been like a tooth abscess and seeing him will be root canal treatment. Unless I see him, the tooth will die. I am going to fall to bits unless I see him.

I also remind myself that I should not turn down

networking opportunities. Dominic and his friends are from wealthy backgrounds and might invest, tell their friends, hand out my cards and flyers, and even buy. I bend my mind to seven-year-old aspirations and my lunch outfit.

My willpower is non-existent I realise. The spirit may be willing to forgo a good man, but the flesh is not.

* * *

He helps me cart some more enormously heavy flat packs back home. The bed is being delivered. It was much more fun shopping with Dominic than it would have been on my own. He doesn't object or criticise my taste and as a result of our labours we are nearly late for our lunch date, and the Vermont family is there before us. I am amused to find that I have met them all before.

Dominic obviously adores his god-daughter. 'For heaven's sake, girl, you'll squash me to death. Being seven is far too grown up! You're twice the height and twice the weight you were last week.'

When she lets go of him, I give her a big squeeze and then shake hands with her parents.

'Where's Cronk then?' I say to Arabella. 'Too cold to take him out? Especially as the coat has all those holes in it.'

Mum Jen blinks and then vaguely remembers a weird woman on a train. Dad and Dominic just blink and look bemused.

With much laughter, lots of 'what a coincidence' exclamations and while the pizza orders are sent to Italy by boat and train and come back about a year later, Dominic gives Arabella an Ecolore recycled plastic tote bag. He too is intrigued as to its contents because I wouldn't tell him what was in it.

While one small girl goes and experiments in the rain in a recycled plastic poncho with a matching tote and matching wellington boots, mother hovers protectively by the door and I discover that Peter is not only Dominic's partner, but also his first wife's brother, and they were at Oxford together. I have to rethink my first impression of him as a bad father.

'How could you have thrown Mr Bird to William?' I ask. 'Isn't that asking for trouble from a puppy?'

He looks mortified by my severity. 'Yes. Can't think how I can have been so stupid. Mr Bird was covered in grey rabbit fur and William reverted to his ancestors in about two seconds flat.'

'Well,' I say, 'the funeral went part-way towards reinstating you.'

'It was all very traumatic. But the funeral was excellent,' Dominic says. 'I never quite understood why Mr Bird was covered in rabbit fur.'

'Softer?' I suggest. 'Feathers would never stay on. Children would inhale them.' The waitress brings us more nibbles while we wait for the continental delivery and, as usual, I am hungry enough to eat the whole plateful, but just manage to be polite enough to pass it on.

Eventually, Italy delivers, and it is a merry lunch with the birthday girl obviously tickled pink with Uncle Dom's brilliant presents. Mum Jen picks up one of the discarded labels.

'So this is your business? Ecolore?' She flicks a smile in Dominic's direction. 'Now I get why he needed shoe size and height. Surely you don't make all these things yourself?'

I shake my head and explain how it all works. '… So the design is my copyright, and any changes are supposed to have my agreement and I should get the profit from them.'

I didn't mean to change the stress of my words, but she must have heard something in my tone because she turns her head towards me in interrogation. I laugh.

'Long story! It doesn't always happen like that.'

Jen seems intrigued by the sustainability aspect, but eventually a restless seven-year-old gets us all moving and we walk back to our respective destinations. I hear Jen's whisper reminding Arabella, in her new outfit, to thank Uncle Dom for her birthday presents, and she gives both Dominic and me a hug and a kiss as we part ways. I can see he really loves this little girl and although I don't know many children, I have a longing for more of the child's touch.

I stop in front of a little house which has enormous clumps of herbs growing next to the pavement, bursting with post-rain scents. Closing my eyes, my mind is soaked with colours, drunk with memories of Greek sage and thyme on holiday with Mike, guiding my blind mother through the water meadows along the River Itchen, the cool abrasive mint brushing our legs and flooding me with the smell of palest primrose, the moistness of spongy moss, of dragonflies and river weeds curling and streaming in the strong but unseen current. The woody, flowery oil of trailing rosemary, the prostrate plant which overflowed Mum's garden wall and spilled into the outside world, where strangers brushed against it and released the fragrant streams of blue, the exact colour of its flowers. I am not aware of the tears on my face until he says, 'You were crying when I first saw you.'

I swipe at my eyes and pull my fortifications around me. 'I was not. I was under the shower, and no one was looking at my face.'

'I was,' he says. 'And you were crying.'

Well, why don't you kiss me then? Say you love me. Touch my face, hold my hand.

'What utter rubbish. I don't cry. And what is more, you were sniggering afterwards.'

He protests. 'They were. I wasn't.'

Damn you, Dominic, just lay a finger on my skin and I'll come crawling. 'Well, you would say that, wouldn't you?'

'I wasn't because you were crying.'

I'm not going to admit to being weak. I'm not having him feel sorry for me. And I can't let him see what I'm feeling inside.

Turning towards the station, I squint up at the overcast sky. 'I must go. I've got to work out how much stock I can keep at the flat and that won't happen unless I go and do it. Saturday may be a weekend for most of the world, but sadly, not for me.' The petulance in my voice must be as obvious to him as it is to me.

'I'll drive you,' he says quietly. I think he's hurt and my throat thickens.

'No,' I snap. 'I'll take the train.' This isn't how I wanted the day to end. The lunch, Arabella's pleasure at her birthday present. Time, precious time, with Dominic, which I was now busy spoiling.

He shrugs helplessly. 'OK, if that's how you want it.' He turns with the obvious intention of walking me there. For heaven's sake, Dominic, tell me off, slap me down, get angry, don't be so nice. I don't deserve niceness when I'm so nasty, and I don't know why revealing weakness should be so difficult or make me so unpleasant.

'You don't need to come to the station.' My ungraciousness is awful and I try to mitigate my bad manners. 'You'll get so wet and you're nearly home now. After all you've done for me this morning you must be longing to sit down and watch the cricket – really, you don't need to come.' I see his shoulders drop a little. 'It was a great pizza and sticky toffee pudding and I think Arabella loved your brilliant presents.'

There's a little half smile as he acknowledges what is meant to be an apology.

'I think she did.' He inclines his head to give me a faint

but friendly kiss on the cheek. 'Have a lovely supper with your friend.'

Why do I get the feeling he knows both friend and supper are a figment of my imagination?

My sadness at having spoiled something precious knows no bounds and I stare unfocused out of the train window wanting to rewind, craving to take back words which can't be recalled.

Chapter Twenty-Six

He had texted a thank you for choosing Arabella's present and I had drafted an apology for my bad manners and then not sent it. In the end, I just texted*, 'Thanks for lunch and the furniture. Sorry I had to go.'* Poor Wendy has been the patient recipient of an outpouring of self-hatred. Even the laying of my new carpet has failed to raise my spirits.

He phones, as if I had done nothing to be embarrassed or ashamed about. I am learning a bit about not taking offence because it is a personality trait in Dominic that is very attractive.

'I met your father yesterday,' he says in a matter-of-fact tone of voice.

'Really?' I'm knocked sideways by his phone call, but even more shocked by this news. 'Where?'

'Here. In Winchester. He lives here apparently.'

I don't know why I should be so surprised as we have always lived in Hampshire, and he used to have an office in Basingstoke. Alarm that I might have bumped into him while walking the streets of Winchester seizes me and Southampton suddenly seems a much safer place.

'How? I mean, how did you know it was my father?' There is an odd feeling in my stomach, like a lift dropping.

'I was having lunch in a restaurant, and he knew my lunch guest and she introduced us.' A totally unexpected sensation of dismay hits me. *She?* Who? Surely, I didn't say that out loud. 'The surname Hunter—' Dominic goes on.

'—is very common!' Did I shout? 'How on earth did you discover he was my father?' I hope my voice has returned to its normal pitch. 'I can't believe you said, "Oh, I know someone called Cassia Hunter. A relation, by any chance?"'

'No, of course I didn't.' He sounds patient and amused. 'We had a pleasant conversation about Winchester, and retirement and what he'd retired from, and what sort of family we had, and how we'd both lost our wives and I had a son called Patrick and he had a daughter called—'

'Dominic, did it really come out like that?'

'Yes. Truly, it did.'

'And? You didn't say you knew me. Please. Tell me you didn't say you knew me.' I can hear the apprehension in my own voice. A distinct wobble.

'I did. Stop freaking out. I gave you a terrific write-up and told him you had a successful business. He seemed rather surprised.'

'I bet,' I say snappishly. Another thought occurs to me. 'Did you tell him the company name?'

'He asked, and yes, I did. What's wrong with that?'

'Because he could look it up and find me. Not that he'd want to.' Why am I so twitchy about this? 'I think it was very disloyal of you.'

'Disloyal of me?' There is a faint emphasis on 'me'. 'Why is it disloyal to tell him how successful you are?'

I wish he wouldn't be so mild. 'Because I'm not successful, and I will kill you if you told him where I lived.'

There's a smile in his voice. 'No. I didn't tell him that. Though he asked.'

'He *asked*? Why would he ask? He threw me out, for God's sake! He hates me! I hate him. It's the last thing he'd want to know!' The pitch has risen again, and I am so agitated that my phone is quivering in my hand and my heart clattering in my chest.

'Cass!' Dominic says firmly. 'Stop being such a wuss. I

didn't tell him where you lived. He seemed pleased you'd made a success of life, and we had a pleasant conversation for a few minutes. Then he went to a single table, and we continued with our lunch. Full stop.'

We continued *our* lunch? Who is this she? He called me a wuss! I am not a wuss. I am angry. Furious. How dare my father come to live in Winchester? How dare he seem pleased I'd made a success of life, especially when the whole of life was going down the plughole. He'd told me countless times that I would never make a success of life which is why I'd set out to prove him wrong and now I find that he was right.

And who is this she?

'And by the way,' Dominic adds. 'He walks with a stick.'

I nearly say 'Good and I hope whatever it is hurts' and thankfully manage not to. Dominic already knows I'm a foul-mouthed witch and I don't want to worsen my reputation.

'Why?'

'I don't know,' he says primly. 'It was one thing I didn't ask.'

* * *

Wendy smells more than usually apple green today. She has poured each of us a large glass of wine and we are surrounded by boxes of tights.

'You walked out on him, and he needn't have come back,' she says, ripping open one of the packets and unfolding the tights with a flip across her workshop table. 'Ooh! Nice!' She reverts to Dominic. 'It was the perfect opportunity to let you go if he suspected you had problems with your eyes, wasn't it? It was what you said you wanted so he could have just not contacted you again. He could have walked away after your furniture disaster, but he didn't. He needn't have contacted you after you were bloody rude to him at that child's birthday lunch, but he did.' She slides her hand down one leg of the tights and stretches the fabric over her fingers. 'Honest to God, these are fabulous! Your designs are just beautiful. Do they really not ladder or snag?'

'Well, if you attack them with scissors they'll go into holes, but the fabric doesn't ladder as such.'

'They're one hell of a price.'

'They last ten times longer than ordinary tights, so people won't mind paying ten times the price. And supporting the sustainability aspect will be even more desirable. I hope.' My thoughts return to Dominic. Wendy has a point. He needn't have continued to make contact. He could have let me walk away. It was my rejection, not his.

'But when he came back, was it because he felt sorry for me? He suspected I had problems with my sight.'

Wendy puts the tights down and faces me. 'Cass, it is not a crime to be sympathetic – compassionate – but your stupid angry pride is at one end of the tightrope and Dominic's love is at the other, and you really do not make it easy for him to walk it. If you're not very careful you may swing that rope so hard that he'll fall off and he really will leave. For good.' She is clearly frustrated. 'Why shouldn't Dominic know about your RP? Why shouldn't anyone know? Of course he'll be sorry about it, just as I am, but he loves you and you love him. Pity doesn't come into it. Obligation, being kind, doing the right thing – none of it comes into that particular equation.'

I pick up the tights and slide my own hand in, the colours swirling on my skin, like Wendy's words swirling in my mind. *My stupid angry pride.* I know that Dominic is not like my father, or like Mike, but my expectation of Dominic was that he would feel pity, so much so that he simply couldn't leave me, being too much of a gentleman to leave a lady in the lurch. But Wendy has reminded me that he loves me, and I love him, and perhaps that is all that matters in the end.

Have I already swung the rope too far?

* * *

I miss him.

I wish I had kept a hold on my tongue. I wish I was not living in my own flat but was tucked up in Winchester in his house and in his bed. Ever since he told me my father lived in Winchester, I have been reluctant to go there. What if I bumped into Dad? Would I even recognise him after twenty years? What was the likelihood of him recognising me? What a pathetic, angry, fearful reaction to Dominic's information. And who was the woman he was having lunch with?

Disturbed nights, despite my new bed, are not improving my powers of reasoning. I am restless and discontented, so when Sam rings to say they have a spare seat for *Macbeth* at the Mayflower Theatre and would I like to come, I leap at the chance. I would like to think of something else other than missing Dominic, avoiding Winchester and getting money back into the business. My furniture and carpet buying spree has seriously depleted my remaining funds and the tights have yet to take off.

All dressed up, and with very careful make-up, I meet them in the foyer. And there is Dominic who I haven't seen or heard from for what feels like years but is in fact only a few days. My heart lurches and heat surges up my face. Does my make-up conceal the flush? How ridiculous that just the sight of him reduces me to an incoherent wreck, wanting to throw my arms around him and shriek for joy. I have been so bad-tempered recently I am embarrassed to be so ecstatic, but he grins at me as if he knows exactly how I feel, and he doesn't look at all surprised to see me. There has been strategic planning, I think. But really, I can't help grinning back. It is so good to see him, and he doesn't appear to hold my horrible chippy behaviour against me.

We have supper at the Italian 'Eat All You Want for the Price' next door to the theatre, where I have seconds of everything. Being in love is supposed to make you lose your appetite, but mine has doubled. We discuss the evening's very odd production, all in modern army uniform. What, we wonder, would Shakespeare have made of it?

I realise that Dominic has by no means backed off from my chippiness but has waited patiently for me to get over it. I can't believe that he is still friendly when I behave so badly. I am acutely aware of him on the bench beside me. I can feel the warmth of his leg next to mine, and the hairs on my arm lift when he reaches for his wine glass. As Zev drives us back to the flat afterwards to see the effect of my alterations, my hand almost has a life of its own, wanting to creep across the seat to grasp Dominic's fingers.

I want Dominic to like what I have done. Never before have I much cared what anyone else thought of how I looked or what I wore, or whether my taste coincided with theirs, which it normally didn't, but I care about Dominic's opinion. There is still the creamy smell of new carpet as they stand in the centre of the sitting room and take in the expanse of blue and the floor-to-ceiling curtains in graded verticals of blue through to green. There is a total absence of chintz. There is an absence of much else, in fact, as I still have only the most basic furniture and there is not much to sit on except bean bags. However, the bean bags are part of my design showcase too, consisting entirely of recycled and sustainable materials echoing the curtains and the blue of the carpet. My visitors are satisfyingly impressed and seem amazed to discover that I actually made the curtains. I wonder how much longer I'll be able to see well enough to use the sewing machine and feel sad that a hobby I really love will inevitably slip away from my capabilities.

'Fab!' Sam says, trying out a beanbag.

Dominic bends to smooth his hands over the carpet. 'And this is recycled plastic bottles! Exceptionally soft. It's delightful. And a lovely colour.' He stands to look at the curtains. 'The material is extraordinary – gorgeous. I'm guessing the light comes streaming through it in daytime. I think they are lovely. Reminds me of the aurora borealis.' He turns towards me. 'It's beautiful, Cass. Clever you.' That's music to my ears. 'So different and the room suits modern minimalism as much as it did antique furniture.' I don't remember Mike ever being so generous. 'No regrets about selling? You don't want to change your mind?'

'Nope. No regrets.' There are regrets, of course, because now the bones of this flat have been delineated, how long will I see them for? 'Come and see the rest – slightly different!'

The blue carpet is laid throughout, but I have used different materials and designs for the curtains. I am using the small room, Mike's old dressing room, as my bedroom and the master bedroom is floor-to-ceiling hanging and shelving. Stuffed with colour.

'The warehouse,' I say, throwing my arm expansively around the room. 'As I have given up the car, the old container became very inconvenient as well as expensive. At least it's all in one place now.'

Dominic shoves his hands in his pockets and swings round on his heel. 'That's a lot of stuff. How did you move it all?' He follows me into the kitchen and gets mugs out of the cupboard as I put the kettle on.

I grin. 'A man with a van, and several friends and it's a lot less stuff than it was.'

'I'd have helped, but you didn't ask me.' He sounds reproachful.

Hesitating, I mutter, 'I didn't think you'd want to.'

He's watching me, his face a little sad I think, and when the kettle boils, he fills the cafetière. 'How many viewings have you had?'

I sigh. 'Three. I've dropped the price now.'

He indicates the warehouse. 'Is this working?'

'Yeah, pretty well. I have to run the business from somewhere, and this is the least expensive option at the moment. Zev said I should let the flat, but then where would I go? Letting, reorganising the business – it all takes a lot of time which I can't afford just now.' Quite apart from not seeing properly. 'The good news is that I've reduced the stock substantially, reduced my overheads, sold the car – all £900 of it' – I put the cafetière and mugs on a tray – 'and if no other disasters occur, I should balance the books by the end of the year.'

Dominic smiles and picks up the tray. 'And the only person who is surprised is you.'

Zev takes his mug. 'These bean bags are extremely comfortable to sit in, but how the hell do you get out?'

'With inelegance,' Sam says.

They extract themselves after half an hour or so with protestations about required sleep and early starts and I suspect that there has been organisation and pre-arrangements and scheming about the whole evening.

Dominic makes no effort to leave, and my tummy does little nervous bunny hops. My brain is in the bedroom. I changed the sheets on Saturday. It's not tidy. Several pairs of shoes are not in the cupboard. I did not hang up my clothes. Or my towel. I make a supreme effort to keep the conversation at business level.

'I'm glad you like the carpet. If nobody else likes it, it will be an expensive gamble.'

'I do like it. People are much more aware of the environment now and that means they'll look at alternatives.

You will need to work at the marketing.' He gathers up the dirty mugs and takes them into the kitchen. 'There are plenty of people who *would* have gone bust in your situation. Who would have given up, who wouldn't have drawn up a good business plan after such a disaster, who wouldn't have been passionate about what they do, who wouldn't have a well-thought-out exit route.' He turns and spears me with those perceptive eyes. 'Plenty who wouldn't have had the idiocy to punish a thief by writing off their car.'

I can feel my mouth opening. 'You knew?' He's looking at me a bit gravely.

'You reacted oddly when I asked you to Mottisfont. Then you looked guilty. You looked as if you were steeling yourself to say something. And then you dropped in this information that Mike's Aston was a write-off and you sounded guilty. I didn't know why, of course.'

I load the dishwasher carefully and slowly so I don't have to look at him.

'So how did you know it was me?'

'I mentioned it to Patrick. I thought the write-off of a luxury car in that way would interest him. His reaction interested me,' he says dryly. 'He confessed under not too much pressure and was inordinately proud of his achievement.'

'It boomeranged,' I admit with embarrassment. 'That car might have brought back thousands. Too late I realised I'd cut my own throat. I was just so angry about him cheating on me. Angry that he loved the car more than he loved me. It was stupid.'

'Yes. Pretty stupid.' He makes a humphing sound. 'Please don't lead Patrick astray like that again. It was very risky. Both of you could have had criminal charges brought against you and that would have remained on file forever. It would have affected his employment prospects.'

I deserve the reprimand and squeeze my eyes shut

because I am ashamed. Way back when I first met Dominic, I saw a photograph of Penny on his desk. Slight and dark, long hair blowing across a tanned face, a little boy climbing stiff-legged up her jeans, their hands grasping, both leaning backwards, laughter bubbling out of the picture. I am not just an interloper. I have interfered with Penny's family, Dominic's family.

'Sorry. Sorry for asking him to do it. That was a mess up.'

'Yes, well, we all mess up at some point.' When I have the courage to look up, the grey eyes are smiling. 'Did you enjoy your revenge?'

'Not really. A momentary triumph and then it all tasted very sour. How does that saying go? About cutting off your nose?'

'To cut off your nose to spite your face?' He puts the back of his hand against my cheek. 'Don't beat yourself up. Move on.' His head tilts slightly, looking at me a bit quizzically. 'But I wish you'd move on with me.' I find I am not shying away from the slight pressure but leaning into it. Wanting much more than this comfortable friendliness. Wanting not the back of his fingers, but his hands touching me, holding me with desire. Moving on with Dominic is impossible, but there goes that clutch in my innards again telling me – telling me what? He draws me closer, very gently, and his lips are nearly touching mine. And I want you to be so much more than a friend, Dominic. The best lover, the kindest, the most forgiving of men. How this man makes me want to burrow into his arms, to bury my face in his shoulder. My whole body remembers his. Every little particle.

I stamp on the brakes of where my mind is taking me.

'No, you don't.' I hope I sound brisk and humorous. 'You haven't thought it through.' My fingers have crept up to his. 'You know I'm not a nice person. I'm revengeful and angry.' He's got my fingers laced into his and won't let me pull away. 'I'm entirely unsuitable, even as a lover. Odd ideas. Strange looking.' My next appointment at Moorfields skulks like a monstrous black vampire at the edges of my soul. 'I would bring nothing to your party, your friends and family would be horrified.'

He interrupts. 'Rubbish. So far, everyone who's met you, Patrick especially, thinks you would do me the world of good. And I know for a fact you still lust after me.' There is laughter in his voice.

That's rather intriguing. 'How do you know that for a fact?' He turns me towards him, holding both my hands at chest height, his thumbs across my fingers. The pair of us marooned in the middle of the kitchen.

'Do you know,' he says dreamily, his eyes on our entwined digits. 'You have the most beautiful hands I have ever seen.' I pull, but he doesn't let go.

'Don't avoid the question.'

He grins. 'You were not pleased to hear I was lunching with another lady.'

I pretend bemusement. 'What *are* you talking about? It's none of my business who you lunch with.'

'Indeed.' Somehow his face is very close to mine again, and my breath shortens as my lungs contract. 'I am a man of the world, Cass; I can tell when the woman of my dreams wants to cast herself into my arms.'

'Oh, *really*, Dominic. Don't rot me up.'

'Tweak your tail.'

'Talk utter drivel.'

'I'm not talking drivel.' He puts a finger up to my lips. 'You want me as much as I want you. I want to spend the rest of my life with you. Be your best friend forever.'

I can't be brisk and humorous anymore. 'We can't, Dominic. It's not possible, however much you want it. I'm really, really sorry, but I can't.'

I don't feel he is surprised, but he doesn't back off. 'And your reason is?' I don't reply.

'The Aston fiasco really did give you a criminal record?'

'No. Honestly, we weren't caught.' I'm having to think. 'You're a sober banker. I'm mad. I am unsuitable.'

He puffs a little laugh. 'The sober banker's mad wife. You've said all that before. So your reason is?'

I narrow my already reduced vision. 'You sound as if you want a particular answer.'

He smiles. 'I want the truth, certainly. Unsuitability doesn't count. It could be said that I am unsuitable for you. Are you in love with someone else?'

'Oh! You know quite well I'm not.'

Suddenly he pulls me into his chest. Encloses me in his arms, his hands rubbing my back, like a child being comforted. 'Cass, be brave. Tell me your reason. The worst that could possibly happen is that you achieve what you think you've been trying to achieve for weeks. Tell me the reason.' There is nothing sexual about his embrace, there is not even friendship. There is just love, in every form possible.

I absorb the amber scent of him, feel the soft cashmere of his sweater against my cheek, hear his quiet steady breathing and the regular thump of his heart at my ear. I think he is trying to give me courage. Drawing myself out of his comforting arms I turn to the window. Below me, the streetlamps spill splintered stars into the darkness and I can make out an imprecise figure slowly walking a dog. Soon I won't see even that.

I sigh. Wendy had said, 'Why shouldn't Dominic know?' At least he'd know there was a good reason why I left him. Why friendship can be the only way forwards.

'I'm going blind, Dominic. Really blind. It's genetic, it's incurable. I can't have children because I might pass it on. I can't stay with you. I won't.' I turn slowly, to face the inevitable pity. To face the concern, the apologetic embarrassed backing off, the final acceptance.

Of course, his face is not that clear, but it's not unreadable either. There is no apologetic embarrassment, but there is comprehension and in some strange way, relief and pride.

I stare at him uncertainly. I can feel the frown of bemusement on my own face. 'Did you know? Did Wendy tell you?'

That slow loving smile. 'No, I didn't know, not for sure, and though I asked Wendy, she wouldn't tell me, though she did say I shouldn't give up on you and you did have a reason. I suspected something was wrong when you went to Moorfields, and you wouldn't tell me about it.' He draws me back into his arms. 'You told me you loved me, and always would. I know women are reputed to change their minds at the flick of a switch, but it didn't quite add up. There had to be a reason. When Mike took the furniture, Wendy phoned and said you wanted *me*. I didn't believe you'd suddenly fallen out of love with me.' I find myself drawn back against the warmth of his body. 'So, now you've actually managed to confess … would you like to tell me about it?'

'I can tell you, and you'll understand, but it won't change anything. I can't get more involved with you – no more than being friends.' I drop my forehead onto his chest so he can't see my face. 'I'm going blind and this is a one-way ticket for me, and I will totally understand if you can't remain in friendship mode – I'm not sure that I can. Even if there is trust and truth.'

I grip his hand, making the point that I had taken his words about the nature of friendship to heart and tell him the bare bones of retinitis pigmentosa. What I see and what I don't see, and how this dark surround is narrowing, imperceptibly creeping across the receding end of the tunnel. How the colours are bleaching out, the image becoming faded sepia and less defined. How outlines and patterns are gradually distorting into strange shapes. How light splinters into stars. How terrifying the dark is.

'I am not going to spoil your life, your career, by becoming dependent on you for everything, especially as I know that you'd never kick me out.' I make a silly face at him, trying to lighten this heavy moment. 'I know what it's like to be totally dependent. My mother was dependent on my father for a roof over her head – for everything financial – and dependent on me for everything else. It's huge. It's bigger than you can imagine. I love you too much to do it.'

His arms are so comforting, and he doesn't withdraw in any way. I allow my tense muscles to normalise a little.

'I hear you,' he says quietly. 'And I'm not going to argue, at least not at this minute, although I strongly disagree on almost every point. I don't think you could take much arguing. Let's just say that we are here for each other, that just being friends is sufficient for the moment.'

I look at him, seeing clearly and without distortion, the person most valuable to me, whatever form he takes, lover or friend, mentor, guide, source of wisdom, constructive critic. Infinitely more valuable than all the things I have been struggling with and for; my business, my achievements, triumph over Mike's betrayal, my sight.

Lifting my head, I kiss the tip of his nose. 'You are the best of men, and I am more grateful for that than you could know.'

Chapter Twenty-Seven

He's done another of his 'friend' things and as a Friend of the National Gallery has invited me to go to the Durer exhibition with him. Dominic loves figurative drawings, I have discovered.

The audio tells me that Durer's parents had eighteen children. I am not even going to have one. I am standing in front of his *Praying Hands* and although I find myself bending close to this miracle, the removal of the cataract means that there is no cloud to obscure the extraordinary pencil strokes. The dark nimbus of my vision focuses on the veined worship in the long, steepled fingers; there is such strength in their frailty. I am moved almost to tears.

We move forward, through the flawless woodcuts, me reluctant to leave the long-nosed gaze of his self-portraits yet drawn on to the amassed body of Renaissance work.

'It is quite different, seeing these for real.' We are perched on a leather seat surrounded by exquisite art. I am exhilarated by seeing first-hand, even if not very clearly, what I have only ever seen in books. Someone moves close to us, and I smell pale pink.

'Dom?' a voice says, and we both look up.

He gets to his feet. 'Hello, Jen. How lovely to see you. We could all have come together, had we known!' He turns to me.

'Cass, you remember Jen – Arabella's mum?' He glances at Jen. 'The Pizza Italia experience.'

'Of course,' we both say, smiling. I like her, but the meeting has disoriented me, the delight of the exhibition lost in social norms and I feel it all slipping away. A few minutes of talk, and a suggestion to meet for lunch in Jermyn Street. They are so at home here, the streets and galleries and restaurants all known, ideas proposed, discarded, agreed. Jen is elegant and classically smart. I am just outrageous. How could they possibly have included me, with my hair streaked with reds, sporting red jeggings with diagonal multicoloured stripes? I'm wearing my elegant black army boots which are extraordinarily comfortable if I am on my feet for hours on end.

'Do you mind?' Dominic says as Jen moves on with a wave in search of Peter.

'I think it's a case of do *you* mind,' I indicate me and my outfit. 'Not exactly Jermyn Street. I thought we'd be sitting outside on a lion with a sandwich and our feet in a fountain.'

He chuckles. 'Much too cold. Jermyn Street will sit up and be tickled pink.'

Naturally, neither the maître d' nor the waiters turn a hair and Peter kisses me on the cheek. He and Jen appear unfazed by their brother-in-law's companion, and I admire their cool. Peter doesn't seem to have taken offence at my turning down their investment offer and I suppose that Dominic has by now told him why I did so. We all compare notes on the exhibition, order our meal and then the two men get chatting and Jen and I do the female bit.

'You heard I saw your father a while back and introduced him to Dom?' she says. 'Such a coincidence meeting you and then realising I knew your father.'

'Extraordinary!' I say, wondering why Dominic hadn't mentioned it was his sister-in-law he was lunching with. 'Winchester is such a small world. How do you know my father?' I don't wish to expand on the father/daughter non-relationship but wonder if Dad has.

'Some dinner party, ages ago. He and his wife were there.' She glances up at me briefly. 'Would that have been your mother?' I shake my head. 'We've bumped into him occasionally since then, but I understand the marriage didn't last. I gather he's a useful older single man when hostesses are trying to even up the numbers, there always being more single women than men.'

Dominic must be a useful single man too. I smile faintly. I expect Dad's wife number two eventually discovered she'd attached herself to a control freak and made a fast exit.

Jen is looking at me, but I can't quite make out her expression. It's not avid curiosity I don't think, but more perplexity.

'It was interesting,' she says slowly. 'He didn't seem to know anything about your business, or where you lived, or anything about you, which is unusual. For a father.' I say nothing, hoping all this will go away. 'Dom told him you had a good business, and I could see your father was surprised. Intrigued. A bit sad too, I thought.'

Sad is a strange word to use. I don't remember him ever being sad. 'Yeah. Well. I haven't seen him for a while.' I try to keep my voice light and cool. If she thinks I'm a heartless uncaring daughter, so be it. I am. But once more the memory of Mike's extraordinary rant about my father surfaces, like oil on water. I thought I really had dropped it in my brain dustbin, but here it is again, demanding to know what my father can have done to create enough vitriol to make Mike seek me out, charm me, make me fall in love with him, steal from me. Enough vitriol to take revenge, through me, for six years, for something my father had done. What I feel for my father doesn't entitle anyone else to hate him more than I do. What the hell did he do to Mike's parents?

I feel a hand on my arm. 'Cass,' Jen says. 'I'm so sorry.

Whatever it is, I've opened up something painful, and I wouldn't have done that for the world. Forgive me.'

I try to focus and bring myself back to the present. Jen's concern is so obvious that the two men have stopped their conversation and are looking from Jen to me. I blink and pull myself together.

'No, it wasn't you at all,' I tell her. 'I'm fine. Honestly. It was just something I remembered.' I grin at them. 'Dad and I get on better at a distance, but that's nothing new or unusual between fathers and daughters.' The moment I say it, I could bite my tongue. Arabella adores her father, and he adores her.

I turn the conversation and ask after Arabella, her school, Cronk, William the Labrador and where Mr Bird is buried. The men resume their talk and Jen and I are relieved to be on more stable ground. The waiter brings wonderful food and the wine is in a different league.

'What colours are lunch?' Dominic asks me.

I close my eyes and breathe in. 'Maroon and primrose yellow, periwinkle and pale mauve, orange and green, orange and blood red.'

Laughter obliterates all thoughts of Mike or my father.

* * *

The sun has lost itself in low grey cloud and we all walk back from the station in a chilly red-smelling wind to our respective houses. I would have stayed on the train and gone on to Southampton, but Dominic says he will drive me home later. This is stupid. Neither of us should be deluding ourselves that we just feel friendship when both of us want so much more. But any time in his company is like a mug of hot chocolate in a snowstorm and I am so, so cold inside.

'What happened at lunch?' he asks, producing tea and Jaffa cakes.

I produce a blank look. 'What happened at lunch?'

'Something Jen said about your father? You were – upset.'

I shake my head. 'Not really about my father. I haven't spoken to him in eighteen years. Nothing to get upset about. But …'

'But?'

I turn my head so I can look directly at his face. 'I thought I'd binned it, but it all got tipped out again when Jen said she'd met Dad.'

'Mike's blame game?'

I nod. 'That connection between them. Because I don't know what it is, or what it means, it's like a poisonous thorn. It keeps coming back, I know it's there even though I think I've dug it out.' Dominic waits.

'Money – greed – I could understand. But why my IP rights? Why destroy Ecolore? Why make a perfectly good business founder, especially when it was providing financial benefit to him?' I gather my thoughts and memories. 'I didn't understand his motive. I still can't, it seems so pathetic, so founded on entitlement.' I take a long pull at my tea.

Dominic is frowning. 'Did he expand more on your father "being the reason"? What entitlement did he think was owed him?'

I circle my hands around the warmth of the mug.

'He said Dad had ruined his parents and stolen his birthright.'

'His birthright?'

'He told me quite early on that they had had a lovely house in the Cotswolds which had to be sold. He was bitter about it, but I assumed that was on behalf of his parents.' I glance up at him, mortified by my greenness. 'But now I know he wasn't bitter for them. He blamed them for losing everything he had been expecting to get.'

Dominic sucks in a breath. 'That really does smack of entitlement. You never met them, did you?'

'Nope. No visits from them or to them in the whole six years. No Christmas or birthday presents in either direction. I sort of assumed – got the impression – I was too wacky to be introduced, or maybe they had disowned him because of us living together. Because I had no family either, I suppose I didn't find it so strange.'

I shake my head at my failure to recognise the oddity of Mike's relationships and wonder why I had assumed it was my oddity, not his, that had been the problem.

Dominic is unhygienically mopping up biscuit crumbs with a licked finger. 'I can only think that your father, as an IFA, induced them to take an investment risk which went wrong. But losing on an investment shouldn't have meant selling up. I wonder …' He stops on a sudden thought, and then continues, 'But it is still a mystery why Mike should have chosen to punish you for something your father might have done.'

'Just because he could? Maybe he was disappointed that he hadn't killed him. And Dad didn't know that he'd been targeted for a reason and that could have been frustrating for Mike. Just as I was frustrated that Mike didn't know it was me who drowned his precious car.'

'Maybe,' Dominic says wryly. 'More likely that he couldn't extract money from your father, but he could steal it from you. Stealing your IP was just making trouble.' He puts our mugs and plates on the counter and says persuasively, 'Will you stay for supper?'

'I ought to get back,' I say reluctantly. I am longing to stay for supper. And the night. But I must stick to my decision. 'It was a lovely day and a lovely lunch. And the Durers were utterly fabulous. Thank you for taking me. But I must do some work tonight.'

He doesn't argue but drives me back and escorts me to my door as if there is a possibility of someone lying in wait on the well-lit stairway. An old-fashioned gentleman. Mike was very modern I recall.

As I open the flat door, he says, 'I think you need to talk to your father, Cass.'

I am silenced by surprise as he kisses my cheek and turns away, descending the stairs without looking back.

My cheek frizzles from the kiss, and my lips burn with envy of it. It is a bereavement. I so nearly call out and invite him to stay.

Chapter Twenty-Eight

It takes a few days to admit that Dominic is right. And I only admit it to myself, not to him. I can't go the rest of my life avoiding Winchester town centre in case I meet my father. I am a big girl now, successful in my own right – as Dad doesn't know how close to the wire I have come – and what have I to be nervous of? Sticks and stones and all that guff. Words can never hurt me, not like they used to.

His words, when I was twelve, when I had repainted my room in rainbow colours and rearranged all the furniture. *What ghastly colours. And the idiocy of putting the bed head under the eaves. Not that banging your head will make you any more intelligent given your present state of stupidity. I want this whole room painted white by tomorrow evening, and don't expect me to be paying for it.*

First, I discover where he lives, which isn't at all difficult given Google. Then I lurk in an art gallery and card shop on Parchment Street, about fifty yards away, trying to gather enough courage to knock on the door. Which I don't achieve. Henry Hunter leaves his house and limps slowly towards the centre. I may be a big girl now, but all of me is trembly and I've stopped breathing for so long that my face feels scarlet.

He's going for a drink in the pub and I will sit down beside him like a grown-up person and we will talk. About his retirement and my business. About his ex-wives and my ex-lover. And about my ex-lover's parents and what the hell he did to them.

Instead of the pub, he goes to the Waitrose food hall and then he limps for home, stick in one hand, bag in the other. The leg looks as if it hurts. Recalibrate, Cass. I overtake him easily.

He doesn't see me standing at his door until he's put one shiny brogue on the bottom step. There is surprise but no recognition.

'Can I help you?' he says politely.

'I hope so, Dad.' I hope my voice doesn't sound as shaky as I feel inside. I haven't spoken to this man for eighteen years, and as I look at him, I feel like a teenager again, wanting his approval, unable to obtain it, and angry as a result. But I am not a teenager now.

After a little pause, he says, 'Cassia.' And then after a longer pause, 'Do you want to come in?'

Neither of us knows how to begin. I appraise his perfect little house; the furniture shines with the pale yellow smell of polish, and the cushions are plumped. Tasteful, although not my taste. I decline a drink; he pours himself a gin and tonic even though it's only a quarter to six. Of course, he's nearly twenty years older, but even so, I think he has aged much more than that. His handsome lined face is soft at the edges, like a worn playing card, the once dark hair receded and grey. His good figure is thinness rather than fitness.

He puts his glass down carefully and sits in a wing chair. His smell, the colour of lapis lazuli, brings sudden familiarity.

'I met a friend of yours. Paget, I think the name was. He said you'd made a success of yourself.' He stares at me as if he can't quite equate my appearance, which I have toned down a bit for his benefit, with the teenager he kicked out.

'Yes.' I am non-committal. 'I've got a good business.' I

glance round the sitting room. 'You married again, didn't you?'

'She didn't stay long. Couldn't stand having me in the house after I retired.'

'You always were a control freak.' I find I have smiled at him to take the sting out of the truth. 'These houses are nice. How long have you lived here?'

'Eight years or so. The wife found a cleaner, and I've kept her on. But I shall have to move to a flat or something. The stairs are becoming too difficult.'

'Because of that?' I indicate stick and gammy leg. 'What is it? Knee joint?'

He grimaces. 'Every joint and every bone. Smashed to pieces.'

I am disconcerted. 'Smashed to pieces? Whatever happened? A car accident?'

'In a manner of speaking. A hit and run. Spine, pelvis, hips, and all. I was in Southampton General for nearly six months while they glued me together.'

'Oh! How horrible. I'm sorry.' I find I am genuinely sorry. However much we had fought, I wouldn't wish that sort of pain on anyone. 'When did that happen?'

'Six years ago. I wasn't going to retire so soon, but I was sixty-five so it wasn't unreasonable.'

Six years ago. While I was busy running my successful business and getting together with Mike, my father must have been near enough dead in the local hospital and I never knew. I am flooded by guilt. I shouldn't have just walked out on him, after that last row.

After Mum died, I didn't have to be silent to protect her. I found my vocal cords. Even now I hear the echoes of words neither of us should ever have thought, let alone uttered. *You killed her. You gave her cancer. You made her blind. You blighted both our lives. You are a philanderer. You are Scrooge – mean and greedy and uncaring. You are a monster.* My skin flames with shame. Somehow those terrible unjust accusations against him must be dealt with.

She ruined my life and my career. You have no idea what it was like to live with her whining, her excuses to do nothing because she couldn't see, her refusal to help herself, her incessant demands on my time, my money, my energy. Where had I been, who was I with, how much money had I spent. As if I hadn't earned every penny that she then spent on her pet projects, rebuilding the garden, buying stuff we didn't need, employing gardeners and cooks and cleaners, refusing to help herself.

I had never acknowledged that he might have had a point. My memories of Mum had been of someone who confided in me. How unkind he was, how thoughtless, how unloving, how demanding. He might have been a bully but had my mother's attitude aggravated our mutual animosity?

Looking back, I wonder about both my parents. I wonder how much of each of them this daughter has inherited.

'Did they get the driver?'

He shakes his head. 'No. I never saw the car or the bastard driving it. Caught me from behind. On purpose. Never heard a thing till it was too late, and he was long gone by the time anyone found me.'

'That's awful. I'm really sorry,' I say again, ashamed to remember how I had wished that his leg hurt. 'Where did it happen?'

'Winnall Moors. I was on my morning run to the reserve. No traffic to speak of.' He takes a slug of his gin. 'Ah well. That's life.'

'Or nearly death,' I say soberly. Somehow, I don't want to embark on Mike Benton or his parents now. 'I didn't know you lived in Winchester until Dominic Paget told me he'd met you.'

'Is he your boyfriend? He's much too old for you.' How

quickly his critical character reasserts itself, but I am in control of myself and am careful not to react.

'No. He's an investment banker, and I wanted expansion funding. Which he offered me. My partner and I have a flat in Southampton.' Perhaps now was the moment. 'He's called Michael Benton.'

I am watching him carefully, but there is no reaction to the name.

'Partner!' His contempt is clear. 'The modern euphemism for an inability to commit to anything.'

Oh! The hypocrisy! I nearly remind him of his non-commitment to two wives and a daughter, but just manage to bite my tongue.

'His parents live in the Cotswolds. I think you knew them.' He looks puzzled, but I have no idea whether it is genuine or not. 'It might have been a long time ago.'

'What was the name again? Bentley?'

'Benton.'

His eyes screw up a little in thought. 'Benton. Benton. It rings a bell.'

'Something financial?'

'Maybe business. Can't remember. Why?'

I don't think he's lying. 'No matter. Were you out buying your supper?' He nods. 'I'd better leave you to it then.'

'Yes. Could you put the pie in the oven before you go?' It's not a demand, it's a perfectly reasonable request. I am no longer a bolshy teenager and he can't control me anymore. I put his pie in the oven.

I have to ask my question before I leave, however difficult.

'Do you know what Mum's eye condition was? Why did she go blind?'

He shrugs. 'No. No idea. She just went blind.'

I am astounded. 'Really? No idea? She must have had treatment, or seen a consultant or something?' He must have had some knowledge, some curiosity, surely? He frowns as if trying to remember. 'It happened very gradually. There were endless pairs of new glasses so she must have been to the optician.' I remember the glasses. The house was awash with them.

'And have you had any problems with your sight?'

'No. I've got reading glasses, but no problem. Why? Have you?' Oddly, there is a note of concern.

My turn to shrug. 'Yeah. A bit. Just wondered.' I look at my watch rather pointlessly as I can't read it. 'I must go.' After twenty years, I still have no inclination to give him a hug or a kiss. 'Bye Dad.'

As I open his front door he calls after me. 'You can come again if you want.'

How kind. I think I don't want, but maybe it's time to relinquish this ancient grudge and try to get a better perspective on their marriage and their parenting.

* * *

Dominic had said, 'Good for you!' in a surprised tone of voice when I told him I had been to see Dad. He obviously thought I was far too pig-headed to have listened to his suggestion. We are walking now in the New Forest because he apparently wants to know more about the visit to my father. Even though I am relieved he has not stepped over the friendship line I stipulated, I am more than saddened by it. My diagnosis has no happy ending. I must become accustomed to the friendship because having him as a friend is better – much better – than nothing.

'Was it as bad as you expected?'

I smile because I can hear the teasing note in his voice. 'No, of course it wasn't. It was just one of those demons that needed facing and you booted me in the right direction.

He limps because of a hit-and-run accident. I almost felt sorry for him.'

The earth bursts with the overwhelming scents and colours of autumn, dark musky puddles giving way to churned mud, smelling red and black where the ponies have trampled, the brambles drooping with blown fruit, rose hips like drops of blood jewelling the leafless branches. The smells are woody and ancient: greens and browns, charcoals and creamy greys.

My hearing seems to be as heightened as my sense of smell and the whole forest resonates with birdsong, wind, the delicious slurping of our boots through mud, cracking twigs, the whispering of falling leaves. Dominic's voice and his amber scent. There is a taste of winter on my tongue. Less seeing, but as my consultant had said, more of everything else.

'Mike would never do this.' My scarlet wellies are standing up well to the slippery ground, though the silver stars are nearly obliterated. 'So I hardly ever came. I'm sad at what I've missed on my own doorstep. It's so utterly beautiful.' A group of ponies cross our path, ignoring us, and I take lots of pictures, of them and, more surreptitiously, of Dominic. I want a photo of the sun spearing through bronze and scarlet leaves and ask him to take it because the cloudy effect in my other eye makes me uncertain about visual effects. The contrast of light and shade merge gently into my own lost clarity and, in my mind, I see a design of various autumn leaves, blown, spinning, wafting in a gale. My pocket is full of them, ready to draw.

'When is that second cataract going to be done?' he asks, moving to get a better perspective.

'After Christmas. They're giving me a date in January I think.' He hands back my phone and takes a picture of me with his own.

I think back to my brief visit to Dad. 'He had no idea

why Mum went blind. Just remembered her endless visits to the optician and hundreds of pairs of useless glasses. When I told him I thought he had known the Benton parents he thought it rang a vague bell, but whatever had happened he'd forgotten. Or he said he had.'

Dominic kicks a fallen branch out of our path. 'I did a bit of sleuthing myself which was partially successful, I think. Benton is not a common name, but it's not that unusual either. You said you thought his mother's first name was Virginia.'

'I think it was Virginia, but I'm not sure. It was on some form he had to complete and I think it began with a V. Vanessa?'

'Could it have been Veronica? I found a Kenneth and Veronica Benton on the Lloyds Register for 1980. But it might be entirely unrelated.'

I stop and think back, as sudden clouds darken the sun. 'It could have been. Yes, it could have been Veronica.'

'There are ways to discover if someone has been scammed or defrauded or just been plain unwise. Would you like me to take it any further?'

There is a sudden rattling of rain on rhododendron leaves, and instinctively I duck and lean into him as drops hit my face. Then as quickly as they came, the sun gleams out again and I straighten, back to friendship mode.

I hesitate, thinking that this whole idea of investigating my ex-partner's parents must be something he could do without. 'You're a busy man in a busy job. It's an imposition to ask you.'

'You're not asking,' he says mildly. 'I'm offering. Mike raiding Ecolore seemingly had something to do with your father and Mike's parents. There may be some explanation as to why he went to such lengths to make a relationship with you, and to try to ruin you. But inquiries may come to nothing and it may be wiser to just drop it and get on with your life.'

‘I suppose if I could find his parents, I might find the link between them and Dad. I’d like to discover why all this happened, why Mike targeted me. It feels like unfinished business. I still want to know *why*.’

Chapter Twenty-Nine

The following Saturday we are walking again, this time clambering up the wooden steps of St Catherine's Hill. All the daily walking I am doing has paid off in fitness and I can keep pace with him, although I certainly can't talk and climb at the same time. We stop to savour the views of Winchester, the intermittent shafts of sun through wind-racing clouds make the Itchen floodplains wink and ripple wetly through the drizzle. Beautiful, although it is as if I were underwater with no goggles. I can't believe I am so warmly happy – inexplicably happy – to be with Dominic in this wet, red-scented coldness. There is nobody else here and we settle on a bench, my Ecolore poncho protecting me from the damp wood, and Dominic, his legs stretched before him, sitting on the edge of his Barbour coat.

'The Bentons, probably Mike's parents, came to grief in the Lloyds LMX disaster in 1990. Your father was a young Lloyds broker in 1973 and had advised Kenneth Benton to become a name. When Lloyds crashed, the names had to pay up.'

He could, of course, be telling me this over the phone. Or by email. But he didn't. He invited me for another friendly walk, another friendly pub lunch by a warm fire, another friendly Saturday together. Red warning lights flash in my subconscious; this is dangerous ground, Cass. Thin ice, a fuse about to light, a tyre about to blow.

He sighs. 'People had to sell their family estates, homes,

cars, horses. Yachts. Villas in Spain. Some people committed suicide because they simply couldn't pay. They hadn't ever bargained on a rainy day at Lloyds.'

'And Mike's parents had to sell up to pay their debts.' I don't even bother to make it a question. 'The family estate. Mike's inheritance. The birthright. They wanted something for nothing, all stemming from greed.'

'Not necessarily greed. Ignorance too; inexperienced brokers who didn't realise how the system worked, but who gained from every new name they brought in.' He sounds sad. 'There were loads of perfectly nice but ill-advised people who were ruined, and Mike's parents were possibly – probably – one of those casualties.'

I shove my chilled hands deeper into my poncho pockets. 'I can understand now what he meant about losing his inheritance, but it doesn't explain why he targeted me and not my father.'

'I doubt he could have forced your father to reimburse him, as it were. Whereas there was you, a beautiful, desirable, and successful businesswoman.' He can hear my fizzle of disbelief and there is a smile in his voice. 'Very simple really, he gets the girl and gets the money too.' He turns serious and puts an arm round my shoulder. 'I've told you before, don't feel bad because you loved and trusted someone.'

I had loved Mike and even now I believe he had loved me in his own slightly weird way, at least for three or four of those years together. Trustworthiness is a different characteristic. He wasn't trustworthy. Do I trust Dominic? Yes, I do. Could my judgement be wrong again? No, it couldn't. I just know.

I should move away, but I don't. His arm feels warm and protective. As if it belongs. It's an effort to keep my voice light.

'So do we know what happened to the Benton parents? Was it just the house they lost?'

'Their losses were considerable, but they managed to cover them. I have no idea how they paid. They eventually got out of Lloyds in 1993.'

I calculate. 'Mike was fifteen in 1993. Old enough to resent a change of lifestyle for the worse.'

He grunts in agreement.

We climb on, up to the earthworks of the Iron Age fort, and contemplate the lumps and bumps that were once great ditches and defensive walls before turning for home through the naked dripping beech trees. I slip on a wet stone and Dominic's arm is round me again, preventing a fall and tightening enough to swing me into his chest. His face is very close, and I stop breathing, heat rising. I am held in a long timeless place, a space with no dimensions, full of amber scents and silence. I cannot, I will not let myself drown in this space, this scent, this silence.

I feel his fingers tighten on my shoulder blades, but he doesn't kiss me, and the red wind blows cold on the wetness on my cheeks.

* * *

I did a bit of sleuthing to find Kenneth and Veronica Benton's address and phone number and nearly went to visit them, but the prospect was so daunting and the weather so horrible that I phoned them instead.

'I had this surreal conversation with my ex-partner's father,' I tell Dominic. 'We don't know each other from Adam, but out of the blue I'm asking them if they have a son called Michael and telling them that my name is Cassia Hunter and I lived with their son for six years and he's a thief and a criminal.' I take a deep breath. 'Obviously, it didn't come out quite like that, but you know what? He wasn't surprised, he wasn't angry with me, he apologised for

Mike, and he commiserated with me! The whole thing was extraordinary. Weird.' I finish the seam on a duvet cover for my new bed, made from some of my designed fabric, turn the sewing machine off and come to sit beside Dominic. 'I'm convinced they knew nothing about what he'd done to me. He didn't even know Mike had a partner. I didn't speak to his mother but according to him, she had spoiled their only child. Mike had no time for them, never came to see them and didn't care about them. Neither of them had seen nor heard of him since 8th May 2012. Six years ago.'

'That's very precise,' Dominic says, frowning.

'His mum remembered, because it was two days after her sixtieth birthday and she thought he'd come because of that, but in fact, he'd brought his car down for them to sell and said they could keep the money.'

'Did he tell you how your father was involved?'

'Yes, just as you discovered. Dad introduced them to Lloyds, and they went bust. Kenneth Benton isn't my father's greatest fan. I suggested that Mike's motive for defrauding Ecolore might have been to try to regain and return some of their losses, but he said that was not the case. Mike never did send them any money.'

'So if they haven't seen him since 2012, they don't know where he is?'

'Nope. It's a dead end there, not that I care where he is. They haven't got any money of their own, let alone my money. But I wondered about that very precise date, and why he wanted his parents to sell his car and keep the money. It's very out of character. Why sell his car? He would have been more likely to sell it himself and keep the money towards a bigger and better one. I asked Kenneth Benton if there was anything wrong with it.'

'Anything wrong with it? Like what?' Dominic is puzzled.

'He said the garage couldn't find anything wrong – it

went like a bird. The only thing that reduced the value was a dent in the bodywork. It occurred to me that a car gets dented if it hits something, so I asked where the dent was. He thought on the front nearside wing.'

'Ah.' He is getting my direction. 'Were you thinking …?'

'Yes, I was.' I start to match the buttons to the duvet buttonholes. 'It definitely got me thinking. So via Google, I find that the local paper reported that a man was the victim of a hit-and-run driver at the junction of North Walls and Durngate, on 8th May 2012 between 7.25 and 7.43 am. The day Mike took his car to his parents and asked them to dispose of it, rather than him. Could be a coincidence, but I don't think it's very likely, do you?'

What could possess a driver to hit a man from behind *on purpose*? It would have been murder if Dad had died, and it was only luck that he hadn't. A little tremor shudders through me as I think of a car battering down an unsuspecting jogger. Whether it was Mike or not, it's still a horrible thought. I tie off and cut the thread. It has taken me twice as long to sew that button on as it would have done six months ago and I have drawn blood from my thumb. If my eyes have deteriorated that fast, will I be able to sew at all in another six months?

'No,' Dominic says, sounding appalled. 'I don't think it's likely. And it would explain Mike's comment that it wasn't just you that he'd punished. Thank God he didn't try the same thing on you.'

* * *

Dorset's Avon beach smells greeny grey of salt, seaweed and sand. It is chilly and sparsely populated and we have turned up the collars of our coats. No one could accuse Dominic of being a couch potato.

'I went to Winnall Moors to look,' he says. 'The pavement on the left runs behind trees until the entrance to the Durngate car park. Fairly easy to drive behind him, then accelerate at the junction.'

'No way of proving it, though, as there were no witnesses.' I stop to pick up another piece of plastic and add it to the carrier bag full of rubbish. 'What bothers me is that it is more than likely that for six years I lived with a psychopath who tried to murder my father and, as you so rightly said, might perhaps have tried to murder me.' I shudder both mentally and physically and Dominic encloses me with a comforting arm.

The moment is interrupted by a passing child who has seen us collecting rubbish and runs over with a flabby piece of swimming armband for the carrier.

'I like your boots,' the child says. I can't see whether it's a girl or a boy.

'Thank you,' I say. 'They are made out of the plastic rubbish we collect.'

I notice again how easy Dominic is with children, how he enjoys their company and how children immediately relate to him. After a conversation during which a new eco warrior is born, Dominic and I walk back to The Blue Lobster to meet Zev and Sam for a pint of prawns. It is strange how these three men have become such good friends to me. And one of them would like to be more than a friend, although he has done nothing about it for weeks. I try to tell myself that this lack of pressure is a great relief.

The warmth of the pub steams up my glasses and sets Dominic sneezing; his habit of sneezing in sixes amuses me. Pulling off my emerald coat, my red hair tumbles from the hood and they all admire the new colour. 'Cass the chestnut tree!' Sam says. 'You look dazzlin', darlin'!' I kiss his bald patch.

The prawns arrive, along with a mountain of buttered brown bread, and as usual, I am famished.

‘What colour do the prawns smell?’ Sam asks.

‘Maroon. This whole place smells maroon. I think all fish are maroon one way or another.’ I consider a moment. ‘Slightly off haddock verges more on the purply though.’ Munching on a fresh prawn I think of the rotten ones. ‘I wonder what happened to the curtains. I never got to open the bags with prawns in them so they must still be there.’

There is a mixture of reactions. A snort of laughter from Sam, a single ‘tut’ from Zev and a pseudo-frown of disapproval from Dominic.

‘Cass rang the Benton parents,’ he says to Zev and Sam. ‘A sad little story of unwise investment – but it had an interesting slant.’ He scrutinises a gigantic prawn before dipping it in the homemade mayo. ‘This mayonnaise is extremely good.’ Zev and Sam hold their own prawns motionless for a moment until he comes back to the point and explains what I have discovered.

There is silence while Zev and Sam digest the information.

‘Hmm. Interesting,’ Zev says. ‘Six years is a long tail. There won’t be any forensic evidence, so it would be circumstantial at best. Even if we knew where he was, it would be difficult to get him extradited and into a UK court. A dishonest con man is one thing, but attempted murder might be much more difficult to prove.’

My chest is so tight it makes me catch my breath. I try to look at myself from a distance – the years I had followed Mike’s lead, done what he wanted to do, the times when he’d never asked me what I wanted to do, the decisions he had taken, the decisions I had not. My business policy, Mike’s suggested alterations, the flat. Looking back, I am astonished and sickened by my abdication. Any joint decision was subtly altered by him. It had all seemed so reasonable at the time, and I am disgusted at myself. The denigration of my business and my skills; the laughter which I now think was mocking, the ease with which he took my trust, my friendship, my love, my money. After all those years of living with my controlling father, convinced I had understood what he was doing and could resist his manipulation – I was much too savvy to be caught that way again. So how, *how*, could it have happened? Six years of being taken for a ride. That familiar surge of humiliation sucks the air out of me.

I am suddenly aware that Dominic has taken my hand in his. Had I said something? Across the table, Zev looks troubled.

'Why was I so stupid? Why didn't I see what he was doing?'

'Because people with that sort of personality disorder are adept at it,' Zev says quietly. 'They are narcissists. They are con men. If it was recognisable, nobody would fall for it. But they do; thousands of perfectly sensible people are conned every day, online, on the telephone, by letter, face to face.'

'But six years!' Anger vies with mortification. 'I wanted children with him. At least he spared me that, I suppose.' I can hear a pathetic note of bitterness and pull my hand free, thumping my fists down on the table. The pints of prawns jump slightly.

'Rats and off haddock were excellent retaliation.' Sam is pragmatic. 'His birthday party nearly had him wetting his pants, and I bet he's never stopped regretting he'd ever orchestrated meeting you.'

'He still nearly ruined my business.' But the indignity of being so gullible is ebbing away in the warmth of their friendship, leaving me cross rather than furious.

'But he didn't achieve it,' Dominic says. 'Move on, otherwise he'll have achieved what he set out to do. Ruining your business was only a means to an end and that end was to ruin your life, so don't let him.'

Of course, he's right, and I must stop scratching at this scab and making it bleed. Move on, Cassia Hunter, rebuild your life. No. Moving on means it's got to be a new build, not a rebuild.

Chapter Thirty

We have returned, wind-tired and prawn-full, to the flat, and Dominic has been thinking about smells and colours and sight.

'Could you annotate your colours,' Dominic says, picking off tired blooms from one of my tired house plants. 'From a chart, so the official numbers can be matched to your own description? It would be a huge work, a magnum opus, and take a long time I think, but you need to do it sooner rather than later.'

Oh! Oh! Here is the male of the species trying to fix the problem. 'I think I do that anyway.'

'Or do you see the colour you want in your mind, then go to the chart, match it and then specify the number?'

'That's the same thing, isn't it?' I can't quite see where he's going with this.

'No, I don't think it is. When you can't see, except in your head, how can you specify exactly what colour you want? You remember colours but not so easily numbers. You need a code which both you and the manufacturer can exactly pinpoint, don't you?'

'Got it in one,' I say dryly, pouring boiling water into the teapot. Carefully, slowly, away from me. I've seen on the internet a kettle which boils one cup of water and then pours it into the cup. I will buy one in due course, funds allowing. 'Easy with eyes, not so easy without them.' I lie awake at night, sweating about this exact problem. 'Colour is no use if I can only see it in my head.'

'I'm not so sure,' he says slowly. 'Beethoven was completely deaf by the time he was forty-six. Think of all the music he wrote, especially the symphonies, when he couldn't hear a sound.'

I am doubtful. 'But he could see to write the musical notes, and he knew what the notes sounded like. It's not the same.'

'No, of course it's not the same. We need to find a way of transcribing what you see in your mind into physical colour. It must be possible.' We. He said 'we'. Mr Fixit again. 'I think you told me you don't smell colour, but smells are colour?'

I think again about that. 'That's right. I don't smell the colour, but I know what colour things smell.' I screw my face up trying to put into words something I have never analysed. 'That simply doesn't make sense, does it?'

He is staring at me. 'Yes. I think it does make sense. Can you visualise the smell – of mown grass for instance – when you can't actually smell it?'

Shutting my eyes, I give it a go. 'Fairly well. It's a dark blue. Come springtime I could pinpoint it on a colour chart.'

'You don't use every colour in a colour range, do you?' he went on. 'There must be thousands of shades, you just have to look at those little cards in a paint shop, but if you knew the name of one range, say yellow, couldn't you somehow pinpoint which yellow it was by what smells of that yellow?'

I lean my head back and give my blurry curtains the once over.

'Yes. Oh yes, I could do that. I think I do it already. I can go to a named colour and there are about eight different pages of that colour, each named as well as coded, and on each page about eighty codes within the range.'

'Good Lord! Six hundred and forty-odd. Do you use them all?' He seems astounded by the idea.

I grin. 'Definitely not! There are some perfectly horrible shades, and I wouldn't touch them with rubber gloves. Putrid rat for instance.'

His eyes crease up. 'So if you printed an enormous colour chart, you could write "Mown Grass" on the appropriate dark blue and then specify a design element to be coloured mown grass?'

'Mmph. Yeah.' Could I? Could I specify precise colours which I can no longer physically see and choose? Yes, I think I could.

'When you smell something and it has a colour, is it always the same colour for the same smell?'

'Yes. But I think some different smells are the same colour.'

He thinks for a moment. 'So a bag of coal will have the same colour as a coal fire?'

'I think so. Probably. But until I smell them, I don't know for sure.'

'I remember you saying that individual people have a colour – a smell?'

'Yes. A colour of their own.' I smile. 'Patrick smells orange and you smell amber.'

'Sounds the same to me.' He looks puzzled.

'Oh no! There are several gradations in between.'

'And does each gradation have a name?'

I consider names. 'Sort of. I'd use words like light, dark, vivid, bright, deep.' I grin again. 'Don't think those descriptions would be much use to anyone else though. Colour wheels and charts allocate symbols and numbers and when I'm designing and need to stipulate a particular colour or range, then I'd use, say, the RGB chart. For instance, there are sixty-five grades of raspberry.'

He responds with an amazed lift of his eyebrows. 'So

could you write "Fish" on maroon, "Fillet Steak" on one orange and "Patrick" on a different orange?'

That makes me giggle. 'Off haddock on purply maroon. It probably depends on the cooking. What spices and herbs are in there. But yes.'

Dominic puts a handful of plant rubbish in the bin and turns to me.

'Cass.' I can hear a sudden sober tone to his voice. 'I mean it. I think you should start constructing a palette with those sorts of names annotated to particular colours. If your business is to survive, let alone thrive, you need to be proactive now.' He takes a breath. 'You think I'm trying to manage you. I can see it in your face. Here comes another Mike. But I'm not, really I'm not. You have a fantastic talent, which is going to have to be directed into new and different channels. Eventually, you may need to work with another designer, especially if you can't see to draw, but there are loads of ideas you could prepare for. I would just hate to see you wishing you'd done something sooner when you could still see.'

I must admit that over the last few months my peripheral vision has slowly decreased and darkened. The tunnel is getting longer. No matter how enlarged the font, letters are double, triple imposed, flickering and shifting and bending. Sixes turn to nines; fives turn to eights. Images turn into different images. Multiple letters or numbers are impossible to keep track of. Steps are not where I expect them. Pavements are a snare and a delusion, the uneven slabs tripping me up and turning my ankles. He's right. If I leave it too late, I'll be left wishing I'd been more prepared.

That panicky feeling of multitasking a few too many tasks fills my chest.

'It's a case of time. Time to design, time to think of new ideas, time to sell the old ideas, time to find new materials, time to negotiate better prices for them, and time to market myself. Time to design an entirely new system of colourisation and then to computerise it.'

I close my eyes because I don't want him to see how daunted I am, and then I feel his arms encircling me and my head is against his shoulder. It is a good place to be. A comforting, friendly, supportive, undemanding sort of place. But it doesn't really solve anything. And it certainly doesn't solve my lustful inclinations. I know that this friendship is not enough; not for him and not for me.

'But you can do it,' he says quietly.

Chapter Thirty-One

Wendy has ordered thirty metres of a new fabric to be delivered by Christmas, and I'm hoping my outlay will be made up into must-have sustainable clothing and, along with the non-snag tights, quickly sold to her wealthy clients. She apparently still feels responsible for my welfare. Although I have been living in my own flat since my RP was confirmed, both my love life and my work life are far from perfect, and she is concerned.

'I'm going to my mother for Christmas. She wants to stay at home, and there's enough room for us three girls in her house. If you didn't mind sharing a room with me, you could come too. Think how jolly it will be. Five miserable women all fighting to get the turkey on the table.'

You can tell when a friend would make you welcome and give you the best time they could, but – it would be easier for them if you didn't. If I'm honest, the thought of Wendy's elderly and grieving mother, plus her two sisters, is daunting. The explanations, the false jollity none of us would be feeling. And for them, this strange, clumsy friend, with her funny clothes, and inexplicable bad temper. No, I say, terribly grateful and all that, but no. I want to make the most of the business holidays by getting on with some designs and continuing Dom's idea of charting my colours. Already it has been a surprisingly hilarious undertaking and I find I have actively sniffed and named nearly a hundred shades.

This magnum opus has not, so far, been particularly time-consuming. Once the colour wheel was printed and tacked up on my office wall, I started adding smells with little Post-it strips. From a distance, the chart looks like it's been sliced up with a razor.

* * *

My sight is slipping into a guessing game. Straight lines curve and dent. Pictures are crooked on the wall; verticals slide to the diagonal. Door handles lie in wait to bruise my hips. As the days shorten, I dread the low light. Occasionally fear attacks me like a rabid animal.

And yet I am learning to dictate with punctuation and without too much repetition. I can print verbally onto pink and yellow paper and discover that technology in general is far from perfect. I am learning to feel – edges, dimensions, height, width, texture. As the consultant had prophesied, my other senses seem to be enhanced. I cannot read easily on my phone or computer but behold! They speak! The computer robotically reads me text and tells me all sorts of things, some of which is useful, much that is not.

I can still design – create shapes, sense the subtleties of colour and dimensions – but for how long. How will I translate shape and colour and dimension when I cannot see?

Dominic remains a friend and a humorous one at that. What would I be, *where* would I be without that friendship? But how I wish it was more. There are regular phone calls and emails from him. Invitations to art exhibitions, meals, theatre and cinema. Sometimes it is just a walk, sometimes with Arabella, who dances restlessly in and out of my vision. Dominic's arm often seems to find itself under my hand and occasionally his fingers become entangled in mine, but he stays on the friendship side of the line. My sight is worse on dismal winter days and early darkness means that I am nervous about going to unfamiliar places.

* * *

Mid-December he discovers I am going nowhere for Christmas and asks me to join him and Patrick.

I decline graciously. This is my choice, I tell him. I have turned down countless offers. Well, a blood-red three to be precise, and I would be a cold teabag in any company. Dominic grunts and says nothing but at ten am on 23rd December my phone burbles.

'Patrick has just announced he is going to his girlfriend on Christmas Day, and I am going to be on my own. I have bought Christmas for two, and it will all go to waste.'

This is an obvious ruse to stop poor Cass from snivelling alone in her empty flat. He must have a raft of family he could go to, everybody does, except me, and I don't believe in Christmas and all the razzmatazz. It's just an excuse to make people spend money. Mike and I used to have an expensive Christmas lunch at a good restaurant, and then he would cook treats for us in the evening and we'd watch a good film on Netflix.

'This is not me either asking for or dishing out sympathy,' Dominic says rather tartly. 'The wretched boy is obsessed with her – says she's the next Einstein – and when she asked him to join her for Christmas, he practically licked her feet. He says of course he won't go if I'm going to be on my own, but his expression! I know quite well that I will be the most unpopular father of the year if I insist he stays, or even if I play the lonely parent. Which I will be.' There is a pause. 'Cass, please come.'

I sidestep. 'Have you met the girlfriend?'

He sighs. 'No. We've spoken briefly on the phone. Patrick says she is rather plain, but her brain makes up for it.' He discards Patrick and his girlfriend. 'Will you come?' He sounds hopeful. 'And dress in something amazing?'

'Why don't you go to your family?' I'm beginning to lose certainty.

'Because my sister lives in Canada, and my mother has flown out to stay with them for a month. My brother is a doctor in Truro, and he's on duty.'

'Why aren't you going to Jen and Peter?'

'Because they're in Scotland with his parents.' He sounds sad. 'Couldn't you survive me for just one day?'

'Dominic! That's very underhand! You simply cannot want a silly, depressed woman on Christmas Day.'

'You're the only woman available just at this moment, and if you come you won't be depressed.'

'Only silly.'

'Well, you are being silly, turning down my amazing free-range turkey and a bottle of Châteauneuf-du-Pape. And I will be putting a silver sixpence in a small Christmas pudding, with which there will be good alcoholic brandy butter.'

'Can you guarantee I'll get it?'

'Brandy butter? Why wouldn't you?

'No, you idiot. The silver sixpence.'

He chuckles. 'No guarantee, but if you do, your wish will come true. And if I get it, I'll get my wish. You can't turn that down, can you?'

'No,' I say slowly. 'I can't turn down a wish come true.' I wish, I wish, I wish this man could be my lover and not just a friend.

I can hear the smile in his voice, and I am glad I have allowed him to persuade me, even if it is just a random act of kindness. He has played the friend so well that I am now not sure that he wants to be anything else. 'Well, thank you.' I sound a bit stiff. 'Shall I appear about twelve thirty?'

'Preferably not. I'll come and get you at about ten thirty. OK?' Before I can even yelp in protest he goes on. 'Church at eleven, but it's a family service so quite short. And make sure you dress up – the kids will love it. Have you got a holly-green wig?'

I emit a shriek. 'To church? You'd lose your name! Excommunicated for sure! And I haven't been to church since Mum …'

I have a flashback to the funeral. My restless father, longing to get on with his life without the inconvenience of either wife or daughter. The dark mulberry smell of swinging incense, the heavy robes of Father George, the automated Latin Mass and chants, the altar boy walking backwards holding an enormous missal, the meaningless insincere flow of pious condolences. Church had never been my bag, despite my mother insisting I attend. My heart sinks.

Dominic says gently, 'It'll be lovely, you'll see. Lots of carols. It's Christmas Day and I promise you'll enjoy it. I'll be there at ten thirty.' He puts the phone down so I can't back out. What does he mean, 'dress up'? I now feel cross and manipulated and decide to teach him a lesson. After all, it's no skin off my nose to shock the pompous religionistas.

He rings the bell at ten thirty, but I hover at the bathroom mirror, unaccustomedly dithering about what I look like. I do want to prick the religion balloon, but at the same time, I am slightly ashamed about shaming Dominic. After all, he is having me to Christmas lunch, and considering how bad-tempered I am, and how I've hurt him, and what a mess I've made of life, that is pretty kind even if it also has a whiff of benevolent commiseration.

To my surprise, he is not in a suit. Surely pillars of the church can't visit the Almighty tieless and in chinos on Christmas Day?

Kissing me on the cheek he says, 'Happy Christmas,' and looks me up and down. 'Perfect. I'm so glad you found the wig.'

By the time he's got me into his car, the smile has become a grin. 'Don't look so nervous, Cass. They won't eat you, and you won't eat them.'

The church is exactly what I was dreading. Old, with a steeple. The car park is full but he finds a slot. I tug my very bright coat across me and have a crisis of conscience and nerves.

'I'm sorry. I shouldn't have. I can't. I mean I won't …'

Dominic opens the enormous oak door and pushes me inside. 'Don't let all the warm air out, woman.'

Colours swirl; the blue smell of candles, green piney resin, primrose yellow wood and oddly, bright yellow mince pies, flood through me. There is a cacophony akin to a school playground. Children are playing tag up and down the aisle, yelling their heads off. Father Christmas onesies and fairy princesses are in the ascendant with an assortment of toy lambs and other strange animals being tossed over heads and bashed into parental faces. The parents are equally as noisy and there is a lot of hugging going on. Mum's church, so far as I could remember, was always icy cold and had rows of black wooden benches about six inches deep. As a child, I couldn't get my bottom to stay on, or my feet to the floor. Here it is palpably warm, and there are pale wood chairs with blue upholstered seats filled with chattering grannies, teenagers and babies. The whole place is awash in Christmas decorations, flowers, tinsel, an enormous Christmas tree heavily clothed up to age ten height, and more lightly and elegantly dressed further up. There is an enormous stable and crib at the back. That at least looks like a sober Holy Family, the only piece of religion I can see.

Some lady throws her arms around Dominic and kisses him roundly on both cheeks, closely followed by other ladies, all of them shouting, 'Happy Christmas'. Their spouses, mostly attired in Christmas sweaters with flashing lights, confine themselves to handshakes and back-slapping and as Dominic repeats, 'And this is Cass,' to my amazement they all shout, 'Happy Christmas, Cass!' and I get roundly kissed as well, by both spouses. I am speechless.

Two little girls appear, not fairy princesses, but in enchanting long blue velvet dresses with blue satin sashes. They tug me onto a spare chair and give me the third degree.

'Why is your hair green?'

'Why are your dresses blue?'

'Our auntie got married and we were bridesmaids. Why have you got green hair?'

'Don't you like it?'

'Yes!' they both say together. 'Why are you wearing green lipstick?'

'Cos it matches my hair,' I say gravely. 'Just like your sashes match your dresses. Don't you like my lipstick?'

'Oh yes!' says one fervently. 'Have you got it with you? Can I try?'

I lie through my teeth and say I haven't got it with me. What would the parents say?

'What are your names and how old are you?'

By the time this information is forthcoming, there are more children, and several teenagers, flopping about all over the surrounding chairs, stroking my wig and commenting favourably on my make-up. A small boy of about four has no qualms about pulling my coat away and giving my outfit his serious attention. This is a surreal situation and I wonder if I inadvertently consumed ganja for breakfast.

Band music which I now realise has been playing in the background suddenly becomes loud and demanding and Dominic appears, gently removing several children from the neighbouring chair before sitting down beside me. The cacophony lessens to a more subdued burble and I begin to realise this is not church as I had ever known it, or in my wildest dreams ever imagined it. Half an hour and a mince pie later, we depart, leaving a trail of promises of green lipstick, nails with holly berries and multicoloured wigs.

'I am exhausted!' I tell the driver.

He glances over at me, and he's laughing. 'I said the kids would love you. They all loved you. It wasn't that bad, was it?'

It's ridiculous, but I find myself turning sober. 'But it can't be normal, can it? Church is not supposed to be like that. I mean, they were genuinely nice, and I had sort of gone to …' Tailing off, I am truly ashamed of myself.

'I know. Take the mickey. Shock them all to the core. Ruin my reputation. Get me excommunicated.' He is amused. 'I think it's supposed to be exactly like that. That's why I go there.'

He doesn't talk about it anymore, though I am full of curiosity about guitars and children being allowed to shout answers to daft questions from a lady vicar. The whole thing had been extraordinarily unholy and pragmatic and unnervingly moving. Confused.com.

The table is laid already, everything in the kitchen is prepared, and yellow smells emanate from the oven making me salivate in anticipation. Christmas cards are on every surface and tucked into the books on the shelves. I've had about twenty. Dominic has about two hundred.

'I forgot the crackers,' he says without too much apology. It's not even midday, but he pours champagne. The gas log fire is wonderfully realistic, warm, and welcoming.

There is a small Christmas tree in the bay window with a mass of singular hanging ornaments on it, but no tinsel or coloured balls. I have the feeling each item is a memory.

'You didn't live here with Penny, did you?' This house

is one of the few subjects we have never discussed in any depth.

'We were students when we married – well, postgraduates – our draughty barn flat had no heating and the water froze in the taps in winter.' He grins at the memory. 'We loved it. Patrick arrived and thrived, but when Penny got pregnant again, my mother-in-law became all bossy and put her foot down.' He gets up and tops up my glass. 'By that time, we were both doing OK career-wise and we started looking. We found a lovely house, but she was killed before we bought it. It took me a while to get my head round losing her and the baby. Eventually, I found this place, and Mum found a cleaner. We managed.'

What a lot he isn't saying. I suspect that this house is exactly as he bought it, and without Penny, he didn't have the mental energy to upgrade the seventies kitchen and bathrooms while coping with a motherless five-year-old.

'What are you going to do about the Southampton flat?' Is he changing the subject back to me because he finds it too painful thinking about Penny's death and his lost daughter? I can relate to his broken hopes and dreams, but mine are not on such a terrible scale.

'Nothing came of my efforts to sell in the autumn, so I've taken it off the market and will try again in the spring. I want something smaller but I haven't found anything suitable.' I try not to let my voice go downbeat. 'I'd like to live and run the business from one place, but I'm not clear whether it would be legal or not. I don't want to ask in case it isn't! Finding somewhere is rather daunting when all my brain power is directed at trying to get Ecolore on the road again.'

'There's no legal reason why you shouldn't have a home-based business, but mortgage companies can be tricky, and some councils don't like it. And permission depends on all sorts of factors – parking, customers, noise. That sort of thing. Zev would help you with that when the time comes.' He gets up to refill my glass. 'So would I, come to that.' He disappears to the kitchen and pans rattle.

That's a kind thought, even if I am an independent woman who doesn't need that sort of help. After a moment or two, I follow the yellow smell to the kitchen doorway. He is spooning hot fat over roast potatoes and a small turkey.

He indicates some jars on the counter. 'Would you like to be in charge of that lot?' As I put bread sauce in a pan, and a spoon in the cranberry jelly, he turns chipolatas wrapped in bacon in the meat juices. 'M & S are fantastic. All the bits, ready-made. Perfect for bachelors. And bachelor girls too. Even the very small Christmas pudding can be microwaved. My mother would be horrified.'

'I bet she wouldn't,' I say. 'It's just that back in the day there was no alternative. Have you heard if she's enjoying sitting back and letting your sister do Christmas?'

He flicks a glance at me. 'She doesn't say. Knowing Merryn, she's probably getting Mum to do it all from scratch. I love food but I eat to live, rather than live to eat. There are other things I'd prefer to do than preparing food.'

I nearly say 'What?' and think better of it.

He snaps a small knife off a magnetic rack. 'Do you like or loathe Brussels sprouts? I've got broccoli and beans as well.'

I take the knife from his hand. 'I love sprouts and oddly they smell the colour they are.'

The sprouts are little baby ones. They will taste sweet.

He returns the roasting pan to the oven, and we return to the fire and the topping up of glasses. The champagne bubbles are rising more slowly now, fire flames flickering through the gold. I have a sense of timelessness, ease, of something unusual in my spirit, and wonder if it is happiness.

* * *

Lunch is delicious: primrose yellow, leaf green, lavender, citrus yellow and dark navy. Dominic gets the silver sixpence and the unspoken wish. I consume too much brandy butter and Châteauneuf-du-Pape.

We walk briefly in a bitter wind to make us feel less indolent and the return to the fire is therefore especially agreeable. It makes him sneeze. Three times, then enough gap for half a sentence, then another three. I give him my Christmas present: a toddy lifter I found in a bric-a-brac shop. It is smooth and plain but the glass glows ruby red.

'I love it,' he says. 'I haven't got a coloured one.' He seems genuinely pleased and I find him running his fingers over it at odd moments. His present to me is an Alexa Echo Dot which I am thrilled with because Mike has taken ours and I miss it.

We eat M & S Christmas cake for tea and smoked salmon with lemon for supper. I have told him about progress on the magnum opus, and my night blindness, how the edges of my sight have shrunk, and the centre splinters into a kaleidoscope of black and white and grey. We have discovered so much more about each other without even asking for information and uncovered yet more layers of interest and knowledge, and what makes us laugh or cry.

I have also found I have a craving for a family and an envy of his.

When the pre-arranged Uber arrives at ten o'clock, he takes me in his arms behind the still-closed door and holds me close.

'Might you think again, my beautiful Cass?'

I lay my head against his steady, beating heart. 'I think all day, every day. And the answer still has to be no.' I choke down the pain. 'You know it has to be no.' I can feel his sadness and my own regret is an agony.

He sighs, and I can feel it, deep down in his lungs. 'It doesn't have to be a total, absolute no.'

The driver rings the bell, and I reach around Dominic and open the door. 'It does,' I say wretchedly. 'We both know it does.' I have had the best Christmas I can ever remember, but as the fractured headlights stream past the taxi on the black motorway, I think it has been the saddest one too. A man-friend is just as wonderful as a girlfriend. But very different. I just yearn for him to be a lover too.

Chapter Thirty-Two

Dominic, quite without intention, has managed to make me feel guilty that Dad had probably been alone at Christmas, and now I think I ought to go and visit. For half my life I have hardly given him a thought and now I feel bad about him being alone at Christmas!

And although I suspect it was a malicious effort to upset me, ever since Mike's nasty inference that my father loathes me because Mum had a fling with someone and I am not his daughter, the possibility of it being true has niggled at me.

Could Dad's treatment of Mum have had a reason? Could Mum have gone for comfort and love elsewhere? In which case, was I Dad's daughter? Did he think that he was hatching a cuckoo in his nest? And would that explain his attitude towards me? And does it matter anyway?

I buy a decent bottle of wine, put it in a Christmassy bottle bag, and dress up. I might as well show him what Ecolore is about before dropping my bombshell question.

'Very kind of you,' he says, clearly surprised by both my visit and my offering. 'I was in fact entertained by friends on Christmas Day, but thanks for the thought. They have no children, so they invite me most years.' He adds, almost humorously, 'I can on occasions make myself pleasant and socially acceptable, even if you never experienced it.'

I look at him sharply. Is that an admission of fatherly failure? Jen had said he was a 'useful single man'.

We have cups of tea, and to my amazement, he comments positively about my blue wig, which is similar in colour to his own smell.

'Smart. Classy,' he says. 'The fringe suits you.' I have a fleeting memory of my untidy beige mother; was her mousiness another thing that annoyed him?

What I want to ask him becomes more difficult to frame by the minute, but oddly it is he who enables the conversation.

'When you came before, you asked about people called Benton – said your partner's parents knew me. It took a while to remember but I think a couple called Benton were Lloyd's clients back in the nineties when I was a broker, and they took a hit.' He taps a finger against his teacup. 'Can't remember their names though.'

'Kenneth and Veronica?'

'Kenneth. Yes, I think so.' Their taking a hit doesn't seem to bother him unduly. 'You going to marry this Benton man?'

'No.' I'm wondering why I don't mind the thought of him knowing about Mike and what he's done. 'No, I'm not. It turned out he stole a huge amount from my business and interestingly it was because of you.'

Dad looks up sharply. 'Because of me? I don't know him, do I?'

'No, you don't. But he blamed you for his parents' bankruptcy and decided that I, as your daughter, should restore his financial loss. It was a bit of a surprise, I must admit.' I can hear his indrawn breath and he shifts uncomfortably in his chair. 'But more than that, I think he may have been the hit-and-run driver who smashed you up.'

I have silenced my father, who is staring across at me in amazement. Eventually, he says, 'How did you come to that conclusion? The police found no evidence at all.'

So I tell him about Mike's gleeful statement that it

wasn't just me he punished and that I discovered he took his car to his parents to sell on the same day as Dad's accident.

'I don't think it can possibly be proved, and as he has skipped the country with my money, the police won't catch him now, but I think it's more than likely it was him that hit you.'

He grunts, thinking about it. 'Bad judgement on your part, choosing a man like that,' he says sourly. 'Lloyds was always a risk. What goes up must come down. They risked too much and didn't think of the consequences.'

Well, he's right about my judgement. To my surprise, I don't feel I have to react like I used to. I'd have been furious as a teenager. And I've no particular right to start telling him he had a responsibility towards his clients.

'He said something else. About us. As a family.' Am I mad, to be verbalising this innuendo of Mike's? Just as I am making the effort to mend fences and make some sort of relationship with him?

'Someone like that wouldn't have anything good to say about our family.'

'True,' I agree. 'But it bothered me.' Taking a deep breath, I come out with it. 'He said you loathed me because I wasn't your daughter and you'd had to bring up a cuckoo in the nest because Mum had got pregnant by someone else.'

There is a protracted stunned silence, and I can feel his outrage. 'My God, Cassia! How dare you even give that house room! It's not true. Of course it's not true! I didn't loathe you!' He is patently troubled by the word, as indeed I had been. 'You drove me demented because you wouldn't do what the hell I told you to. Ever! You always went your own way, and it was never mine. Like your clothes, and that hasn't changed, though I must admit you carry it off well.' There's a faint smile. 'But I didn't loathe you, or hate you, or even dislike you.' He suddenly laughs. 'I adored you when you were little. It was when you developed a mind of your own that we crossed swords. You're my daughter all right, no doubt about that.'

He didn't loathe me. Why do I feel so released by his certainty? So relieved? The word had been nagging me like a shard of glass. To be loathed would be so horrible, there would have to be a cause for loathing.

'How are you so sure I'm your daughter?' I am still wary of my father. I haven't forgotten his treatment of me as a teenager, but I must admit that I was certainly a rebellious one. I am rather sad that I don't remember him adoring me when I was little.

He laughs again. 'As a child, you looked exactly like me. Your mother had photographs, God knows where they are now, but you had the same expression as me, the same shape of face. And you were as bloody-minded as I was. You and I fought like tigers because neither of us would ever give in. Exhausting.' He breathes in deeply. 'It was a waste of time fighting those battles. We should have kept our ammunition dry for the things that mattered, but I didn't see that at the time. Perhaps you don't when you're young. It takes a bit of life experience to recognise what's important and what isn't.'

So why did I give in to Mike? Because it was too exhausting to go on fighting? 'You treated us really badly.' I'm not quite prepared to be mollified.

He thinks for a moment. 'Maybe I did. Yes, I guess that's true. You were both everything that drove me nuts. You did nothing but fight and your mother wouldn't fight at all.'

* * *

When I get back to the flat, I search through Ugly's drawers and find the three old photo albums. I have never examined them closely before, but I do now. I want to confirm Dad's apparent certainty that I'm not anyone's child but his. There was a time when I'd have been glad to have it proved I wasn't his child. I'm not so sure now. For the first time, I look closely at those faded, slightly out-of-focus faces. There are almost none of them together in the same picture, but Mum and Dad looked perfectly happy when they were young, and both appear delighted with their squat, plain and scowling baby.

There's a picture of me, aged what? Two? Three? In dungarees, standing at the top of a slide, a grin smeared across my face, poised for launching. Highly dangerous at first sight, but now I see, right at the bottom of the photo, a pair of open hands. I fetch my magnifying glass and peer more closely. Big hands, a man's hands. Dad's hands? Ready to catch a toppling toddler. Mum had always given the impression that he was never there, that he never helped, that he never cared. What did I remember? What had I chosen to remember, and what had I chosen to forget? I open the Red Box and take out those strands of red and yellow wool, and choose to remember a great long scarf, wound round and round till his face was covered, and Dad going out the door on his way to the train, two long scarf tails streaming behind him. I don't remember him saying thank you, but so what?

And he's quite right. There is a distinct resemblance between him and me, and none at all that I can see to my mother, except for my concave nose.

Chapter Thirty-Three

We are in a second-hand bookshop and had only been having a ping-pong sort of conversation between the teetering racks and book-bowed shelves. Since Christmas, and my second cataract operation, I have sensed a mounting tension in him, making me increasingly uneasy; I know in my spirit that our relationship is both tenuous and unsatisfactory. Friendship is essential but not sufficient.

I indicate the three books he is holding. 'What have you got?'

He looks down at the spines and his tension is laced with astringency. '*The Key Above the Door*, *Salmon Rivers of Scotland* and "How to Live with a Bloody-Minded Blind Woman". What have you got?'

I'm perturbed by his tone and try to lighten the moment. 'Large print. Not that I will read it, even though it's better without the cataract.' Even large print is exhausting so I haven't read a book for months. 'It's Audible only these days.'

'Let's go then,' he says. 'We need to talk audibly.' I grip the shelf with stiff fingers to steady myself. His normally soft voice is almost harsh, and I have a strong sense of apprehension.

He carries the bag with four books in it back to his house. Sadness and a sense of failure fill me as we heat a carton of soup and fresh French bread. I think I know what's coming.

'I really have tried to be just a friend.' He sounds tired. 'I have given myself stern lectures, but this friendship simply isn't enough. I don't want to be just a friend. I love you. I want more than friendship; I want to be with you, to be part of your life, and you to be part of mine. I want to make love to you, to touch you and feel you. I want to share my home and my family and thoughts and plans and a future with you. But I don't think I can manage to go on just being a friend. You left me because you hadn't the courage to tell me the truth, but unless you change your mind, I'm going to break off this … whatever you call it. Friendship. Relationship. Because I have finally found the courage.'

His words silence me. My eyes fill with unwelcome and alien tears and his unhappiness reverberates like a stone in a tin can.

'If you can't – won't – be more than a friend, I'm going to stop seeing you because it's just too painful. I don't understand why, if you say you love me, you won't stay with me. I've come to think that actually, you don't love me. Or not enough.' The sadness is edged with frustration now. 'Just because you've got RP doesn't seem to me to be a good reason for not being together. There must be thousands of people whose partners are blind who still love each other, live together, and have a fulfilling life.' He puts his soup spoon down so forcibly it clangs discordantly on the bowl.

'So I think I'm calling time, Cass, unless you change your mind very soon. I told my family that I loved you, they know you're going blind, and they would support me and you through whatever difficulties might lie ahead. It doesn't have to be impossible. You needn't be blighted by it when you could find new outlets and new skills. But to spend the rest of my life purely as your friend is more than I can bear when there is no good reason to do so. I've waited and waited. I thought we loved each other. But now I'm not at all sure.' I am frozen, unable to articulate anything because this is the first time I have seen him like this. Not just frustrated, but angry.

'Why in God's name are you so stubborn about this? Why must the fact that you're losing your sight prevent us from being happy together? What is your reasoning?'

Because I can't have your child and I know you'd love one. Because I am terrified of what lies ahead in the darkness. Because I am afraid that I will turn out like my mother, and you will become like my father. To see that happening, and to be the cause of it is more than I can face. Why can't I say this?

He has waited out my silence and his exasperation really has become anger. 'If you won't even try to explain, I have to assume that you don't feel as you said you did after you and Mike split up. I wonder if you even know what loving is.'

I physically lurch away from him because that hurts like a slap in the face.

'I do. I do know. I do love you.'

He looks at me with a sort of hopeless bewilderment. 'I don't think so. If you did, you wouldn't do what you're doing to me.' His shoulders drop and he looks utterly drained. 'This time, it'll be me leaving you.'

The wretchedness that drags down my mind and body is so great that I feel as if I'm drowning. It's not just blindness that is so terrifying, though that is bad enough, it's what will happen to me – to us – if I surrender to this desire.

'Will you think again?'

My mother, wiping her tear-wet face with a dirty tea towel, a broken jug and a pint of milk spreading on the kitchen floor, and Dad's foot crunching on shards of pottery. Her sobs, his shouts, my hatred.

'No,' I whisper.

* * *

I am designing using the new colour chart. I concentrate hard on the little multicoloured butterflies flitting over photograph frames as I would otherwise focus on the total and final loss of Dominic. The sharp pain of his absence has mulched into a background ache and the winter chill seems to have gone as deep into my heart as it has into my bones. These days I'm always aware of my financial cliff edge, so with the heating turned off the flat is perishingly cold, and my feet are unglamorously encased in a pair of enormous boot socks. My vision has declined steadily since the summer, and all my paperwork takes twice as long as it used to. I seldom get to bed before midnight, partly because when I'm in bed all I can think of is that Dominic is not. These days I need to be so exhausted that I can't lie awake longing for him.

Wendy continues to be furious with me.

'You're mad to have let him go, Cass. Can't you recognise a gem when you see one? You spend six years with a bone bracelet and then throw away a diamond necklace. Anyone would think you had dozens to choose from, but I'm telling you he's a chance in a lifetime. One in a million.'

'Considering your usual views on men in general and husbands in particular, I don't think you're in any position to comment,' I say aggressively.

'You bet I'm in a position to comment! I had a bone bracelet too; I just didn't find a diamond necklace. Didn't think they existed. Your reasoning is ridiculous.'

'My reasoning is not ridiculous.' I feel exhausted by having to defend it. 'You have no idea what this feels like. I'm becoming a different person; a scared, incompetent person. Not the person Dominic thinks I am or wants me to be.'

'Rubbish!' Wendy spits. 'You may be scared, but you're not incompetent. Pull yourself together. There's nothing worse than self-pity.' Oof. Wendy doesn't pull her punches. Self-pity is certainly an unattractive characteristic. I am chastened by her disapproval. This is not the first time she has sown the seeds of doubt about my decision.

I return to my tablet determined to finish the day's work, but my concentration is interrupted when the phone rings, and as usual, I'm nervous that it may be a disgruntled creditor or someone I have let down by cancelling orders. I have long since given up wondering whether it might be Dominic.

A pleasant sounding woman introduces herself as Ursula Anderson, an interior designer based in Cheltenham, a friend of Jen's, and she is interested in hearing more about my recycled carpets and sustainable fabrics.

Networking pays off! Adrenaline surges and I try not to gush my responses as I tell her about the advantages, the content and colours, the pricing and manufacturers.

'What about carpet retailers?'

I sense that, like Wendy, she is a hard-headed businesswoman and suck my lips in as I admit that none will stock colours. 'Retailers don't believe that people want a colour statement on their floors. It's all bland creams, beiges, greys.'

I hear her sniff. 'So this carpet type is available, but only in standard and limited shades?'

'Sadly, yes. I've had one set of colours made up and they look gorgeous, but the retailers say there won't be a market and they'll be left with unsold stock.'

'I see.' She sounds displeased, as indeed I am. 'Where are the samples and what colour ranges?'

'I could only afford to have reds done, and there are fourteen shades from pale to deep. I've got them here. In Southampton.'

‘Can colours not be produced to order?’

There is a pulse hammering in my throat. ‘Yes, of course. But it would have to be a definite order and the samples are expensive.’

I have no idea if the manufacturer would do a limited colour run and think it unlikely, but I’m not going to say so. She’d like to see the samples. Next week. I gulp.

‘In Cheltenham?’ I can’t drive there. Taxi? Courier? We agree on a day and a time, and I will bring colour charts and fabric samples as well. In the meantime, information will be emailed.

I am shaking as she rings off. Is this good news or bad news? I never asked what sort of interiors she designed for. Just doing local houses, or offices or what? By the time I have sent her photos, product descriptions and prices, I am split in two. Half of me exhilarated to think that at last this idea might come good, and half terrified that I have again bitten off several mouthfuls too large. Computer cases and wellington boots are small beer compared with expensive carpet. I take a grip on my nerves. Without risk, life is not worth living. So they say. I want to tell Dominic and there is an empty hole in my excitement because I’m not going to. Wendy’s angry words echo again in the silence.

I bring forward my hair appointment with Rupert and the wonderfully avant-garde nail stylist, Abigail. I may turn off the heating, but there are some things I won’t compromise on.

* * *

Ursula Anderson has high street premises, painted a creamy pale blue. The big bow window reveals an enticing interior of high-quality furniture with unusual, quite modern upholstery and curtains. It looks welcoming and unintimidating which is quite a feat for an interior decorator, and it smells of burned umber: potpourri. The taxi driver helps me unload the samples and my laptop and paperwork, and Ursula, tall, thin, with beautifully cut blonde hair, ushers me into a spacious back room with a large, cleared table.

She handles the carpet samples with knowledgeable fingers. 'These have a good texture. Do you have the manufacturer's details? Cleaning, staining, fading, durability? And the shades are beautiful. Very subtle. I agree with you: in certain circumstances, there is no reason why carpets should not be the focal point, rather than paint colour, or decoration.' Her eyes narrow and I can see her visualising. 'Colour on the floor and maybe the paintwork. Neutrals in the furnishings.'

She seems to be interested in my sustainable and eco projects and looks closely at the fabrics. I show her photographs of the curtains in the flat and her attention sharpens.

'Ah! I like that design! That interests me more than singular colours, lovely though they are. Among other clients, I am bidding for a new conference centre and there must be design in the flooring to take up wear and spillage damage, however easy to clean it is.'

'And curtain fabric and upholstery design and colour to echo the carpet?'

And we are off, on my favourite subjects, and I take reams of notes and try to squash down the mounting excitement. After all, there are no orders, and she is only putting a toe in the water. In any case, she will be only one of several bidders for the conference centre. I am a middleman, and I know from experience that middlemen are avoided or cut out wherever possible. That is why design copyrights are so necessary.

'I'll need colour samples, like these …' She indicates the

strewn table. 'We'll discuss colours in a minute. And some designs. Modern, geometric, curves. Nothing flowery. Nothing traditional. How quickly could you have those done?'

Panic rises. Speed would not be my major problem. Ursula is looking at me sharply. I am aware that she is older, more experienced, and probably savvier than me.

'There's a problem with that?'

'No problem with designs, or colours.' I'm going to have to come clean. 'It's the samples. My finances are – stretched. If I did computer designs would that be acceptable?'

The fact that I would find it difficult to pay for more carpet samples might be enough to lose me this contract.

Once more I tell myself that life without risk is no life at all.

'My partner of six years stole my business. He virtually bankrupted me. Then he disappeared, so I'd have to ask you to advance me the cost of actual samples. I had good financial reserves, but now I have none and I'm having to start from scratch again.' I look down at the beautiful designs on my nails. 'I will quite understand if you don't want to do business with me. But I hope you will.'

There is a long silence. When I look up, Ursula Anderson is gazing unfocused at the samples, the tips of her fingers stroking her jutting chin. She is not sympathetic. She is making calculations.

'Give me designs and colourways for carpets and curtains and seating, to suit this conference centre.' She reaches behind her and slaps open a file to some artist's impressions of a big modern extension. 'It will be attached to a hotel in Bournemouth. Get them to me within seven days. Leave the manufacturers to me. Then we'll discuss.'

She is reminiscent of a dragon. Charming but alarming. I am wrung out like a floorcloth. Twisted into spirals of damp sweat and dry mouth. Can I achieve this in the short timespan she has given me?

Yes, you can, Cass Hunter. This is what you have been aiming for, before this disastrous year. Of love lost. And love found and lost. This is a project which you know in your heart has potential and is viable. Just because life has fallen apart doesn't mean that you need to behave like wet blotting paper. You can seize this chance and make it a success.

I will do this. Even if I'm blind.

* * *

When the designs go off to Ursula, I catch myself staring at them on the screen. Have I done enough? Are they suitable? Will she like them? Will the hotel like them? Have I got the right colourways, and the right formatting? Some days I feel positive, and some days I don't.

Sometimes I feel so positive that I convince myself that being blind won't affect me. I will be the epitome of pushing through difficulties, continuing to work and achieve. A feeling of urgency whips me into a frenzy of productive ideas and plans whether I get this conference centre project or not. I will be an example to those who are struggling with their sight. Self-pity is not in my lexicon.

But quite often I am assaulted by frustration and panic as to how I can take design into a realm of darkness. Once or twice, waking from a nightmare, almost always searching for an elusive Dominic, pure, unadulterated fear of the future has enveloped me to the extent of making me run for the bathroom. I find myself on my knees, chilled to the bone, throwing up into the loo, cold sweat on my skin, hands shaking, eyes leaking. These panic attacks are the times when I long for my diamond necklace, to be enclosed in Dominic's arms. But at the same time, I am thankful this weakness is hidden from him.

It has taken me weeks to pummel my magnum opus into a working model. Until recently, smells and colour were an unacknowledged fact of life. Now, I consciously annotate the salty wind, the cigarette smoke and snuffed candles, the burning leaves, the broccoli and garlic. The most surprising smells have the same colour, like the friendly cat downstairs who smells the same pale yellow as furniture polish. I discover that I smell more yellows than any other colour. It will never be truly finished of course; there will be perpetual tweaking.

I think it's brilliant, and my favourite fabric printer can't stop chuckling. I can name all the colours I need, and the computer picks them out and puts them into the designs. I practise with my eyes closed although I have so little peripheral vision now that I hardly need to. My pride is as great as if I had just completed a PhD, and I long to show Dominic and thank him for having the idea in the first place and then for making me do it.

Wendy's words continue to echo in my mind. I spent six years with a bone bracelet and now I'm throwing away a diamond necklace in case I become a bone bracelet. Am I completely mad?

* * *

To my great surprise, because it felt such an unlikely outcome after so long a silence, Ursula Anderson likes my designs and colourways and so apparently does the Bournemouth hotel because she got the contract.

Of course, there are changes and modifications, but suddenly there are deadlines to meet, manufacturers to instruct, and copyrights to register. Piles of samples clutter up the flat. It's not the world's most lucrative deal, but my natural optimism is in the ascendant again. The rocky business storm is calming with the Christmas sales trickling into Ecolore, and the non-snag tights have taken off. Everything in the garden should be rosy, but without Dominic to share it with, the flowers are windblown and rain splashed.

Wendy has sold her shop. I knew she couldn't wait for my flat to sell. Although she got a better deal than my original offer, I am disappointed that she couldn't hang on longer. When this flat sells, and there are viewings now, I would have had the money.

Not all of Mike's furniture has sold. The black pictures have returned, piled face to the wall, and once I have vacuumed out the spiders, I ring the gallery that represents Milo Szorski-Czyz.

'Oh yes!' the gallery assistant cries. 'Milo's work is much sought after. We always have a certain number, though they fly off the walls all too quickly and we can't get enough. If you can visit, I'm sure we could help you source something you'd love.'

I explain that it's me helping them, not the other way round. I can assist in providing them with three of Milo's black period. There is an immediate cooling, and the gallery, unfortunately, cannot repurchase.

'OK. They'll just have to go to the charity shop,' I say, hanging up. It is clear that no one in their right mind would want them. It is also clear that Mike was an idiot. I take photographs, copy Milo's blurb and auction them on eBay at twenty per cent less than the original price. To my amazement, there are other tasteless idiots out there who start a bidding war and I end up with some useful loose cash. Dominic would love this story, but he won't hear it. I miss him.

The rest of Mike's pictures, sculptures and brown furniture, antique or not, sell for peanuts compared to the caviar prices he bought at, and what doesn't reach their reserve comes winging home to Southampton where I put them on eBay too. I would so love to share these moments of hilarity, the excitement of seeing auction bids escalate, and the astonishment I feel when some stout conservative matron displays a deep desire for a Mayan fertility goddess sculpture. Perhaps Dominic, with his interest in archaeology, would like the fertility goddess too? I hope not, but I don't know. I wish I did.

Chapter Thirty-Four

Jen Vermont rings to congratulate me on the conference centre contract.

'Ursula is thrilled to have got that hotel contract and thinks your designs are wonderful. It's a huge coup for her and for you.'

'I never thought of it being so important for her,' I say, rather astonished that the Dragon Lady hadn't taken it all in her stride.

'You bet!' Jen says. 'And we want to hear all about it. Come and have lunch with us on Saturday and bring pictures and some of the fabric to show us.' I hesitate. This lunch could be extended to Dominic too, which would not be good, but Jen appears to know that we no longer have a relationship.

'I promise Dom won't be here. He's going away.' I wonder vaguely whether there is a subplot here. I like Peter and Jen very much, but they are Dominic's friends and I am only an acquaintance.

Over lunch, I realise I am right as they use the opportunity of Arabella's absence on a shopping spree with her grandmother to try to sort me out.

'He's miserable, Cass.' We have eaten a vast lasagne and salad and now Jen puts an enormous pudding covered in meringue on the kitchen table. 'He loves you and says you love him too. You're both free to be together, so why don't you? Your sight problems are horrible for you, but loads of blind people get married, do amazing things, achieve degrees and hold down jobs. Why shouldn't you? It's just another incredible achievement.' She fills bowls and pushes a jug of thick cream towards me.

I sidetrack. 'Oh my goodness, that is utterly delicious! What do you call that?'

'Queen of Puddings,' Peter says happily. 'Everyone's favourite. Go on, tell us, why shouldn't you be with Dom? You were both so happy when you were together. What went wrong?'

'I got the diagnosis,' I say slowly, and then feel the need to expand on my apparent illogicality. 'But it's what went wrong with my parents that terrifies me. My mother became totally dependent when she went blind – and my father became a monster. I think he had always been controlling and bad-tempered but when she was blind, he was truly awful. If I turn out like my mother, I may drive Dominic to be like my father.'

There is a stunned silence. Then Peter puts his spoon down and says, 'What absolute rubbish! All of us are people in our own right, not clones of our parents. You're a capable, talented woman, and you are not your mother, and Dominic is neither controlling nor bad-tempered. The complete opposite in fact.'

William has put his head on my lap and closed his eyes. It will only last about thirty seconds but still feels comforting.

'But me being blind would be an appalling disadvantage to him. And – and all the other things.'

'What other things?' Jen asks.

'The ten-year age gap. And I can't have children because RP is genetic.'

And a raft of other things I can't put into words. My lack of judgement in falling for Mike. My childish revenge, Dominic's faith, my doubts. His kindness, my vindictiveness. His maturity, my immaturity. Jen puts the remains of the Queen of Puddings in a bowl for Arabella's supper and drops the newspaper on the table for Peter.

'The age gap is irrelevant,' she says briskly. 'We've got married friends with twenty-five years between them. OK, he'll fall off his perch before her, but in the meantime, they're very happy. And I'm very sorry you feel you shouldn't have children, but that is your unavoidable sorrow, not Dom's, and has no bearing on whether you marry him or someone else. He has Patrick and we have Arabella. The fact that neither of us has another child is no reason not to enjoy what we do have and, frankly, I'd have no desire to start all over again with babies, even if I could, and I very much doubt Dom does either.'

'I know for a fact he doesn't,' Peter says. 'There was a girl who was very keen on him, but she wanted children. The relationship didn't work.'

'Oh!' I'm having to rethink. 'But he loves children! He adores Arabella. He's always stopping to talk to the toddler next door.'

'Just because he likes children doesn't mean to say he wants another of his own,' Peter remarks dryly.

I think about that as I start washing up the pans while Jen fills the dishwasher and then starts whisking pancake batter for tea. It seems to be non-stop food in this household.

'So, what other things are stopping you?' she says.

'What on earth will his family say? I am not suitable. He's a professional man, his brother and sister would have a fit.'

Peter crushes the paper onto his lap and stares at me. 'Do stop talking nonsense. His mother will love you, and David and Merryn will too. Patrick is besotted by your clothes and how wicked you are. Why would they have a fit if you were together?' He raises the crumpled paper and then puts it down again. 'And what has suitability got to do with anything? Why aren't you suitable? And who the heck cares whether you're suitable or not?'

I take a quick look down at my retro seventies trousers, made of patchwork offcuts from the last batch of my fabric designs. I think they're terrific but suspect most people think they are downright peculiar.

'Well, you're his brother-in-law. You might care. After Penny.'

Peter sighs and tries unsuccessfully to fold the paper which by now looks as shambolic as he does. 'Penny would have wanted him to be happy.'

'Look.' I am trying to be resolute. 'He cannot, he really, truly cannot get involved with someone who is well on the way to being blind. Can't you see it would be disastrous for him? I'd be dependent on him for everything.'

The paper is crumpled down again on the kitchen table. 'You are being ridiculous, Cass. Why should you be dependent on him for anything? You will learn to do everything you need to. If you were on your own, you'd learn to do them. You've already learned how to do lots of things you once used your eyes for. And two of you together will be much better than just one of you trying to do it by yourself.'

'But that's exactly it.' I can hear myself getting strident as I try to regain the conversational high ground. 'What a pain! He'll end up resenting me and how I hold him up and hold him back.'

Peter shakes his head. 'He won't. And you won't hold him up or hold him back. You're not the pathetic sort, and he wouldn't have fallen for you if you were. He wants to do it with you, not for you.' He sighs. 'Cass, he loved my sister, but there is life after death you know. I'd be the last person to say he shouldn't have any happiness after what he's gone through. He's fallen in love with you, and we were hoping it was mutual.'

'Is it mutual?' Jen says.

The doorbell goes. Ping, p-ping, ping. Ping, p-ping, ping. Ping, p-ping, ping.

'They're back,' Jen says resignedly.

'I'll go.' I could do with an intermission.

Arabella is hopping on the doorstep and without even a 'hi' makes a lightning streak to the kitchen shouting, 'Are you doing the pancakes?' There is an affirmative.

The older lady still on the doorstep says, 'Hello. You must be Cass.' She is looking at my trousers. My clothes goeth before me. 'I'm Arabella's grandmother, Peter's mother.' Therefore, Penny's mother. 'What perfectly splendid trousers!'

In the kitchen, everyone gets kissed and hugged and Arabella hugs me too, which is warming. After coming last in several games of Racing Demon, mainly because I can't differentiate suits and numbers, I am persuaded to get the laptop again and Jen and Granny pore over the hotel designs. Tea is made, I chop hunks of lemon and put honey, chocolate spread and sugar on the table and we eat pancakes which smell pale lilac as they come off Jen's griddle.

'We were trying to discover if Cass is as much in love with Dom as he is with her,' Jen says, to my acute embarrassment, as she slides another plateful of lilac pancakes onto the table. 'She's being reticent.'

'Don't you know?' says Dominic's first wife's mother, giving me a sharp look.

I empathise with the rabbit in the headlights. My voice has deserted me. This discussion is out of order and has nothing to do with any of them.

Arabella breaks into my paralysed silence. 'Do be in love with him, then you can live really close and take me to school instead of Mummy so they can see I'm not making you up.' She is not interrupted by me, so continues. 'You could pick me up in the afternoon too and take me to McDonald's.'

'There you are, Cass,' Peter says. 'That absolutely has to clinch the deal. How could you possibly resist?'

I relocate my voice-box and my dignity. 'Thank you all for your interest in my private life.' Glancing at the kitchen clock, I think it must be getting dark outside. 'I really must go.' Thanking them for a delicious lunch and tea, I gather my jacket, computer and bag and make a disorderly exit.

Halfway to the station, a car draws up just beyond me and getting out, Jen blocks my path. I can't analyse her expression, but her body language is all determination and I have to stop as I can't get past her.

'Cass, Dom understands the complications. He says he's been in love with you from the day you met.' I wonder if he told them the circumstances of the day we met. 'The fact that you're going blind is not irrelevant or dismissed, and yes, he's talked to his mother and David and Merryn and Patrick about what it would involve. He's quite aware you don't want him to be a crutch. He's not sorry for you and he is not trying to control you. But he is in love with you, and he thinks it's mutual.'

I swallow down the lump of uncertainty that fills my throat.

'Of course I love him. That's why I can't stay with him. The problem isn't just the fact of me being blind. It's what being blind will do to us. To us both. I love him too much to take the risk.'

A stream of traffic is deviating irritably around her Range Rover and passers-by are having to walk around us too as we have this life-changing debate in the middle of Winchester. I'm surprised some don't linger to hear more.

Jen throws her head back. 'Any relationship is a risk. Marriage and children are a risk. It's a miracle any child reaches adulthood, the daft things they do. Life is a risk.

Take the risk, for God's sake, it's better than regret.'

I stare at her silently. I had this conversation with myself about risk a few weeks ago and decided that life without it wasn't worth living. Do I need to rethink my present perspective?

The light is shifting and everything around me is beginning to flatten into contour-less monochrome. I must get the train before I fall over.

Jen lifts her hands as if I were pointing a gun at her. 'Please, please don't wreck this opportunity of happiness for him. Or for you. Don't leave it too late.'

* * *

Sunday morning I leave all the little jobs I ought to be doing to look after themselves and walk down to Ocean Village to sit on a bench overlooking the marina. The salty, oily smell is creamy green, different to a beach smell, and the choppy water munches and slurps around the hulls of seldom-used ocean-going yachts as my thoughts munch and slurp around my past assumptions and decisions, just as they had done for most of last night.

I don't have to be like my mother. And Dominic is not like my father. I have managed to make both Dominic and myself miserable with my fears and my confused priorities. I may be going blind, but surely, I am sufficiently robust to cope with it. I love him too much to want to be the liability I might be, but I also love him too much to let him go. Dominic was willing to live with me, blind or not. I have skills and talents which along with his, would make life manageable. Peter says suitability is not an issue. Come on, Cass Hunter. Get over the fact that neither Mum nor Dad was brilliant at parenting, that Mike made a fool of me, that my business was brought down to ground zero, and that I shouldn't have children. In the great scheme of things, these are useful life lessons, they don't need to define me. Loving someone defines me.

I look down at my legs stretched across a puddle in the concrete. These faux leather emerald boots may be waterproof, but they aren't warm. I will discuss recycled warmth with the shoe designer and sort out my future.

Chapter Thirty-Five

Easier said than done. Jen had said he was going away, and he had. His house was empty, and the lights were off. So I have to wait; frustrated, impatient, and nervous. Unable to use technology to do this difficult thing. How will he react to yet another about-turn by Cass? Will he even believe it? He was at breaking point when he left me, maybe he has already put me in the past tense.

On Tuesday late afternoon, after visiting the shoe designer in London, I get off at Winchester and it is cold and drizzly. This is the third time I will have gone to his house and fully expect it to be as empty and dark as it was last Sunday night. I hate the dark; my eyes don't cope well with streetlights or headlamps, and I can't see the pavement slabs or the kerbs. The rain-slicked, windy streets with strange figures hurrying home seem alien and the wintry smells of wet dogs, rotted leaves and damp leather underscore the utter loneliness of him not being there.

As I come down from the bridge and walk towards the exit I see him, standing on the London-bound platform. He has his arm around a woman's shoulders and his head is bent towards her, listening. His figure is as indistinct as everyone else's, but I know it's him. The way he stands, both feet solidly planted, the shape of his body, the angle of his head. I have stopped involuntarily, passengers passing me in a stream, until I am the last and only person on the platform.

The London train comes in; the woman hugs him and he kisses her and hands her suitcase up into the carriage. My heart as well as my body grinds to a halt with dismay and desolation. I am too late. As he waves goodbye, I know I must escape and force myself to turn and go up the stairs again. My feet are so slow, the treads so high.

Too late. You left it too late. You stupid, stupid woman. Why should he have waited? He told you friendship wasn't enough, and you made it clear that friendship was all you were prepared to give. You've got what you asked for, and he's found what he was looking for. Only yourself to blame, Cass Hunter.

Why can't I see anything, and why is my face so cold? Why is all of me so cold? Hold onto the rail or you'll fall. Only twenty minutes until the next westbound train. Only a lifetime of being too late. God, these stairs are so steep, and my feet are so heavy.

'Cass! *Cass!*' The shout confuses me. It's the first time I've understood it's my name, but it's not the first time it's been shouted. I still can't see anything at all, but I'll have to get used to that. When you're blind you can't see.

Quick heavy tread on the concrete steps. A firm hand on my arm. An amber cloud.

'Cass?' I think he turns me towards him, and I hear the sharp intake of his breath. 'Cass, what's wrong? Why are you here? What are you doing?'

I try to pull away, but he's holding me, and then I feel his hand on my face, warm fingers wiping across my eyes. 'Darling girl, what's wrong? Why are you crying?' I'm not crying, am I? And why is he calling me his darling girl when I'm not?

'Nothing's wrong. I'm going home.' My voice sounds like a cobweb. Fragile but sticky.

There's a tiny pause and he says, 'Did you go to the house, and I wasn't there?' He sounds bewildered and I haven't got the mental capacity to even begin to explain. I shake my head and again find that I can't see anything.

Somehow, I am down the concrete steps, his hand firmly holding mine and we are outside the station, even though my goal was the train to Southampton. I get put into his car and the warmth of it makes me shudder after the cold. Splinters of light spear into the darkness, and then I know by the stronger amber smell that we are inside his house.

'What on earth has happened?' He is kneeling on the floor beside the chair he's put me in and wiping my face with a tissue. Now I can see a bit. He twists round and a moment later the fire bursts into warming life. 'Cass, I'm sorry if you came and I wasn't here. Mum and I were shopping for my late Christmas present before her train. Tell me what's happened. Why are you so upset?'

There is a delay in comprehension. Like lift doors which hesitate so long to open that you think they're never going to. I know I am staring wordlessly at this anxious man, who obviously thinks that I have witnessed a murder, or have inadvertently started World War Three.

'Oh!' I say. And that is all I can think of to say. Dominic is patently none the wiser, but I think he feels that my catatonic state is improving as there are kitchen noises and then a mug of tea is put into my hands. The end of my world has now dissolved into embarrassment.

'Sorry,' is my next utterance. Dominic's anxiety is morphing into hopeful amusement.

'Why don't you tell me what is going on? "Oh" and "Sorry" are not very explanatory. Have you had a row with your father? Is that why you're in Winchester?'

'No. Oh no.'

'Has Mike come back?'

'No.' This is just too awful. There is no way to avoid this mortifying situation. 'I wanted to say sorry.'

'You just have, but what for?'

I'm not sure. For getting it wrong. For getting him wrong. For being pig-headed, for not believing in me, in him. For being plain stupid.

'Sorry for hurting you.'

There's a little frown between his eyes. 'Apology accepted with thanks. But why did I find you crying your eyes out at the station?'

I take a gulp of air. 'I thought – I saw you – with someone. I thought—' I squeeze my eyes shut because, somehow, I must get this over with. 'I didn't know it was your mother. I saw a woman, and you hugged and kissed her, and she had a suitcase, and I thought—'

'You thought I'd found another lover?' There is an unamused snort. 'Very flattering that you think I could have managed that in such a short space of time. And were you crying because you were so easily displaced, or was it jealousy?'

Oh, good grief, he's set me off again. I seize the tissue and swipe vigorously at my face. Even when Mum died I didn't cry, so that Dad couldn't accuse me of being weak. I've done nothing but cry for the past half hour.

'Don't. Please don't. I came to say sorry.' Swallowing down the huge lump in my throat, I gasp, 'I am so sorry,' and get unsteadily to my feet. 'I'm going back now. Thank you for the tea.' Groping for the door because again I can't see anything beyond a watery blur, I find he is standing in my way. 'Sorry for what, Cass?' He adds quietly, 'I need to hear you.'

He says he needs to hear me. Please God, if this is the last chance, don't let me be too late. Please let him hear me.

Opening my mouth, all that comes out is a dry croak. I swallow and manage a whisper. 'Sorry I left you. I came to – to ask you if I was too late. Is it too late to change my mind?'

To be what you wanted me to be. To love you in spite

of what I am, what I might become, in spite of what it may do to harm you?

Neither of us seems to make the first move. We have just come together. Both of us very still in each other's arms. His cheek against mine, the five o'clock shadow faintly rough on my skin, the amber scent of him thick in my throat. I am lost in that scent, lost to any form of willpower or self-control. But I am found in him. I am filling up with relief, contentment, with coming home, with loving him.

His voice is thick too. 'I love you. I have loved you from the first moment I saw you. I love every eccentric particle of you. Love your mad outrageousness, your clothes and hair, your rotten judgements and terrible choices. Love your sound and fury and never giving in and determination to get where you want to go whatever life throws at you. I love your big bottom and your dippy nose and your blurry eyes.'

His voice is as light and soft as his hands. 'I love you, Cass, in all those ways. I want you to be a daft friend for Patrick, to be part of my family, to accept my business suits and boring job.' His lips are travelling over my face, and every millimetre of me is sensitised and aware. 'I hate it when I'm not with you. I never used to mind being alone if I couldn't have Penny, but now I do. I see you everywhere: in the garden, in the street, in the car, doing your nails. In bed.'

He stops. Swallows. He isn't the confident man of the world just now. 'I know I'm not what you would have chosen, I have an unexciting life with an unexciting family and an unexciting job. But we can make it work. I could try being more exciting.' The humour is there, but only just.

He hasn't even mentioned that my dippy nose will soon be in the middle of two blind eyes. I am car-crashed by a torrent, by a tsunami, of love and gratitude and total defeat.

I lean into him, so surprised by his words. He's not what *I'd* have chosen? That can't be right. I'm the one who's going blind, the unsuitable one with my purple thigh boots and crazy nails and coloured hair. I'm the one who returns a wolf whistle and dances on tables – though I have never danced on tables on account of my height, poor balance and bad eyes. Surely, I'm the one who would have to change; to buy normal clothes, put on normal make-up, to colour my pale mousy hair a conservative auburn and have it styled by a normal hairdresser. The one clicking my way tentatively through life with a white cane, stumbling and falling, needy and demanding, scared and angry.

'Oh Dominic! Please don't ever be more exciting.'

How strange that I can sense the hope in him, even though I can't see it clearly. Perhaps it is the way his body straightens, the way his breath snags, the way the smooth skin of his face relaxes over the bones. He draws me close again and I feel all of him, all of me, hard and urgent: thighs, stomach, breast. He has pushed up the loose sleeves of my sweater and the touch of his thumbs on the inside of my forearms brings an almost terrifying wash of desire – a fizzing tangle of screaming nerve ends.

The imperative, the burning, the urgent is slowed by him, his kisses linger as we undress each other, relishing the moments which lead to fulfilment, savouring the taste of each other, the skin, the contours, the muscles, nerves and bones. He is a giving man, a generous man. He enjoys giving me pleasure and will not hurry so that I long to give him pleasure too. The soft hair on his chest, the smoothness of my moisturised legs, my subconscious knowledge that just to touch the edge of his shoulder blades is enough to make him groan. His fingertips down my ribs and over my belly reduce me to a shuddering, melting essence.

Later, his whisper is hardly distinguishable. Slurred and heavy with the aftermath of love.

'I got the silver sixpence.'

Chapter Thirty-Six

Dominic is on his back under his kitchen sink, among the cobwebs and their denizens, trying to repair a leak. I turn off his big torch as he slides out from the cupboard and creaks to his feet, using me as a post. Putting the heavy wrench on the countertop he scrubs his hands with washing-up liquid. I am mesmerised by the simple act of him washing and drying. Turning, he pulls me close, his hands slipping under my sweater to explore bits of me that go rock-hard in an instant.

'If I don't make love to you again soon, I'm going to explode.'

Nothing to what is going to happen to me. My skin is electric as he touches it. My belly rippling with desire and the rest of me making it quite clear that the fuse is lit.

He pulls my head into his chest, fingers combing through my red streaks. 'Cass Hunter, I love you; blind, eccentric, and a crazy arachnophobe.'

'And I love you; sensible, conservative, sneezing in sixes.'

His hands cup my face and tip my mouth to his. 'I won't be bored, that's for sure.' He smiles that slow smile which turns my insides over like a dropping lift. 'Even if marriage is still a step too far for you, "Come live with me and be my love?"'

'Will you promise to remove every spider within a mile of me?'

'No, but I'll remove every one I see. And I'll bring you

truckloads of conkers, and a new spider catcher whenever you break one in a panic.' He puts the wrench away in his toolbox. 'Peter will be convinced that your capitulation is entirely due to him.'

'He helped.' I have to smile. 'And Jen. And Wendy. Wendy has been furious with me; said I'd had a bone bracelet for six years and had thrown away a diamond necklace.'

He laughs. 'How descriptively flattering. Now, Mum will come back from visiting my aunt in London and David says he can drive up this coming weekend. Will you make sure you don't have anything else lined up?'

Not for the first time, apprehension takes a clenched fist to my insides. 'They'll want to see you. Not want to make small talk to some strange woman.'

He tips my chin up and kisses my nose. 'I've just spent a week with Mum, pouring my heart out, and David knows all about you too. They're coming to see you, not me, to inspect the goods, discover if you are as blind and peculiar as I say you are. I'm going to leave you in their tender care and take myself off.'

'Take yourself *off*? Where to? You can't! You *wouldn't*!'

His eyes crease up with laughter. 'I wouldn't. I really would not dare. Now, have I cured this leak?' He turns the tap on and inspects the pipe for drips.

I am still acutely uneasy about meeting his family.

'Dominic, what have you said to them? They can't be happy about you getting involved with someone who's going blind. They must suspect I'm a gold digger, only after your money.'

Closing the under-sink cupboard, he turns off the tap and kisses me again. 'Aren't you? Actually, I'm after *your* money.' He twines his fingers into mine. 'Do stop twitching about my relatives. Even if they disapproved, it wouldn't change anything. It would make me sad because I like my family, but they won't disapprove. They've been trying to find me a woman for years.'

'I daresay they have, but probably a woman they approve of.'

He puts his hands on either side of my face until our noses touch. 'Cass, your father and that bloody Mike have twisted your perception of yourself into a completely back-to-front version. You are beautiful, intelligent, innovative, creative, positive, outgoing, humorous, determined and feisty. Even sexy.' He evades my cuffing. 'Your clothes and make-up are part of your personality. You are also tactless, untidy, impetuous, angry, vindictive and revengeful.' He makes a sorrowful face. 'After all, nobody's perfect.' He kisses me thoroughly again, tongue and lips and his body pressing close. 'Everybody who meets you loves you, and Mum and David and Merryn will too.'

I may have a craving for a family, but a family is outside my experience, and I can't get my head around the fact that his family might like me, let alone love me.

'OK,' I say slowly. 'If you say so.'

He looks at my face with sympathetic amusement. 'They *want* to like you, and they want you to like them.' This seems extraordinary to me.

'But Patrick hasn't communicated with you for weeks. He must be horrified and upset.'

Dominic is quite unconcerned. 'It would never occur to him to tell either of us whether he thinks we are a good idea or not. What do you think he and Miss Einstein have been doing all this while? Conducting computerised moon rocket tests? Patrick is an uncouth twenty-two-year-old who has no interest whatsoever in my love life, but only in his own.'

I leap to his defence. 'Don't be mean. I love Patrick. I mind what he thinks.'

Dominic grins. 'I love him too. But I can assure you, he

won't be thinking about us, or only to feel relieved that he's not responsible for my well-being.'

'Have you truly told them I'm going blind?'

'Yes.'

The monosyllable doesn't tell me much and I try to gauge his expression which I think is amusement.

* * *

His mother smells the green of new beech leaves, has short silvery hair and her excellent figure is in pull-on jeans with a navy cable sweater. The impression is that she likes to be comfortable, and she is not at all disturbed by being about six inches shorter than me. I call her Mrs Paget, and she tells me to call her Maggie. Dominic hasn't allowed me to dress down very much, which leaves me as the brightest light in a winter landscape but neither she nor David reacts with any sign of astonishment. Not by a raised eyebrow do either of them express dismay at Dominic's new companion. David looks like a thinner version of his brother; direct grey eyes and oddly, a similar ambery smell. The conversation is polite and generalised until Dominic takes his mother away to advise on spring plantings for the garden and I am left nervously with David.

'Dom says you've got RP. I'm sorry. That's a horrible thing to happen, especially for someone in your business.' He's a doctor, I remember. 'Are you scared by it?'

Wow. Suddenly not polite and generalised. I can feel my breath shortening. 'Sometimes. But I don't tend to dwell on it.' Not half. 'There's too much to do.'

'Including rescuing your business.' Those intent eyes are kind. 'We were shocked to hear about what your partner did to you.'

I find myself smiling. 'Yeah. He may have got away

with my money, but he lost his reputation, his job and his new lover and had to leave the country. I'm clawing my way back from the brink of disaster.' I pull in some air and am not polite and generalised either. 'Look, you must think I'm on the make with Dominic, but I'm not. When the RP was diagnosed, I tried to stop. To leave. We tried to be just friends.'

David shrugs. 'I know. And he was miserable. He's a big, grown-up boy able to make his own decisions about the big things in life. He loved Penny and we all grieved for her, but why should that tragedy rule the rest of his life? He loves you, and if you love him why shouldn't you be together?'

I get up and go over to the window. Dominic and his mother, swathed in anoraks and muffled with scarves, are pointing to various plants and pulling at shrubs. The miserable February weather is not conducive to gardening and as I watch they turn back to the house.

'What does your mother think? She can't want him to be involved with someone like me if he doesn't have to be.'

'Mum wants him to be happy.' His voice is even. 'She wants whatever will make us happy. And if she thinks you'll make him happy, then that's what she'll want.'

I turn round and stare at the out-of-focus man in the armchair. 'I didn't have a family that wanted happiness for everyone else. It takes some getting used to.' I'm still puzzled that he has the same smell as Dominic. 'Are you older or younger than Dominic?'

He grins. 'We're twins. He's older by a minute or two.'

Twins! Surprise makes me blink. 'That must explain why you both smell amber.'

'He told me you had synaesthesia. It's not that rare, but it is fascinating. Have you always been aware of it?'

'No, but I've always known I have a very acute sense of smell. I suppose it's connected. My art teachers became curious about my textile colours and my painting.' I'm much more curious about him and Dominic being twins. 'What's it like being a twin? You're not identical. But do you have similar tastes – similar ideas? He never told me you were twins!'

He flicks a sideways look at me. 'Twins can be felt as exclusive. Sufficient unto themselves. A special relationship that even partners can't break into. But Dom and I are not identical. We don't have the same interests. He is a classicist: books, art, music, history. I do Glastonbury and football matches.' He grins again. 'We aren't alike, but we watch each other's backs.' Was there a friendly warning there?

Dominic and Maggie have shed their anoraks and thaw out beside the fire. She asks about Ecolore. Dominic tells her that my designs for carpets and fabrics have been chosen for a Bournemouth conference centre.

'That's quite a coup,' says Maggie, sounding impressed.

Dominic takes David off to his study to look at something and I am left with Maggie, who seems to be genuinely interested in what I do.

'Tell me about these fabrics and how plastic is recycled and used.'

As usual, my enthusiasms get the better of me, and gradually I become happily talkative and relaxed.

Maggie's eyes are gleaming. 'It sounds fascinating and fun.' She hesitates a little. 'I don't want to meddle, but Dominic was so sad when you left him. It broke his heart. Now he's a different man. So happy. You are sure this time, aren't you, that you'll stay with him?'

My stomach contracts in apprehension. Stay with him? I would stay with him forever but happily-ever-after is an illusion.

'I thought he'd told you. I have a genetic problem. I'm going blind and I shouldn't have children because I'd pass it on. I want him to be able to leave me without any complications, without guilt, with no hard feelings.'

'My dear,' she says gently, 'of course he told us you've got RP. I'm sad for you that you feel you can't have children, but that doesn't stop you and Dominic from being together and being happy together.' Her nose wrinkles in wry commiseration. 'And don't kid yourself that it's possible to leave a relationship without complication, guilt or misery. It isn't.'

'But a blind partner is not a very good starting point, is it?'

'It's a rotten starting point and I am so very sorry that you are starting there.' Maggie sounds very firm. 'But it is just that, a starting point. There are lots of points to come, hurdles to be jumped and difficulties to be tackled. The higher the hurdles the greater the achievements.'

'I couldn't agree more,' David says from behind me. I hadn't realised he and Dominic had come back into the room. 'Some hurdles are really high, but not yours I think.'

I turn my head so that I can see him. There was a strange note of sadness, almost bitterness, in his remark.

Dominic pulls Maggie out of her chair. 'Let's go get lunch and leave these two to their philosophical discussion.'

I suspect that I will be putting my foot where my mouth is, but it was David who had opened the subject. 'Dominic says you have a girlfriend in Devon. Do you have hurdles there?'

'I do.' His voice is even. I speculate that she's married and won't divorce.

'Tell me about her.' I'd be glad to have the spotlight taken off me.

'We were at school together. She works on her parents' dairy farm. Just outside Truro. She's a paraplegic.'

'*What?*' I really am stopped in my tracks. I think paraplegia is paralysis from the waist down but am not sure.

I had read Jojo Moyes's *Me Before You*. For two brothers, two tragedies and now a probable third. How could that possibly happen in one family?

He's looking at me with a tilted head, eyes sympathetic, mouth a little humorous. Older, wiser than me.

'She broke her back competition diving – just a wrong position, not hitting anything – when she was twenty-two. We were at school together and I'd always loved her. That's when I decided to be a surgeon. I was going to cure her.' But he is a doctor, not a surgeon, I think. And this was twenty-five years after it happened.

'So you see, Cass, I've spent a good part of the intervening years not quite achieving the Mr title and trying to persuade Arden to marry me.'

I am ashamed of myself. I could still walk and dance, still smell the colours, taste the snow, and still make love. How dare I wallow in self-pity?

'I'm so sorry.' My face is aching, and I rub my cheekbones. 'And she doesn't want to pin you down to that commitment?' I wish I could see his expression more clearly. 'I don't want to pin Dominic down to that commitment either. When I'm blind, I want him to be able to leave with no complications. Don't you think that's the right decision? To make it easier for him?' Am I hoping he will think differently from his mother?

'The right decision for him?' He shakes his head. 'No, I don't. Arden thought the same. She said she would not encumber an up-and-coming doctor with all the extra difficulties, complications and heartbreak entailed in marriage to a very disabled wife. She said I'd get over her. Find someone else. Have a two-point-four happy family. And all that's happened is that I didn't get over her. When you fall in love, you can't do much about it. Time doesn't heal. The scar is always there, and it hurts, pressed or not.' His voice is sad. 'I speak from experience. I think it would be the same for Dom. He wouldn't get over you. He won't leave you whether you marry or just live with him, because he loves you, however blind or unsuitable you think you are.' He has the same shaped smile as Dominic. *He won't get over you.* The words resonate in my mind. I know I won't get over him either.

There is a long moment of silence, and he is watching me. 'Cass, can I suggest something which I think would make you feel much more optimistic about losing your sight?'

I could say, 'Yes you can,' or 'No you can't.' But instead, I mutter 'What?' It comes out apprehensive, if not ungracious.

'Make friends with blind people. Use social media, discover the forums, the FB pages, the local groups. Discover what they think, how they manage, who they trust, what scares them and what encourages them. Learn from them, find the gadgets, *design* the gadgets. Offer to train them in design, drawing, and sustainable materials. Tell them how to use your colour palette, what Dom describes as your magnum opus.' He smiles at my surprised expression. 'He does talk about you. A lot.'

I take a few moments to digest what he's said. Learn from blind people, use their knowledge, find their requirements, design what they need, and teach them my skills? That had never occurred to me.

'A two-way process,' I say slowly. 'Learn and teach.' I find myself smiling at him. 'Thanks for the heads-up.' A faint wriggle of excitement and optimism begins to squirm in my tummy.

Chapter Thirty-Seven

As time goes on, I discover new things about our relationship. Dominic does not tell me what to do, or why I should do it. He asks for my opinions and takes them seriously. He does not load me with guilt-inducing presents, or indeed inducements of any sort. He is unfailingly kind, thoughtful, non-pushy, but thankfully, amorous. My throat tightens with pleasure at the sound of his voice, and just the thought of him touching me makes my stomach flutter.

Nearly all of Mike's possessions have sold, some well, and the cash was a welcome and much-needed bridge until the flat sold at last. As the money was banked and my business temporarily transferred to an industrial unit, the last residues of Mike's betrayal slipped away. Now I can send a substantial cheque to his parents. I don't suppose for one minute that it will make up for what happened to them, or make Mike's rejection any less painful, but it makes me feel slightly better.

'He's not worth the effort of despising,' I admit to Dominic who is teaching me how to prune his buddleia.

'Too exhausting?'

I think about that. 'It just feels like a waste of time to get uptight about what he's done when my present is so much happier than my past.' My hand slips into his and he transfers his secateurs to his pocket. 'Yes, too exhausting to go on hating him. And anyway, he didn't destroy me or Ecolore, thanks to you.' I go on snipping. 'I'm going to see my father again next week. I need to understand a bit more about how my parents' relationship got into such a horrible mess. Maybe it wasn't entirely Dad's fault. Looking back, I think she was a bit of a victim and although he did treat us badly, perhaps he was frustrated by her "poor me" attitude, and the way I always took her side and never tried to understand how he felt about it.'

I can feel Dominic nodding in agreement. 'Putting oneself in another man's shoes does give perspective. Anger and hatred are exhausting.' He holds my back to his warm chest, his hands pinioned across me, his chin nuzzling into my collarbone.

I ruminate a bit more. 'My lovely consultant said something I didn't really take in at the time. I suppose I didn't believe him.' I can feel Dominic's head tilt questioningly. 'He said blindness can be a curse or a blessing and it was up to me to choose whether to be a victim or a victor. At that moment I could only see it as a curse but I'm beginning to understand that it's something new that I can, and must, embrace and turn into a blessing. I think it was Professor Hull who wrote, *'It's a gift. Not a gift I want, but it is a gift.'* I need to take that on board.'

He runs his fingers back from my temples and I close my eyes, luxuriating in his touch.

'And I think it's true to say that to have a fresh start in a new life we need to drop the baggage from the old one.' His mouth is now on my bright red hair. 'I have taken my own advice. This house is also on the market.'

I am startled, but not dismayed. 'Wow. That's two of us homeless then!'

* * *

Dominic has changed. Younger, riskier, more sociable. The weariness has dropped off him. And yet I know that living together, blissful though it is, is not quite enough for him. Dominic loves family, and he wants a continuation of family life. Gradually I am learning that like anything else, you have to work at family. I'm probably never going to have a very close relationship with my father, but we don't have to be completely estranged. Every now and then I drop by his house, and on each occasion, we find it easier to talk. He has asked about my business but so far has refrained from offering unwanted advice. When I eventually told him about my diagnosis I was surprised and pleased by his reaction.

'You're not like your mother. You'll fight blindness like you fought me and come out on top.' The humour is unmistakable. 'I probably wasn't the best role model, introducing you to combat at such a young age.'

I am fairly certain that that is as near an apology as my father will ever get. I give him a sincere smile. I still haven't managed to give him a hug though.

* * *

Looking for forums for the blind on Google, I am astounded to discover over one hundred, featuring leadership and career advancement, mentoring, networking and connecting and much more. For some days I do very little work and a great deal of Facebooking. There are an awful lot of people out there like me, and every one of them is inspirational. Dominic watches me getting inspired and generates a production line of chocolate biscuits and mugs of tea.

'Could you come with me after work tomorrow?' he asks. 'It's a surprise. Put on your wildest clothes and be prepared to use your wildest imagination.'

'I could,' I say. 'I love surprises.' My wildest clothes! It must be a party, though why I should need wild imagination I don't know. As always, I am amazed that this seemingly conservative man wants me in wild clothes, making waves and shocking his friends.

Another thing about Dominic is that he takes my business seriously, and if I have commitments, he doesn't ask me to break them. He will normally text me before phoning to ensure that he's not interrupting a meeting. I have learned a lot about good manners and thoughtfulness from Dominic and am still unlearning a few habits Mike introduced.

On the way to this surprise event, I ask him something I have been pondering over. 'What would you think about having a dog as well as me? Would it be too much to cope with?' I can feel his surprise as he glances briefly over at me. 'I've always wanted a dog or a cat. Or any pet really. Dad wouldn't even consider it, so I don't really know what it entails. I take it there's a lot of puddles, poo and chewing?'

He laughs. 'That's fairly accurate, I think. I'd love another dog, but we do have quite a lot on our plate right now.'

'I wasn't thinking quite yet. More establishing the principle. I was looking up Guide Dogs and they need volunteers to take and look after a puppy, mainly Labradors or retrievers, for a year or so. Walking and socialising it with people and animals. Then it goes back to them to be fully trained before going to a blind person. That way, we needn't be taking on a dog's whole life. It could be a finite commitment.'

'Or maybe a lifetime commitment if it comes back to you?'

I grin and shrug. 'I don't know how it works, and of course, we may be – probably are – entirely unsuitable. Neither of us may have enough time and I may not see well enough to do what's needed.'

I can hear from his voice that he likes the idea. 'No doubt we would have to be thoroughly assessed, but why not try it? I'd love to have a dog again.'

I have a creeping excitement about the thought of a puppy. And perhaps a kitten too. Or even of a future guide dog. 'I'll ring them and find out more.'

We must be early for the party as there is only one car in the driveway. In any case, it is only six o'clock. The house is a single storey, curved around an untidy courtyard garden, modern but built along traditional lines with lots of big windows and patio doors and thick oak beams. Friends of Dominic's I haven't met before?

A smart young man in a trendy suit meets us at the door, wielding a set of keys. Dominic introduces me and adds, 'Cass doesn't know why she's here.'

'Ah!' he says with a grin. 'No expectations then.'

I am almost totally silent in my wildest clothes as we scrutinise this abandoned empty house. The floors are dark wood; cold and echoing, the naked bulbs feeble yet glaring. It may be quite a modern build but internally it is badly designed, shabby and has a kitchen from hell. Dominic's main interest seems to be the wine cellar, shaped like a bottle opener with drainpipes for bottles all down the outside of a spiral staircase.

Trendy estate agent and untrendy Dominic don't say much either. I get the impression they may have done their talking already.

It is completely dark by the time we leave the house and I grab Dominic's arm for safety as we are shown a big shed in a small paddock at the back which, despite the cobwebs, I am glad to get into as the wind is bitter.

'Paddock for a pony, planning permission for a swimming pool and a granny annex.' The young man wields a strong torch and his voice echoes in the chilly space. I stare around it for a long time, a familiar kick tightening my stomach. The excitement of a new design and the thrill of a fresh idea always makes me breathless. I have a natural aptitude for filling empty spaces, whether one dimension or two, with solidity, shape and colour. This empty space looks warehouse, showroom and office-shaped to me.

* * *

There are other visits of course. Other houses, other bungalows, other flats, other villages.

Estate agents seem to think that if you specify a requirement, it means that you could manage without it. So in my imagination that first peculiar house is stripped out, redesigned with the planet in mind and the swimming pool discarded in favour of business premises.

'Cass, will you please stop dithering. Choose a house to buy or design a house to build. We need to live somewhere.' It's humour, not irritation, but still, he senses me crumbling and turning towards me, shuts his laptop lid down with a snap.

If he hadn't enfolded me in his arms I wouldn't have cried. But he did, and I did. Right down from the inside, messy sort of crying. Eventually, having been shuffled onto the sofa, armed with man-size paper hankies, and just held, I begin to run out of snot and hiccups. Then there is just silence and sniffs and his arms around me. I must look like a witch judging from the eye make-up on the tissues.

'Sometimes I'm just so bloody frightened.'

'I know,' he says. 'I know you are. Nevertheless, you go on, frightened or not. And I'm going with you.'

He turns me to face him. '"*Courage is not the absence of fear, but rather the assessment that something else is more important than fear.*"'

'Who said that?' I am still sniffing.

'I did.' His cheek is against my hair, and I can feel him smiling. 'Roosevelt, I think.'

I lean my forehead against his chest and think about what is more important to me than being blind. Dominic is the centre of my universe. What courage it must take for him to take a risk on me! I heave in an enormous breath and sit up straight.

'OK. I don't think I could design a house from scratch. Not in the required time frame. But that first house had something. Though it does need a lot doing.' I feel a bit anxious about letting my ideas loose. 'The paddock would be good if we did have a puppy, and those buildings at the back – are you desperate for a swimming pool?'

He is trying not to laugh. 'Only in a heatwave with a naked woman in the shower.' He leans forward and kisses my dippy nose, hands lightly holding my still damp face. 'A potential showroom, office and warehouse on the premises was the icing on that particular cake. I could see the cogs going round as you looked at it.' He tucks a damp strand of scarlet behind my ear. 'But the house, my darling, needs stripping out, redesigning, rewiring, replumbing, reroofing, re-everything. Saving the planet as you go. You have a lot to do.'

'Dominic, we can't do all that! The cost!' I am genuinely horrified.

'Tell you what,' he says reflectively. 'You pay for making the Ecolore premises out of your flat sale. Do the planning and design for the house as well and save me a fortune in architect's fees.'

My stomach flutters as if there is an aviary of budgies in there. I am exhilarated and astonished that he considers me competent to design an eco-sustainable house suitable for a blind person and an investment banker. I am astonished that he is taking this risk. That I am taking this risk. I am breathless but can't analyse this heart-stopping sensation. Anticipation? Terror? Excitement? Gratitude? Love?

I retrieve his wastepaper basket and fill it with soggy tissues. I don't feel at all soggy now.

'If we're buying a house,' I say tentatively, 'perhaps we should think about a wedding date?'

'What an excellent idea, and not before time,' he says, pulling me close again. My insecurities and uncertainties vanish into an obscurity even deeper than the mists which cloud my eyes.

Chapter Thirty-Eight

It's not as if I haven't been here since Christmas, because I have. He's dragged me here often. Perhaps dragged is a bit strong because they've been happy visits, full of laughter and welcome, and I've enjoyed them. But somehow it feels like a totally unknown place. I've met the lady vicar lots of times but today she seems – not a stranger, but – different. Smiling and laughing, but serious too. Wearing all that weird robe stuff with a glittering sash thing slung over her shoulders.

I'm wearing some pretty unusual stuff myself; a far cry from the trad white bride, so I'm not complaining about the vicar's dress sense. And I am cosy in my high-necked, long-sleeved fur dress, the colour between heliotrope and violet, with four full-length pale rose panels. This dress has kept three hundred and fifty-eight plastic bottles out of landfill. It's late April and there's a howling gale in the porch, making the windblown cherry blossom skirl around the paving, the sensuous emerald scent whirling in my throat. I know that the church is pink with blossom too, and that cherry blossom will always bring me back to this moment. How can nearly twelve months have brought me so far? From the anger and despair and betrayal to this locus of love, peace, hope and acceptance.

Sam is giving me away and I grab his hand as Wendy twitches her creations – mine and Arabella's – to her satisfaction, and then disappears inside. The 'Arrival of the

Queen of Sheba' is unleashed with considerable decibels. I know that between us, Dominic and I have a lot of family and friends crowding the blue upholstered chairs, and some of them have been significant players in getting me to this point. Matriarch Maggie, Patrick and the entire Paget clan, Cornwall to Canada, even Arden in her amazing electric chair. Peter and Jen, Zev and Sam, Wendy, Stefan and his extended family, Eddie and Jade.

The vicar waits for a limping latecomer to enter before we set off, but the late arrival hesitates beside us, and he smells the colour of lapis lazuli.

'Hello, Cassia. Hope you don't mind me coming.'

His face is a blur, but that's irrelevant. My insides tumble: something has hit me in the solar plexus, and I am short of air. Only one person hadn't answered the invitation.

There is an eternity of silence before he puts his hand on the door.

'Good luck. You've got yourself a nice chap. Kind of you to ask me.'

I manage to heave in oxygen and crush Sam's hand to a pulp. 'Dad. Would you like – would you walk me down the aisle? As you're here?'

I wait. Arabella waits. The vicar waits. Sam's hand disengages gently, and he goes inside. What if Dad refuses? Then no one will walk me down the aisle. Does it matter? A coiled memory of past dismissals twists in me.

The 'Queen of Sheba' is even louder as Dad takes my arm, and I briefly think that this is the first time I have touched my father since I was a child, and it really isn't so difficult. His limp slows us down from the musical gallop and the soft caress of the fabric against my skin warms me. I can smell sky blue from myriads of tea lights, emerald from the cherry blossom, the paler green smell of late white narcissus and Dad's lapis lazuli. The lady vicar proceeds decorously through the massed ranks of smiling faces towards my amber Dominic, foursquare at the centre of my tunnel vision, his brother David at his elbow, waiting for me at the altar step.

THE END

Acknowledgements

My husband, children, and in particular my talented, encouraging daughter-in-law Trudi, all of whom have wondered why it has taken me nearly three years to write *Colour Blind.*

My wonderful, supportive and wise editors, Kia Thomas and Kirsty Parkinson, and Joanna Barnard for her immensely helpful critique. And to Jane Dixon Smith for the gorgeous cover and the formatting.

To Helena Bowie of the eagle eye, and the members of 'We Write Stuff' who have patiently listened to the monthly extracts and endured and commented on uncountable drafts of back cover blurb, and to Charlie Cochrane for unstinting help and wisdom.

Thank you all.

Also by Charlotte Milne

Dolphin Days

Come in from the Cold

About the Author

Charlotte Milne grew up in the Scottish Borders. Her naval father and artist mother had vast quantities of books, from the unsuitable to the incomprehensible. She read all of them and then the contents of the school library, writing her own romances along the way.

After an education which ground to a halt at seventeen, she trained as a secretary at 'The House of Citizenship'. From humble beginnings at The National Trust for Scotland, she travelled to Africa and became PA to the Dean of Makerere University in Kampala, returning to the UK as Personnel Manager for an American software house. Then came marriage, children, and a house with an overlarge garden in the Hampshire countryside.

In pre-Covid life she and her husband travelled extensively but have exchanged the globe-trotting for a more tranquil life in a retirement village near Southampton, within reasonable reach of their children and seven grandchildren. Foreign travel now only consists of visits to their beloved cottage in Wester Ross, Scotland.

Her first book *Dolphin Days*, a contemporary romantic novel set in Greece and the UK, was published in 2017. Her second novel, *Come in from the Cold*, was published in 2018, and is set in Wester Ross.

All royalties from these books go to 'An African Dream', Charity No. 1123231 www.aaduganda.org

Dolphin Days

Artistic young antique dealer Melissa fails to recover a precious Byzantine manuscript stolen from her in Greece. Instead she finds herself accused of theft by wealthy architect Nicholas.

Struggling with financial disaster, a dangerous attraction to an embittered Nicholas, and guilt over a family tragedy, Melissa is determined to put the past behind her and sets out on a new career in design and illustration.

But it seems that Nicholas has not only destroyed her career as an antique dealer, but his unwanted interventions may also wreck her new aspirations.

Melissa is tempted to trade her professional talents and career for the security of marriage to kind, devoted David, but as she gets to know Nicholas better, her resolve wavers.

Will she overcome her lack of confidence, build her career and find the love she longs for?

ISBN: 9 781979 129152 (Print)

Come in from the Cold

Wartime love and murder throw a long shadow.

In 2012, Annie Devereux, humiliated and bruised by her divorce, retreats to David Mackenzie's cottage in the Scottish Highlands to research the mysterious wartime history of her grandfather, John Elliott, serving on the Arctic convoys supplying Russia in World War Two.

In 1942 John comes off convoy a sick man and is billeted on nineteen-year-old Mhairi to recuperate, setting in motion tragedy and unforeseeable consequences for future generations.

David, still grieving for his dead wife, is intrigued by Annie's discovery of a connection between his grandmother Mhairi and John Elliott. As Annie and David begin to peel away the hidden memories of ninety-year-old Mhairi, dark secrets surface.

Soon Annie has a fateful secret of her own. There are rough seas they both need to navigate towards healing and reconciliation before she and David can come in from the cold.

ISBN: 9 781916278509 (Print)

All books available from Amazon in print and e-book.

Printed in Great Britain
by Amazon

15802350R00203